HIS FIERY ANGEL

RAKES & REBELS: THE ST. BRIAC FAMILY, BOOK 4

CYNTHIA WRIGHT

OLIVERHEBERBOOKS

His Fiery Angel

The St. Briac Family, Book 4

Cover design by Dar Albert at Wicked Smart Designs

Published by Oliver-Heber Books

0 9 8 7 6 5 4 3 2 1

CHAPTER 1

HYDE PARK, LONDON, ENGLAND, MAY 1838

"*L*ook!" Camille St. Briac nudged her younger cousin, her voice an urgent whisper. "The sweetest long-tailed tit is perched in that dogwood tree near the Serpentine."

Extending her striking Wedgwood monocular, which resembled a very short telescope, she waited for Emeline's reaction.

Emeline lifted the monocular and blinked against the brass eyepiece. "Sorry. I don't see anything in that tree, but I confess my thoughts are elsewhere. If we don't start back to Grosvenor Square very soon, we shall be late for the garden party celebrating our new monarch. Rumor has it Queen Victoria herself will attend."

Camille suppressed an urge to wince. *A garden party.* Why must life be so fraught with deadly dull obligations? All she wanted was to remain in the vast green park, searching out rare species of birds, making notes, sketching, and enjoying the brilliant morning. However, it seemed all of England was otherwise engaged, for the coronation of Queen Victoria was just a few weeks away and the celebratory season of parties, balls, routs, and assemblies had begun.

Of course, Camille had no wish to disappoint the beloved relatives who had invited her to travel from her family home in Cornwall and spend several weeks with them in London. It seemed everyone was obsessed with the coronation, but truly she would rather hide patiently in the bushes near a nesting swan than dress up and make polite conversation with a lot of pretentious aristocrats.

Furthermore, if there was one thing worse than stuffy chit-chat, it was the *men* whose eyes lit up as soon as Camille arrived at any party. For as long as she could remember, adults had showered her with compliments about her physical beauty, as if the accident of her tawny-gold curls and Parisian-blue eyes were a great accomplishment on her part.

Nothing could be further from the truth. Now that she was grown, Camille found that her looks had become a millstone, a distraction from her strong intellectual convictions. Worse, her appearance caused men to undress her with their eyes on a daily basis, which was highly annoying.

Of course, Camille admitted to herself, she was human. *Unfortunately.* Last year ago, she had succumbed to the ardent attentions of a dashing viscount, and it had ended so badly that, ever since, she did her best to block the incident from her memory.

"What's wrong?" Emeline asked. "Don't you want to meet our new queen? After a procession of stodgy kings, it is so refreshing to think that Victoria is only eighteen years old! Her youth adds luster to festivities like today's garden party."

Camille bit her full lower lip. "I know I ought to be more excited...and grateful to be included," she said apologetically.

"Perhaps you should endeavor to open your mind a bit to new possibilities. Mama thinks you could have your pick of eligible noblemen if you would give them even an ounce of encouragement," Emeline ventured.

"It feels very odd to hear this speech from you," Camille protested. "I happen to know that you are barely more interested in the *ton* than I am. Admit it! I'll wager you'd rather be in Lyme Regis, fossil-hunting with Mary Anning, than curtsying to our new queen."

Coloring, Emmie said, "Perhaps. But I am also a female, embarking on my first real season. I don't see why I must choose between science and romance. Why can't I enjoy them both?"

Suppressing an urge to reply honestly, Camille forced a bright smile. "If anyone can have it all, it's you, Emmie. I shall enjoy watching you set the *ton* on its ear."

Emeline was blessed with raven curls, sparkling violet eyes, and a lithe figure. Although her strong-willed father, Justin, had conspired to delay her first season as long as possible, their lives were about to change. Suitors bearing gifts would begin lining up outside the St. Briac family's newly established London home, across Grosvenor Square from Emmie's grandparents, André and Devon Raveneau.

"And why shouldn't you enjoy romance, too, my dear cousin?" Emeline persisted. "Mama couldn't help noticing that the Earl of Hartcroft paid a great deal of attention to you last week at Almack's. He's very handsome and he's extremely interested in botany." She waited for a reaction before adding, "Like your father, Gabriel!"

"How nice." Camille nodded politely, then turned toward the rat-a-tat sound coming from a nearby ash tree. Grateful for the distraction, she lifted a gloved finger and whispered, "Up there. Do you see it? You can tell it is a great spotted woodpecker by the smudge of red on its belly."

Emeline nodded indulgently. "You are indeed in your element."

This drew a sigh of pleasure from Camille. "Very true. These are perfect moments, to be treasured."

The two fell silent, watching and listening to the big woodpecker, until the spell was broken by the sound of carriage wheels on the narrow lane bordering the Serpentine.

"Bother," Camille said, frowning.

Usually, it was very quiet in this section of sprawling Hyde Park, especially in the morning. Most of the *ton* who came to see and be seen didn't appear until at least four o'clock, and their domain was a good distance away, in Rotten Row. Few of them could be bothered to seek out quiet corners of nature like this one.

Even as Camille had these thoughts, she saw a yellow, open barouche come into view, occupied by an elegant older lady. Beside her, a wire-haired wolfhound sat upright, his black eyes slowly sweeping back and forth.

"It's the Countess of Rockbridge," whispered Emeline, a note of awe in her voice.

Camille narrowed her eyes, aware only of the woman's elaborate headdress that sported a white bird's wing, strikingly edged in black, on each side. "Good God, how *could* she?"

"What do you mean? What's wrong?"

"That horrid woman is wearing the wings of a kittiwake on her hat!" Camille whispered hotly. Without pausing to consider what she was doing, she rushed forward from the concealing trees and shook her fist at the coachman.

"Halt! I must speak to her ladyship." She tried not to betray the depths of her rage. "It's very important."

Although the elderly coachman drew on the reins,

he looked back at the countess for permission before bringing the matched greys to a stop. Lady Rockbridge lifted her quizzing glass and peered out at Camille who hurried to reach the barouche.

"Who are you, child?" demanded the countess. "Are you in distress?"

For once, Camille was grateful for her angelic beauty. "Yes, my lady, I am in great distress." She reached the side of the barouche and paused to catch her breath. "I am shocked to see that your headdress is grotesquely decorated with the wings of a kittiwake."

The woman blinked in dismay. "A *what?*"

"It is a beautiful black and white gull that nests on sea cliffs, especially in Cornwall."

"I think you must be mad." The countess scowled and touched her headdress. "Do you have any idea how costly this was? It was created just for me by one of the most exclusive milliners in all of England." She let each word fall like a stone.

Appalled, Camille thought of the birds she had watched each spring since childhood, and tears stung her eyes. "It is a crime against nature to kill so splendid a bird! No doubt he was nesting in the cliffs, tending his innocent hatchlings! The villains who murdered this kittiwake probably left the babies to *starve*. I demand that you remove that hat this instant!" Camille's heart was pounding as she gave up any pretense of courtesy.

The wolfhound narrowed its eyes and emitted a low growl.

"I most certainly will not!" shrieked the countess. As the coachman turned to look back, she commanded, "Baines, proceed! This instant!"

However, before the barouche began to roll forward, Camille impulsively reached inside and caught hold of the countess's headdress. She didn't think about what she was doing, she only knew that she had to stop the woman from parading about London wearing the wings of this poor, slaughtered bird.

"Help! Help!" Lady Rockbridge implored. "I am being attacked!"

* * *

BENEDICT HAWKE WAS PREOCCUPIED as he guided Max, his chestnut gelding, toward the path edging the Serpentine's western boundary. It was a clear, bright morning, but he could think of little other than the probability he would be late for an important ten o'clock appointment. Why hadn't he left sooner?

At the very moment Benedict urged Max into a canter, a shrill female voice reached his ears.

"Help, help! I am being attacked!"

They rounded a stand of ash trees to behold a low-slung, open barouche occupied by a plump older woman and an Irish wolfhound. His memory flickered as he realized the occupant was the Countess of Rockbridge. From the high driver's perch, the ancient coachman was turning, trying unsuccessfully to reach back and fend off a female who had both hands raised to the occupant's head.

With a groan, Benedict reined Max in as they came alongside the barouche. "What's happening here?" he demanded, hoping to settle the problem quickly, without taking the time to dismount.

The occupant of the equipage cried, "This madwoman is attempting to *steal* my priceless headdress!"

He reached down and caught the girl's arm, easily lifting her away from the barouche. Her bonnet fell back as she whirled around to look up at him, and Benedict found himself staring at the most exquisitely beautiful female he had ever seen. A thousand shades of gold and caramel mingled in the loosened curls that tumbled down the back of her enticingly fitted, loden-green riding habit. Her eyes were a stunning shade of blue, with thick lashes and delicately arched brows. She could have been the embodiment of Botticelli's Birth of Venus if her expression was not so fiery.

"Unhand me!" she commanded.

"Hold still," he countered as Max began to sidestep, "unless you wish to alarm my horse and risk injury."

Just then, another female rushed at him from the trees, shaking her fist. She was younger, but nearly as lovely. "Don't you dare harm my dear cousin, Camille!" she threatened.

Benedict released the beauty and straightened in the saddle, hands raised in mock surrender. "I have no intention of harming anyone. I heard cries for help. I am late for an appointment, but I cannot continue on my way until I am satisfied that none of you are in danger." He could have added that this was not a role he relished. If anyone else had been available, he would have gladly let another man play rescuer. "Someone tell me what this is all about."

The attacker, who was apparently named Camille, fixed him with her sparkling eyes and pointed to the lady in the barouche. "The Countess of Rockbridge's hat is decorated with the wings of a *kittiwake*!" She said this as vehemently as if she were accusing the older woman of murder.

Benedict focused on the white and black wings affixed to the hat and blinked in surprise. The girl was correct, he realized, which was an amazing fact in itself. There were no kittiwakes in the vicinity of London. He wouldn't have guessed one female in the entire city would recognize the disembodied wing of a humble kittiwake.

Dryly, Benedict addressed Camille. "I don't think it

is wise for you to rip the hat from her ladyship's head, whatever the origin of the feathers." Reaching down again, he lightly caught the spitfire's arm and signaled to the elderly coachman to move on. To the countess, he suggested, "Why don't we all just forget this unfortunate episode ever happened."

"My good sir, I hardly think I can be expected to do that!" Lady Rockbridge looked as if she wanted to command that her assailant be locked away in Newgate.

Benedict summoned one of the devastating smiles he reserved for emergencies and was gratified to see the countess's outraged expression soften.

"Hmm." Her ladyship sighed uncertainly. "Very well." Turning her gaze toward the angry girl, she pronounced in haughty tones, "Do not imagine that you could stop me from wearing this hat even if you *had* wrested it from my head! I would simply order another. My milliner tells me these smart-looking white-and-black wings will soon be the newest fashion."

With that, the barouche rolled away over the crushed limestone path, and Benedict's beautiful captive twisted free. He was surprised to feel the strength of her arms under his fingers.

"How dare you?" she challenged.

Benedict had a great many questions of his own, but each passing moment only further delayed his arrival at the appointment that might well change the course of his entire life.

"As much as I would like to continue this lively discussion, I must bid you ladies farewell," he said in ironic tones, nodding first to the raven-haired girl, and then to Camille. "Kindly refrain from attacking any further passersby."

With that, Benedict touched the brim of his hat and rode off, pressing his knees into Max's flanks. Moments later, he was relieved to discover a path that cut across the meadow toward Park Lane.

Perhaps he wouldn't be so very late after all.

* * *

CAMILLE FROWNED at the sight of her cousin, staring after the odious stranger, her face aglow.

"Cam," she murmured, "who was that man?"

"I neither know nor care," Camille replied shortly. She resumed pacing back and forth along the waters of the Serpentine.

Still gazing into the distance, Emeline mused, "I must say, he has all the hallmarks of a devilish rake…so handsome, sardonic, and self-assured!"

"Self-assured?" muttered Camille. "I think you mean arrogant."

"Hmm, yes. He is the kind of man who would take command of any room he enters, yet I do not recognize him." Her cousin looked dreamy. "How could it be that he has not been seen out in London society? His clothing was a trifle disheveled, did you notice? Perhaps he is a scholar."

"Dash it!" Camille rounded on her. "There are more serious matters at hand than the identity of an overbearing male who has allowed a *feather thief* to go free!"

"Feather thief? Are you referring to Lady Rockbridge? Surely, she did not steal the wings affixed to her headdress. She is not the thief."

"Not literally, perhaps, but now the countess knows the truth. If she continues to wear that hat, she is as guilty as the thieves themselves!" Camille drew a deep breath, her thoughts turning to the kittiwake who had been cruelly murdered for something as frivolous as a lady's hat. She thought of the frolicsome gulls who had swooped about the cliffs near her family home in

Cornwall, making their nests on rocky ledges and then sitting in them through much of the spring, waiting for their eggs to hatch. Hot tears choked Camille as she imagined the feather hunters sneaking up on the nesting kittiwake whose wings adorned Lady Rockbridge's hat. Were they shooting them with rook rifles? Flinging nets over the unsuspecting birds, or clubbing them to death as they tended their fluffy chicks?

Camille's mind instinctively recoiled from the sickening images, but in the next moment she stiffened her spine. She must not turn away from this horror, cringing, pretending that what she couldn't see with her own eyes was not happening. Lady Rockbridge had asserted that there would soon be other hats featuring black-tipped kittiwake wings. If Camille didn't act to stop this slaughter, who would?

"What's wrong?" Emeline was watching her with an expression of concern. "You should not allow a man to upset you so."

"A—man?" Camille blinked, and when she spoke her voice was thick. "Oh, you mean *that* man. He was of no consequence." She shook her unbound curls for emphasis. "On the contrary, I am thinking of the countless kittiwakes who are tending their young, unaware that danger lurks all around. If Lady Rockbridge is correct, the feather thieves are already gathering on the Cornwall cliffs."

Emmie nodded sympathetically while stealing a glance at the delicate watch pinned to her bodice. "Indeed, it is a shame...but meanwhile the hour advances, and we are due in Grosvenor Square."

"I cannot possibly socialize at a time like this. The kittiwakes are in danger, and I cannot expect anyone else to come to their rescue!" Camille clenched her slim hand into a fist. "I must return to Cornwall immediately and do what I can to help these birds who cannot fight for themselves."

CHAPTER 2

$\mathcal{A}$ wrenlike maid silently led Benedict down the hallway toward a paneled door. His heartbeat accelerated as he imagined the heavy portal swinging open to reveal an incredible new future.

If indeed this came to pass, it wouldn't be the first time. Benedict's entire life had been a series of unexpected turns that could have proved disastrous, but he had navigated them with increasing skill. Each new path took him farther away from his origins.

Thank God, he thought grimly.

Passing a tall case clock, Benedict glanced over and breathed a sigh of relief. He was only a few minutes late. If he handled things right, it wouldn't matter.

The maid stopped before the door and scratched softly.

"Come," barked a voice from within.

The door swung open to reveal a dimly lit room lined with cluttered bookshelves. Near the window, a long table displayed countless corpses of stuffed birds laid out in rows, beaks up, labels tied with string to their twiglike legs. In the center of the study, behind a desk strewn with papers, a pale, stout man with receding brown hair rose halfway from his chair.

"Ah. You must be Hawke," he said with a distracted nod. "Come in and take a seat if you can find one. I am John Gould."

Benedict approached. He had met Gould before at the Zoological Society, where the great man had recently resigned as superintendent of the ornithological department. It had been one thing to mingle in a large group of scholars, quite another to be face to face with the ornithologist who was revered for his five-volume *Birds of Europe* as well as his partnership with Charles Darwin, helping to identify key specimens gathered by Darwin during his groundbreaking voyage of the *Beagle*.

"I am grateful to you for seeing me today," Benedict said. Just as he began to extend his hand in greeting, Gould dropped back into his chair.

"Your letter was very persuasive, or so my wife claims. She insisted that we invite you here."

As if on cue, footsteps sounded just as a slim young woman appeared, carrying a tea tray. When Benedict jumped up to assist her, she gave a soft laugh. "Don't worry, Mr. Hawke, I'm very strong. I have to be to manage four small children."

He took the tray nonetheless and watched as Elizabeth Gould swept aside some of her husband's papers to make room for the tray on his desk. After pouring tea for all three of them, she took a chair beside Benedict's and raised her cup.

"The tea has grown cool, I fear. We expected you at ten o'clock."

They were both watching him. Benedict gave a nod of wry contrition. "I apologize for my lateness. I hesitate to share the reason; the tale is so outrageous..."

"Now you *must* tell," urged Elizabeth, brushing back an errant brown curl.

"While riding through Hyde Park on my way to this

appointment, I was forced to stop and intercede in an altercation." He paused. "The Countess of Rockbridge had been waylaid by a hot-tempered young woman who wanted to destroy her headdress."

"How bizarre," marveled Elizabeth. "Whatever for?"

"She was upset because the hat was decorated with the wings of a kittiwake. As I approached, her ladyship screamed, begging me to rescue her."

Even John Gould looked up at this and blinked. "Deuced odd. Who was this female? Did you know her?"

"I did not, sir. I've been away for the past few years, on birding expeditions in America and Brazil, arriving back in London just yesterday. I only recognized the Countess of Rockbridge because I had encountered her a few times in my youth." He decided not to waste precious time explaining about his upbringing, when his father was the head gardener at Tremethyck Park and Benedict had crossed paths with all sorts of nobles, including Lady Rockbridge. Time was passing, and they had already strayed too far from the purpose of his visit today.

"Perhaps the irate lady who caused the disturbance was one of those crusaders against the use of feathers in women's fashion," offered Elizabeth Gould. Turning to her husband, she asked, "Didn't you meet one of them a year or two ago?"

Gould shuffled some papers. "Yes. As I recall, she was the daughter of botanist Gabriel St. Briac. Quite a beauty! The chit was crusading against the feather trade." Pausing, he squinted into the distance. "Cassandra, perhaps. No...Camille."

As much as Benedict wanted to change the subject, this information made him sit up straighter. "Did she happen to resemble Botticelli's Venus?"

"Exactly," Gould confirmed with a chuckle. "The face of a goddess but the temperament of a firebrand."

"That is a perfect description for the female I encountered in the park," Benedict said in sardonic tones.

"She visited me with her cousin, Anthony St. Briac, who had been on the *Beagle* expedition with Darwin. The chit heard I'd worked with Darwin to correctly identify the finches he collected in the Galapagos Islands, so she believed I must be just the person to join in her cause. However, when Miss St. Briac entered my rooms at the Zoological Society and saw the vast array of dead and stuffed birds, her regard for me withered instantly. She pronounced that she wanted nothing to do with ornithology if it meant *killing* wild, glorious birds." Gould coughed. "She boldly informed me that I was evil, no better than the demonic feather thieves, then turned on her pretty heel and marched out."

"Amazing. " Benedict's lips twitched. "It would seem that Miss St. Briac's views have only strengthened in the intervening years. I'm glad she didn't learn that I too am an evil ornithologist." The clock chimed in the hallway, alerting him that his interview with Gould would soon be over. "But I do not wish to take up your time talking about that outrageous young lady. I know you must have a crowded schedule, given your impending expedition to Australia."

"Yes, there is so much to do." agreed Elizabeth. She looked at her husband. "Mr. Gould often remarks that his brain is quite jumbled. As you may know, we sail in a few days and will be away in Tasmania and Australia for two full years."

"I do know." Benedict waited, his heart pounding in his ears, unwilling to say anything that might use up more precious time. In the distance, he heard a baby begin to cry.

"Ah, Eliza is awake," murmured Elizabeth. "I will go

to her." When she glanced at Benedict, he saw that her eyes were agleam with tears. "Soon enough we will be parted, for I must go with my husband to Australia, sketching and painting the birds that are sighted. My baby and two of our other children will stay behind with my mother."

He stood as well and nodded to her, thinking that she was a very unique female to set out on such an arduous journey that would separate her from her children for two full years. "I thank you for the tea and conversation, Mrs. Gould."

After she had hurried from the study, Benedict looked back to find his host shuffling and stacking a new pile of papers. He prayed that there would be no further interruptions.

"Let us speak frankly," Gould said. "I've read your detailed letter, applying to join our expedition as my assistant. However, I have also had an excellent application from John Gilbert, my colleague for many years."

Benedict stopped breathing. He knew Gilbert, who had worked with Gould as a taxidermist at the Zoological Society. "I have the utmost respect for Mr. Gilbert, and he would be an excellent choice, no doubt," he managed to reply, "but I should remind you that I have spent years abroad, exploring and discovering rare species of birds in places like the bayous of Louisiana, where I worked alongside John Audubon himself. Birding in Britain is tame stuff by comparison, and the Australian bush will prove to be a challenging wilderness."

Gould's double chin wobbled as he nodded repeatedly. "I realize that. Because many colleagues have cautioned me about the trials we will face in Tasmania and Australia, Mrs. Gould convinced me it would be prudent to hire *two* assistants instead of one." He paused to allow this to sink in. "Would you be ready to depart in one week's time, Mr. Hawke? The *Parsee* sails with the tide Monday next."

Benedict swallowed, stunned. Was it possible? Adrenaline coursed through his veins, and his mind spun ahead, making plans. Yet his voice was deceptively calm as he replied, "One week? Of course. I am honored to accept."

* * *

CAMILLE PLACED A FOLDED chemise in her open portmanteau just as the deep French-accented voice of Justin St. Briac spoke from the doorway of her bedchamber.

"What's happening here, *mon ange*? I've been sent to collect you. The others wish to depart for the garden party, but clearly you are not ready."

Turning, she couldn't help smiling at the sight of him. "As you may perceive, I have other plans." She sent him a beseeching look, for if anyone would understand her contrary nature, it was Uncle Justin.

Camille had been enchanted by her uncle ever since the day he first appeared in her family's Cornwall home when she was four years old. Justin could be outrageous, but his magnetic presence lit up every room he entered, and he had played a starring role throughout Camille's life.

Most recently, when Uncle Justin and Aunt Mouette invited Camille to come to their new London home in Grosvenor Square, he'd written her a convincing letter:

"*Mon ange*, there is a better reason for celebration than the mere coronation of the new queen or even our Emeline's first Season. You see, Mouette and I were married twenty years ago this very month. You were present on our wedding day, and now you must come to mark our anniversary."

Camille had felt tempted yet uncertain. She was content in Cornwall, at Elysium, her family's clifftop estate where she could not only avoid London's marriage mart, but also spend her days in nature, tramping for hours along paths bordering wildly beautiful cliffs, green and mysterious tidal creeks, snug little valleys strewn with wildflowers and sheep, and ancient churchyards where birds had nested for centuries.

Yet as she grew older, her parents began to ask why she didn't want to socialize with other people her age, and they encouraged her to go to London and enjoy herself. In truth, they didn't quite know what to do with her. Although Mama and Papa knew that Camille was not like other females, they were unaware of her heartbreak at the hands of the Viscount Upton, for he had courted her in secret.

My dear, I yearn to hear you call me by my given name, Roger...

During those brief, golden weeks, Camille had been deluded enough to think Roger was in love with her. When the truth painfully revealed itself, Camille had retreated farther than ever into her own world.

Tears pricked her eyes now at the memory. It seemed best to keep on as she had been doing. In any event, even if she did meet someone socially, as soon as she spoke of her passion for birds and her desire to banish the feather industry, men looked at her as if she had gone mad.

Yet Mama and Papa had repeatedly urged Camille to accept Uncle Justin's invitation to travel up to London, and she hadn't known how to refuse. "I will try to keep my mind open to new experiences," she assured them before climbing into their post chaise. Papa had done everything in his power to smooth the way for Camille, even insisting that Helivet, their aging coachman, should drive her and her maid, Lillian, safely to London.

"It is important that you do this," he told her. "I know you may feel uneasy, but life grows in unexpected ways when we take a chance and do something new, taking a path we hadn't planned to travel."

"Yes," Camille's mother had chimed in with an irrepressible smile. "For example, I stowed away on Papa's ship and went to France with him in the midst of the Napoleonic wars. If I had obeyed convention and stayed behind, I am quite certain none of us would be here together now."

Camille had pasted on a smile. *Romance...again. Everyone thinks that is the only answer for a female of a certain age.*

Today she felt the truth of that again. Having hurried back to Grosvenor Square after the horrid scene with Lady Rockbridge and the overbearing man on horseback, Camille realized she didn't belong in London... especially not during the Season, when frivolity ruled.

As Uncle Justin came toward her now, Camille went to meet him.

"You have *other plans*? What the devil does that mean?" he demanded with mock severity.

Justin was looking more piratical than usual, his smoke-gray eyepatch set at a rakish angle and his thick, silvery hair rebelliously unruly. Camille put a hand on his arm. "I beg you to attend me, Uncle."

When he cocked his head and waited, she hurriedly told the tale of that morning's incident in Hyde Park with Lady Rockbridge's shocking kittiwake-decorated headdress, and the arrogant, interfering man on horseback. As Camille reached the end of the story, she flung out an arm toward her portmanteau.

"Clearly, I must return to Cornwall. I am the only

person who will fight to save the kittiwakes! I know of a colony even now, nesting in the cliffs near Polruan." She felt the color rising in her cheeks. "Lady Rockbridge asserts that kittiwake wings are in great demand by exclusive milliners. Oh, it is so shocking! I cannot stop imagining the hired villains who may, at this very moment, be raiding the cliffside nests and killing those unsuspecting birds...leaving the chicks to starve." Camille let out an angry sob and felt Uncle Justin wrap an arm around her shoulders.

"Do you know," he murmured in a low voice, "that you are a bit mad, *mon ange?*"

Her eyes burned. "Perhaps you imagine that I am powerless because I am female."

"If I made such an assumption in this family, I would be stoned," he replied ironically. "Yet I must wonder, in this case...what exactly do you intend to do when you return home? Perhaps the kittiwakes are but an excuse to flee London."

Camille drew a breath, searching her own heart. "There may be some truth in that, but more important is my need to help the birds and discover who is behind this terrible enterprise. I can assure you, I *will* find a way."

"I don't doubt it," Justin agreed.

Sensing his support, Camille dared to add, "My one great problem at the moment is how to travel back to Cornwall...posthaste." She paused. "I don't suppose you have any ideas, dear uncle?"

"You are very bold, but of course I like that about you." He patted her cheek. "Perhaps we might speak to your cousin Anthony. He and Frederica are expecting a baby this summer. They won't be going on any expeditions of their own for some time, and their young Brazilian servant, Rafael, may find it dull to be confined at home. Perhaps we might persuade Anthony to spare him for a time."

"Oh, yes, I like Rafael very much!"

"Your maid, Lillian, must accompany you as well, but I'll wager she won't like it. Mouette suspects Lillian is enjoying a romance with Joseph, our footman."

The maid's romantic entanglements were, at that moment, of little interest to Camille. "But what of Aunt Mouette? Do you think she will agree to this plan?"

As if on cue, a voice spoke from the doorway, and Camille turned to see Mouette standing there, hands on hips. "My darlings, if you imagine I might try to stand in the way of any scheme you have hatched, you underestimate me. After two decades of marriage to a stubborn, incorrigible pirate, I know when to step aside."

"*Eh bien*," pronounced Justin with a flourish. "You may help Camille finish making ready while I go to Charles Street and speak to our son about Rafael. We must endeavor to send this determined beauty on her way by daybreak."

"Oh yes!" Unable to stop herself, Camille added, "If not sooner!"

* * *

RIDING BACK to his lodgings in St. James, Benedict was consumed with anticipation for the almost unimaginable adventure that would begin in mere days. It was the opportunity of his life. *Australia, for two entire years, in the service of the great John Gould!* If someone had given Benedict a chest filled with gold, he wouldn't have felt half so exhilarated. Oblivious to the crowds and stink of London, he envisioned instead the wild bush of Australia under clear cerulean skies, sightings of birds he had only read about, probable discoveries of entire new species. Joy squeezed his heart as he gave his imagination free rein.

Benedict was mentally packing for the long voyage when Max abruptly came to a stop in the middle of Piccadilly. A passing phaeton veered to one side, and the driver shouted an obscenity. With a start, Benedict realized that they had missed their turn. Thank God at least Max was paying attention.

"I'll see to it that you have an extra helping of oats tonight," Benedict promised as he found a place to turn back.

They passed the shop of Benedict's bootmaker, George Hoby, and continued down St. James to a modest hotel tucked among the gentlemen's clubs. By the time Benedict had stabled Max and quickly ascended the steps to his own rooms, it felt as if the hours were rushing by too quickly. The prospect of preparing for the Australia expedition in just a few days' time felt daunting. Thank God for wise old Fletcher, who had been organizing Benedict's life since he'd been assigned as his scout at Oxford, more than a dozen years ago. While Benedict pursued birds and other natural wonders as far as possible from England, Fletcher hovered in the background, attempting to interest his employer in fine clothing. Although he'd yet to succeed in that endeavor, Fletcher had proven invaluable at managing Benedict's domestic agenda at least as well as any wife.

Of course, there were other, more intimate benefits to be gained from marriage, but Benedict had never lacked females who were willing, even eager, to warm his bed. Since he had no intention of becoming permanently shackled to any of them, he had thus far enjoyed the best of both worlds.

Just as Benedict reached the door to his rooms, the portal swung open, and he saw Fletcher standing there as if he were answering a knock.

"Don't tell me you recognized my footsteps, Fletch."

"I did, sir." The faintest of smiles touched his mouth. "It has ever been thus."

Scanning the small parlor and adjoining bedroom, Benedict noted the open trunks, looking for the special one filled with his zoology books. "I see you have begun packing. You must have foretold that my meeting with Gould was successful." He clapped him lightly on the back. "We are going to Australia, old fellow! John Gilbert and I will both serve as assistants to Gould." He paused, sighing, allowing the words to sink in. "My dream is coming true!"

At this, Fletcher paled, closing his heavy lids as if the world had come to an end. Was it his health? Perhaps the older man might be worried that he could not withstand two years in the wilderness. During his tenure as Benedict's scout at Oxford, Fletcher had suffered a fall down a set of stairs. Once his fractured leg healed, he'd been reduced to using a walking stick when he went about his duties and had never fully recovered his previous strength. Benedict had protected his faithful scout ever since, covering for him in front of others and, later, keeping him in his private employ. Fletcher had developed a set of therapeutic exercises which he performed faithfully each day, but still he had grown a bit frailer with each passing year.

"Oh, sir..." Fletcher moaned. His long chin trembled.

"What is it? Are you ill? Injured?" Leaning forward, he put one of his own strong hands on the manservant's black-clad arm.

"No sir." Cautiously, Fletcher opened one watery gray eye just enough to focus on Benedict. "It's much worse than that."

"What the devil do you mean? I haven't time for riddles. We have a thousand things to do before the *Parsee* sets sail in a mere seven days." Benedict couldn't suppress his soaring spirits. "It's going to be the adventure of a lifetime!"

Was that a tear he saw in the older man's eye? Perhaps one of Fletcher's aged relatives needed him. Bloody hell, was he about to announce that he could not accompany Benedict to Australia?

"I demand that you tell me what's plaguing you," Benedict ground out in deadly tones.

Fletcher drew a small, folded letter from inside his black coat and held it out with trembling fingers. "A young boy traveled on the stage to bring this to you, sir." Wincing, he added, "From Cornwall."

Benedict's heart plunged, as if he'd been pushed from a cliff. With a rising sense of dread, he took the letter and stared at it. Sealed with smudged green wafer, it was addressed to him in an urgent hand he recognized as belonging to his sister, Prudence.

"You might have refused it," Benedict said hoarsely.

"But, sir, you are too honorable for that."

"I am far from honorable and well you know it. I was a fool to come back to this same hotel, to let her think she could reach me." Rising suddenly, he paced across the small parlor, wishing there were a fire burning in the grate so he might toss this damned missive into the flames and never know what Prue had written.

Benedict had spent years putting distance between himself and his family. He had no grudge against Prue, who was married to the Polruan ferryman and had two small children. It was his father he couldn't bear. He'd suffered Pa's company as long as necessary, and when Benedict had escaped to Oxford, he had vowed never to return.

"We are going to Australia," Benedict announced, in spite of the crushing pain in his chest.

"So you have said, sir," replied Fletcher in soothing tones.

"I'll read the cursed letter, but it won't change a thing. We are *going* to Australia." He strode to the window and angrily broke the seal.

Dearest brother,
I need you. Our father has suffered a severe attack of
apoplexy. A stroke, rendering him helpless, and I cannot
carry on alone. I implore you to return home with all possible
speed.
Ever your sister, Prudence

CHAPTER 3

*E*lysium.

Camille emerged from the glass conservatory filled with an assortment of flowers and plants and stepped outside into the charming, sunlit kitchen garden. Surrounded by high brick walls, it had always felt like a secret, even magical place. Camille paused to breathe, and her heart rose. Elysium meant a *place of perfect happiness*, and her family home embodied that definition, at least as fully as any mortal dwelling could.

It was spring in Cornwall, brisk and fragrant with the scents of new plants, each one tended by Gabriel St. Briac, Camille's father, and maintained by a small band of trusted gardeners. There were three acres of flowerbeds and vegetable plots, laid out in geometric shapes and bordered by neat paths of crushed limestone. Even now, Papa was digging a hole for a new Italian fig tree while her mother, Isabella, harvested a crop of raspberries. As they worked together in the fresh air, Papa glanced over toward Camille's mother and sent her a secret, sensual smile, an invitation to be alone with him later. In that moment, it was as if they were in a world of their own.

Camille sighed. If Elysium was something of a

dream, her parents' marriage was one as well. Somehow, they usually managed to put each other first, bending and compromising. From a young age, however, Camille had known she could never be like them, and the heartache she had suffered with Lord Upton had reinforced this. Camille didn't need any man to help her accomplish her goals. She possessed more than enough determination on her own.

"Hello, darling," called Isabella, Camille's mother. "You've come just in time to finish picking these berries. The light is perfect at this hour, and I must capture it before it's gone." She gestured toward her easel, which was set up near the glass orangery.

Camille kissed her mother, took the basket, and wandered closer to Papa, who was watching her with a rueful smile. "Why are you looking at me that way?"

"I still can't get over the idea that you have really come back…so soon after we sent you off to London." He brushed some dirt from his canvas-gloved hands as he spoke. "Tell me again about the emergency that compelled you to leave before you attended even one ball or other coronation event."

She narrowed her eyes slightly. "One might guess that you and Mama don't want me, considering the reception I've gotten."

"I know you too well, *ma fille*. You cannot turn this conversation around so easily."

"Weren't you listening last night when I explained? I told the entire story while Rafael and I were eating Madame Kerjean's delicious *cotriade*." She didn't bother to wait for his response. "I've come back for the kittiwakes!" In a rush, Camille again repeated the tale of Lady Rockbridge and the odious man who had thwarted her efforts to remove the kittiwake headdress.

"*Mon Dieu*, what a tale." He glanced heavenward. "It sounded so fanciful, I thought perhaps I'd dreamed the entire conversation." Drawing off one glove, Gabriel smoothed his hand over her long, shining curls. His voice was husky as he continued, "How eccentric you are. The road may clearly stretch out before you, but you invariably choose an alternate path through the underbrush."

This made her laugh. "Oh, Papa, I'm so glad you understand me."

"When you were five years old, we discovered a nest of newly hatched woodlarks, toppled by a spring storm, and you were determined that we must rescue them." His expression was tender. "I never guessed that you were unveiling a lifelong obsession."

Camille pressed her lips together, fighting a sudden urge to weep. "Oh, those tiny babies. I may never forgive myself for not protecting them better." The memory rose up in a wave. Camille had been very small yet proud when she had discovered the nest on the woodland floor and had shown it first to her sister, Louise, and then to her parents. She had been so adamant that they must help the newly hatched woodlark chicks that Papa had agreed she might bring the nest back to Elysium. All the adults had been preoccupied at the time with family matters concerning Uncle Justin and Grandmère Cerise, so her parents hadn't noticed when Camille tucked the nest of tiny birds into the branches of a blackberry bush and, later, even brought them worms to eat. The next morning when Camille went outside to visit her tiny patients, she'd been horrified to find the nest lying on the gravel path, upended and empty.

She would never forget the pain and guilt that tore her little heart in two. Papa had held her, assuring her that it was part of nature, that no doubt it had been a hawk or owl, or even a fox, that took the little birds... and they wouldn't have known what was happening.

"They didn't suffer," he had murmured, stroking her hair, "and in any event, without their mama, they probably could not have survived."

But Camille was inconsolable. From that day forward, she'd felt a deep urge to make amends, and wild birds became her passion and purpose. It seemed wherever she went, there were sick or injured birds and threatened nests. Sometimes she'd enlisted her Aunt Julia, who lived at nearby Trevarre Hall, to advise and assist her. Julia had been rescuing woodland animals for decades, and when Camille was by her side, she felt perfectly normal.

"Thank goodness for Aunt Julia," Camille now said to her father. "Since that terrible tragedy with the woodlarks, she has helped me to save so many other birds. I tell myself that the deaths of those helpless chicks had some meaning after all."

"Of course, *chérie*. Thanks to you." Papa wrapped an arm around her slim shoulders and held her against him, but something in his voice made Camille glance up. For an instant, she thought she saw a glimmer of concern in his midnight-blue eyes, and something else as well. Was he *humoring* her?

"What is it? Do you think, like everyone else, that I am a bit mad when it comes to birds?"

"Not a bit." He widened his eyes and firmly shook his head. "I admire your dedication to a cause. It's just that your mama and I hope you will seek other kinds of fulfillment...before—"

"Before it's too late and I become a hopeless spinster?" Camille broke in.

"We are your parents." Gabriel inclined his head slightly and said gently, "Perhaps we worry a bit about the time when we will not be here any longer. It isn't easy to be a female, alone in this world."

Before Camille could reply, they were interrupted

by the sounds of barking and a boy's laughter. The arched door in the brick wall opened with a loud creak and her young brother, Damien, rushed through, pursued by the family's black curly-coated retriever, Zeus. They had been frolicking in the woods that lay outside the walled garden, a world of grand adventure for children. Memories swirled up, recalling a past when Camille had tagged along after her older sister, Louise, and their many cousins, traversing the swinging rope bridge over a ravine, playing in an old shepherd's caravan that overlooked a butterfly meadow, and cheering as Uncle Justin taught her cousin Anthony to fence in a leafy clearing. How fortunate they all had been to live in the charmed, loving world of Elysium.

Zeus and Damien raced toward her, and her brother threw himself into her arms. His chestnut curls smelled of a young boy's sweat and high spirits. He'd been born when Camille was nearly sixteen, fresh evidence of their parents' enduring passion.

"Hide me, Cam!" he cried, while Zeus began to bark again.

"From what?"

"Him!" Laughing, Damien pointed over one shoulder just as a disheveled, dark-haired figure burst through the garden door. As he spoke, her brother tried to conceal himself behind Camille and their father.

"Does that rapscallion think he can escape from *me*?" The speaker was Rafael, the young Brazilian servant sent by Anthony to escort Camille back to Cornwall. Rafael was only fourteen years old, and even though he liked to swagger about and pretend he was already a man, he was clearly enjoying this opportunity to relax and engage in some boisterous play. Approaching Camille and her father, he pointed a sharp twig at them. "I demand that you turn over to me the fugitive criminal and his black stallion!"

Zeus began to bark again as if he understood exactly what Rafael was saying. Camille felt a rustling behind her cambric skirts just before Damien emerged, hands raised in surrender. Before leading his prisoner away, Rafael glanced back at Camille.

"My lady, have you need of me?"

"Not at this moment, but I would like you to accompany me at mid-morning. I am eager to walk the cliffs in hopes of discovering the colony of nesting kittiwakes."

"I cannot guess what a kittiwake might be," he mused, then brandished his tree branch. "Shall I bring a weapon?"

"Absolutely not," Camille cautioned. She stepped away from her father before adding in a whisper, "However, if we discover the evil feather thieves, we shall doubtless require *real* weapons in the future."

* * *

IT IS LIKE A NIGHTMARE, thought Benedict, looking around from Max's back as the steed carefully descended Fore Street, the steep thoroughfare bisecting the village of Polruan. People he hadn't seen for years emerged from their cold, damp cottages to stare openly as he passed, clearly not recognizing the son of Josiah Hawke, once the head gardener at Tremethyck Park.

Benedict wanted to say, *That's right, you don't know me and I bloody well don't know you.* He'd never wanted to come here again, never wanted to lay eyes on his father again, and yet here he was. Forced to give up the opportunity of a lifetime in Australia…to come instead to this hellhole and visit Satan himself.

The street felt as precipitous as the nearby cliffs overlooking the Channel. With each careful placement of a hoof, Max took Benedict deeper into what felt like a pit with no escape. In truth, he knew Polruan was a pretty village. Many called it picturesque. His own sister was happy living here, in a narrow house with flower-filled window boxes at the foot of Fore Street. Across the lane was the ferry operated by Prudence's husband, Caleb Johns. Every hour, Caleb took passengers across the river to the larger, ancient town of Fowey.

As they reached the bottom of the hill, Benedict glanced over to see Fletcher watching him from the back of his less impressive-looking mount.

"Why are you looking at me that way?" he demanded.

"You are scowling so that I feared you might be taking ill," the manservant replied.

"You know perfectly well why I am scowling. I'm trapped." As his sister's house came into view, Benedict's chest tightened with dread. "Pa has had an attack of apoplexy, Prue says. A stroke. What exactly do you think it means?"

Fletcher cleared his throat. "My uncle suffered a similar attack. Afterward, he was unable to speak intelligibly, walk, or…look after himself." His voice trailed off.

Benedict stared in disbelief. "But he recovered."

"Not really." The manservant averted his gaze. "However, Uncle Stephen was quite elderly."

"Right." Should he press further? "How old, exactly?"

"Oh, at least two-and-seventy, sir."

His stomach clenched. Only two years older than Pa.

"I will wait with the horses, sir," Fletcher said. With slow deliberation, the older man dismounted and held the reins of both horses.

Benedict looked around as if expecting a groom to

appear and take their mounts, but of course Prue and her family lived a simple life, doubtless without servants of any kind. The last thing he wanted to do was enter that house alone, yet what choice did he have?

"All right. Fine." His mouth was dry.

Fletcher sent him a sympathetic look just as the door to the tall, narrow house opened and a young woman appeared. Her raven hair was tucked under a kerchief, and she balanced a toddler on one hip. A voluminous white apron partially concealed her swollen belly. Prudence! Good God, he hardly recognized her. She must be due to give birth very soon.

"Benedict! Oh, you have *come*."

He managed a tight smile as he went forward to greet his sister, rather grateful for the dozing child who blocked him from getting any closer. Benedict struggled to remember when he had last seen Prue. Perhaps after the death of their mother, when he had dared to come back here. The memory of that visit sent a dark chill through him that he quickly banished, back to the cellar in his heart where he kept so much old pain locked away.

"Of course, I came," he said. "What sort of blackguard do you take me for? I am your brother, after all."

She was staring at him in a most disconcerting way. "And *he* is our father." No sooner were the words out than Prue visibly softened. "I'm sorry. I know…it's not an easy situation between you two."

"That's a massive understatement," he said coolly, then gestured toward Fletcher. "My man will stay with the horses."

She nodded. "Let us go inside. You and I must talk, and of course you'll want to see Pa."

Inside the dimly lit parlor, Benedict drew a breath. The air was damp and smelled faintly of sour milk, no doubt from the baby's spit-up.

Prue was laying the baby down in a nearby cradle. "By the way, this is your niece, Jenny." She stood up and seemed to follow his gaze as he surveyed the cluttered room. "I am sorry the house is in such disarray. Since we were forced to bring Pa here, I've been busy from dawn to dark and into the night. I scarcely have time to eat or sleep, yet I must think of the unborn babe." Her hand touched the curve of her belly.

"You need help," he said.

"Indeed." She cast him a sidelong glance. "That's why I sent for you."

What the devil was she expecting him to do? Cook supper? Burp the baby? Scrub the floor? Fine, but if Prue thought he would play nursemaid to their cruel father, she was sorely mistaken.

"You might as well show him to me," Benedict muttered. "Waiting won't make it any easier."

His heart sped up as she led him to a doorway behind the parlor.

"I had to make a bed for Pa in here," Prue said, fingertips on the frayed curtain that served as a door. "This was going to be Gareth's room after the new babe is born, but now he will stay upstairs with us."

Even as she spoke, a moan rose from behind the curtain. Prue seemed to forget all else as she entered.

"Pa, don't fret, I'm here," she said gently.

Looking past his sister, Benedict saw the narrow cot pushed against a wall in what must have once been a sort of storage room adjoining the kitchen. In the bed lay a shrunken version of his mean, cold father, the man who had made his life hell for so long. There were pillows behind his head and a blanket rolled up to support the bent, bony knees poking out below the hem of his nightshirt. A worn quilt was cast aside. Pa's left arm was flexed at the elbow and tucked against his chest, as if it were useless. Worst of all, he was staring at Prudence, his mouth agape.

Benedict wanted to turn around and leave, to ride away up the steep hill and never come back. But that was not an option—at least not yet.

"Look who has come to help us." Prue put a hand behind Pa's head and turned it slightly. Benedict saw that the left side of his craggy face drooped a little, but there was a hard, familiar glint in his black eyes.

"Uh," he gasped.

"Aye," she agreed, smiling. "It's our own Benedict."

When Prue gestured for him to come forward, Benedict did so but stopped when he was just out of reach. Blood thrummed in his ears. He was cold as ice. "Hello, Pa. I'm sorry to see you in this state."

His father made a sound that might have been "Bah!" and closed his eyes.

"I'll just go and get you something to eat," Prue said, gently replacing Pa's head on the pillow.

Benedict followed her into the kitchen. He wanted to tell her that this was sheer torture for him. Unbearable. But when he thought about the burden his sister was carrying, he bit back the words.

"What is it you are planning, Prue?" he asked her. "For me, I mean." This was the benefit of conversing with a sibling: he could get right to the point, and she would understand each layer of meaning.

"If you were a different sort of person, I would beg you to take him back to his own cottage and take care of him there." As if sensing that he was about to emit a harsh laugh, she raised a hand to silence him. "But of course, I know better."

"Even if I were so disposed, Pa would rather die than be left alone with me," Benedict said. "We will hire help for you." Perhaps he might not have to stay in Cornwall after all. Was it humanly possible for him to ride back to London in just forty-eight hours, in time to sail with the Goulds to Australia? His heart leaped at the possibility.

Prue quickly quashed that dream. "Do you imagine you can toss coins at this problem and make it go away? After Oxford, you went sailing around the world to search out not only new species of birds, but also beautiful women to bed, relieved to be free of your family responsibilities. But who do you think assumed them in your place?" Pointing a finger at him, she kept her voice low with a visible effort. "I did. Your *sister*!"

"Allow me a word. Our parents were living in their own cottage these past ten years, overlooking the Channel," he protested. "On their own!"

"Do you think it was easy? More than once, Ma came to my door in tears over something he had done. And after she keeled over dead last year, Pa became more difficult than ever."

"That's a nice word for it," Benedict muttered.

"I don't blame you for wanting to escape, but now I *need* you. Jenny is scarcely weaned, and the new babe will come in just a few weeks. Gareth is not yet four. He must be tended, watched so he doesn't do something reckless. And Caleb is no help, for he is away with the ferry from first light until full darkness."

He felt as if she were hitting him over the head with each point. "I understand."

"I cannot do this alone any longer."

"All right, I will stay, curse it." Hot lava bubbled deep inside him. "But not in this house."

"You can stay at Pa's cottage, but do not imagine you'll spend your days gazing out over the Channel and recording the birds you sight."

"You have made your bloody point," Benedict ground out. "I will do the best I can."

"Like most men, you would prefer to leave life's real

work to women." Prue looked heavenward, and her eyes gleamed with tears. "However, I suppose I must be grateful for whatever assistance you can manage."

After uttering those hard words, his sister swayed forward. As she leaned against his chest and gave a choked sob, Benedict's resistance melted away.

"I will give it a go, Prue. I'll do what I can," he said in a low voice before slowly lifting one hand to rub her back. "That's all I can promise."

CHAPTER 4

$\mathcal{A}$s Benedict rode back up Fore Street, just ahead of Fletcher, he felt numb.

"If I may ask, sir, where are we going now?" the manservant asked when they reached the grassy promontory above Polruan. To their right spread a magnificent view of the Fowey Estuary as it joined with the English Channel. A stirring sight if one were in the mood to appreciate it.

Benedict was not.

"Pardon me, sir, but did you hear my question?" Fletcher called.

"I did." He drew in on Max's reins and squinted into the wind blowing in from the Channel. "We'll be staying in the cottage where my father lived before his attack."

"Ah. I don't believe I have been there. I remained in Oxford, helping to care for my uncle, when you came south the last time…to bury your mother."

It was the manservant's way of asking for more information. Suddenly Benedict was thirsty. He took out a flask of whisky, drank, and offered it to Fletcher who shook his head.

"You'll recall that my father was the head gardener

at Tremethyck Park, the noble estate not far from here where we lived during my childhood," Benedict said. "My earliest memories are of wandering the grounds. Before I could write, I kept a small notebook where I drew crude pictures of the birds I saw." He paused to absorb the sting of memories. "The Dowager Countess of Far lived in her own house on the estate, and she came to believe that I had promise. It was she who arranged for me to have a tutor, and then to attend Oxford, in spite of Pa's strong disapproval." He felt a flash of anger, remembering how Pa had mocked his scholarly pursuits and, later, his aristocratic classmates at Oxford. Benedict might privately admit that his life-long passion for ornithology was rooted in those formative years in the gardens created and tended by his father, but he would never say it aloud. Even if he did, Pa would doubtless make a cruel joke of it.

Or...he would if he could still speak or think clearly.

The whisky simmered in his gut. "My father may be a son of a bitch but he was a gifted gardener. When his knees gave out and Ma's health began to fail, the Dowager gave him a cottage overlooking the Channel, where he and my mother could live out their days."

"Ah," nodded Fletcher. "And that is where we will stay?"

"For now."

Benedict nudged Max with his knees to follow the coastal path toward Lansallos Cove. Waves crashed against the rocks below, clumps of vibrant pink thrift were budding, and Benedict glimpsed gulls and kitti-wakes nesting on niches in the cliffs. In the distance, his parents' charming Gull Cottage came into view, perched above the blue expanse of the English Channel.

"I vow, sir, I have never seen a more beautiful spot in all my life," Fletcher said in tones of wonder.

Benedict breathed deeply of the sea air, but his chest felt tight. He wanted to get to the cottage, drink another flask of whisky, eat some of the food they had packed in a saddlebag, and go to sleep for the rest of the day and night. Longer, if possible.

But what about Prudence? The memory of her pinched, exhausted face tugged painfully at his heart.

"I didn't come to look at the view," he told Fletcher as they continued along the path bordering the cliffs. "Let us hope that the cottage is habitable. One never knows with Pa."

* * *

ON A CLIFF near the smuggling village of Polperro, Camille sat in her mother's neglected art atelier and gazed out a row of tall windows to the windswept English Channel. Long ago, before Camille's parents had fallen in love and married, her mother used to steal away to Lupine Cottage to sketch and paint. Easels, canvases, palettes, and brushes were stored near the window views. The opposite wall was taken up with a chaise of mahogany and woven cane, softened by crimson velvet pillows.

Although Lupine Cottage was also where Camille had trysted with Lord Upton on one life-altering occasion, she urged herself to put that in the past, where it belonged.

"Thank you so much for bringing my books up here," she told Rafael as he carried in the last stack from the two-wheeled gig they'd driven over from Elysium.

The boy spoke in courtly, Portuguese-accented English that made him seem older than his years. "What do you mean to do in this place, my lady?"

Camille had explained to Rafael many times that she was not a "lady", but he seemed to like the sound of it. "I need a place to be, away from home," she explained. "We may spend hours on the cliff paths, looking for the kittiwake nests and also the feather thieves. If we grow tired or it begins to rain, we can seek shelter here, and then I can read and sketch." She paused to dust off a small table and added, "Besides, Lupine Cottage is too pretty to be left empty."

Rafael nodded, looking very serious. "You are right, my lady. I like it here. I could live very happily in such a place."

"It is like a doll's house, I think, more for pretending...and I imagine you would soon find it too small." She gave him a wide smile. "You are right, though, it's very inviting. Shall we bring some provisions? Look, there are a few dishes in this tiny cupboard."

Before he could reply, Camille heard a familiar squawking call from the cliffs outside. Hurrying over to open the door, she stepped out into the cool, brisk air and saw herring gulls swooping down toward the water, fishing for their baby chicks. Her heart accelerated as she imagined the smaller, gentler kittiwakes nesting on cliff ledges not far away.

Camille turned back to Rafael and called, "It's time for us to begin our real work here. Let us walk along the cliffs. I feel hopeful that today we will see the kittiwakes. I can already imagine them, sitting on their nests, happy and unaware they are in danger." She paused, her usually sunny nature clouding over. "But there is no time to lose. Even now, the villains who are responsible for monstrous hats like Lady Rockbridge's may be lurking nearby."

* * *

BENEDICT WAS STARTLED to hear a knock at the cottage door. Looking outside, he saw his sister standing on the step. Behind her, the blue expanse of the English Channel sparkled like diamonds in the morning light.

"Prue!" Suddenly he was aware of the towel round his neck and the razor in his hand. "I didn't expect you."

A little boy of about four peeked out from behind her faded yellow skirts. "H'lo. I'm Gareth. You be my Uncle Ben'dick."

His sense of discomfort intensified, but he extended his free hand to Gareth and shook it. "I am, yes. Nice to meet you, Gareth." Meeting Prudence's clear gaze, Benedict realized he must invite them inside. "Please, come in. What have you done with the baby?"

"Her name is Jenny," Prudence reminded him. "Caleb's mother was kind enough to watch both Jenny and Pa so I could visit you."

He felt oddly trapped. "I am sorry to say I'm not prepared to entertain guests."

"Don't be ridiculous. I know that." She threw him a look of mingled affection and annoyance before turning sideways to fit her bulk past him in the doorway. "Do not imagine you can put me off."

"Ah, Prue, I'd missed hearing you speaking to me that way," he remarked with heavy irony, closing the door. "Sweet words only a sister would utter."

Fletcher, who was in the small bedroom tying his own cravat, poked his beaky nose into the parlor.

"This is my man, Fletcher," said Benedict. "He would gladly serve you tea and cakes if we had any."

"Good morning, madame." The manservant bowed as if Prue were a noblewoman. "I was just about to step out and, one hopes, fetch our baggage. It is due to arrive on the next stage."

"Perhaps you can find us some provisions as well?" suggested Benedict.

"My father keeps a small wagon behind the cottage,

I believe," Prue said to Fletcher. "You must make free to use it."

"Thank you, madame," murmured Fletcher. "I shall do that."

Prudence had taken a seat on a worn, stained settee which looked to be much older than the cottage. She motioned toward a basket near her feet. Benedict hadn't noticed it before, but now the aroma of warm pasties wafted up to him. He generally didn't care for the crescent-shaped savory pies, but at that moment, he would have settled for anything, even watery, gray porridge.

"You must be hungry," Prue said. "I brought meat pasties, a fresh loaf of bread, a crock of butter, and some blackberry jam." As an afterthought, she added, "You will find that Pa has a small garden as well. I think the berries will be ripe soon." She glanced at Fletcher. "When you go down into Polruan, seek out the ferryman who is my husband. Caleb will direct you to our village market and help you transport your belongings from the posting inn."

When Fletcher had gone, Gareth began circling the cluttered parlor, peeking around the furniture. "Ember!" he called again and again.

"Who is he talking to?" asked Benedict.

"Pa's cat," replied Prue. "I'm certain he's hiding. No doubt Ember won't emerge until he knows you are gone forever."

"Pa has a cat?" The notion of his father caring for a domestic pet was absurd.

"Ember came after Ma died," she explained. "Pa only let the cat stay because of its mean disposition. Its claws are sharp as razors, and he was convinced it would not only kill rats but also attack intruders. In truth, however, I suspect that Pa was lonely and has been glad for the company."

"Hmm." Benedict cocked a skeptical brow. Prue was doubtless working to soften her heart toward Pa, to make it easier to take care of him, but Benedict knew the truth and so did she.

Their father was a cold-hearted bastard.

He put away his shaving things and carried the basket of food into the small kitchen at the back of the cottage. The room was filthy. After a moment, Benedict located a knife and cut a thick slice of the fresh-baked bread. The yeasty fragrance made his mouth water. When he'd spread butter and jam on it and finally took a large bite, it seemed that food had never tasted better. Returning to the parlor, he sat down near Prue and finished eating. "That was ambrosia. I'm grateful."

"You'll need your strength if you're going to help me care for Pa," she said. Her forthrightness made him draw back. "Would you like to come home with me today and get started?"

"I can't come yet. I'm only half-dressed and—"

"I will wait."

"Prue, for God's sake." Jumping up, Benedict paced across the room. It was too damned small for him to put much distance between them. "I can't, not yet. Actually, I need to talk to you about this. I have another, better idea. You see, Fletcher has a lot of experience with this sort of situation. His uncle had a similar attack, and Fletcher helped care for him."

"You must be in jest." Her expression was stony. "You mean to send your *manservant* to help with the care of your father, who is unable to do anything at all for himself...not even speak—or piss?" She paused to let this sink in. "What will you be doing in the meantime? Riding out to Fowey or even Truro, in search of an unsuspecting female to seduce?"

He narrowed his eyes. "I haven't done anything like that for years."

"But for someone like you, what other pastimes exist in a place like this?" she wondered calmly. "As I recall, that's exactly what you told me when you persuaded Rowena Bligh to come to your bed. I thought her father was going to have you drawn and quartered."

"Your memory is stunning." It was a devil of a thing when your own sister remembered the tiniest detail of the events you wanted most to forget. "However, I will be otherwise occupied during this visit. I am writing a book." Actually, he'd just decided this while lying awake in the middle of the night, but no need to tell Prue that he hadn't actually put pen to paper yet.

"Really? What about?"

"The title is *Birds of Coastal Cornwall*." Seeing that she was clearly unimpressed, he went over to sit beside her. "Curse it, Prue, am I not *here*? I was supposed to sail to Tasmania, and then on to Australia with John Gould's expedition. It was a magnificent opportunity, but because you asked me to come, I did so. You might give me a little credit."

"Oh, Benedict..." She closed her eyes and sighed as if he had set a heavy weight on her shoulders.

"You will have to allow me to do this my way," he said.

"Yes. I can see that." As Prue rose slowly to her feet, Benedict reached out to help her. She touched a hand to her swollen belly. "I wish I might have the array of choices you give yourself."

"Fletcher will help you, no doubt much more than I ever could. And we both know Pa would rather be boiled in oil than open his eyes to find me sitting at his bedside all day long."

"In your own way, you can be as difficult as he is."

Benedict put a sun-darkened hand to his shirtfront as if she'd landed a mortal blow. "Oh, cruel."

"I am your sister," she murmured, gesturing to

Gareth to come to her side. "I will say what you cannot: I love you…but I also know you. You cannot hide behind a shield with me."

* * *

TRAMPING along the grassy cliffs behind Rafael, Camille was very glad she had brought along a pair of old breeches and some boots when they left Elysium that morning. It was a long walk, up and down the rugged coastal path, from Polperro to Lansallos cove and then on to Polruan. She wanted to be able to climb the rocks, if necessary, especially if they spotted nesting kittiwakes. Frivolous skirts and feminine slippers were out of the question.

"You are very strong, my lady," Rafael remarked as he paused to catch his breath.

"Indeed I am. I've been walking here all my life!" she replied, glowing.

In the distance, they glimpsed the mouth of the Fowey Estuary where it merged with the English Channel. Small boats bobbed on the water, and on the high, distant bank perched the round tower of St. Catherine's Castle, constructed by King Henry VIII three centuries ago, to defend the coastline against threats from France. On the east bank, just over the next hill, the village of Polruan unfurled down a steep slope to the water's edge. Her own home, Elysium, was several miles east, but other family members lived closer. Her Uncle Sebastian and Aunt Julia resided nearby at Mama's family estate, Trevarre Hall, while Papa's brother, Justin, owned Frenchman's Haven in a lush valley north of Lansallos.

For Camille, this entire stretch of coastline was infused with golden memories, and she would go to great lengths to protect it from the thugs who meant to kidnap and murder beloved residents like the kittiwakes.

"Just ahead are the cliffs where kittiwake colonies have nested in the past," she told Rafael, clambering up the path. "They spend the winters out at sea and only come ashore during nesting season, pairing off with the same mate year after year." Her insides churned as she thought again of the terrible people who wanted to murder kittiwakes simply to decorate their absurd hats. It was unthinkable.

Just then, Camille stopped, listening. In the distance, she heard the familiar lilt of "kitti-*wake!*"

"What is it?" asked Rafael, his black curls blown in every direction by the sea breeze.

She pressed a forefinger to her lips and pointed toward the sound. The call came again, then again. Unlike the wild squawking of the herring gulls who barged right into the village to search for scraps of food, the kittiwake's call was as playful as the birds themselves, Camille thought.

Just then, a small white gull with black-tipped wings made a circle in the air above them and disappeared around the next point of land. Camille's heart sped up. "Did you see him? Follow me but be very quiet."

They scrambled over a series of large stones and emerged into the open, gazing down on the side of a cliff riddled with rocky ledges. Below, Camille saw dozens of kittiwake nests, each one guarded by a least one parent. Gesturing to Rafael that they should crouch down, she took her monocular from the pocket of her breeches.

"Look at them," she whispered, peering through the brass-rimmed lens. "So precious."

In some of the nests, tiny, down-fluffed pale gray chicks were visible. The kittiwake parents fed them worms. Camille watched for only a few minutes before gesturing to Rafael, back toward the cliff path. He followed her, waiting as she pressed her hands to her cheeks and paced back and forth.

"I have to find a way to protect them," she said softly, a note of steel in her voice.

"I don't see how you can do that," he replied. "The birds are wild things."

She had seen a cottage in the distance, perched on the brow of the hill near Polruan. If memory served, an older couple lived there. Perhaps they would help in her quest? Without another word, Camille started toward the cottage. As they drew closer, she saw an exceedingly fine horse grazing outside a small, crude structure that might serve as a stable. A little shiver ran down her spine as she remembered the man in Hyde Park who rode a chestnut gelding exactly like this one.

"Wait," she murmured to Rafael, and stopped under a windswept pine tree.

Just then, the cottage door opened, and a tall figure emerged. Camille's mouth went dry. She didn't need to look through her monocular to confirm that it was the arrogant man who had stopped her from plucking the kittiwake hat from Lady Rockbridge's head. He was tall and strong, with wide shoulders and a roguishly handsome face. As she watched, the sea breeze ruffled his already disheveled black hair.

"It's *him*," she said too softly to be heard. What was *he* doing here? Where was the old couple who had owned the cottage a few years ago? "Let's go back."

She had no sooner spoken the words than the mysterious stranger turned his head, as if he sensed her presence and already knew her identity. Camille knew a surge of panic as he stepped onto the path in front of the cottage and started toward her. Should she turn and run away? Already, the odious man was just a few long strides away.

Camille glanced toward Rafael and put a finger over her lips to indicate that he should be silent and hide behind a nearby tree. By the time she looked forward again, the man was just feet away.

"Who the devil are you?" he demanded, coming close enough for her to stare into his deep green eyes before they raked her body from the toes of her boots to her breeches-clad legs to the curls escaping from her woolen cap. He blinked in disbelief. "By God, you're a girl!"

Camille's cheeks grew hot as she was swept by a disturbing feeling: alarm mixed with something even more dangerous. It was, Camille realized, a thrilling flutter of attraction. She tried to mentally shove it away from her awareness.

"Whether I am a female or not, it's none of your affair," she said defiantly.

He leaned closer, and she inhaled his heady male scent. It was confusing that someone so arrogant could also be potently attractive.

"Wait," he muttered. "It's not possible. You can't be the mad vixen from Hyde Park…"

She straightened, lifting her chin "I am certainly not a *mad vixen*."

"What are you doing here? Did you follow me?"

"Ridiculous!" Camille scoffed. "I suspect it is you who followed *me*."

Just then, over the stranger's wide shoulder, Camille saw a movement in the doorway of the cottage. A statuesque, dark-haired woman, great with child, emerged. A little boy held one of her hands, in the other she carried a basket. The woman lifted a hand to shade her eyes and swept her gaze over the landscape, pausing when she spied the man.

"Benedict!" she called. "Are you coming?"

"Yes," he replied, but didn't move until the little boy

began to run toward them. The man, whose name apparently was Benedict, put up a hand to halt his progress. "Stay there, Gareth."

Camille's heart skipped a beat as she watched him walk away without another word, back to the woman and child. The woman, obviously his wife, slipped her hand through his arm, and the boy pulled at his mother's skirts.

"My lady?" came a tentative voice close by Camille.

She gave a little start, so caught up in the scene by the cottage that she'd forgotten all about Rafael. "Oh, it's you! Thank goodness that man has left us alone."

"Who is he? Do you know?"

"He is the odious stranger from Hyde Park, the one who stopped me from destroying Lady Rockbridge's hat with the kittiwake wings." Her thoughts were spinning. "It appears that he and his family live right here, near the very cliffs where the unsuspecting kittiwakes nest! No wonder he interfered that day in the park. It cannot be a coincidence. I believe that this man called Benedict may be responsible for the deaths of these lovely birds. I suspect he sells the wings merely to enrich himself!"

Rafael narrowed his dark eyes. "I must agree, my lady, that man did have the look of a scoundrel about him. His neckcloth was not even tied properly!"

"Exactly! A scoundrel," Camille agreed, heading toward the coastal path that would take them back to Elysium. "Let's go home. I am suddenly ravenous, and I shall need a great deal of food in order to devise a *plan*."

$\mathcal{I}$sabella St. Briac swallowed a bite of onion tarte and cast surreptitious glances toward her daughter. It seemed that, perhaps for the first time, Camille wasn't hungry for Madame Kerjean's legendary tarte. The aged cook had brought the recipe with her from Brittany, the birthplace of Gabriel and Justin St. Briac, and Camille had adored it since babyhood, when her father had let her sample tiny bites. Today, however, her generous, aromatic wedge of tarte went untouched.

"I don't think you have eaten a bite of food," Isabella remarked with a frown. "Are you ill?"

Before Camille could reply, her brother Damien reached toward her plate. "If you don't want yours, I'll take it," he offered with a grin. Isabella reflected that he might be only eight years of age, but the boy was already a rogue.

Camille pushed the plate toward him. "I'm not hungry."

No sooner had Damien taken possession of her supper than he passed a bite of tarte to Zeus, who waited, tongue lolling expectantly, under the table.

Meanwhile, Gabriel turned to their daughter. It was

his turn to question her. "*Ma petite*, what ails you?" he asked gently.

A long moment passed before Camille relented and regarded them with her deep blue eyes. Isabella could see her mind working, deciding whether to confide in them. At length, she spoke.

"You already know that I am very worried about the kittiwakes, and I've come back to rescue them from the villains who would kill them for the most shocking and frivolous of reasons." She closed her eyes and grimaced at the thought. "Rafael and I went out today to see if we could find their nesting spot, and in the process, we encountered that odious man!"

Isabella and Gabriel glanced at one another before he spoke in a tentative voice. "Are we supposed to know what man you mean?"

"Of course!" Color rose in Camille's cheeks, and Isabella was struck anew by her daughter's rare beauty. Her unbound, golden-caramel hair tumbled around her slim shoulders in a riot of loose curls, and her exquisite, fine-boned face was luminous. "I *told* you, Papa, don't you remember? I am referring to the man who interfered in Hyde Park when I tried to wrest the hat from Lady Rockbridge's head."

Trying once again to imagine this scene, Isabella wanted to smile.

"Are you saying," Gabriel began carefully, "that the man from Hyde Park was on the Cornwall cliffs today?"

"Yes, yes, that's exactly right! Perhaps you know him. He lives in a stone cottage with a slate roof, near the cliff path, just above Polruan. It is situated alone, beside a group of windswept pine trees." After a short pause, Camille added, "Oh! I almost forgot, I also saw his wife and small son. She addressed him as Benedict."

Gabriel exchanged another look with Isabella. "The

only cottage I know of in that area belongs to an elderly couple by the name of Hawke. He was a gardener at Tremethyck Park. The Dowager Countess gave him the cottage when his wife's health failed, and he couldn't work any longer."

Camille shook her head. "I don't remember them."

Ignoring her, Isabella continued, "Mrs. Hawke was in ill health for a long time. I believe she passed on last year."

"Hmm." Camille frowned. "Are you both certain you don't know a local man named Benedict with rather wild black hair and a forbidding countenance?" After a brief pause, she added helpfully, "Rafael said he has the look of a scoundrel, and I couldn't agree more."

"I do not know any such man," said Gabriel. "On the contrary, barely a fortnight ago I saw old Mr. Hawke sitting on a bench outside that cottage, all alone on the hilltop. There was a gray cat next to him."

Camille was pensive. "Well, there was no old man today, yet I know what happened was not a dream."

"What do you mean to do?" Realizing that her daughter was capable of rash behavior when pursuing a cause, Isabella pressed, "I hope you don't mean to put your own safety at risk on account of the kittiwakes. What if this man you think you encountered today is dangerous?"

"I don't *think* I encountered him, Mama. I know it!" She pushed away from the table. "I must confer with Rafael. There are plans to make."

"But Rafael promised to teach me how to play Hazard this evening," protested Damien.

Shocked, Isabella momentarily forgot about Camille and her birds. "Hazard! Oh no, Damien, you are too young for games of chance."

Her son gave her a grin that could only be described

as raffish, despite his youth. "Rafael knows all sorts of things."

"I'll bet he does," Gabriel said with grim amusement.

"Perhaps a boy of fourteen knows more of the world than we might wish Damien to understand," Isabella remarked. She knew her son had been rather lonely. His two sisters were much older, and Louisa had been living away from Elysium for years. No doubt Rafael made for enticing company, but what other knowledge might he impart to their young son?

"I don't think a game or two of Hazard will transform Damien into a gamester," Gabriel said wryly.

The twinkle in his eyes made her smile. Remembering their daughter, she looked around, but Camille had slipped away while Isabella was distracted.

"*Cherie*," murmured Gabriel, lifting her hand to his lips, "if you must worry about any of our children, choose Camille. There's no telling what sort of trouble she may get into if she continues to interfere with the feather thieves."

"I couldn't agree more. I was about to ask you to do something to stop her, Gabriel!"

Her husband drew a breath and shook his head. "If you imagine I can *forbid* her, especially at four-and-twenty years of age, you are dreaming, my love."

* * *

Upstairs, Camille slipped into her bedchamber, closed the door, and leaned back against the paneled wood, smiling as if she had just eluded capture. Her room was as lovely and welcoming as ever, yet it seemed she didn't belong here now. The crowded bookshelves, the graceful Sheraton bed she had chosen at age thirteen, the blue satin chaise longue in front of the tall windows...why did all of it seem like part of the past?

Her eccentric French grandmother, who was now elderly and in failing health, had helped to decorate the room. It was Cerise St. Briac who had found the ivory-and-blue striped silk for the swagged window curtains, but Camille had drawn the line when Grandmère brought her a 'special gift'—a yellow, long-tailed canary in an elaborate cage.

"I know how much you adore birds," her grandmother had proclaimed, clearly pleased with her thoughtful choice. "He sings quite nicely."

But of course, Camille had been horrified by the thought of keeping any bird caged. It was almost as repellant a concept as the stuffed birds her cousin Anthony, a respected naturalist, displayed in a glass case in his library. She had politely thanked Grandmère, but as soon as the old woman departed, Camille declared that she meant to set the canary free.

Yet, Papa had pointed out to her that she could not release a domesticated bird into the wild. "Our little friend wouldn't last a day," he said, fixing her with his blue eyes that were so like her own. "I propose we keep his cage in my tree-filled *orangerie* and let him out every day to fly about and enjoy some freedom inside the walls of glass."

Camille had named the tiny bird Pierre, and throughout his years in Papa's glass *orangerie*, she cared for him and loved him deeply. He had trilled at the sight of her, eaten from her hand, and even perched on Papa's shoulder while he gardened.

A strange wave of sadness swept over Camille as she thought about Pierre and tried to imagine what had been inside his tiny heart. He had been loved, but was he ever truly happy, truly himself, living among humans in a glass prison?

It seemed that all God's creatures, herself included, needed only to discover their own place in the world...

and be allowed to live in peace. Camille wasn't certain yet exactly where she belonged, but in the meantime, she could find a purpose by protecting the sweet kittiwakes.

* * *

BENEDICT SLEPT RESTLESSLY during his first few nights at Gull Cottage. Every small noise seemed to wake him, though often it seemed only to be the sound of waves striking the cliffs.

Invariably, he gave up trying to sleep when dawn broke. On this morning, faint sounds came to him from the other side of the cottage, and Benedict donned a dressing gown and padded barefoot from his bedroom. The faint clatter of pans led him to the tiny kitchen where he beheld Fletcher sitting on a stool next to a basin of soapy water, a towel tied round his bony midsection. His blackthorn walking stick was propped against the long table.

Benedict blinked and ran a hand through his tousled hair. "What the devil are you doing, old man?"

"I am scrubbing the kitchen, sir," proclaimed the manservant in austere tones. "Next, I will prepare your breakfast, after which I shall return to the home of Mrs. Johns."

He felt a twinge of shame, for Fletcher's own health was precarious at best. It didn't feel right that he should be laboring this way. "Did you sleep?"

"I did indeed, but as you know, sir, I require half the sleep of other men." He dried a large, chipped bowl and set it on the long worktable that now appeared to be spotlessly clean. Nearby, a pot of hot tea was swathed in a towel. Fletcher did not ask Benedict if he cared for tea, for he already knew the answer. Moments later, he handed him a cup of the steaming brew with a splash of milk.

"You are a prince, Fletch." Sipping the brew, Benedict felt grateful for this welcome moment of normalcy even as the rest of his world tilted precariously beyond his control.

The corners of Fletcher's thin mouth flickered momentarily. "It is kind of you to say so, sir. Might you care for porridge?"

"Again?" he grimaced. "Is there still no ham?"

"The butcher has promised me some today." Fletcher took out a pan. "I do have some fresh berries for your porridge."

Benedict wanted to back out of the room, but he knew he must ask about Pa. "You returned from Prue's late last night."

"Yes, sir. You were reading and I didn't want to disturb you."

"Well." His mouth was dry. "I should have inquired about my father." He braced himself to hear the manservant's report.

"Mr. Hawke is…the same, although I did think he showed a bit of expression when I mentioned your name." When Benedict made no reply, Fletcher continued, "I believe I have been a considerable help to your sister. Mrs. Johns is able to go about her day while I look after Mr. Hawke."

Benedict didn't want to think about what that might entail. "I appreciate that," he said hoarsely. "More than you know."

"As we have discussed, I am better suited to the task of seeing to Mr. Hawke's needs, and you have other, more important work to do, don't you? You are writing a book," Fletcher said with a nod, then turned back to the porridge. "I'll bring your breakfast to your desk, sir."

The tightness in Benedict's chest eased as he came into the parlor. In the past three days, the cluttered room had been transformed into an airy study. He'd moved his parents' long dining table near the windows that overlooked the coastal path and the English Channel, affording him a stunning view throughout the day and evening. His workspace was at one end, while his books and ornithological specimens were arranged along the other side. There was still room for the ugly settee on the far wall. Benedict had been inspired to cover its stained upholstery with one of his mother's woven shawls, so it was presentable enough to entertain a guest or two if it were absolutely necessary.

Sitting down at his makeshift desk, Benedict spread out the papers and looked at them. Although he had prepared copious notes for his book, *Birds of Coastal Cornwall*, he felt rather uninspired.

He tried not to think of the Gould expedition, sailing that very day on the *Parsee*, but images crowded into his mind, nonetheless. There were John and Elizabeth Gould, leaning over the rail as the ship launched, waving, poised on the cusp of a brilliant adventure.

Benedict pressed both hands to his eyes and smothered a groan. "Fletcher!" he barked. "I'm going out."

"But sir…"

Turning, he saw the manservant standing in the doorway, holding a steaming bowl of porridge in one hand. "Just put it here on my desk. I'll eat when I return."

* * *

AT DAWN, the coastal path was bathed in a golden light that should have lifted Benedict's spirits. Lavender and azure softly streaked the sky, and the broad expanse of the English Channel glittered in the distance.

Because he needed quiet to observe the birds, Benedict fed and watered Max but decided to postpone his usual morning ride. Instead, he slung a leather bag over one shoulder and set out along the cliffs on foot. If the opportunity arose to gather specimens to study for his research, Benedict meant to take full advantage.

A chilly wind blew up from the Channel. Benedict wore a wool coat he'd owned for more than a decade, and he'd pulled an old tricorne hat of Pa's down over his thick hair. He thought he might walk to Trelawne Manor, an estate near Polperro where there was a large rookery. It might well be a good place to start, for rooks were fascinating birds, yet he found that he felt little interest in them today.

As he followed the winding path above the cliffs, Benedict glimpsed ships in the distance, perhaps sailing from London to a port as distant as Hobart, Tasmania, where the *Parsee* would eventually arrive. His heart twisted in his chest as he imagined himself standing on deck, shoulder to shoulder with John Gould, making plans for the bold exploits that awaited them.

A moment later, Benedict heard the birds before he saw them. *Kitti-wake!* came the cries, sounding especially shrill to his ears. He had just rounded a bend in the path when he looked down and saw the nests. As if by design, they balanced on shallow ledges that descended like rugged, uneven steps, carved by wind and waves into the side of the cliff. *Amazing*, marveled Benedict. There were parents, feeding their tiny pale gray chicks who needed no camouflage due to the remote locations of their nests. Nothing seemed amiss, yet the cries continued, and Benedict clambered up on a high rock for a better view. Partway down, on one of the cliff ledges he saw the culprits: a trio of men with nets who had already captured at least one male kittiwake and were shoving it into a canvas bag. The bird's mate was flying at the feather thieves in an effort to protect her hatchlings.

Who the devil were those men? Even from a distance, he could hear their coarse accents, see their ragged clothing, and realize that they were louts. The one who had stuffed the kittiwake into the bag wore a striped sailor's cap.

A second man reached down and produced a long pole with a hook on the end. As Benedict watched, the miscreant aimed it at the captured kittiwake's agitated mate. Rage boiled up inside him. Seeing a crude path that led partway down the sloping cliff, he scrambled down it, determined to stop them.

Yet, it quickly came to him that it would not be so easy. Who exactly were these men? It seemed impossible that they were working on their own. Someone must have hired them.

"Wait!" he called, and the trio looked up in unison. Benedict tried to force a smile. "It looks like you might need help."

The stocky, thick-necked man in the striped hat froze, holding the long pole at his side. "Who're you?"

"I am new to these parts, and I need work," Benedict replied, doing his best to adopt the accent of a laboring man rather than a scientist. "I'd be good at this! Can ye use me?"

* * *

"SHH!" Camille cautioned softly, putting a hand on Rafael's arm. After a moment, she whispered, "Do you hear that? It is a kittiwake, in trouble!"

They were standing on the coastal path, wind whipping around them.

"I hear it, my lady." Rafael nodded. His usually tanned face looked pale today.

She excitedly reached inside the pocket of her breeches for the Wedgwood monocular. When she glanced back at Rafael, she saw that he was grimacing and clutching his stomach. "What's wrong? Are you ill?"

"I do feel sick," he admitted. "Mayhap I ate too many kippers at breakfast."

"Go back then. I'll be fine on my own!"

"But my lady, what if you get into trouble?"

"I have been here a thousand times before. What trouble could befall me?" She gave him a little push. "Please, do go *now*. I wouldn't want you to be sick on my shoes."

The boy nodded and turned back toward Lupine Cottage, perched high above Polperro. "I will just lie down for a bit, my lady. But I beg you to stay right here. Do not try to climb down the cliffs."

"Of course not!"

Camille watched him go, then quickly returned her attention to the distressed kittiwake. The call continued, sounding increasingly urgent. Finally, unable to help herself, Camille started toward the edge of the cliff, following the sound. She clung to the edge of a huge rock and leaned forward, scanning the scene below.

Her breath caught at the sight of more kittiwakes than she could count, their black-barred wings flashing in the morning light. Most of them appeared oblivious to any threats as they shared plunder with the chicks, tucked in nests on stone ledges carved by the elements. However, looking farther south, Camille located the single, alarmed bird. He was flying in a circle over a small group of men who stood on a promontory partway down the cliff, occasionally diving down to squawk and menace them. Camille squinted into her monocular.

Outrage surged inside her as she saw one of the men reach into a nearby nest and grasp the male kittiwake. His beefy hands clenched his helpless victim's neck. Horror seared Camille as the brute ripped the wings off the bird, stuffed them into his bag, and flung the maimed kittiwake backward over his shoulder.

Angry tears burned Camille's eyes as she watched the murdered, bleeding gull spiral down to land in the English Channel. The hatchlings, who surely must be terrified, made small screeching sounds. The man merely pulled his striped sailor's cap lower on his fat head and moved on to another nest. Facing him was a tall, broad-shouldered man in a tricorne, his profile turned away from Camille's view. He shook his head and put a hand on Striped Hat's sleeve.

Camille took the monocular from her eye and drew a deep breath. Remaining silent another moment was simply not an option. If she did so, she would be complicit. That she could never be! Without another thought, Camille started down the sloping cliff path. The early morning mist had left a slick sheen on the rocks, but she barely noticed.

Suddenly, the tall man turned, and their eyes met. Camille's pulse raced as she recognized her now-familiar enemy, Benedict. It was just as she had suspected all along: this scoundrel was in league with the gang who were killing the kittiwakes in the most brutal way possible. When she thought of what she had seen, thought of the helpless, orphaned chicks who would doubtless be left to starve, raw fury seared her heart.

"You! Stay away!" he shouted, pointing at Camille.

Oh, he was despicable! Without a pause, she continued her precipitous descent toward the rocky ledge where the men were gathered. She saw Benedict's chiseled features darken, first with anger, and then something that might have been alarm.

Ignoring him, Camille came close enough to lean forward. Reaching toward Striped Hat, she demanded, "Give me that bag, murderer!"

Just as she grasped the filthy burlap fabric, Striped Hat tugged back and shouted, "Leave it, Missy!"

She felt something moving inside the sack, and her heart twisted with the realization that a kittiwake must still be alive inside, struggling to escape.

"I demand that you let go!" she cried.

Striped Hat yanked hard, and as he did so, Camille lost her balance on the wet pebbles, her booted feet sliding out from under her. For one harrowing moment, it seemed she might be able to right herself, but gravity was too powerful. She tumbled sideways toward a nearby boulder, unable to stop her forward momentum. A moment later, everything went dark.

CHAPTER 6

*G*ood *God!* Looking down at the breeches-clad female who lay crumpled against a boulder on the stony ledge, Benedict felt momentarily paralyzed by shock. She was completely still, eyes closed. Could she be dead? His heart thundered as he absorbed this terrible possibility.

"I will see to her!" he warned the others, even as he approached the mysterious beauty who had been plaguing him since their first meeting in Hyde Park. Why couldn't she heed his warnings and stay away?

Kneeling on the rocks, Benedict swept an assessing gaze over the girl's motionless form. He was adept at examining birds with fragile, jointed legs no bigger than toothpicks, and he used those skills now. His long fingers were agile as he encircled her neck and, ever so gently, felt each vertebra, from the base of her skull to the small of her back. Her hair had tumbled from its pins, and long, gleaming curls spilled over her face and shoulders. When Benedict looked more closely, he saw the smear of blood near her scalp. A bump had begun to rise.

"My lady, can you hear me?" he asked, voice low,

coaxing, but she did not respond. Remembering that John Gould had said her name was Camille St. Briac, Benedict tried again, softly whispering, "Camille…open your eyes."

Her long lashes fluttered as she stirred, then tried to sit up.

"No. Don't move. Just rest." To his surprise, she obeyed, relaxing against him without ever fully opening her eyes. "I'll take care of you."

Benedict glanced back at the boorish trio of feather hunters who stood nearby, mouths agape. "I will look after her…" He focused on the group's leader who held the sack. "I want to meet with you later. We may be able to help each other." Seeing the man's dubious expression, Benedict added, "I am living for a time on the clifftop. I see everything that happens—and I need work."

"Oh! Aye, let us talk." A gust of wind caused the fellow to pull down his striped cap just as drops of rain began to pelt them. "Meet me at the Old Ferry Inn for a pint."

"In Bodinnick?"

"Aye. At dusk."

"What's your name?"

"Jem."

Seeing Jem look around as if in search of another kittiwake to capture, Benedict said, "Go while you can, afore they come looking for this young lady. Clearly, she is a person of quality." He lifted his brows as if to convey his own distaste for the upper classes and hoped they would accept the portrait he was presenting of himself.

"Aye." Jem gestured to the other two men to follow him but paused after one step. A frown creased his weathered face. "But—the wench won't die? If she be quality, there'd be questions."

"I hope not." This seemed to hurry them along. When the trio had scrambled out of sight, over the cliff top, Benedict gently gathered the girl into his arms, grateful that she wore breeches rather than voluminous petticoats and skirts. How pale she was! As the wind picked up, raindrops fell faster and faster, and the rocks were slick. It was risky to try to carry her out of here now, alone, but what choice did he have?

Sheltering the beautiful Camille against his chest, Benedict rose easily to his feet and began to pick his way up the steeply sloping, rock-strewn cliff.

* * *

IT WAS the headache that broke through Camille's unconscious state, forcing her awake. Her head throbbed in time to her heartbeat. Slowly, reluctantly, she opened her eyes and blinked until her vision cleared. Where in the world was she? She lay on a lumpy, narrow settee in a small, paneled room that smelled of books and damp. A scratching sound commenced from across the room, and her heart jumped. Warily, she turned her head, wincing, and made out the silhouette of a tall, broad-shouldered figure standing before a long table that faced the room's only window. The man bent forward, his pen scratching softly on a paper.

Dear God, where was she? Remembering the horrible louts who had been clubbing kittiwakes, Camille felt a rush of panic. Had they taken her to their secret lair?

At that very moment, the tall man turned toward her. Camille closed her eyes. Terror squeezed her chest. Footsteps came closer. She focused on breathing evenly, praying her captor would not guess that she was awake.

"Camille," whispered a deep male voice. His tone was…surprisingly gentle yet familiar. "Can you hear me?"

Fingers touched her shoulder. Panic replaced by a frisson of curiosity, Camille opened her eyes.

"Ah, there you are." A pause.

She felt the power of his smile deep inside, like a drink of sparkling wine. When he removed gold-rimmed spectacles, it came to her—it was *that man*, Benedict! "Let me go," she whispered.

This drew a low, compelling laugh from him. "No one is holding you back—though it seems advisable that you rest for now. You've been unconscious."

Camille badly wanted to assert herself, to stand up and march out the door, but she couldn't muster the strength. "What have you done to me?"

His tone was wry. "I think you did it to yourself, advancing full tilt down that cliff to confront the feather thieves."

"Oh…yes." It all came back to her then, right up to the moment she'd lost her footing and tumbled forward. Lifting a hand, she gingerly touched the bump on her head and cringed. "Those evil men…and you…" Her words trailed off.

He was one of the evil men himself, and now she was his captive. It should come as no surprise that he did not respond to her remark. Instead, he asked, "How do you feel?" He crouched beside the settee, sitting back on his heels, and Camille felt the warmth of his breath on her cheek. He brushed feather-light fingertips over her brow. "Are you in pain? Dizzy?"

"Yes, a bit of both," she admitted.

To her annoyance, she felt a rush of tingling warmth, seemingly because this man was near. Her body did not seem to care that he was a scoundrel.

Camille hadn't felt anything like this since she'd lost her head with Lord Upton.

Roger.

Had she been a fool to think she might close off that part of herself forever?

"Since we continue to engage in unplanned encounters, I should introduce myself," the man said wryly. "My name is Benedict Hawke." He waited. "And you are…Camille?"

She licked her dry lips. "Yes. But how did you know?"

"After our first encounter in Hyde Park, a friend guessed your identity. I didn't know if he was right until I called you by your name on the cliffs, after you fell, and you responded."

She felt too muddled to ask more questions, but she did muster enough strength to warn, "Do not imagine that you can keep me here in this helpless state. People will be looking for me. In fact, I expect my father, Gabriel St. Briac, to pound on the door at any moment!"

"He is welcome to do so," he replied with the driest of smiles. "Has anyone told you that you resemble an angel, Camille?"

"Yes, far too often." She tried to scowl. "However, I am nothing like that."

"So I have noticed." Benedict drew closer and gave a low laugh. "Your angelic countenance is misleading."

Oh, dash it. Her nipples tightened and her mouth watered slightly, as if she were hungry—for *him.* Camille felt dizzy as Benedict's chiseled features began to swim before her eyes. Her eyelids grew impossibly heavy, and from a distance she heard herself mumble, "Bother."

* * *

TIME PASSED. How much? It felt as if she were swimming up from the bottom of the English Channel when she finally managed to open her eyes again. The small, plain room was empty. There was no sign of Benedict Hawke—if indeed that was his real name.

The throbbing in her head had subsided, but now Camille was aware of a bruised area near her right shoulder. With an effort, she sat up and moved her feet to the floor. The earlier encounter with Hawke felt like a bizarre dream, especially when she remembered that he had not only a wife, but a child as well. The man had a family, and yet he had brought her into their house and looked at her as if…well, as if he would like to ravish her.

And Camille had shamelessly wished he might try. Her cheeks flamed as her body began to respond all over again, just thinking about it. Roger had once whispered that she was *passionate*—but look where that had led! This was the very reason why she ought to confine herself to looking after birds and forget about romance of any sort. *Ever.*

Drawing a deep breath, Camille looked around the parlor. She remembered the conversation with her parents, when they had spoken about Mr. Hawke, the elderly gardener, whose wife had recently died. Had Benedict taken over his father's cottage?

Across the room, the window overlooking the cliffs was dominated by a long, mahogany dining table. It appeared to serve as a desk, for one end was stacked with papers, books, and an inkstand. The remainder of the table was lined with small objects of various sizes. Remembering that she had seen Benedict writing at that table, Camille decided to have a closer look.

Pushing up from the settee, she gingerly rose to her feet and moved from one piece of furniture to another, holding on to each one for support. Eventually she reached the long table and beheld an array of books and papers covered with sketches and notes written in a strong hand. Near the front of the desk, was a message on a scrap of paper. Remembering the sight of Benedict writing at this table, Camille dared to pick up the paper, but before she could read it, something else caught her eye, on the other side of a tall stack of books. Her heart stopped.

Oh, no! Please, God, no!

Had she simply not wanted to see or feel the horror? For in that moment, she looked beyond the books and focused on a vast array of birds, all quite dead, lying on their backs. Handwritten tags were affixed to a precious little outstretched leg of each murdered gull, wren, sandpiper, owl, woodpecker, robin, and so many more. Camille pressed a shaking hand to her mouth. She wanted to weep. To shout in outrage!

To kill the odious Benedict Hawke and tie a specimen label to *him!*

A rustling sound reached her ears from the next room. Just as Camille turned back to the settee, still clutching the scrap of paper, she glimpsed a lovely kittiwake among the other victims. Its white wings were tipped with black, as if they had been carefully dipped in an inkwell. Images filled her mind of the kittiwake nests filled with eggs and new chicks, depending on their parents for sustenance and guidance. Her heart raced as she thought of the cruel oaf who had been with Benedict on the cliffs, ripping the wings from a struggling kittiwake.

Bile rose in her throat.

Perhaps she had clung to doubts about the extent of Benedict Hawke's villainy, but now Camille knew that reality was more terrible than her suspicions. He truly was a killer of innocent, wild birds. A savage *feather thief*—no doubt the ringleader of the criminal gang she had confronted on the cliffs today.

No sooner had Camille taken her seat on the settee than Benedict reappeared, carrying a tray laden with dishes of food. His tall form was silhouetted in the doorway to what was doubtless the kitchen. He had shed both neckcloth and coat, and his strong, tanned forearms contrasted with rolled-up white shirtsleeves.

Other women might swoon at the sight of such a splendid-looking man. Camille, however, stiffened her spine.

"Ah, you are awake. That's good," he said. His moss-green eyes swept over her. "Have a care. You shouldn't try to walk yet."

No, of course he didn't want *that*. If she walked around, she would discover the evidence of his crimes! The poor murdered birds, ripped from their nests, their families who needed them. No wonder he wanted her to stay on the other side of the room!

He was coming toward her, bearing the silver tray covered with fragrant dishes. Camille inhaled the scents of roasted chicken and warm, crusty bread. Benedict reached her side and flashed a smile that was almost irresistible, but she fought both the pull of attraction and the inner voice that reminded her that she was his captive and might well be in danger.

This man is a devil, she reminded herself as he set down the tray on the settee next to her. There was a small loaf of bread with butter and a tempting dish of stew, crowded with pieces of chicken, carrot, and potato.

"Are you comfortable eating from the tray, or should I bring a small table?" he inquired kindly. He shook out a napkin and spread it over her lap. When

Camille only stared at the food, he spoke again, "You need food to regain your strength."

Her stomach emitted a plaintive sound, a reminder that she hadn't eaten at all today. "I will have only a bite, or two." As he stood by, watching, she tried the stew. It was so delicious, she closed her eyes to savor the flavors.

"It's good, isn't it." It was a statement, not a question.

Hoping to catch him off-guard, Camille casually remarked, "Your wife is a fine cook."

Out of the corner of her eye, she saw him blink in surprise. "What are you talking about?"

Setting down her spoon, Camille boldly met his gaze. "I saw your wife and child recently. They were coming out the door of this house, so you needn't deny it."

One side of his mouth quirked. "You sound as if you suspect me of betraying *you*."

To her dismay, her cheeks felt hot. "I was simply stating a fact."

"You are so convincing I almost believe it myself." To her surprise, he sat down beside her on the settee, the tray separating their bodies, then buttered a piece of bread. When he put it in her hand, his long, tanned fingers brushed hers for one instant. "However, I must inform you, your facts are wrong. I have no wife. The lady you saw was my sister, Prudence, in the company of her young son, Gareth."

Camille bit her lip, reminding herself that even if he were telling the truth, none of this mattered. The only interest she had in this cruel feather thief was putting a stop to his crimes! "I must go now."

"And how do you intend to do that?"

"Do you mean to prevent me from leaving?" Boldly, she added, "Perhaps I am your captive."

"Hardly." He leaned one arm against the back of the settee and arched a brow. "My dear, you have quite a flair for drama."

Camille swallowed the last bite of bread and tried to stand. For a long moment, the floor swayed beneath her feet, and then Benedict Hawke's strong hands were on her waist, and he was guiding her back down on the settee.

"I demand that you send word to my family, without delay," she managed to command.

"Of course." He nodded, unfazed. "Where do you live?"

What was he up to? "My home, Elysium, is a manor house not far from here." She lifted her chin. "If you do not release me immediately you will incur the wrath of not only my father but also my uncles, Lord Sebastian Trevarre and Justin St. Briac!"

"Your warnings are noted." He moved away from her and rose to his feet. "I will send word to Elysium."

"You…will?"

He cocked his dark head and smiled. "If you truly imagined I would force you to stay here, you have misjudged me." Walking to the doorway, he spoke to someone, and to Camille's surprise, a voice answered. Was it possible they had not been alone in the house after all? A moment later, an older man with a wild shock of white hair emerged into the parlor, leaning with one hand on a walking stick.

Camille stared as the rail-thin gentleman used his free hand to fasten the last button on a worn black waistcoat and nodded to her.

"This is my man, Fletcher," Benedict said casually. "He prepared the stew you enjoyed so much." Glancing at Fletcher, he added, "You have the pleasure of meeting Miss Camille St. Briac."

The older man gave a slight but courtly bow. "I am

at your service, Miss St. Briac." Although Fletcher's expression was impassive, Camille discerned kindness in his heavy-lidded eyes.

Benedict said, "The lady desires to return to her home. I would simply take her myself by horseback, but given today's events, it would be safer if she travels in a proper equipage. Do you have time to summon assistance from her family? Miss St. Briac tells me their estate, Elysium, is not far to the east."

"Of course, sir." The manservant nodded. "I will go there immediately, on my way back to Polruan to care for your—"

Benedict cut him off. "Right, good, thank you."

Camille watched as Fletcher approached and retrieved the silver tray. She met his eyes and said softly, "When you reach my home, please ask for a young man named Rafael. It would be better for him to fetch me than my father, who might, uh, overreact to this situation."

When Fletcher left, Benedict removed himself to the garden, as if belatedly endeavoring to preserve her reputation. Camille found that she was glad to rest. Lying on the settee, she closed her eyes, then opened them. Memories swirled…the touch of his fingers on her brow, the low sound of his laughter, his breath caressing her cheek, promising more.

She frowned and made herself think of the countless feathered corpses spread out on the table under the window, then reminded herself that Hawke was a villain, a murderer. Camille must continue to quash any appetites he stirred within her.

It wasn't so hard; she had done it before, with Roger, hadn't she?

Yet Camille would not breathe easier until she was on her way back to Elysium. She was so eager to see Rafael and tell him all that had happened on the cliffs, and then here in this cottage. Suddenly she remembered the scrap of paper she had stuffed into her pocket. Her heart sped up as she took it out and read the boldly scrawled words.

Meet Jem—Old Ferry Inn, Bodinnick, dusk.

CHAPTER 7

$\mathcal{R}$afael arrived at the cottage in a fine gig, pulled by Camille's own bay gelding, Pegasus. Benedict supported her with one arm around her waist in a way that felt good. Too good.

Then she focused on Pegasus, and her heart swelled. "Hello, my beautiful fellow!" The horse tossed his dark mane, turning his head to search for her.

Still half embracing her, Benedict issued instructions for Camille's care, and the boy nodded soberly throughout, eyes averted.

"Given the circumstances, I expected Miss St. Briac's own father to come for her," Benedict said rather sternly. "With a proper, well-sprung carriage."

Camille was amused to see Rafael mutely duck his head in a posture of subservience.

"My parents are very busy," she said. "No doubt they were away from home. And I will be perfectly fine in the gig."

"I only hope this lad can be trusted to keep you safe."

"You underestimate me, sir," Camille huffed. "I am perfectly capable—"

"Please." He cocked a sardonic brow. "I hope you weren't going to claim that you can keep yourself safe."

"In normal circumstances, yes." Her cheeks grew hot under his mocking regard. If there was truth in Hawke's insinuation that she was reckless, Camille would never admit it.

A moment later, Benedict swung her into his arms and gently positioned her in the gig next to Rafael. When he stepped back, watching her intently, Rafael snapped the reins and Pegasus started forward.

"Go easy, boy!" came Benedict's command as they rolled away on the coastal path.

When they were safely away, Rafael looked over at her. "What have you done, my lady?" he scolded in his Portuguese-accented English. "I knew I should not have left you."

"It was an accident." She found that she couldn't meet his gaze.

"Did you not promise to stay off the cliffs?"

"Oh, Rafael, if you had seen what they were doing you would understand!" The drama she had witnessed that morning tumbled from her lips. Once the story was told, she added grimly, "It was terrible beyond description, and that *man* is involved. I know it."

Rafael turned to look at her just as the wind from the sea nearly blew his hat away. "Mr. Hawke? But he rescued you, didn't he? He was so worried for your safety..."

"Fiddle. He is a villain, just as I always suspected. He was chatting with those murdering feather thieves as if they were compatriots. I am convinced that Benedict Hawke is not only involved with their criminal enterprise, but the ringleader."

Rafael looked dubious. "I know you don't like him, but are you too quick to imagine the worst?"

"Don't *like* him?" Camille's head began to throb.

"Didn't you notice the way he behaved a few minutes ago? I despise him."

As the gig crested a hill, Elysium came into view, its handsome brick façade framed by an archway of rhododendrons. "My lady," soothed Rafael, "I beg that you calm yourself. If you have these suspicions, you must take them to the authorities, and they will intervene to save the birds."

She waved this suggestion away. "Do you really imagine anyone else would care about a lot of gulls, or that any law protects them? No! Only I can save them…" Turning beseeching eyes on the boy, she added, "With your help, of course."

He cringed. "I don't know. It all sounds dangerous, risky, and—" After a brief pause, Rafael dared to add, "There is always a chance you may be mistaken about Mr. Hawke, my lady."

"On the contrary, I have proof." She felt as if they were playing loo and she was about to lay down her trump card and take the trick. "I saw a note on Hawke's desk today. He has an appointment to meet Jem, the savage kittiwake killer, today at dusk."

He frowned and shook his head. "I think we should leave it alone."

"If you had witnessed this morning's carnage on the cliffs, you would not suggest such a thing." She took a breath, timing her next words. "If you do not help me, I must go alone."

They were drawing up in front of the manor house. Helivet, the family's elderly coachman, emerged to greet them. Rafael jumped down, handed the reins to the Frenchman, and reached up to help Camille alight from the gig. For a moment, her senses swam, but then she recovered.

"If it is your will, my lady," the Brazilian lad said in an undertone, "I will do it."

She gave him her most dazzling smile. "Oh, Rafael, I knew I could depend upon you!"

* * *

INSIDE THE HOUSE, Claire, the housekeeper ran an appraising eye over Camille's rumpled form. "Mistress, do ye be well?"

"Perfectly," Camille replied firmly, ignoring her own disheveled appearance. "Where are my parents?"

"The master does go to Frenchman's Haven to see his brother."

"To—see Uncle Justin? Has he returned to Cornwall?"

"So it seems," Claire said, nodding. Her ginger curls, now threaded with white, were partially covered by the same mobcap she'd worn for more than two decades. "The mistress were painting today, in her studio, but I believe I do hear her come in a short while ago."

"I'll go upstairs and tidy myself then," Camille said hastily, eager to postpone an interview with her perceptive mother.

The stairs were lined with Isabella's paintings and sketches that featured beloved family members as well as views of their enchanted corner of Cornwall. Camille found herself gazing at them as she passed, each one a memory of her own life. Inexplicably, a shiver ran down her spine, as if the world were tilting just a bit.

In her own bedchamber, Camille longed for a hot bath and a nap, but there was no time. Instead, she poured tepid water into a basin and washed with a bar of French-milled soap. She managed to tame her thick honey-caramel locks with a brush and some hairpins. Soon a long braid was coiled atop her head, and Lillian was summoned to fasten the hooks that marched up the back of her demure green day dress.

"Mistress, you look so very lovely," murmured Lillian, smiling.

"Oh..." Camille glanced absently at her reflection in the dressing table mirror. "Thank you."

Emboldened, the maid added, "Like an angel."

"You're too kind." Suppressing an urge to cringe at Lillian's words, she turned and hurried downstairs to find her mother.

As magical as Elysium's gardens were, the inside of the manor house cast a different sort of spell. The large rooms were haphazard, filled with well-worn furniture and an assortment of mementos from both the St. Briac and Trevarre sides of the family. There were stacks of books on side tables, cups half-filled with tea, and a pair of Damien's shoes blocking Camille's path. Her brother was sprawled across the biggest sofa, munching on figs, while Zeus dozed beside him.

"Really, Damien," she remarked automatically, "you shouldn't let Zeus up on the furniture. He leaves piles of black fur behind."

"I didn't invite him up," Damien replied with a mischievous grin. "And you know he won't budge once he makes himself comfortable."

As if to punctuate this statement, Zeus yawned loudly and rolled onto his back, legs flung in every direction.

"I thought you would never come home, Cam," Damien declared, rubbing the dog's belly. "I've made some new paper ships. We don't even have to go to the lake, we can race them in the Italian pool. Say yes!"

One of her brother's favorite games involved creating paper ships. He could spend an entire day designing and cutting them out. When his new fleet was ready to launch, Damien would begin challenging various family members and servants to race on one of the lakes fed by their father's ingenious ram pump. Whoever stayed afloat the longest was the champion.

"I can't today," she said, wondering how soon she and Rafael must leave to reach Bodinnick by dusk. "Tomorrow, though."

"I'll ask Rafael, then."

"He can't do it either. I need him to…help me with an errand."

Fortunately, their mother entered at that moment. At the sight of her, Zeus widened his eyes in panic, rolled sideways off the sofa, and collided with a tapestry ottoman.

"Zeus," Isabella scolded with mock severity. "Have I not asked you nicely to stay off the furniture?"

"Perhaps he doesn't speak English, Mama," offered Damien.

She glanced heavenward, smiling. "He may not *speak* English, but I think he understands every word." Adjusting her spectacles, Isabella seemed to see Camille for the first time. "Oh, darling, you're here! Let's go out into the garden, and you can help me feed your birds."

Camille flushed slightly at this last remark but followed her mother through the glass doors to the terrace, then down three shallow steps to the walled gardens. She had set up the trays of seed for the titmice and finches who darted about among the plants and flowers, safe from predators inside the high brick walls. When was the last time Camille had refilled the trays or checked on the nests?

"Thank you for looking after them, Mama," she said. "I've been so busy…"

"So I have surmised." Isabella took a seat on the edge of a low stone wall and watched her tend to the birds. A bit too casually, she said, "I confess I have been a bit worried that you might get into trouble in your quest to stop the feather hunters."

Camille knew a strong urge to confide everything that had happened today, even her confusing, conflicted feelings about Benedict Hawke. Where to begin? She turned to look at her mother. "Actually, I saw those terrible men today on the cliffs..."

When she hesitated, Isabella leaned forward. "Oh, my. Is that where you have been?"

Camille swallowed. Suddenly it came to her that if her parents knew everything that was happening, they might well try to intercede out of fear for her safety. Papa was not the sort of father who would lock her in her room or send her away, but if he felt she was in real danger, there was no telling what he might do.

She turned her attention to an apple tree, espaliered against the brick wall, where she had positioned a nesting box among the flattened branches. "Oh, look, Mama. The chaffinch eggs have hatched. The nest needs to be removed or they will never return."

Using a soft brush, Camille began to sweep out another of the little nesting boxes that Papa had helped her to make several years ago. How many tiny chicks had hatched and fledged in this sweet little nook? Behind her, Isabella cleared her throat.

"Did you hear my question?" she asked gently.

Camille continued to clean the little box. "Oh, it's nothing to be concerned about." She gave a little shake of her head. "No one threatened me. In fact, I actually didn't stay on the cliffs very long at all." This was true enough! "I beg you, do not worry. Am I not a grown woman?"

Isabella looked doubtful. "Well, yes, but..."

After repositioning the nesting box, Camille returned to her mother's side. "You must trust my judgement. You and Papa are the most sensible members of the entire St. Briac family, and I am your daughter."

"My dear, I have not always been so sensible. I was young once, too."

"Perhaps, but *I* am four and twenty, not some flighty girl." Camille forced a little laugh. "Really, Mama, what sort of mischief could a dull spinster like me create? You know very well all I care about is birds!"

* * *

THE SUN HAD JUST BEGUN to wane when Benedict, astride Max, set out for Bodinnick. Skirting the highest edge of Polruan, he tried not to look down Fore Street, toward his sister's modest home. He tried not to think about his wretched father, lying on that cot, unable to control his own body. Benedict knew he should care, but he could not. Josiah Hawke had mocked and bullied Benedict from the moment he began to think and dream for himself, and too often he followed up with a physical blow.

When a boy's own father derided him at every turn, words hurt far more than fists.

A strong burning sensation centered in Benedict's chest. *I hate you, Pa.* Saying this under his breath made him feel slightly better. It wasn't enough but it would have to do.

He focused on the narrow track that would lead him through leafy woods, past Pont Pill where tufted cygnets swam in the wake of their elegant mother, and across the pasture bordering a rustic manor house. The River Fowey came into view, shimmering in the distance as they crowned a steep hill that descended into the village of Bodinnick. Near the water's edge stood a whitewashed structure. An ancient sign swinging above its doorway proclaimed: *The Old Ferry Inn.*

As Max picked his way down the rutted lane, Benedict saw that villagers were emerging from their cottages to stare at him. Just as in Polruan, everyone knew everyone, and strangers were eyed with suspicion.

However, he thought sardonically, *if Miss Camille St. Briac should pass by with her monocular and her little bird notebook, she doubtless would be greeted with broad smiles and shouts of greeting.*

This single thought brought Camille's exquisite face alive in his mind. Unbidden, he seemed to inhale her fragrance of meadow flowers and sea air. *Get a grip, man*, Benedict chided himself. He gave a soft derisory snort that caused Max to glance back.

"Don't worry." He stroked the horse's mane with one gloved hand. "I'm only scolding myself. Let us hope that chit has safely returned to the care of her parents, so that you and I can get on with more important matters at hand."

They had nearly reached the foot of the hill when Benedict remembered to don the same tricorne hat he'd worn on the cliffs that morning. Dismounting, he noticed a handsome, older couple alighting at the water's edge from the ferry, which was little more than a raft. How many centuries had it been traveling back and forth between Bodinnick and the larger town of Fowey?

As the couple passed Benedict on their way up the hill, he saw that the lady carried a cage made of willow twigs. Inside he was surprised to see a beautiful swallow-like bird with a black cap and blush-pink breast. Its white tailfeathers resembled slim ribbons. Unable to help himself, Benedict blocked their path.

"My God," he uttered without preamble. "Is that a roseate tern?"

The woman, graceful and lovely at perhaps sixty years of age, stopped and gave him a quizzical look.

Her older male companion spoke first. "Have we met, sir?"

"Forgive my bad manners. My name is Benedict Hawke. I am an ornithologist—"

"Oh, I see," the lady interjected. "You would doubtless like to stuff my splendid bird." She hugged the cage closer to her body.

"Not at all," Benedict protested. "I am a scientist, writing a book titled *Birds of the Coastal Cornwall.* I had learned from John Gould himself that the roseate tern could only be found on the Scilly Islands, their breeding grounds. I am merely surprised to see this handsome fellow on the mainland." After a moment, he dared to add, "I confess, I am curious to know how you came by this specimen."

The man put out his hand. "My name is Sebastian Trevarre, and this is my wife, Julia."

Comprehension dawned. "Ah, yes, you must live at Trevarre Hall." This was the reason they were on foot; their estate was not far away. With his next breath, Benedict remembered Camille mentioning that Lord Sebastian was her uncle. "I am honored to know you both."

Trevarre seemed to decide that Benedict could be trusted, perhaps because he had mentioned knowing Gould. "My wife looks after any birds and animals who need assistance, from orphaned badgers to wounded foxes," he explained. "This tern apparently found his way onto a fishing boat and one of the men put it in this cage. He brought it to Fowey, and when Julia heard, she was moved to intervene."

She nodded. "It's criminal how many rare birds are being captured and killed, or their eggs stolen. Soon all the species we know and value will begin to disappear." Color washed her cheekbones. "I want nothing to do with you, sir, if you believe killing birds is acceptable—for any reason!"

Just then, Benedict heard someone cough behind him. Then came a second cough, sounding so false that he instinctively turned to look. There, loitering under the Ferry Inn's gently swinging sign, was Jem, pudgy eyes narrowed.

Benedict drew a harsh breath as reality dawned: he had come there to meet a bird-killing feather thief.

"I take your meaning, my lady," he said to Julia Trevarre, hoping to quickly end their conversation. "It was an honor to meet you and Lord Sebastian. This fine bird is fortunate to be in your care."

He took a step backward. In the distance, the sun had begun to dip toward the ancient rooftops of Fowey, and petals of golden light shimmered on the river.

Dusk was gathering. It was time for his appointment with Jem.

CHAPTER 8

"Leave the gig here, behind these trees," Camille demanded in an urgent whisper. "We must endeavor to go unnoticed." Without waiting for Rafael to assist her, she clambered down from the seat and took Pegasus's reins into her slim hand.

"My lady, what do you mean to do?" The boy frowned. "Did you not say that you would remain behind with the gig while I walk down to that inn and spy upon the meeting?"

"Don't worry about me," she said quickly. "Just go, and"

Rafael cut her off, his accent strong. "Do not worry? That is what you told me just this morning, on the cliffs, and look what happened."

Many people would be shocked to hear a servant speak to her in such a familiar manner, but ever since Rafael had stowed away to sail from Brazil to England and then persuaded her cousin Anthony to grant him employment, he had become an essential figure in their lives. In truth, he seemed almost like a member of the family.

"All right then, I promise to wait here," Camille said.

Reaching over into the gig, she brought out a gray hooded cape that had once belonged to her sister, Louise. "I will wear this."

"My lady, perhaps you do not realize just how distinctive is your face. So clearly you are a female, a rare beauty, and many doubtless would recognize you."

"Oh, bother." Donning the cloak, she drew the hood over her hair and held the edges close about her face. "Are you satisfied?"

He pursed his lips. "I suppose so."

"But look!" Camille pointed at the setting sun. "It is dusk. Do go, or the meeting will end and you will learn nothing!"

Rafael turned up his coat collar and tugged down the big, flat-crowned hat that they had discovered in a trunk at Elysium. Watching him descend toward the Old Ferry Inn, his features shadowed under the hat's wide brim, Camille prayed that Benedict Hawke would not recognize the boy. *Surely, he will be too busy plotting ways to pillage kittiwake nests to notice the other patrons of the taproom,* she thought derisively. If only she could go herself, then she could know that everything was being done to gather the information they needed. Wouldn't the cloak make it impossible to identify her? The impulse to break her word to Rafael once again was almost overwhelming.

Just then, Camille noticed a striking older couple walking up the twilit hill, carrying a willow cage with a bird in it. With a shiver of trepidation, she recognized her Uncle Sebastian and Aunt Julia! There was no telling what might happen if they identified her. Trying not to panic, Camille turned away to Pegasus, presenting her back to them. It came to her then that Aunt Julia paid close attention to every animal she ever met. What if she recognized Camille's beloved steed?

In the next moment, her aunt spoke, her tone uncertain. "Camille? Is that—you?"

Hidden inside the cloak, she froze. What in the world could she possibly say to them? Yet Julia sounded doubtful. Unless they came closer and managed to see her face, there was no proof.

She heard her aunt whispering to Uncle Sebastian, who made a low, doubtful sound. And then there was silence. Long, heart pounding minutes passed. When at last Camille dared to steal a backward glance, she saw her uncle and aunt disappearing into the woods that surrounded their nearby estate, Trevarre Hall.

* * *

THE SHADOWED INTERIOR of the taproom was stuffy and warm, redolent with the smells of ale, fried onions, pipe smoke, and the sweat of unwashed men. Near the soot-stained stone hearth that covered one wall, Benedict shared a table with Jem and his two partners in crime.

When the tapster set the mugs of ale before them, Jem drank his down and signaled for another. Benedict managed a grim smile and lifted the tankard, endeavoring to conceal his disgust for the entire situation.

"I were that thirsty," Jem proclaimed, and his friends nodded in vigorous agreement.

"Yes." Benedict nodded and drank a bit more. The ale was good enough, but lukewarm. "Thank you for agreeing to meet with me."

"An' what became of that interfering wench? Did she die?"

"No! That is, she awoke and insisted on returning to her home, a fair distance away." This was partially true after all, and Benedict certainly didn't want to share

93

any further details with these brutes. "One hopes that her misadventure on the cliffs taught her a lesson."

Jem shrugged. "Hope ye be right, guv'nor." He paused, darting a look at the other two. "An' what were your name?"

Damn, why hadn't he thought about this earlier? He remembered the surname of his sister's neighbors. "Pascoe. Tom Pascoe."

The trio of ruffians stuck out their grimy hands and he shook them. Jem leaned closer, starting his second quart of ale.

"Pascoe do be a common enough name in Polruan. Surprised I never met thee."

"I been living in Kent since boyhood, just returned for a few weeks' visit."

Jem nodded and raised his tankard. "Good enough. We do need a clever bloke like thee. Used to have another fellow to oversee the raids, but he's…gone away. Glad to have ye join us, guv'nor."

Benedict digested this information as Jem's third ale was served by a fellow with a brimmed hat pulled low over his brow. Did this mean the band of feather thieves had no leader?

"I see," he said. "But why me? Shouldn't you lead the men, Jem?"

"Nah!" The vast quantity of ale was turning his face red. "I be best at snatchin' the birds when they are busy with the chicks. Don't want nothin' to interfere. Ye would not *lead* so much as watch the men t' see it all be done right." Pointing at Benedict, he paused, narrowing his eyes. "They be known to steal each other's birds."

Benedict felt his lip begin to curl but managed to force a smile instead. "Ah. I see."

"For weeks, plans be set for a raid," Jem assured him. "Friday next. There be a full moon." He paused and used his striped cap to wipe sweat from his brow.

"Near dawn, the cliffs be covered with them birds, bringing breakfast for the chicks. We can bag enough of 'em to fetch a right fortune from the millinery trade."

"You must have a very good connection there," Benedict remarked.

"Right, guv'nor!"

Benedict's pulse accelerated. If he played his cards well, he could intercede to stop the kittiwake slaughter and also discover who was paying for the feathers.

"It does sound promising," he allowed.

"Ye will do it then."

"Oversee the raid on the kittiwake nests? Yes, I will do it," Benedict confirmed in a low voice, momentarily distracted by the rather odd servant who moved nearby, bumping against his chairback. Not wanting to make his agreement seem too easy, he said, "That is, as long as I'm rewarded properly."

"Oh, aye! The feather folk will pay." Jem winked for emphasis.

Feather folk. Good God. Benedict began to lean forward, ready to press Jem for more, but managed to rein himself in. Instead, he drew a deep breath and spoke in a conversational tone.

"Of course, I'll need the coin before we conduct the raid." He paused before adding casually, "I would be glad to make time for a meeting with those, uh, feather folk you speak of."

"Nah, none of that. They do keep themselves private if ye take my meaning." Jem reached inside his stained coat, brought out a leather purse, and tossed it down on the table in front of Benedict. "Ten guineas to start. The more birds we do get, the more will they pay."

As Benedict stared at the purse, the hairs on the back of his neck stood up. *This must be how Judas felt.*

"Heed my words." Jem pushed unsteadily to his feet as he spoke. "Come Friday, be on the cliffs above the nests, one hour before dawn. I do be there with six blokes, mebbe more. All ye must do is lead the raid, we'll do the rest." He limped a few steps away, then turned back to gesture toward the purse that lay untouched on the table. "Ye wouldn't want to forget about that, guv'nor."

Benedict couldn't help thinking of Camille as he lifted the pouch and put it in his coat pocket. What would she say if she could see him? This thought only deepened his sense of unease. The only way to stop the slaughter and discover who was really behind it was to pretend to be one of them.

Benedict paused to consider this for a moment. He might know what his true motives were, but who else would believe it? Certainly not Camille St. Briac. If his ruse had a chance of success, he realized with a pang, he must avoid that provoking beauty at all costs.

Rising, Benedict started toward the door, his passage through the taproom crush made easier because of his height. Just then he caught sight of a brown, flat-crowned hat. It was the lad who had served his ale. As if sensing Benedict's stare, the boy turned back just long enough to reveal a slice of his profile.

In the next instant, he disappeared, seeming to slip through the entrance door. By the time Benedict also emerged into the shadowy evening, there was no sight of the boy. Perhaps he hadn't gone this way after all? Benedict's heartbeat kicked up as he thought back to that very afternoon, when the Brazilian lad, Rafael, had come to fetch Camille at Gull Cottage.

Bloody hell, this couldn't possibly be the same person! His mind was playing tricks on him, all because of Camille St. Briac. He began to wish he had never encountered her that morning on the cliffs, never carried her back to Gull Cottage after her fall. She was like a vine, twisting among all his thoughts...and desires.

Benedict warily touched the leather purse in his coat pocket. What had Jem said? *The more birds we do get, the more will they pay.* He felt chilled in the warm summer air. How the devil could he remain in the midst of the feather thieves, gaining their confidence, yet somehow stop them from slaughtering the kittiwakes?

Reaching for Max's reins, Benedict was certain of one thing. In order to keep his wits in the coming days, he must stay far away from the irresistibly reckless Camille St. Briac.

* * *

CAMILLE PEEKED out from behind the oak tree just as Rafael came trudging up the steep lane. "Oh, thank goodness," she said, momentarily closing her eyes in relief. "There you are!"

Although he looked quite ridiculous in the wide-brimmed hat that dwarfed his head, the expression on his face stopped her from saying so. Rounding the thick tree trunk, Rafael glowered at her. "Did you not promise to wait in the gig?"

She blinked. "In all the excitement, I forgot. I'm human, you know."

Rafael pressed his lips together as if to suppress an inappropriate comment. "We must hide until he passes," he said, turning away toward the gig that was hidden nearby.

In the same moment, Camille heard the sound of approaching hoofbeats on the rutted dirt lane. Glancing between two nearby tree branches, she saw Benedict Hawke riding up the hill. His face looked stormy under the point of an old-fashioned tricorne. Realizing that her hood had fallen back, she scrambled to find the edges and cover her head before he caught sight of her.

Rafael seemed to sense what was happening. He stopped in his tracks, tore the recognizable hat from his head, and knelt on one knee to examine his boot. Camille held her breath. If Hawke saw them and realized what they were up to, there was no telling how far the villain might go to silence them.

She had to keep pushing aside the sensual stirrings she'd known that morning in Benedict Hawke's cottage, reminding herself instead that he was capable of true evil. After all, he had stood by as his fellow feather thief tore the wings from a kittiwake and flung the maimed bird into the English Channel! Truly, that was evil incarnate.

The hoofbeats passed by and, after a moment, Camille exhaled. She watched as Rafael rose from his crouch and gestured for her to follow him into the thicket where the gig was concealed. Pegasus lifted his head at the sight of Camille and, when she put her hand out, he nosed it, clearly relieved to see her.

"Get in, my lady," said the Brazilian youth.

"But wait," she whispered urgently to Rafael, "before we go, you must tell me what happened! Was I right? About that awful man?"

He glanced away. "I fear so."

Camille was swept by a wave of excitement mixed with dread. "Why? Please tell me."

"It is as you suspected." Rafael sounded almost regretful. "Hawke is indeed one of the feather thieves, but he has told them his name is Pascoe...and he agreed to lead a group when they execute a dawn raid, pillaging dozens of nests."

"W-when?"

"Friday next."

As this sank in, Camille pressed a hand to her

mouth to stifle a cry of horror. When she could speak, her voice was steely with resolve. "We will not let this happen."

"But—how?"

"I don't know yet." Undaunted, Camille climbed into the gig and took up the reins. "However, I shall devise a plan, and I promise you, it will succeed!"

CHAPTER 9

s Camille and Rafael returned home from Bodinnick in the little gig, they discovered that the windows of Elysium were ablaze with light. From within, laughter carried to them on the warm summer air, and Camille recognized the assertive tones of her French grandmother's voice as well as a deep, chiding reply from her Uncle Justin. It seemed that a good share of the St. Briac family must be gathered here tonight.

"Is there a party, my lady?" asked Rafael.

"Oh, no, it's only some family members. When Uncle Justin and Aunt Mouette are in residence at Frenchman's Haven, they frequently stop while passing by. Of course, Mama always insists that they stay to dine with us."

Sighing, Camille climbed out of the gig and handed the reins back to Rafael. "Usually I would adore their visit, but the last thing I need tonight are a lot of questions from my relatives," she said. "I wish I could steal up the back stairs to my bedchamber and avoid them entirely."

"My lady, your family doubtless wonders where you have been," he pointed out.

"Oh, yes, that's an excellent point," Camille agreed wryly.

"Have you thought of a plan yet?"

"Of course, I would like to threaten that wretched Benedict Hawke at gunpoint, forcing him to help us, but that would doubtless be a mistake."

"I must agree," the boy said warily. "Is it possible Mr. Hawke might listen to reason?"

"Hmph! I highly doubt that." She wanted to dismiss his idea out of hand, but an inner voice suggested that her headstrong tendencies could prove dangerous. "I shall ponder this tonight and confer with you at dawn, Rafael. Perhaps, as you say, there is a less perilous way forward."

With that, she folded the voluminous cape and put it in Rafael's hands, then walked up the steps. It was easy enough to slip into the manor house, for her parents' small staff were all occupied tending to the guests. Camille paused to scan her reflection in the entry hall mirror. At times like this, she was glad for her looks that others described as beautiful. Her luxuriant hair was easily smoothed, her cheeks were naturally rosy, and once she gave her skirts a shake, she was quite presentable.

Strolling through the dining room, she saw that the table was set with Mama's best china and crystal, but the guests had not yet been seated. Camille followed the sound of voices into the big drawing room. Her extended family came into view, a few occupying the same long sofa where Zeus liked to nap. Camille saw her parents and Damien, Uncle Justin, and Aunt Mouette. Even Grandmère was present this evening.

Camille donned a radiant smile as she entered the room. "Hello everyone!" she called. "How lovely to see you all."

Papa was sitting in his favorite, well-worn tapestry

chair, while her mother and Uncle Justin occupied a nearby settee. After quickly greeting the others one by one, Camille approached her father.

Gabriel St. Briac lowered his brows. "Where have you been, Cam?"

She perched on the arm of his chair, kissed his cheek, and whispered fondly, "Don't be gothic, Papa. I am not a child."

"We'll discuss this later," he said, eyes narrowed.

"I can promise you that I have been attending to matters of importance, and I was not unaccompanied. Rafael is assisting me."

"That's very cryptic."

Hopefully this was enough to placate him for now. Turning her head, she saw her mother watching them.

"You must go and change into a fresh gown," said Isabella, "and join us all for supper. Sebastian and Julia will arrive soon. And your grandmother is with us, so it is rather an occasion."

Since the death of Xavier St. Briac last year, Camille's widowed grandmother had suffered a decline, spending her days lying in a darkened room, moaning. But of course, it had always been difficult to discern whether her illnesses were real or conjured up for dramatic effect. Now Cerise appeared to be completely restored to health, alert and sitting upright, as she sipped an aperitif and conversed with Aunt Mouette.

Camille silently gave thanks that Grandmère was not wearing one of her shocking, feather-adorned headdresses. The most horrible one of all had been decorated with the glimmering skin of a hummingbird.

Papa gave her a nudge. "Did you hear your mother?"

"Oh, yes, I'm sorry...but I cannot stay for supper. I am tired." As both parents opened their mouths to protest, she added quickly, "I am suffering from dyspepsia."

"Are you indeed?" Her father looked skeptical.

Camille rose, hoping to make her escape, but stopped at the sound of her Uncle Justin's deep, French-accented voice.

"Izzie," he was saying casually, "I forgot to mention that I encountered Lord Upton at White's a few days ago. He asked to be remembered to you and Gabriel..." Pausing, he glanced her way. "And Camille."

Her heart jumped at the mention of Roger, and she hoped none of them could discern her inner turmoil.

"Oh yes," Mama was replying, apparently oblivious to the heat spreading up Camille's face. "His lordship was a frequent visitor here last year. We all became quite fond of him. I believe he planned to propose marriage to Lady Barbara Framstead soon after returning to London."

"Excuse me," Camille murmured, glancing toward her parents, "I apologize for interrupting, but I must go. I am not feeling quite the thing."

Moments later, back in the stair hall, she leaned against a wall and waited for the wave of anguish and shame that inevitably followed any reference to Roger. This time, however, Camille felt only the slightest twinge. Instead, she was much more aware of a vibrant cascade of thoughts and plans, all dealing with the threatened kittiwakes...and that scoundrel, Benedict Hawke.

* * *

BENEDICT SAT at his makeshift desk overlooking the cliff path, surrounded by papers and notes for his book as well as an assortment of ornithological specimens. He glanced up to dip his pen in the inkwell when slight movement in the distance caught his attention. Removing his spectacles, he gazed through the rain-spattered window and saw a white-and-black kittiwake swoop low beyond the cliff's edge, then disappear from sight. *Gathering breakfast for the chicks*, he thought.

"Perhaps you would be interested to know that your father shows signs of improvement," Fletcher said from the kitchen doorway. Moments later, he appeared with a breakfast tray and crossed haltingly to set it on the paper-strewn desk.

Benedict decided to ignore the manservant's remark about Pa. "It smells as if you've outdone yourself, old boy." Indeed, the large plate boasted saffron buns, coddled eggs, and a helping of some sort of fish pie.

"Thank you, sir," Fletcher replied. His thin lips twitched only slightly. "In truth, I made the pie to take to Mr. Hawke. Your sister tells me it is one of his favorites."

Benedict poked his fork at a thin, intact pilchard that seemed to be staring at him. *At least it's not a kittiwake*, he thought darkly. "In that case, it's very generous of you to share this bit with me."

He could feel the manservant's uncertain gaze. "I didn't expect that you'd like it, sir. I could leave half the pie here."

"No, no, I wouldn't think of it," Benedict said magnanimously. For good measure, he added, "Go on to Prue's. I know she is grateful for your visits."

Fletcher stood there, watching him, clearly undecided about whether to say what was really on his mind. Benedict turned back to his breakfast. There was a pot of coffee, and he poured the steaming, fragrant brew into a cup.

"If there is nothing else, you should go, old fellow," he said pointedly.

Another heavy silence ensued. Benedict was on the

verge of shouting at the manservant when Fletcher spoke.

"Sir, do you truly mean to go through the day without a neckcloth?"

Surprised by this sudden conversational turn, Benedict put a hand up to his open collar. His lack of interest in clothing was a frequent point of contention between them. "Fletch, I am *alone*. If I don't care about the blasted neckcloth, neither should you."

"I see. I shall go then, sir."

When at length Benedict was alone, he tried to concentrate on *Birds of Coastal Cornwall*. He stared at his list of birds and wondered if he ought to include the roseate tern, which appeared to have found its way to the Cornwall mainland. He was deep into his notes when a knock sounded at the door.

For a moment, it seemed he must be hearing things. Perhaps it was a branch, blown by the wind, for Benedict knew he had not invited anyone to Gull Cottage.

The knocking commenced again, followed by an all-too-familiar female voice. "Mr. Hawke, I beg you to open this door!"

When the bold caller did not receive an immediate response, she appeared suddenly in the window, just a few feet in front of Benedict's desk. It was, of course, Camille St. Briac, wet with rain, waving and gesturing for him to let her in.

Benedict rose and went to the door. Secretly he was pleased to receive this particular uninvited guest, but he would never let her know this. On the contrary, he threw open the door, reached out to grasp her cloak, and pulled her inside.

"What the devil are you doing, turning up in a rainstorm at the home of an unmarried man?" He badly wanted to grasp her arms and shake her a bit for emphasis, but he didn't trust himself to touch her. God could not devise a more kissable mouth than hers, and the mere thought of her body, concealed under that cloak, sent a surge of heat through him.

"How churlish you are!"

Churlish? Why had she chosen a word best suited to an ill-tempered old man? "And you are very bold."

"Indeed, sir, yet I do not exaggerate." And with that, Camille St. Briac untied her sodden cloak, removed it, and hung it on a peg as if he had invited her in. She wore a simple gown of periwinkle printed cotton that served to accentuate her rich blue eyes. A pure white muslin tucker, edged in lace, made a collar around her pretty neck. All of it was quite prim, yet he found her intensely alluring.

He was thirty years old and had thus far managed to elude the romantic designs of many respectable young ladies. The very thought of being with the same person day after day and accepting her affections made him as uncomfortable as a scratchy, homespun shirt. Since boyhood, Benedict had been restless, especially when people tried to get close to him. Much easier to go off on another scientific adventure and share passionate nights with women he would soon leave behind.

Benedict looked at Camille St. Briac and tried without success to detach himself from the moment. What was it about this singular female that aroused both his temper and his carnal desires? He took a long breath, unclenched his fists, and exhaled.

"May I ask again what brings you here today?" he asked evenly, watching as Camille strolled over to his desk. "Perhaps you were caught in the rain and had no other source of shelter?"

"No, I intended to come here, though I did not expect the rain." She bent her head, looking at his notes.

Benedict came up beside her and reached out to

turn over the papers. "If you don't mind, my manuscript is private."

"I see. And what about these murdered birds?" Her luminous blue eyes settled on the specimens he had laid out in rows on the desk, their beaks and tiny feet pointed toward the ceiling. Scornfully, she added, "Before you shot and killed them, they no doubt wished for privacy as well."

He stood over her, angry and yet shamed by her words, the strength of her spirit. Noticing that the rain had stopped outside, Benedict wondered how quickly he might send this vixen on her way.

"See here," he said sternly. "I am a scientist. An ornithologist! I only possess these specimens because I need to study them. I am writing a book"

Camille put up a silencing hand. "Please, spare me this Banbury tale. We both know that all of this nonsense is but a cover for your true pursuits."

Infuriated, he shook his head. "You are wrong."

"If you were truly serious about writing such a book, you would not be shut up indoors at this desk, but outdoors tramping over the cliffs, along the secret paths that lead deep into the woods and tidal creeks. You would be dedicated to witnessing the birds of Cornwall in their natural habitats. It would require many months and a lifetime's worth of patience." She gave him a challenging stare. "And if you should discover a new species of bird, you certainly would not *kill* it! You would sit quietly in a place where you could observe, sketch, make notes, and reverently give thanks for this beautiful living creature."

He refused to react to her lecture. "That is all very nice, but not the way of a true ornithologist." Meeting her fiery gaze, he added, "Your opinions about my work do not alter the truth. I *am* writing a book."

They were standing close together, and Benedict

remembered when she had been lying on the settee and he had breathed in her scent of meadow flowers and fresh sunlight.

Camille licked her lips. "No doubt you are used to starry-eyed females believing every word you say, but I will not be taken in by your..." He was gratified to see her visibly swallow and glance away from him. "...male enticements."

"Clearly not," he replied with heavy irony, well aware that she was weakening. The temptation to touch her was almost overpowering, yet he resisted. "I shall ask a third time: why did you come here? Simply to challenge my scientific methods—and profess your determination to resist me?"

* * *

CAMILLE WANTED to slap Benedict Hawke. Even pushing him would feel excellent, but of course she could do neither. Instead, the moment had come when she must lower herself to beg on behalf of the kittiwakes.

"Why did I come here?" she repeated.

Hawke only lifted his dark brows in reply, waiting. So arrogant! He might be sinfully handsome, she thought, but his appearance would be frowned on in polite society. He hadn't bothered to don a neckcloth, he wore riding clothes that had seen better days, and his hair was rather wild, as if he used only his fingers as a brush.

"Actually, I came here to appeal to your better self," she said.

He gave a harsh laugh. "What makes you think I have one of those?"

Remember the birds, Camille admonished herself. "May I sit down?" She took a rickety chair near his desk. "I am here on behalf of the kittiwakes who are threatened by those terrible men. I have reason to believe that you may be involved somehow in their…" She swallowed the angry words that threatened to spill forth. "Their…nefarious pursuits. No doubt you have your reasons for joining in, but I must ask—nay, *beg* you, sir, to desist."

He sat at his desk, chair angled toward hers, gazing impassively back at her. "I am afraid I don't know what you are talking about."

Camille clenched both fists, her cheeks growing warm. "I have not come here to hurl accusations at you, for that would serve no useful purpose. Instead, I am asking you to help me save the kittiwakes and their innocent chicks from slaughter." She straightened her back. "Will you do the right thing and join me?"

Something flickered in his eyes before he glanced out the window. "If you are expecting some sort of heroic intervention, you have the wrong person, Miss St. Briac."

"Do I?" Camille summoned every ounce of self-control to refrain from shouting. "Perhaps you are unaware of the truly evil purpose for this massacre of countless innocent, beautiful birds. You must not know that those villains are ripping the wings from live birds and tossing their bodies into the sea merely to acquire wings for *ladies' hats!*"

Just as her voice rose on the last two words, a muffled but pitiful, high-pitched cry reached her ears. Both of them looked around. It came again, and again, seemingly from under Benedict Hawke's desk.

"Listen to that," exclaimed Camille. Rising, she pointed toward the wide planks near Hawke's feet. "It sounds like a cat, crying under your floor!"

He blinked. "Ah. Well, it may be Pa's cat. I was told it ran away before I arrived here."

She remembered then that this cottage apparently belonged to his father. "Aren't you going to see if the poor thing is trapped down there?"

"I suspect it must have another way out…since it clearly didn't pry up the floor to enter."

"Mr. Hawke!" Camille cried, even as the cat continued to yowl. "If you do not lift that board, I shall!"

He glared at her but rose to his full height. "I'm not certain I have ever encountered a more vexing female than you, Miss St. Briac." And with that he knelt and, without hesitation, fit his fingers under the end of one board, almost as if he knew all about the mewling cat's hiding place.

Moments later, a dark opening was revealed, and she saw a small soot-gray cat inside, its head thrown back as it emitted yet another plaintive cry. Was it sitting on a step? "Goodness! Look at that. Do you suppose it is a smuggler's hole?"

Before Benedict could reply, the cat sprang out and landed on his thighs, claws extended. Hawke bit back a curse. With one dark hand, he lifted the animal into the air and lightly dropped it onto the floor nearby. The cat gave a dismissive sniff, sauntering off toward the kitchen.

Grimly, Benedict said, "If I hadn't been told that the creature belonged to my father, I wouldn't let it back in this house."

Camille badly wanted to ask more questions, especially about the dark open space under the floor. She was about to suggest they could take a closer look with a light of some sort, but Hawke was already putting the boards back in place.

Instead, she ventured, "This is your father's house, then?"

"Unfortunately, yes." He frowned. "I've only come here because he is ill. My sister is caring for him in the village." His face darkened further as he added, "I was about to leave on an expedition to Australia with the great ornithologist John Gould when I was summoned here. It would have been the adventure of a lifetime."

Camille blinked. Did he care more for the opportunity to sail off in search of birds than for his own father? Before she could ask more questions, Benedict Hawke reached out a hand, gesturing to indicate that she should rise.

"If you don't mind, I have a lot of work to do," he said. His voice was cool, but when he touched her hand, a current of heat passed between them. "In the future, I must ask you to refrain from stopping by uninvited. Do we understand one another?"

"Perfectly." Lips compressed, Camille withdrew her hand from the warmth of his and forced herself to press on. "You do not intend to assist in my efforts to save the kittiwakes who nest on your nearby cliffs?"

"I don't know how you came to believe that I might play a role in your crusade," Hawke replied enigmatically. "I have enough to do here, tending to my own affairs...and you would be wise to do the same, Miss St. Briac."

She felt a chill. "Is that some sort of threat?"

Hawke shrugged his wide shoulders almost imperceptibly. "More like a warning for your safety. I can only guess what those men might be capable of if a female like you should attempt to interfere with them again."

"I see." Camille pulled her damp cloak from the peg and slipped it on, feeling both numb and furious. "I will see myself out, sir."

She opened the heavy door, marched outside, and pushed it closed as forcefully as she could. In the distance, beyond the windswept pine trees, she glimpsed the figure of Rafael. He stood in the tall grass, holding the reins for his own horse and her bay gelding, Pegasus. When he saw her, he raised a hand in a slight wave.

Tears unexpectedly stung Camille's eyes as she lifted her skirts and half-ran along the wet coastal path to reach them.

Rafael took one look at her face and asked warily, "How was your meeting, my lady?"

"Terrible. I should never have listened to you!" Her voice broke. "Benedict Hawke is an ogre."

Rafael touched her arm in sympathy. "At least you did the right thing."

"Fiddle!" Camille pulled away. "That man has a heart of granite. There is only one remaining course of action." Her heart was beating fast. "My idea may sound...extreme, but at least you cannot say I didn't first try a more civilized approach."

She saw Rafael's eyes widen in alarm. Before he could speak, Camille hitched up her skirts and mounted Pegasus. Holding the reins, she turned the horse eastward. "Let us go to Lupine Cottage. There is a great deal to do before Friday, when we shall carry out my battle plan!"

"You want to do *what?*" Rafael's dark eyes were like saucers as he stared in at Camille.

They were inside Lupine Cottage, faintly illuminated by a pair of oil lamps. Clouds gathered outside as more raindrops began to spatter the windows overlooking the vast English Channel.

"You surprise me!" Camille gave a little laugh, as if that might serve to calm him. "Are you not the same boy who masqueraded as a highwayman to help my cousin Anthony retrieve his runaway love?"

Rafael frowned. "Indeed. But my master is a grown man, capable of looking after himself. When he sent me with you to Cornwall, I was charged to keep *you* safe."

"And so you shall," she said breezily. "By helping me to waylay the odious Benedict Hawke."

"Waylay?" Eyes wide, he added, "Would the proper word be *kidnap?*"

"Well, perhaps," she agreed, and hurried on. "However, we shan't harm him. We shall bring Mr. Hawke here, to this remote cottage, and thereby stop him from leading the feather thieves on their terrible raid of kittiwake nests."

"But what makes you think that will be enough, my lady? Won't they just go ahead without him?"

Camille had no wish to discuss this part of the plan, for she knew Rafael would shake his head in outrage. Instead, she soothed, "I have thought of that, and I have a plan which I will reveal when the time is right."

"That sounds...ominous."

"Rafael, your English is vastly improved since first we met." Laughing, she spread a handmade map on the table before them and moved the oil lamp closer. "Here is the route you will take on Friday. I will meet you here to receive our prisoner."

"D'you imagine I can overpower him on my own?"

"No, of course not. I shall assist you!"

"Ah, good, my lady." Rafael nodded, but there was a gleam of mockery in his dark eyes. "I'll not worry further about this mad scheme of yours."

"I'm glad to hear it," Camille said firmly.

"Indeed, I feel certain you will realize that it is impossible. That man is stronger than both of us put together, and I shudder to think what he might do if he's angry."

"Fiddle! I have no intention of allowing that scoundrel to best me. He may be stronger, but I am far cleverer..." Camille paced over to the window and stared out at the cliffs and the rain-tossed English Channel. "I shall prevail over Benedict Hawke and his band of villains."

* * *

ON FRIDAY EVENING, Benedict put down his pen, closed his books, and stood up. Dusk was gathering, and in just a few hours, Jem and his crew would begin arriving on the cliffs to conduct their raid on the kittiwakes' cliffside nests.

It would be a challenge for Benedict to bring off his scheme to stop, or at least minimize, the raid without arousing Jem's suspicions. His heartbeat kicked up as he mentally ticked off the steps of his plan...while reminding himself that his bigger goal was to discover the identity of the true mastermind behind the kittiwake slaughter. Someone was willing to go to great lengths—and expense—to provide exclusive decorations for costly millinery creations. When Benedict remembered the wings being ripped from a kittiwake, and then the still-living bird spiraling down into the sea, fury burned at his core.

Inside the tiny kitchen, Fletcher was removing his apron and hanging it on a peg. The older man was looking especially worn and frail, and if it were any night but this one, Benedict would urge him to stay here, to rest, to care for himself instead of others.

But this was not just any night.

"I suppose you're off to sit with Pa?" Benedict inquired. Lately, as Pa had become more fretful in the middle of the night, Fletcher had taken to staying at his bedside so that Prue could sleep. She needed her rest to contend with two little ones and the baby that would soon be born.

Fletcher looked at him, dark smudges under his eyes. "Aye, sir. I've left your supper on the hob, still warm."

The last thing Benedict could think of tonight was food, but he smiled and nodded. "I appreciate that." He wanted to offer to go tomorrow night in Fletcher's place, but the words would not form on his lips. The very thought of sitting for hours next to Pa, breathing the same fetid air, sent dark torrents of dread through his body. "Try to get some sleep tonight, old man."

Perhaps, he mused, *it would be good to hire someone else to help Fletcher with Pa.*

Minutes later, after hearing the gig roll away down the pebbled track, Benedict poured himself a brandy. He drank it down in two swallows and savored the burn as the liquor made its way down. The gray cat, Ember, was sleeping on the settee where Camille St. Briac had lain unconscious not so long ago.

Benedict wandered restlessly outside and inhaled the fresh sea breeze. Could he sleep tonight, knowing what was ahead?

Just then, a cry reached his ears from beyond the stand of pine trees. "Oh dear, help me!" The voice was high-pitched, yet strangely familiar. There was a pause, followed by a scream.

Benedict looked around for a person who might be assisting the person in distress. Seeing no one, he began to run toward the trees, lured closer by intermittent, pitiful moans. In the distance, he could see the dark silhouettes of a horse-drawn gig against the violet-tinted sky. Perhaps the lady in distress had been traveling along the cliffs. Had she gotten out for some reason and fallen?

"Please, help me!" came the voice again, sounding almost ghostly now.

A twinge of doubt made Benedict slow his pace. Reaching the pine copse, he scanned the tall grass, looking for an injured female, but saw nothing.

What the devil is happening here? he thought. In the next instant, before he could turn, a rough cloth, perhaps a sack of some sort, came over his head and quickly imprisoned his arms. The scratchy fabric covering his face smelled of moldy potatoes. Someone pushed him to the ground and sat on his back, even as he struggled with all his might to get free. He felt a rope winding round his legs, and he kicked, but too late, it was already knotted tight.

A hard object, like the barrel of a pistol, jammed between his shoulder blades. "Be still, be silent—or die!" ordered an odd, rough voice, sounding like neither a man nor a woman.

"Bloody hell," shouted Benedict, and redoubled his struggle. "You threaten the wrong man!"

As if from a distance, he heard a low voice mutter, "I knew this was a mistake, my lady." An exchange of hushed whispers followed.

Benedict flung himself backward, hoping to catch his attackers off-guard, but when his head struck something hard, he knew a sudden sense of doom. He tried to curse again, but it was too late.

* * *

CAMILLE WATCHED in horror as Benedict Hawke's tall, broad-shouldered form slumped forward in the tall grass and lay still.

"My God, what did you do?" she demanded of Rafael, sudden tears filling her eyes and choking her voice. "Have you killed him?"

"Killed him?" echoed the youth. He stood over the body, clenching the barrel of the pistol in one hand. "I tried to push back when he flew back at me with such force. I think he just collided with *this*." Rafael stared at the heavy pistol butt as if it had a life of its own.

"Perhaps he's simply dazed." Surprised by the force of her own emotions, Camille rushed forward from her hiding place behind a nearby tree and knelt to fumble under the burlap sack for Benedict's wrist. The warmth of his skin and the throb of his pulse sent a tide of relief coursing through her body. *What is happening to me?* More tears stung her eyes.

"Should I remove the sack?" asked Rafael. "In case he can't get air—"

Camille knew a strong urge to free Benedict and try

to take him back to his cottage. Yet the temptation to forget all about their plan to thwart the feather thieves brought her up short. "No, we cannot waver now. He could come round at any moment, and if we have freed him, it will all be over."

"I knew we should have asked Helivet to help," he fretted. "The coachman is very loyal to you, my lady."

"I will remind you again, Helivet's strongest loyalty is to my father. I could not take a chance that he might divulge our plan, ruining everything."

Rafael rolled his eyes, as if he wished someone like Helivet *had* told her father.

"See here," Camille scolded in a whisper, "we cannot stand here jabbering about this. We must get him into the gig and carry on with our plan."

"But the plan was for us to hold him at gunpoint and force him to get in under his own power. How can we ever carry someone like him?"

Camille held up a silencing hand and hurried over to the gig. Under the seat, she found the voluminous gray cloak she'd used as a disguise in Bodinnick. Shaking it out, she returned to Benedict Hawke's side and gestured to Rafael to help her shift his weight from side to side until he lay on top of the woolen fabric. To-gether, they were able to use the cloak to haltingly slide their prisoner across the soft grass to the gig.

"Is it possible that his weight increased since he fell unconscious?" Rafael complained.

"Just be quiet and help me."

Getting Benedict Hawke inside the small equipage seemed impossible, but through sheer determination the pair eventually were successful. Their captive slumped back against the seat as Rafael jumped up be-side him and took the reins. Camille, who wore trousers and a boy's cap, was relieved to mount Pegasus and lead the way back to Lupine Cottage.

Thankfully, night had descended under a heavy curtain of clouds. Even if they should happen to encounter anyone on the cliff path, it would be difficult to get a good look at Benedict Hawke, who was confined inside a large burlap sack...just like one of the proud birds he had intended to capture and kill.

* * *

BENEDICT'S first thought when he came around again was that his mouth was very dry. Dry as dust. His wrists burned under the ropes that bound him to a wooden chair, and his head hurt like the devil.

It was pitch black, but that might not signify because they'd blindfolded him. *They.* Who had done this to him, and why? Did they mean to kill him? Had they already tried?

He wondered how long he'd been sitting here, tied to a chair, in the dark. He wracked his muddled brain, trying to piece together the events after he'd heard that female call of distress. They had trussed him up, yanked a scratchy bag over his head, threatened him, and then somehow, he had hit his head. Once or twice, he'd swum back to consciousness: jouncing over the cliff path in a well-sprung equipage, being grabbed by people on both sides and led into a cold, damp room; hearing low whispered conversations between his prison guards. But who the devil would do this—and why?

The answer came to him like a blow: Camille St. Briac! Of course, *she* must be his captor. He saw her again, sitting across from him in his cottage, her exquisite face pink with emotion as she pleaded with him.

I am asking you to help me save the kittiwakes and their innocent chicks from slaughter. Will you do the right thing and join me?

How could he have been obtuse enough to think Camille would accept his evasions and denials, and then just go away? What a fool he was to imagine that she was like any other female he had known.

Every inch of his body ached, as if someone had taken a hammer to him. Just as sheer exhaustion was tempting him to close his eyes, a tiny sound made the hairs on the back of his neck stand up. There it was again, the faintest creak of...a door? Benedict straightened his back and lifted his blindfolded head, heart pounding.

"Who is it?" he demanded angrily.

The visitor made no reply, but soon enough he knew the answer: *Camille*. Something subtle changed in the air. He felt her moving around. As she lit a lamp, a faint, comforting sliver of light appeared under the length of black silk tied round his head.

He inhaled a mere hint of her scent. It had not been blended by Floris, the London perfumer. Rather it was part of her, an expression of her nature and innate beauty. Resisting the urge to submit to her spell, he curled his lip.

"Vixen."

She gave an involuntary gasp before, he imagined, pressing a hand to her mouth. He could feel her indecision.

"Oh, I know it is you," he continued in a deadly calm voice. "Heartless wench, did you mean to try to kill me?"

More silence, but he sensed her drawing closer.

"At least have the common decency to give me a drink." He paused. "Brandy if you have it."

He could feel her thinking about it. Next, there was the clink of a glass, the sound of a stopper being removed from a decanter, liquid pouring. Benedict licked his dry lips. When she brought it close, then touched the rim of the glass to his mouth, he felt an involuntary shock of arousal. She was standing very near, her breasts inches away from his face...and he knew she felt it too.

The brandy might have been Paris's finest, and he savored the glow as it spread through his body. In a low, seductive voice, he murmured, "Camille. I know it's you." As he spoke, his cock awoke and stiffened.

She was walking away, across the room. Where the devil were they? Surely not in her parents' home. He wanted to implore her to come back. At length, she did, hovering near him.

"How did you know?" she whispered, sounding tentative.

"Because." He drew a harsh breath. "Because I have wanted you since the day we met in Hyde Park, my dear vixen. My senses are attuned to you...carnally speaking."

The air between them was warmer, vibrating with his confession. "If you are trying to shock me, you will not succeed." Camille swallowed, audibly. "Also, I am not a vixen. Please don't call me that."

"But only a vixen would do what you have done to me today." God, how much he wanted to reach for her, pull her onto his lap, to teach her how to kiss and feel her respond.

"Sir, you are the villain in this piece, killing the defenseless kittiwakes." Her voice rose. "Someone had to step in to save them. I asked you to help me, but you refused. I had no choice but to remove you from the cliffside attack that will occur in just a few short hours."

It all made sense now. "I see. You and your young henchman nearly killed me. You imprisoned me in a deuced sack"

"The same sort of burlap sack that your men force the poor birds into. How did it feel?"

He decided to ignore her question. Until this night's work was accomplished, he could not divulge the truth. "You then brought me to this place, ruthlessly bound me to this chair, and left me blindfolded...possibly to die." He paused, feeling her heartbeat in the space between them. "Why did you come back before the raid?"

"Perhaps I simply wanted to be sure you were...all right. However, I did bring a pistol, so do not imagine you can escape."

"Please don't point it at me," he said acidly.

"I have it close by, just in case." Her voice rose defensively. "See here, I'm very sorry if you have suffered today, but the blow to your head was an accident. *You* caused it when you threw yourself backward."

"Ah, yes," he bit out. "I am the responsible party."

"I must go now." She was backing away. "I only came to be assured that you were alive and well."

"Alive perhaps, but hardly well." Benedict drew a breath, easing his tone. "Look at my wrists, my ankles. The rope has cut off the blood to my extremities, and my shoulders are twisted backward in an unnatural position. I've been like this for hours."

"I-I hadn't thought of that."

"Your young assistant was unnecessarily brutal with the ropes."

"He doubtless feared you might otherwise be able to loosen your bonds. Let me have a look."

Camille's soft meadow-blossom fragrance wafted back to him, and he felt her hovering near, studying his arms, his tightly bound wrists. She touched his chafed flesh with cool fingertips. Then she began to struggle with the ropes, tugging just enough to give him some relief.

"Is that better?" Camille asked.

"Do not expect me to thank you." Benedict flexed his fingers and sighed. "Although I might if you do the right thing and release me."

"Of course, that is out of the question. I must tighten your bonds again before I leave here...though I confess, seeing you like this certainly gives me pause." Silence, then, "I mean, when you refused to help me and I devised this scheme, I felt angry and determined. I didn't fully consider what it might feel like, in reality, for you to be tied to a chair for hours."

His heart leaped, only in part because she was clearly having second thoughts about holding him captive. In a low voice, he coaxed, "Camille...It is just the two of us here, alone, late at night. Let us speak openly."

"I can't imagine what you mean."

"I think you can." He gave her the slow, secret smile that had melted the resistance of countless beauties. "You said it yourself. You are no innocent, but a woman of..."

"Four-and-twenty," she supplied a trifle breathlessly.

"A woman," Benedict repeated. He could feel the arousal that flared inside her, like a flame bursting to life from a neglected ember. "You have mistreated me abominably tonight. However, once free, I will not exact revenge or go to the constable...if you do one thing for me." He paused. "Kiss me."

"You are a scoundrel."

"Do not pretend that you are shocked, Camille. Indeed, you are a firebrand, more used to doing the shocking yourself." He paused. "How many men have kissed you?"

"If you imagine that I am completely ignorant of love, you are quite wrong."

"Ah, that's a relief. Now I can kiss you without fear that I am crossing some invisible boundary." He paused.

"Grant me this single wish and I will forgive you for a night of torture."

Her silent hesitation was all the answer Benedict needed, and his heart pounded as he waited for her to come to him.

CHAPTER 11

"*I* must be mad to agree," Camille said softly. "This is blackmail, you know."

Benedict gave the low laugh she found quite irresistible. "You make me sound very sinister, and yet it was you who ordered me blindfolded and bound to a chair." He paused. "Why shouldn't you grant me a kiss or two to make this torment bearable?"

"Or *two*?"

"Sit down and allow me to practice my powers of persuasion."

Considering this, Camille felt an involuntary, intimate pulse of arousal.

"You needn't hesitate," he added maddeningly. "We both know you want to."

"That's an outrageous thing to say." She perched on the very edge of his hard-muscled thighs. For one instant, Camille thought of her parents. What would they think if they could see her now? Their reaction was unimaginable. Just in case one of them should come to her bedside during the night, Camille had left a note, explaining that she had decided to sleep at Lupine Cottage and would return in the morning. If Papa had already read it and he rode over here to check on her, there would be hell to pay.

"Just one brief kiss, and then I must leave." Somehow, the notion that he was completely restrained, unable to see or touch her, made it all seem less real, like a scene out of time.

"Turn toward me."

The man sounded for all the world as if *he* were the one in control! Yet perhaps it was true, for Camille felt powerless to resist. His face was just a few inches away, and she studied the chiseled lines of his jaw, the shape of his proud head. In the shadows, a tendon was visible in his neck, and she could see the first scattering of black hair at the base of his throat. How like him, she reflected, to have neglected to don a neckcloth.

His mouth, masculine yet sensual, quirked slightly on one side. "I am basking in this moment, feeling you near me," he murmured.

Suddenly her throat went dry, and her heart raced.

"Just one kiss," Benedict coaxed. "After all, you have rendered me harmless. I cannot even touch you."

The air between them was charged with something utterly thrilling. It drew her forward. "One kiss," she breathed.

In the darkness, time seemed to stop as she leaned closer and brushed her lips to his. It was only the merest contact, yet his mouth yielded and grew warm, and she felt him emit a low groan. Suddenly Camille found herself in deep, uncharted waters. Her kisses with Roger had certainly not elicited this response from her.

Against her mouth, Benedict whispered, "Let me taste you."

She felt the edge of his tongue tracing the seam of her lips. As heat and longing blossomed between her legs, she melted into his kiss. His male scent, faintly musky with sweat, rose to her. When his tongue deftly entered her mouth, exploring, Camille responded with growing passion, and they kissed for long, blissful minutes.

"Yes," he muttered at length, "touch me. No one can see."

This felt dangerous, yet she could not resist. She leaned closer and ran her hands over Benedict's wide shoulders, yearning to open his broadcloth shirt and discover his warm, rough skin, the muscled surface of his chest. Camille still wore the same boy's clothing she'd donned for his abduction, yet she had never felt more keenly female. Her breasts were swollen, her nipples tight, alive with sensation. She needed him in dangerous ways she didn't fully understand.

"Closer, love."

Camille knew it was mad to succumb. What if all this was meant to render her so witless, she would set him free?

But now he was kissing her again, and his mouth was like a drug. Driven by sheer need, she yielded to his plea for closer contact. Moving one slim, breeches-clad leg sideways over his lap, she found herself straddling him. They were face-to-face, inches apart. At that moment, her crotch came in contact with Benedict's hard ridge of arousal, straining against the confines of his trousers.

It was a shock. Inside her, uncertainty conflicted with scorching desire.

"By God, you're killing me," Benedict groaned. "I need to touch you. That's all I ask." He paused, and it seemed they were both holding their breaths. "Sweet minx, won't you free my hands…just for a bit?"

She wanted this more than anything. The wet,

aching place between her legs needed it desperately. And it was more than just raw desire. Even her heart wanted him to touch her, to show her how he felt.

"Oh! I..." came her choked reply. Why did she hesitate?

Turning her head, Camille stared across the room to the windows overlooking the moonlit English Channel. In that emotional moment, she looked back through time.

She was here in Lupine Cottage, unexpectedly alone with Roger, after the two of them had been walking on the cliffs. As they sat together on the chaise and he gently kissed her, it felt natural, sweetly stirring. Gradually, however, he turned persuasive, his voice rough with need. He begged for kiss after kiss, and as her body responded, he coaxed her to lie back, kneeling above her. Camille now seemed to watch herself from a distance as Roger firmly clasped her hand and pressed it over the bulge in his trousers.

"Please!" he had whispered hotly. "Let me show you how much I love you." Rubbing himself against her hand, Roger added, "You can trust me..."

"*Camille?*" Benedict's voice brought her back sharply to the present. "What's amiss?"

Clearly, even though he couldn't see her, he sensed the change in her mood.

Scrambling to her feet, Camille shook her head. "I cannot do this. I will not!" She looked at his strong body, tied to the chair, eyes blindfolded, and knew a flare of confusion. Had Benedict's intoxicating kisses been nothing more than a means to gain his freedom? "*This* should not be happening. I never intended...I mean, I brought you here only to stop you from leading that terrible raid." Backing away, she added, "It's nearly time. When we have thwarted your men, I will send Rafael back to set you free."

As she pulled her coat and cap from a peg by the door, Benedict spoke. "Camille, I am not the villain. Let me go. You can trust me."

Camille heard an echo of Roger saying the very same thing. *Trust!* How easily men cheapened that precious word.

Before Benedict Hawke could say more, she opened the cottage door and fled out into the night.

* * *

CAMILLE LEANED FORWARD ASTRIDE PEGASUS, her knees gripping his flanks as she guided the horse westward along the cliff path. Tears burned her eyes even as the cool night wind dried them.

Fool, fool! She chided herself. At least one good thing had come of her humiliating interlude with Lord Upton. It now served as a warning, and she ought to be grateful for that.

As she rode on, turning inland to bypass a treacherous stretch of the coastal path, Camille reached a crossroads near the tiny village of Lansallos. This was where she and Rafael had agreed to meet, yet there was no sign of him. Was she early? Camille rode to higher ground and looked out over the Channel. With a shock, she realized that the first glimmer of sunrise had begun to show behind the clouds. Soon enough the men would be gathering on the cliff above the kittiwake nests.

Of course, she wished Rafael was by her side, but she could not wait for him. No doubt he would join her soon, and in any event, there was little he could do to help her.

Tonight, Camille couldn't trust anyone else to navigate this precarious situation. She, alone, must carry out their plan.

* * *

As Camille tied Pegasus to the low branch of a pine tree near Gull Cottage, she became aware of distant, muffled voices. Her heart began to beat wildly. Where were they? Soundlessly, she ran to the edge of the bluff. The clouds had moved to reveal silvery moonlight and the first light of dawn.

Camille looked down toward the stony ledges, carved by nature into the cliff face. Far below, in a tiny cove, two long boats disgorged men onto the sand. One stocky figure, identifiable by his striped cap, held a lantern. He motioned for silence and pointed the crew toward an upward path a short distance from the rock shelves lined with kittiwake nests.

To Camille's horror, she saw that many of the killers were carrying clubs, and a few were armed with rook rifles. How could humans be capable of such cruelty?

She felt sick as she saw that the birds had already begun to gather breakfast for their chicks. They wheeled and dipped, silhouetted against the ethereal glow of sunrise. The adult kittiwakes seemed to sense that humans were approaching, for those who had gone in search of small fish and worms now circled protectively back to their nests. Camille wished she could call out to warn the graceful, gentle birds to stay away, for they were in far more danger than their chicks. The feather thieves prized only the white, black-barred wings of the mature kittiwakes.

Jem was pointing his men upward, toward the clifftop, where he doubtless expected to find Benedict Hawke waiting to lead them. At that moment, cold, fat drops of rain began to pelt her from the clouds. Taking a deep breath, Camille reached up with both hands to pull her cap more securely over her pinned-up curls, then started down the rugged pathway to meet them.

"Ho there!" she shouted in the deepest voice she could manage. "D'ye be Jem?"

"Mebbe." Jem squinted at her suspiciously.

"Yer leader sent me to tell ye the raid's called off! Someone tipped off the authorities and they be on their way."

"Leader? Who d'you mean?"

Camille blinked, confused, then remembered that Tom Pascoe was Benedict's assumed name. "Pascoe sent me, paid me a shillin' t' warn ye."

"Why is he not here?" Jem demanded.

The rain was falling harder, and from farther down the cliffside came short, nasal warning calls between kittiwake parents and their nestlings. Camille felt a rising sense of panic but struggled to hide it. Just as Jem lifted his lantern in the rain, bent on a closer look, she saw one of his gang clambering over the cliffside toward the kittiwake nests. In the next instant, the thug raised his club and brought it down heavily, bludgeoning one of the proud birds. It was all she could do to suppress an enraged shout of protest. Her heart was racing as she started forward.

"Never mind about Pascoe! They be coming, I tell you! You must all go!"

"D'ye mean the customs men? What do they care about a lot of dirty gulls?"

She felt a moment's panic but forced a firm tone. "They be lyin' in wait for free traders who're landin' by here!"

"But we only got one bird!" one of the gang protested. "And we ain't free traders!"

Nodding, Camille pretended to consider this. "Do any of you men be wanted by the law for other... reasons?"

They all began looking at one another, clearly nervous now.

Before any of the small group could make a reply, a shout came from farther down the side of the cliff.

"Over here!" cried one of the plume hunters, and Camille saw him point toward a ledge with several crowded nests. As he and another great oaf headed in that direction, brandishing their clubs, the kittiwakes raised a chorus of squawks.

Unable to bear another moment, Camille pushed past Jem and hurried down the path, bent on stopping yet another cold-blooded murder. If only Rafael could be here to help! It came to her that she had been foolish to think she could stop this raid all by herself, even with the aid of the small pocket pistol she had brought from Elysium tonight.

"Halt!" she cried, pounding a fist on the bigger man's back, not caring any longer if they guessed she was female.

"Huh?" The brute paused in the act of raising his club over the nest of frantic kittiwakes and glanced back at her.

"I said stop. *Stop!*"

"What have we here?" crowed the man's wiry companion, looking her over from head to toe.

Camille glanced down and, to her shock, realized that the rain had molded her clothing to the unmistakable curves of her body. As the savages came closer, she reached inside the coat for her pistol but was horrified to find her pocket was empty. Dear God! She started to search another pocket before it came to her that, dazed after the kissing interlude with Benedict, she had rushed out and left the dratted thing behind on the table! Panic coursed through Camille's veins. Even as she looked around for a rock to brandish, the two men grabbed her. The bigger one wrenched her arms back while the other one put his hands on her breasts. What did they intend to do to her?

"I'll see you both hanged if you don't release me this instant," she threatened. Her shoulders felt as if they might come out of their sockets.

Her attackers looked at one another and burst out laughing.

"The lass'll see us hang!" cried the big oaf who held her arms.

"Course she will!" his companion rejoined, eliciting more laughter.

The other members of the gang had moved off, seemingly more interested in killing kittiwakes than the assault on Camille. Through the sheets of rain, she glimpsed the distant orange glow of Jem's lantern, swinging to and fro, farther and farther away.

"Lass like you," grunted the tall, brawny man, "out here alone at all hours? Askin' fer it, I'd say."

He attempted to hold Camille's wrists back with just one beefy hand, seemingly unable to resist the temptation to reach around to paw at her breast. Thank God she had donned two layers of clothing against the night air. When her smaller attacker leered and dared to grope between her legs, Camille reacted instinctively and butted her head against him with all her might.

"Swine!" she shouted. "Touch me again and I'll kill you!"

From the corner of her eye, she saw a shadow looming up and felt a wave of sick dread at the thought that someone else had come to join in her assault. But in the next moment, everything changed. The smaller man was yanked away from her, thrown a short distance down the cliff to lie, moaning, on a bed of rocks. A second later, the short barrel of a pocket pistol passed through Camille's vision.

"Unhand her, bastard, and step away" threatened a deep, familiar voice. "I wouldn't hesitate for a moment to put a hole in your chest."

Adrenaline coursed through Camille's body. She must be dreaming! Her rescuer sounded like Benedict Hawke—but that was impossible, for surely he was tied to a chair in Lupine Cottage.

For once in her life, Camille wanted to be wrong.

CHAPTER 12

amille was barely aware of the big thug rushing by, scrambling back to the path, his club and canvas sack forgotten. Before she could speak, iron-hard hands were pulling her along, then lifting her up to a higher ledge where there was an unexpected opening in the face of the cliff.

"In here," ordered her rescuer. And she found herself being shoved into a tiny, dark space.

No sooner had Camille managed to turn around than she nearly bumped into Benedict's towering form. "You! How can this be?" she gasped, peering at him in the shadows. "And you have a weapon!"

"My dear vixen, did you really think you could outwit me?" he replied in sardonic tones, then brandished the same pocket pistol she had mistakenly left behind in Lupine Cottage.

Her heart was beating so fast she could scarcely speak. "I don't understand!"

"You aren't required to understand—or even think. Just obey me for once." Benedict loomed over her, wildly handsome, and laid a finger over her mouth in a way that sent currents of heat through her cold, wet body. "Stay here. Don't move! I'll sort this out and come back for you."

Her brain told her to refuse. Was he not the enemy after all, in league with the brutes who had come with clubs? Yet somehow, on a primal level, Camille knew better. "You won't let them kill the birds?"

"I will not." His deep green eyes searched her face. "I told you before, you can trust me."

She drew a deep breath. "It is very hard, but I shall try." As he turned away, she caught his sleeve. "I told them you sent me, that the revenue men were nearby, lying in wait for smugglers, and Pascoe didn't want to conduct the raid with the authorities so close at hand."

"Ah, so that was your mad plan." He gave a short laugh. "Clever minx."

* * *

BENEDICT EMERGED from the slit-like opening in the rocks and looked around for Jem. The dawn light lent a rather dreamy quality to the cliffside scene and the male kittiwakes who hovered protectively near their nests. Fortunately, it seemed that Camille's warnings might have caused the feather thieves to exercise caution, for they stood in small knots, hands jammed into their pockets, shifting from foot to foot as they muttered to one another.

Jem stood a few feet away from the others, peering through a spyglass out over the Channel. Benedict approached so quietly that the stocky man jumped when he heard his name.

"Oh, it be thee, Pascoe!" he exclaimed. Then, in a hushed tone, he added, "Thankful I am ye have come. There were a warning"

"Right, the customs men are about," Benedict said firmly. "I don't want any of us taking chances at a time like this." Watching Jem, he added, "Mayhap some of these men have reason to avoid the authorities?"

Jem tugged his striped cap lower over his brow. "Mayhap," he nodded, brow furrowed.

"Better to go now, afore they march up the beach. Do not tarry. Dawn has broken, and you all would be seen."

"But if we don't bring the wings to the feather folk," Jem said stubbornly, "we don't be paid."

"If there is one master, I could have speech with him…" Benedict ventured.

"No!" Jem shook his head vigorously. "The master won't speak to any but me."

"Then give me a few hours to see what I can learn about the revenue men."

Jem looked dubious. "And after that?"

"We meet tomorrow morning at the Old Ferry Inn to discuss a new plan."

"Arright then," Jem grumbled. "But nothing does happen without the master's say-so."

* * *

THE ROCK PASSAGEWAY was too narrow and confining to be called a cave, Camille decided as she waited for Benedict. The dank space could barely accommodate one person, standing up, and the stone floor seemed to dip toward a center point where moisture collected. Perhaps Benedict had simply pushed her in here at random, but she doubted it.

Growing restless, curious, Camille edged her way forward, into the murky darkness, but a rustling sound farther ahead made her stop. Her heart gave a wild thump, and then she turned back. It was one thing to be brave, which she was, but quite another to be foolhardy.

Stay here! Don't move, Benedict had ordered.

The sound came again from farther into the narrow abyss. *Whish-whish!* Camille was on the verge of defying his command and fleeing when a tall, broad-shouldered form darkened the entrance to her stone cell. Panic rushed through her like a brushfire.

She turned the other way, even as she realized there was no way out. After one step, a hand grasped her collar and she stumbled backward.

"Let me go!" she cried through gritted teeth.

The intruder easily lifted her up, rotating her body until she was inches away from...*Benedict*. His breath was warm on her face, and Camille felt his heart beating through the layers of clothing that separated their bodies.

"You are the most volatile female I have ever had the ill fortune to contend with," he whispered harshly. "Why must everything be so difficult?"

"Of course I am volatile! I have been imprisoned in this miserable *cave!* And—I heard noises!"

"Be grateful I did not tie you to a chair," he replied in acid tones, "And then leave you alone for hours."

Camille felt heat rise in her cheeks. "I must admit, you have a point."

Unexpectedly, he laughed and set her down. "Let's be away. Follow me."

To her surprise, he squeezed past and advanced farther into the gloomy crevice carved into the stone cliff, away from the entrance. Camille hesitated.

"Where are you taking me?"

"How many times must I tell you to trust me? You'll know soon enough."

Ahead of her, his tall form was being swallowed by the blackness, so Camille forced herself to follow him. "You sound as if this all were some sort of daring escapade, but I can assure you, it is much worse. What those men are doing is horrifying." As she spoke, her booted foot slid on the slick, slightly concave stone ground and she cried out in surprise, losing her footing.

"Sorry." Benedict was beside her in an instant, grasping her arm before she could fall. "I shouldn't leave you alone. Ordinarily, I'd have a lantern, but I had to come here from another…unplanned engagement."

"How can you jest?" Camille cried softly. "And what is this place? It wouldn't surprise me if Satan himself appeared, brandishing his trident!"

"We are in an old smuggling tunnel. They used to roll the small kegs up this passageway, which accounts for the worn-down stone beneath our feet." He paused before adding, "I think it must have been created in the last century."

"By your father—?"

Benedict shook his dark head. "Nay. My parents didn't settle here until Pa stopped working as a gardener." Their eyes met. "There's no time now for that tale. I don't want to take any chances that Jem and his band of outlaws come after us from the cliff side."

They continued on, Benedict feeling his way, until at length he turned back to say quietly, "We've reached the cottage. Hold on."

Camille waited, dimly aware of him stepping onto a strategically placed rock, then stretching up his arms to push on something. In the next instant, light streamed down onto their faces. Blinking in surprise, she realized that they were emerging through the same hole she had seen under Benedict's desk when the soot-gray cat howled to gain entrance to the cottage.

"Can you manage?"

Before she could reply, he grasped her waist and lifted her up. Camille knew a secret, heady pleasure as his strong hands boosted her through the opening in the floor. Moments later, she was standing in the dimly lit cottage, watching as Benedict crouched to replace the floorboards. The cat emerged from another room, tail swishing to and fro, meowing a greeting.

"Hello!" Camille extended a hand to the soot-gray feline. "What's your name?"

Benedict crossed to her side. "My sister, Prudence, tells me he is called Ember." His brows flicked up as the cat rubbed forcefully against his legs.

"Is your man, Fletcher, here?" she asked. It came to her that they were quite alone, and this time Benedict was neither blindfolded nor tied to a chair.

"No, he slept at my sister's house in the village. Prue's time is at hand, but Pa needs someone nearby."

Camille wondered fleetingly why Benedict wasn't the one sitting by his father's bedside, but more immediate questions came to mind. Watching as he went to a small cupboard and took out a stoppered bottle, she blurted, "I cannot wait another moment to learn how you managed to escape!"

He poured a generous amount of tawny liquid into a glass and drank it down. "You are bold beyond belief, my girl. Kidnapping me at gunpoint, tying me to a chair, blindfolded, and then demanding to know how I freed myself?" Eyes glinting, he splashed more liquor into the glass. "You ought to be quaking in fear that I will exact revenge for what you did to me."

Camille's mouth was very dry. "I did it to save the kittiwakes."

"But our kisses had nothing to do with the birds." He advanced on her. "I wonder, are you longing for more?"

"Scoundrel!" Before she could think, Camille brought a hand up to slap him, but of course he caught it in mid-air. "You blackmailed me into...doing those things."

He laughed. "We both know better than that." Leaning closer, still holding her fragile wrist, he murmured, "You revealed many secrets to me tonight, Camille. Some that you may not even realize yourself, but I promise you, I will not forget."

When Camille twisted away, he released her, still smiling in that way that made her cheeks burn. "You are odious."

"Perhaps," he allowed dryly, "but I am *not* the villain of this night's crime, as you must know by now." Turning, he went into the kitchen and gestured for her to follow him. "Circumstances have prevented me from eating since midday last. Now I am hungry."

"I am sorry you missed your supper," she said stiffly.

"A bit late for that." He gave her a wry smile. "There isn't time for a meal. As soon as I am assured that Jem and the others have gone, I want to see to the birds."

Camille's heart leaped at this. She had to stop herself from catching his sleeve. "Do you mean...help them?"

"If possible." With that, he stepped into the small larder adjoining the kitchen. "I confess that I am used to Fletcher doing all of this," he said, rummaging around the shelves.

"I could cook something for you," she allowed. "I love food."

"Ah, a woman of many talents." As Benedict spoke, he found a half loaf of brown bread and broke off a large chunk. There were brambleberries in a pottery bowl nearby, and he carried the food back into the kitchen and set the bowl on the worktable. "This will do."

There was a small dish of fresh honeycomb on the table, and he spread some on the bread. Then, to her surprise, he broke off a piece and offered it to her.

"I really shouldn't, but I can't resist," she said.

"I like that about you," he murmured, eyes agleam with amusement.

Although the cottage was damp and chilly, Camille felt uncomfortably warm. She accepted the bread and honey, and when he offered her the berries, she ate several, savoring the juicy bursts of flavor in her mouth. They stood together in the pale light, eating, until Benedict produced a pint of milk. He raised the bottle to his lips, drank, and offered it to her.

For an instant, she thought of Grandmère St. Briac, who delighted in dictating rules of behavior to her family. She would call it a shocking breach of etiquette for Camille to share this bottle, to put her mouth on the same place as this man she barely knew.

Their eyes met, and she knew he was remembering the acutely sensual kisses they had shared. Benedict nodded, once. Camille averted her gaze, took the bottle, and drank. Was it possible that she could taste him on the glass rim?

"Thank you," she said.

Pausing between bites, Benedict said, "You asked me how I freed myself tonight, and I promised an answer." He gave her a steady look. "It wasn't difficult once you kindly loosened the ropes for me. After your precipitous departure, I finished untying them."

Fool! Camille chided herself. She had fully intended to tighten his bonds again before she left him, but of course he had seen to it that she was drunk with arousal and unable to think clearly. "I see. How very resourceful you are, sir."

"I like to think so, but of course you helped me." He flashed a knowing smile, then showed her the pocket pistol he had used to threaten the brute on the cliff. "I realize that you never meant for me to have this. Quite the opposite, yes? However, your mistake allowed me to save your life."

"I wasn't thinking clearly!" Conflicting emotions surged up in her breast. "You took advantage of me in Lupine Cottage."

"Quite a feat, considering I was blindfolded and tied to a chair."

"You were wicked." Her face felt maddeningly hot. "I mean, I believe you intended only to manipulate me so that you could escape."

"Can you blame me?" Benedict ate one last berry and came around the rough table to look down at her. His voice was husky as he continued, "I can assure you, however, that if you sensed I wanted you, you were quite right."

When he said the words *I wanted you*, Camille felt breathless. Deep inside, longing blossomed. Thank goodness he couldn't know what he did to her! "This conversation is…improper."

"A spinsterish word if ever I heard one," he laughed and started toward the door. "Right, then, I'm going to have a look around outside. Be a good girl for once and wait for me here. I'll return shortly."

She bristled at his words but put her chin up and followed him. "I will go with you."

"See here." There was an edge to Benedict's voice as he removed his hand from the door latch and turned back. "In one day, you've made a devil of a lot of trouble for me. I didn't rescue you from the feather thieves only to have you put yourself in danger all over again. I demand that you stay here."

Camille clenched her fists. "All right, I will wait…"

"Excellent." He sent her a dubious glance but went out into the soft, early morning light.

When the door shut behind him, she looked around the empty cottage and spoke again, softly defiant. "I will wait…for ten minutes only."

What Benedict Hawke did not realize was that no

threat from him could overcome the powerful, protective urges she felt for the kittiwakes. It was as if they were her children. Tears stung her eyes as she silently vowed that she would do anything to stop the cruel feather thieves. Those monsters cared nothing for the lives of these gentle, innocent birds who wanted only to live as God intended, raising their chicks in the majesty of Cornwall.

It seemed that no one could understand what was at stake but Camille herself.

CHAPTER 13

Outside in the fresh mist of early morning, Benedict was drawn toward a cacophony of frantic, nasal *kitti-wake* shrieks. A wave of sickening anticipation rushed over him as he reached the brow of the cliff and looked down. He dreaded what he might see, unable to erase from his memory the image of a wingless, bloody kittiwake being flung out into the Channel.

Scanning the cliff that staggered down to a crescent of pebbled beach, Benedict watched as countless mature kittiwakes flew back and forth over their nests that clung precariously to the rocks. Perhaps more birds had been brutalized in the pre-dawn darkness than he realized? Yet, it seemed that the noise was a reaction to the recent episode of danger rather than a sign that they were being threatened at that moment. From this vantage point, he could see no sign of injured birds, so he went down the path for a better view.

Halfway down, near the place where he and Jem had conversed, Benedict saw the ruined nest. A bludgeoned, wingless kittiwake sprawled on a lower ledge, and in the big nest were two hatchlings that appeared to be dead. He closed his eyes as a long-buried memory tried to force its way to the surface.

"Oh, dear Lord," came an anguished voice from higher up the path.

Camille.

"I told you to wait for me!" he shouted. Already she was descending, and Benedict put up a warning hand. "Stay where you are. Stop! You don't need to see this."

She continued toward him as if he hadn't spoken a word. One hand flew to her mouth in horror, and her eyes were luminous with pain. To Benedict's shock, she went past him, scrambling over the rocks toward the battered nest.

"Camille!" he shouted over the alarmed cries of the kittiwakes. Following her, he grasped the tail of her coat to stop her forward motion. "Leave it. There's nothing to be done."

"Perhaps they are alive," she sobbed, pointing to the miniature nestlings who lay wet and utterly limp in the nest. "We can't simply leave them."

A corner deep inside Benedict went ice-cold. "I'm quite certain they are dead, and even if one might be clinging to a thread of life, there's nothing to be done. You must know that the other kittiwakes will only feed their own chicks, in their own nests."

"Then we will do it for them!" she flung back over one shoulder.

"Surely you must realize that this is part of nature —" He broke off, hearing an echo of Pa's brusque voice speaking those same words.

"That is utter fustian!" Camille blazed. "I have saved more birds than you can count, sir. If one of these chicks has a chance to survive, we *cannot* turn our backs and walk away." After a moment's pause, she added, "If you will not rescue him, I shall do it alone."

"Fine." Heart pounding, he released her coat. "I will help you then."

He edged past her, clambering over the rocky cliff until he reached the nest. The sight of the hatchlings' parent lying a short distance below, disfigured by the feather hunters who cared only for its wings, made him burn with rage.

From behind him, Camille half-sobbed, "The poor sweet papa. He only wanted to protect his babies."

Benedict needed to get away, but that was impossible. Instead, he forced himself to move closer. He gazed down at the two tiny hatchlings. Perhaps only a few days old, the siblings lay bedraggled and unprotected in the rain-soaked nest. One of them was clearly dead, but the other…

"He is alive," declared Camille, edging closer, leaning around Benedict's arm for a better look. Instinctively, he reached for her so that she wouldn't slip and tumble from the side of the cliff. "We can save him."

The voice in Benedict's head rasped, *Little fool! Twist its neck and be done with it!*

He touched a forefinger to the hatchling's breast. "Cold as stone."

"He is not dead," Camille insisted. "And if he is, we shall revive him. Help me!"

She pulled off her cap, tawny curls spilling free, and he realized that she meant to use it to carry the chick. "Bloody hell, I will do it then. Give me your hat." He pointed back to the path. "Have a care on these rocks. I'll bring the bird."

"Perhaps you are not a villain after all." In that moment, her exquisite face seemed lit from within.

Holding the cap in one hand, Benedict gently scooped up the bird, who clung to life by a thread, and nestled it inside the warm cocoon. "Let's be away."

* * *

CAMILLE STOOD NEAR THE HEARTH, impatient for the newly lit fire to spread heat through Gull Cottage. Every moment that passed seemed to increase the odds that the kittiwake hatchling would breathe his last.

She watched as Benedict pulled a straight-back chair closer to the hearth and began emptying a drawer for the tiny chick's bed.

"Do hurry," she murmured.

He sent Camille an ironic glance. "As you wish, my lady."

When the drawer was lined with a worn piece of flannel, Benedict gently lifted the wool cap containing the dying bird and set it inside the drawer. She could almost feel the tenderness of his long, agile fingers, and this act inspired more trust than anything he could say.

Crossing to his side, she gazed down at the mere scrap of a chick. "Thank you," she whispered. Something compelled her to put a hand on his forearm.

Benedict turned to look down at her. "I fear that nothing will come of this but more sorrow for you."

"But you will do everything you can, won't you? I mean, you promised…"

She could see an array of thoughts flickering in his green eyes before they softened. "I cannot promise to bring it back to life."

Camille bent to gaze at the nestling, aching for the tragedy that had led to this moment. "Don't call him *it*. He has feelings…perhaps even dreams." Swallowing tears, she said, "I am going to name him Lazarus."

She heard Benedict draw a deep breath before he walked away, into one of the other rooms, and her heart sank. However, when he returned, he was holding a brick.

"Fletcher warms his feet with this on chilly nights."

He put the brick on the edge of the fire, turning it, and waited, staring into the flames. After a bit, he took it out with iron tongs and covered it in a thick cloth. The drawer was large enough to allow Benedict to put the warm, wrapped brick in one corner.

Watching him, Camille said softly, "Thank you. And now, let us give Lazarus a bit of water. I have experience with that. I will just put a few drops on the edge of his little beak."

When this was accomplished, they stood together, staring down at the hatchling. She could see his tiny breast moving ever so slightly, and once, an eyelid seemed to flicker. "Later he must have food. Grubs, perhaps, or some fish ground into a paste."

"I know that. I will see to it." Another minute passed before Benedict inquired in faintly ironic tones, "Do you intend to keep vigil indefinitely?"

"I confess, it is tempting to do so…" The prospect of leaving the hatchling in his care required a great leap of faith, but what choice did she have? If she tried to move Lazarus now, even to her Aunt Julia at nearby Trevarre Hall, it could spell his death. And, perhaps more to the point, she must go home before her father sent a search party out over the cliffs.

However, before Camille could say any of this, she glimpsed a gray shadow out of the corner of her eye. "Oh, Benedict—we have forgotten the *cat!*"

They both turned to stare at Ember, who sat very still near the kitchen doorway, avoiding eye contact. With careful nonchalance, the feline lifted one white-stockinged paw and licked it.

Benedict drew an annoyed breath. "I haven't gone through all of this only to have the deuced cat gobble up the bird the instant we turn our backs." Without another word, he carefully lifted the drawer and started across the room.

Camille followed only to find herself in what appeared to be a man's simple bedchamber. There was a tall-post bed with linen hangings that would doubtless help to keep the occupant warm when storms blew up from the English Channel. The bed curtains were parted, revealing tousled covers reminiscent of Benedict's own often disordered appearance. A pair of riding boots stood near a mahogany wardrobe.

Benedict carefully set the drawer on a chest and spoke over one wide shoulder. "Close the door."

Her cheeks felt hot. "Oh! Really, I don't know…"

"For God's sake, minx, I only mean to shut out the cat, not keep you prisoner." One brow flicked upward. "Unless, of course, you insist."

Although Camille might generally disparage the restrictions of propriety, being alone in a bedchamber with Benedict Hawke felt dangerous. She was all too aware of the nearby bed where he habitually stripped off his clothing and slept, doubtless quite naked. She swallowed, envisioning him sprawled there, his long, muscular legs tangled in sheets that held his intoxicating scent.

"Are you well?"

Camille heard the knowing tone of his voice. How dare he? She squared her slim shoulders. "Quite well, thank you! However, as you are aware, I should not be here."

He cocked his dark head, amused. "When time allows, I hope you will enlighten me regarding your standards of decorum. Up to this point, you have emphatically dismissed such notions. Why should this moment be any different?"

Her eyes were drawn inexorably back to the bed, and she swallowed.

"Ah. Were you expecting me to take you to bed? Ravish you, perhaps?" As he spoke, he moved a window curtain to let in the morning light. Gradually, a sunbeam spread its glow over the drawer and its tiny occupant. "Fear not. We have more pressing matters to resolve. I thought, now that our patient is settled, you and I might join forces to discover the true villains behind tonight's raid on the kittiwakes."

With that, Benedict went past her and opened the door. When he discovered Ember sitting immediately outside, he stared at the predator and shook his head. "Don't you dare." Then, to Camille, he said, "To protect your honor, I suggest we converse a safe distance from my bed."

* * *

GOOD GOD, had he ever beheld a more artlessly beautiful female? True, Camille could have been the model for Botticelli's Birth of Venus, but even more enchanting was her inner glow, the irrepressible sparkle in her blue eyes, and her refusal to back down from any challenge. As Benedict led her toward his desk, he realized that it was probably a good thing he'd been tied to the chair last night, when Camille was kissing him. If she'd released him, there might have been no turning back for either of them.

That thought was followed by an abrupt surge of arousal, and he forced himself to focus on the present moment.

"Will you sit down?" he inquired, gesturing toward the pair of chairs near his desk.

"I…would rather stand for the moment, thank you."

"Tea?"

"Not at this moment." Camille had moved to one side of his desk and was gazing out the window toward the cliffside path and the shimmer of water in the distance. When she turned her face toward him, her cheeks pinkened. "I must apologize, sir. I misjudged you. This morning, you have proven that you are not a scoundrel or a villain. I am sincerely grateful to you for saving Lazarus."

"I appreciate that." He sent her a wry smile. "Of course, I tried to tell you…"

"But look at *this!*" Her eyes flashed unexpectedly, and she gestured toward the array of stuffed birds lined on his desk. "You will pardon me for not detecting a great difference between these poor murdered birds, ripped from their families, and the kittiwakes you now champion."

Benedict felt a sharp pang of something like guilt, but quickly recovered. "My girl, I will remind you again that I am an ornithologist. As a scientist, I cannot study and understand birds without specimens like these."

"I disagree. There must be another way!" Camille rounded the desk and pointed a finger at his chest. "And do not call me *my girl*. It is demeaning."

In the morning sunlight, golden strands glinted among her long curls. Benedict knew an urge to take her in his arms and kiss her, to lose himself in her. Instead, he took a step backward and muttered, "I shall try to remember that."

"Thank you."

"And now, let us discuss the matters at hand." He strode to a safer place across the room. "You managed to halt last night's raid, but the feather thieves will not stop until their leader tells them to do so. I suggest that we work together to uncover his identity."

Her slim body straightened like an arrow. "Please, do go on. How shall we accomplish this?"

"I think the best way for us to discover the villain is to pretend to be a couple. Such an arrangement would allow us to regularly spend time together without straining the bounds of propriety."

"Oh!" She tilted her head, considering. Her dimples winked at him. "A masquerade?"

"Just so, but of course we would only be *pretending*." He succumbed to an urge to pace.

"Anything else would be out of the question," she agreed quickly. "Those kisses we exchanged a few hours ago were a mistake and should never have happened."

Feeling a twinge of annoyance, he replied, "I would make amends for that episode, but when we kissed, I was tied to a chair...so perhaps you had a part in it as well?"

She bit her lip, saying nothing, but the color that washed her cheeks was all the answer he needed.

"In any event," he went on, "it must not happen again. You are gently born, with a good family; not the sort of female one trifles with. I want your parents to trust me." For good measure, Benedict added, "And the nature of our endeavor must be clear between us. I am not the marrying sort."

His pacing brought him close enough to see her eyes flash. "Neither am I, sir!" she declared. "If you imagine that I am dreaming of marrying you or any other man, you are utterly mistaken. I have planned an entirely different sort of life."

"I see." He bit back a smile. "I did not mean to offend you, but given recent events, it seemed important that we resolve this issue." He wanted to ask her why she was so set on avoiding romance and marriage. Was it possible that such a beauty had never been courted?

Camille spoke first. "If we are going to spend time together, plotting to trap the leader of the feather thieves, we must enlighten my father and mother."

"I would rather not. If we begin telling people, the secret will get out."

"We can trust my parents," she pressed. "In any

event, we really have no choice. They know me far too well to believe I could have romantic feelings toward you."

He bristled at her words. Why would it be so difficult to believe Camille might fall in love with him? "If you insist," he said shortly. "But we will have to assure them that this plan of ours is worthwhile, and you won't be in danger. To avoid complications, I suggest we keep the details to a minimum. Agreed?"

"Yes, that sounds wise. Otherwise, they may be alarmed for my wellbeing."

"I will endeavor to put them at ease." He paused, wondering if all of this was a huge mistake. "Tomorrow I will visit your home to meet your family."

The moment he said the word *home*, she looked out at the sky as if suddenly realizing that the morning was advancing. "Dash it, I must go! If they should discover that I am not in my bed—"

No sooner were the words out of her mouth than a loud knock sounded at the cottage door. Camille put a hand to her breast as Benedict went to discover the identity of his caller.

He paused with his hand on the latch. "You look terrified. Do you wish to hide—in the larder, perhaps?"

"Hide?" She lifted her delicately-clefted chin. "Never."

Benedict threw open the heavy door to behold Rafael, the Brazilian youth who had helped to abduct him just hours ago. Behind the desperate-looking servant stood a taller, much older man with a silk eyepatch, unruly silver hair, and a compelling air of self-possession.

Before Benedict could speak, Rafael caught sight of Camille and rushed in, uninvited.

"My lady! Praise God, you are alive. What has this villain done to you?"

She gave a nervous laugh and crossed to the doorway. "Done to me? Why, nothing at all. I assure you, all is well." She then went into the arms of the tall stranger and, to Benedict's surprise, lay her head on his chest. "Oh, Uncle Justin, how happy I am that you have come!"

CHAPTER 14

"*D*o not be too happy to see me, *mon ange*," said Uncle Justin, holding her away from him and scanning her male attire. "Your friend Rafael was rushing about the cliffs in a panic, looking for you, and he encountered me during my morning ride. He said something about a raid on the kittiwake nests. I agreed to help in his search, but I confess I am not pleased to find you here alone, with this foreigner..."

"Foreigner?" Benedict's dark brows flew up. "I am an Englishman."

"And I am French," Justin parried, clearly enjoying himself. "You see?"

"Kindly be serious," Camille scolded before turning to Rafael. She wanted to ask him if her parents knew she had left Elysium in the middle of the night, but Uncle Justin's presence gave her pause. She certainly didn't want him to know anything about their abduction of Benedict Hawke. "I appreciate your concern, Rafael, but as you can see, I am just fine. Mr. Hawke very kindly helped me to thwart the feather thieves."

"Very kind indeed." Clearly dubious, Justin flared

one nostril and inquired, "And why exactly are you here alone in his cottage?"

Noticing that her uncle had crossed both arms over his broad chest, Camille stood on tiptoe and touched his forearm. "Oh, my dear uncle, when you hear the story, I wager you'll beg Mr. Hawke's pardon for doubting his motives."

"You are a minx."

Behind them, Benedict gave a low snort of agreement.

"Perhaps so," Camille agreed. "Yet my daring nature helped to stave off the raid and rescue an injured hatchling." She tugged at the midnight-blue sleeve of his coat. "That is why you find me here with Mr. Hawke. He was kind enough to assist me."

Benedict cleared his throat but, to her relief, did not dispute her version of events. Indeed, he went one step further and explained about Lazarus, even bringing the drawer out into the main room of the cottage so that they might see him for themselves.

"I had to put the chick safely away from the cat," Benedict explained to her uncle and Rafael.

Camille peered anxiously into the drawer, as if she had not viewed the bird since his transfer to Benedict's bedchamber. It was one thing to hope Uncle Justin might overlook her presence in this cottage, but if he knew she had been alone with Benedict in his bedchamber, she shuddered to imagine his reaction.

Rafael shook his head. "It does not look fit to survive the night. Where I come from, we'd have put the little mite out of its misery."

"You've said the wrong thing, I fear," Benedict warned, sending Camille a wry glance.

"Indeed!" She was heartened to see that Lazarus's pale gray down was fluffing up as it dried. "He is going to recover very well. I would look after him myself, but he cannot be moved. Fortunately, Mr. Hawke has kindly agreed to nurse Lazarus back to health."

Uncle Justin and Rafael both swiveled to look at Benedict, who lightly shrugged his wide shoulders. "I will be working here on a project, so it's no trouble, really."

"Working here?" Justin glanced around the room, his keen gaze settling on the long table lined with stuffed birds.

"I am an ornithologist," he explained, "in Cornwall to write a book about the coastal birds."

"We'll let you get back to it, then," said Justin. "No doubt Camille is anxious to return home before her parents raise a hue and cry."

"Yes, I must go." She looked down at the tiny hatchling, deeply wishing that she might bundle him back into her cap and take him home with her. Could she truly trust this man to look after him properly? Benedict's words on the cliffs, spoken immediately after they discovered Lazarus, came back to her: *There's nothing to be done! It's part of nature.* Yet, it seemed she had no choice. Turning, she fixed him with a penetrating stare. "Mr. Hawke, I expect you to care for Lazarus as lovingly as I would."

"Lovingly?" Rafael made a skeptical noise.

She ignored the boy and wagged a finger at Benedict. "Give me your word that you will not betray my trust, sir."

"Have I not already said so?" came his cool reply. "You may go on your way, Miss St. Briac. Rest assured I shall keep you apprised of your patient's progress."

Their eyes met, and Camille saw golden sparks smoldering in their depths. "I suppose I have no choice but to relinquish my control."

As her uncle led her toward the door, he remarked dryly, "A milestone indeed."

* * *

PLEADING FATIGUE, Camille went to bed early that night and slept deeply, until the sun was high in the morning sky. No sooner had she opened her eyes and thrown off the assortment of feather-soft covers than memories intruded of Benedict...tied to the chair, kissing her, and later saving her from ravishment at the hands of the barbaric feather thieves. Potent feelings coursed through her body as images, words, feelings illuminated her memory. Breathing faster, Camille pushed up to sit on the edge of the bed. She thought about Lazarus, and her heart caught. She prayed that this morning found him not only still alive but improving.

The entire adventure felt like a dream now, but of course it was the most intensely real experience of her life, and there was more to come.

Camille climbed out of bed and rang for Lillian. Benedict had promised that he would visit her today to initiate their pretend courtship, and she had no idea what to wear.

* * *

ISABELLA STOOD in the glass conservatory attached to Elysium, where she could look between the inside of her home and the kitchen gardens outdoors.

Gabriel's handsome face appeared around the doorway. "Is there no sign yet of our daughter?"

"No, not yet. And I cannot think of painting until I see Camille and discover what she has been doing with her time these past two days." She didn't want to reveal that she thought she had heard footsteps on the stairs late last night.

He came past a row of potted lemon trees, drew off his doeskin gloves, and touched her cheek. "Even if we don't like it, I doubt that there is much to be done. As Camille is quick to remind us, she is no longer a child."

"My, how enlightened you have become," Izzie teased.

Just then, Camille herself strolled into the conservatory, looking effortlessly exquisite in a morning gown of lilac shot silk. Her toffee-hued locks were pinned up, charming tendrils framing her face. "Ah, here you two are. Good morning!"

"Is it still morning?"

Her daughter laughed. "I hope so. I am dreaming of one of Madame Kerjean's delectable galettes for my breakfast. I am famished."

Gabriel gave Izzie a slight, quelling pinch on her bottom, and she swallowed all her questions. "Madame adores you. No doubt she will be delighted to cook for you at any hour."

"I know," beamed Camille. "I've already asked her."

The three of them started back inside. As they passed through the morning room, Gabriel paused at his desk to pick up the letters that had arrived in that day's post. The one on top bore the distinctive, bold scrawl of his brother, Justin.

Immediately curious, Izzie urged, "Darling, do open it."

He broke the seal. Inside, there was a sheet of heavy cream parchment with a hand-written message. After reading it, Gabriel looked up.

"It seems Justin and Mouette have decided to relocate their anniversary party from London to Frenchman's Haven, the place where they fell in love."

"But what about Emeline's first London Season?" Izzie asked in surprise.

Gabriel cocked an eyebrow. "Justin writes that he was going mad. He couldn't bear another coronation event and needed to escape from London. Of course, Emeline is very busy with the routs and balls, but it seems her grandmother, Devon, is perfectly happy to look after her for a short time."

"How very difficult Justin can be!" Izzie declared.

"Did you imagine my brother would change?" he replied dryly. "In any event, the anniversary festivities will be held Saturday next, and we are all invited to attend."

Camille spoke up immediately. "That's very nice, but I am not certain I will be available that day."

"Oh, no." Izzie's heart sank. She couldn't stop the words from spilling out. "Darling, I understand that you are free to choose your own path, but we worry that you are living like a nun. Wouldn't this party offer a perfect way for you to mingle in society again?"

Camille looked uncomfortable. "It's just that…I may have other plans."

It seemed the perfect moment for Izzie to express the concerns that kept her awake at night. "Sweet Cam, we are your parents, and we only want you to be happy." She took a breath. "I don't know what happened between you and Lord Upton when he was here in Cornwall last year, but after he left, you began to dim your inner light when in the company of eligible men."

"Mama, please—" Camille's blush was a signal that Izzie had indeed hit on the truth.

"When Justin persuaded you to come to London this spring, I felt hopeful! Really, we all know you could have been the toast of the Season had you wanted it." She couldn't help reaching for Camille's hand. "But you would not have it. Soon enough you were back home, walking alone on the cliff path again for hours at a time."

"Mama, really, I am grateful for your love and concern, but you must know that I am perfectly able to manage my life. In fact..." A tentative smile touched her mouth. "As it happens, I have been getting to know a young man."

"A young man?" Just as Izzie tried to absorb this astonishing news, a knock sounded at the heavy front door. "For heaven's sake, who could that be?"

Gabriel shrugged. "I cannot imagine. I was not expecting anyone." With that, he strolled into the stair hall and opened the front door.

From a distance, Isabella heard a man speaking in deep, smooth accents. "Good day, sir. Allow me to introduce myself. My name is Benedict Hawke. I live in Polruan...in Gull Cottage."

Glancing over at her daughter, Izzie saw that Camille was flushed. She blinked. What in the world could it mean?

* * *

CAMILLE'S HEART raced as she listened to her father conversing with Benedict. Their footsteps were approaching the drawing room. If only she could check her reflection in a looking glass. Had this gown been the right choice?

In the next moment, Benedict appeared in the doorway. Camille's palms went damp. Gone was the disheveled scientist who combed his hair with his fingers and couldn't be bothered to tie a proper cravat. The man who crossed the threshold was impeccably clad in a fitted dark gray tailcoat and buff trousers that skimmed the long muscles of his legs. Freshly barbered, he—or perhaps Fletcher—had clearly made an attempt to tame his curling black locks. Even though Benedict looked arrestingly handsome, a part of her missed his usual disheveled appearance and even his spectacles.

"Good day, Madame St. Briac," he said to her mother. Flashing a smile, he gave a small bow and crossed to Isabella. "Allow me to make myself known to you. I am Benedict Hawke." When he lifted her hand, Camille saw that he was wearing a very fashionable pair of pale-yellow kid gloves. "I've been looking forward to this day. Your lovely daughter has told me a great deal about her parents."

Camille hoped she didn't look as startled as she felt. When they had discussed his planned visit, there had been no mention of Benedict adopting a new, polished persona. Meanwhile, her mother looked surprised, uncertain, and a trifle dazzled. Glancing Camille's way, Isabella allowed him to brush his lips to her bare hand.

"I confess, we have only just learned of your existence, Mr. Hawke." She gave him one of her warmest smiles. "Please, come and sit down. Will you join us for tea?"

Camille knew a pang of sympathy for her mother, who clearly was trying to make sense of the entire situation. As Isabella called for a pot of tea and some light refreshments, they sat down together on two sofas, Camille and Benedict facing her parents. After Claire and another maid had served them, Gabriel fixed the newcomer with a penetrating stare.

"We have not heard how you two became acquainted. Won't you enlighten us?"

Camille found it rather amusing that her usually relaxed and progressive father was behaving as if she had only recently been freed from the schoolroom. Still, she turned to Benedict, her tone tinged with mischief. "You must begin, sir. I feel certain your telling of this story will be far superior to mine."

She saw his eyes flash momentarily before he turned back to her parents and sent them another disarming smile. "In truth, it was your daughter's love of birds that caused our paths to cross."

"Ah," said Gabriel. "My wife and I are not surprised to hear this."

"Miss St. Briac discovered an injured kittiwake hatchling on the cliff path near my cottage, and I assisted her in rescuing it." He turned back to meet Camille's eyes. "No doubt you are longing for an update on your tiny patient. Fear not, Lazarus is improving. This morning, he even deigned to eat a grub that I mashed and fed him with tweezers."

The masquerade forgotten, Camille wanted to throw her arms around his neck, but instead she restrained herself. Beaming, she said, "Of course, you could not have brought me more thrilling news! Thank you, sir."

"Perhaps you should call me Benedict."

To her consternation, Camille felt her cheeks growing very warm. "I continue to be so very grateful to you for tending to my injured hatchling." To her parents, she said, "Mr. Hawke...that is, *Benedict*, is an ornithologist. He has come to Cornwall to write a book about our coastal birds."

Her father remarked, "I seem to recall that you once aspired to become an ornithologist, *ma petite*."

"That was long ago, when I was very young," Camille said, perhaps a bit too hotly. "Upon discovering that ornithology involves not only the killing of birds to use as specimens, but also taxidermy, I changed my mind! I *deplore* those barbaric practices, and I shall persuade Benedict to abandon them."

Across from them, her parents exchanged glances before Izzie ventured, "I gather that, in recent days, when you were off on such long walks, you were actually with Mr. Hawke?"

Benedict spoke first. "True, there have been times when Miss St. Briac was with me, but my manservant, Fletcher, was also present."

Fletcher! She had forgotten about him. "That's right! And often, Rafael was nearby."

"I see," her father said, tapping long fingers against one thigh.

"Allow me to explain the real reason for my visit today." Benedict leaned forward. "Circumstances demand that your daughter and I spend more time together in the future."

Papa's blue eyes widened. "Are you asking our permission to court Camille?"

"Not exactly." He gave a husky cough. "It's a bit more complicated. It has to do with the feather thieves."

Camille came to his rescue. "That's right. I have told you both about the terrible men who are murdering kittiwakes, then using their wings to decorate women's hats. Unspeakably cruel acts, performed for an utterly inane purpose!"

"Yes, we remember," Papa said warily.

"Because Benedict lives so near the cliffside nests, he has encountered various members of the gang," she continued. "We have concluded that these murderers are being directed by another person, and the only way to stop this savagery is to unmask that villain. Mr. Hawke has agreed to help me accomplish this goal."

Her parents were nodding slowly. "Knowing you, Camille, this is quite believable."

"I knew you would understand!" She sent Benedict a triumphant smile. "Of course, we have a *plan*. We will pretend to be courting so that we can work together and share information, and finally uncover the master-mind behind this terrible plot."

Papa's brows flicked up. "Pretend?"

Benedict spoke up then, briefly outlining their masquerade. "I know it might sound mad, but your daughter will not rest until she has stopped the feather thieves."

"*Feather thieves* sounds so harmless," Camille interjected hotly. "They are savage *killers*!"

"Let me see if I have this right," her father said, setting down his teacup. "You two will pretend to be courting...but in truth, there are no romantic feelings between you?"

For a long moment, Camille and Benedict looked at one another, and she saw the smoldering embers in his eyes. Images filled her mind of last night at Lupine Cottage, kissing Benedict, longing to untie him, to feel his arms around her, to let him have his way with her.

"Exactly, sir," Benedict replied at last, manfully meeting her father's narrowed gaze.

"Really, Papa, I am surprised you could ask such a question," she chimed in. "I think you and Mama know me better than that."

"You are a very lovely young woman," Papa said. "And, for God's sake, you are both human. Am I to simply agree to whatever schemes you concoct?"

"I would ask that you trust me to keep your daughter safe," Benedict said.

"Oh, isn't that just like a man?" Camille protested, unable to stop herself from cuffing his arm. "You may beg for Papa's permission until the cows come home, but I am a woman of four-and-twenty, and I speak for myself."

Her mother laughed softly. "I believe that settles it, does it not, Gabriel?" Reaching for another biscuit, she added, "As it happens, we have just received an invitation to an anniversary celebration for Camille's Uncle Justin and Aunt Mouette, to be held at their home, Frenchman's Haven. It would be delightful if you could join us, Mr. Hawke. You can present yourselves to our neighbors and friends as a couple."

"Nothing would give me greater pleasure," came Benedict's smooth reply. Turning to Camille, he cocked his head slightly and flashed a roguish grin. "What do you say, minx?"

An unexpected wave of effervescent joy came over her. "I say *yes!*"

CHAPTER 15

After the tea service was cleared away, Benedict was invited to join Camille's father for a tour of his hothouses and kitchen gardens. Benedict wasn't particularly keen to be alone with the astute Gabriel St. Briac, but there didn't seem to be any way around it.

"As you might guess," Gabriel remarked as he led the way through a sprawling conservatory attached to the house, "sections of the gardens are devoted to birds. Since Camille was in leading strings, she has had a special affinity for birds, entranced by their almost magical ability to fly. Yet her heart aches when any bird is hurt, earthbound, and vulnerable to predators. To her mind, our walled gardens have represented a safe refuge for every injured bird Camille has ever encountered." He paused to grin. "And it continues."

Benedict was wary. There was something in the older man's observant manner that made every remark or question seem like a trap. "I can certainly imagine Camille nursing all manner of birds back to health," he said.

"No doubt she has told you stories?"

"A few, of course."

They came out of the conservatory, into the walled

gardens, the mild air fragrant with lavender, herbs, and roses. Everywhere Benedict turned, there was a sense of orderly enchantment. The neat paths were covered with crushed limestone and lined with riotous beds of poppies and foxgloves interspersed with cold frames, their glass sashes open to the warmth of summer. From the far wall, a low, arched door beckoned, and Benedict wondered what lay on the other side.

"I suppose you must feel quite at home in gardens like these," Gabriel remarked, glancing his way.

Benedict's stomach clenched, as if sensing what was to come. "I am not certain what you mean, sir."

"Isn't your father Josiah Hawke, formerly the head gardener at Tremethyck Park?"

The mention of Pa made Benedict wish he had stayed at Gull Cottage. What the devil had he been thinking? Feeling hot blood rise up his neck, into his face, he managed only to reply, "Yes."

"We visited there years ago, to see Margaret, Dowager Countess of Far after the death of her husband, the Earl." As he spoke, St. Briac paused to study a rosebush. Looking around for one of the gardeners, he pointed to the plant, and the young fellow rushed to fetch a watering can. Satisfied, St. Briac turned back to Benedict. "Lady Far had shown great kindness to my wife when she was very young, after her parents were killed in a carriage accident."

Benedict's eyes stung at the mention of dear Lady Far, his benefactress. During his adolescence, she had moved into the dower house and taken long, daily walks around the estate, silently taking in every interaction she witnessed between Benedict and Pa.

Josiah Hawke had begun his early career at a very low position on the gardening staff at Windsor Castle. Over a dozen years, despite Pa's numerous human faults, he gained a reputation as a gifted and creative gardener. When he was offered the position of head gardener at Tremethyck Park, Pa lorded it over not only his staff, but his family as well. The taller Benedict grew, the more severe Pa's treatment of him became. It was his father who taught him all about nature from an early age, even the art of taxidermy, but as Benedict's interests broadened and deepened, Pa mocked him at every turn.

Lady Far perceived Josiah Hawke's harshness toward his son as well as Benedict's potential to become a serious naturalist. The epitome of dignity and kindness, she had intervened, insisting that Benedict must go away to study at Eton and eventually have a place at Oxford.

"I am not surprised that Lady Far was good to Madame St. Briac when she lost her parents," Benedict said at last. "Her ladyship is one of the finest people I have ever known. In many ways, I owe my life to her. She saw to it that I went away to university, to properly study biology and ornithology." Left unsaid were the words *and get as far away from my father as possible.*

Pa's feathers had been badly ruffled, but once Benedict was far away, Lady Far did her best to smooth things over. When the time came that Josiah could no longer do the physical labor of gardening and Ma was also growing weaker, her ladyship made it possible for Benedict's parents to spend their remaining years at Gull Cottage. It afforded miles of cliff paths and stunning sea views, and the cottage was also located near the Polruan home of their recently wed daughter.

"I made it a point to meet your father during our visit to Tremethyck Park," St. Briac said casually. "I heard that he had made amazing advances with espaliered fruit trees, virtually covering the garden walls at Tremethyck. I wanted to see them for myself, to learn from him, and of course he was quite proud of his accomplishments."

"I've no doubt of that," Benedict said dryly.

St. Briac paused, pointing to the apple and peach trees espaliered flat against his own brick walls. "I have thought of that visit whenever I train and prune my trees. Perhaps two years ago, I heard that Mr. Hawke was living at Gull Cottage. I stopped by one day and knocked on the door. I heard movements inside, but no one came to open it." He lifted a brow. "Your father may be gifted, but he never struck me as a particularly friendly man."

"Indeed. That is quite an understatement." As briefly as possible, Benedict explained about his mother's death, and then the more recent stroke his father had suffered that brought Benedict to Cornwall. "When word came from my sister, Prudence, I had just been chosen to join John Gould's expedition to Australia," he concluded grimly. "It would have been not only the adventure of a lifetime, but also a crowning achievement for me as an ornithologist. There isn't a morning I awake that I don't feel that bitter disappointment again."

He had been staring into the distance as he spoke, lost in thought, until St. Briac said, "Given your passion for your work, I must be grateful that you and my daughter are not truly courting. She could never accept being relegated to second place."

Before Benedict could reply, he saw Camille and her mother emerging from the glass conservatory, trailed by a handsome, lively young boy and a curly-coated black retriever. Camille looked breathtaking, effortlessly graceful in her gown of lilac silk. It took a moment for Benedict to reconcile this exquisite beauty with the trouser-clad hoyden he was used to. But then she headed for an area with a birdbath and trays of birdseed. Benedict watched as she lifted a burlap sack and scooped fresh seed into the shallow trays, smoothing it out evenly.

"Cam has always been like this," her father murmured with a trace of irony. "At times, we wondered if she was switched in her cradle for a wood sprite."

The birds were chirping all around Camille, unafraid, and she conversed with them. "I know what you mean," Benedict said. "I've never met another female like her."

"I highly doubt there are any others." As if sensing that Benedict was about to go to her, St. Briac turned and gave him a hard look. "My daughter is very special. Most people see only her remarkable beauty, but what truly sets her apart are her spirit, intelligence, and courage to be herself." He cocked his head slightly, his gaze still fixed on Benedict. "Quite frankly, her mother and I had begun to doubt that any man could win her heart."

Benedict blinked, wondering how to reply to such serious talk. Should he remind the man that he and Camille were only pretending to be a couple?

"What I mean to say is, even though you say this is all an act between you, my daughter has little experience with courtship," St. Briac said in a low voice. "I would not lock her in a tower and deprive her of romance, even love. Camille is a woman grown and can make those choices for herself." His gaze hardened slightly. "But if you cause her pain, I won't be responsible for my actions."

Benedict opened his mouth to protest but thought better of it. "I understand, sir."

"Good." Before St. Briac could say more, they were interrupted by the dog and its young master. He introduced his son, then watched as Damien raced off with Zeus, flinging open the low door in the wall. "I'd better go after them. I've been constructing a tree house in a wilder part of the estate, but it's not finished yet. There's no telling what risks Damien might take, unsupervised."

As the happy trio passed through the portal in the brick wall and the door swung closed behind them, Benedict felt a bittersweet pain. Young Damien was enjoying the sort of childhood he might have had while growing up on the grounds of Tremethyck Park...if Josiah Hawke had been capable of love.

* * *

"YOU PROBABLY DON'T NEED to feed the birds during the summer," Benedict remarked when he joined Camille. She had closed her sack of seed and was standing near the conservatory's glass wall, watching as a variety of finches, warblers, robins, tits, and sparrows continued to gather. "There is plenty of food for them in nature."

"I know I probably shouldn't do it. Am I spoiling them?" She used both hands to make a charming gesture of surrender. "In the winter, I make special seed cakes for them. The blue titmice and woodpeckers especially enjoy those. Would you like my recipe?"

Remembering the little stuffed corpses lined up on the table at Gull Cottage, Benedict felt a pang. Something prompted him to murmur, "Perhaps you'll teach me how to make them."

Camille tipped her face up and gave him an irresistible smile. "I might."

Bewitched, he looked around to see if they were alone. Past the corner of the conservatory, Isabella had set up an easel and was arranging her painting supplies. "Your mother is an artist?"

"Oh, yes, didn't I tell you? Mama is very talented! The cottage where I held you prisoner was once her painting studio, but Papa built her a new one on the grounds of Elysium after they married." In a clear voice, she continued, "I must inspect my nesting boxes, in case some of the eggs have hatched. Come with me."

Benedict followed her deeper into the garden, noting the glint of sunlight on the tawny curls pinned high on her head. Camille's exposed neck was so inviting, he imagined taking her in his arms, pressing her against the garden wall, and kissing first her delectable mouth, then the graceful line of her neck, breathing in her fragrance. Suddenly he was hard, aching with need for her. It felt new, as if he hadn't been with all those other women, most of whom were hazy memories.

Just then, Camille looked back with a conspiratorial smile. "The nesting boxes were only an excuse to get away from the house, in case Mama or one of the servants might overhear." She stretched out both hands to him. "Come, tell me what happened when you met with Jem this morning!"

"Jem?" At that moment, he could scarcely remember their brief meeting that morning. "Ah. There isn't much news, not yet. I told him I'd learned that the revenue men were on the lookout for smugglers who have been using the beach below Gull Cottage, and there are more surprise raids planned. I suggested that it would be wise to leave the kittiwakes alone for now, until the authorities move on to another location."

Her eyes were wide. "What did he say?"

"Jem agreed." Benedict lifted one brow. "He said his own uncle had been taken into custody by customs officers some years ago and was later hanged. Apparently, the poor man lived for long minutes, an ordeal Jem has never forgotten. He lives in fear of similar treatment."

"I'm sorry for his uncle, but glad for us," she said, eyes alight.

"I asked again to speak to his leader, but Jem said he

had already sent a message regarding last night's failed raid. That leads me to believe even more firmly that the true mastermind lives some distance away."

"Or he could be as near as Fowey," Camille murmured.

"I suppose," he conceded. "Perhaps, if we keep our wits about us at your uncle's party, we'll hear or see something helpful that leads us to him."

"Yes! You might guess that I usually don't care for parties, but I'll own that I'm very excited about this one. I know that we are attending mainly to make our 'courtship' known, but there is always a chance that we shall make a great discovery!"

Her blue eyes shone with determination. In the service of defenseless birds, Camille could be not only brave but reckless, and Benedict was glad that he now had an excuse to stay close to her. "What about our masquerade?" He traced her jawline with one fingertip. "Will it be difficult for you to pretend we are…"

"In love?" Her eyes danced. "I think I can do that."

He gave a low laugh. "Are you flirting with me, minx?"

"Oh! I might be." Camille swayed a bit. "I confess I have very little practice."

Perhaps that was what made her so different from the other women he'd known. Benedict was used to repartee spiced with knowing glances that told him a female was experienced in the ways of seduction. Now, just looking into Camille's eyes, alight with both innocence and desire, he felt another primal jolt. Good God, he wasn't even certain if real love existed, but perhaps lust alone could make him a believable suitor.

He leaned toward Camille, and she parted her lips, as if it had suddenly become difficult to breathe. "Shall we seal our bargain with a kiss?"

"Well, perhaps," she whispered, a blush creeping over her cheeks. "Just one. For luck."

You are making a big mistake, Benedict told himself, but of course he didn't listen. After all, he had been aching for this since last night, when she'd subjected him to sheer torture: tying him up and then sitting on his lap and kissing him until he thought he'd bloody die, done in by his own unsatisfied need.

"Right," he murmured now, his voice husky. "Just one." Curving one hand around Camille's waist, he slid it to the small of her back and drew her closer. Her body was warm and responsive even through the silk fabric of her gown, and he was instantly hot and hard again, burning to press himself between her legs. She melted against him, eyes closed, long lashes fanned above her cheekbones.

"Careful," he warned. "I am no longer your captive."

"That's true," came her whisper, "but we *are* in my family's garden. Hardly private."

Her breasts seemed to brand him through the layers of their clothing. He wanted her too much. Deftly, he cupped her delicate jaw in his free hand, angling it slightly for better access to her sensual mouth. *One kiss.* He touched his own harder mouth to hers, gently. Then with infinite restraint, he kissed her slowly, slowly, his tongue grazing the seam of her lips. Camille made a small sound of surprise, then opened to him. In the sizzling moments that followed, Benedict sensed the gathering wetness between her legs, the need she felt but might not fully understand.

"Hello?" came a man's voice. Gabriel St. Briac! "Cam?"

Benedict stepped back as Camille turned to look down the pathway, telltale color staining her cheeks. Zeus bounded into sight and a moment later, her father appeared in the dog's wake.

"Here I am, Papa," she said.

He seemed to glance between them, but his expression was friendly. "No doubt you two were discussing your plans to save the kittiwakes," he remarked. "Sorry to interrupt, but I knew Cam would want to know about the nest of unidentified eggs Damien and I discovered in the woods."

"Oh, yes," she exclaimed. "Do show me. I hope nothing has happened to the parents!"

"Speaking of orphaned chicks," Benedict said, drawing on his kid gloves. "I should get back. Lazarus will no doubt be demanding his luncheon."

"Indeed," Camille said. "It would have doubtless been better for you to stay nearby and offer drops of water every quarter-hour."

"You'll be pleased to know I tasked Fletcher with that," Benedict replied wryly. "But he does have other obligations at midday."

She gave him a nudge. "You must go then!"

As their eyes met, Benedict nearly forgot that her father was watching them. "If you imagine you can dictate to me," he said lightly, one brow arched, "you are in for a surprise."

Laughing, Camille rejoined, "In any event, I shall try!"

CHAPTER 16

"*I* think you like him." Camille's mother said it very casually, as if she were commenting on a new pair of slippers.

Camille was seated at her dressing table while Lillian pinned her curls into a fashionable arrangement above her ears. In the mirror, she saw the maid's eyes widen, but of course Lillian made no comment.

"Him? Who exactly do you mean?" Camille asked, feigning confusion.

"Why, Benedict Hawke, of course. I realize that you two are enacting a mere charade of courtship, but I will tell you plainly that I sensed a real spark when he was here for tea."

With that, Lillian smoothed a last errant curl from Camille's brow, gathered up her hair accoutrements, and excused herself, adding, "I'll return in a bit to help you finish dressing, miss."

"Do you see, Mama, you have frightened Lillian away, and I am still in my chemise and petticoat." Camille pretended to scold when they were alone. "I hope we won't be late for Uncle Justin and Aunt Mouette's garden party."

"As you know, we aren't leaving for more than an

hour. I don't think Papa has even begun to bathe and dress." Isabella took a spray of late bluebells and white sea campion from a vase by the bed, wiped water from the stems, and crossed over to pin them in Camille's curls. "There, now you won't need any sort of head-dress. Feathers are all the rage at the moment, I fear."

Her temper flared. "So very wicked!"

"Darling, I hope you won't say anything to the guests. Remember, your own Grandmère may be one of the worst offenders."

She clenched her teeth and sighed. "No, you are right. I must stay in character. I'd like everyone to think I've fallen in love and gone soft in the head, so I won't be suspected of hunting down the mastermind behind the feather thieves. I will attempt to focus all my attention on Benedict, but I assure you I'll have one ear open, just in case there is something to be learned today."

Standing behind her chair, her mother nodded, but her gaze was far away. "If you are truly determined not to fall in love, Cam, what sort of future do you envision for yourself?"

"What's wrong with the life I already lead?" She knew she sounded defensive, but it couldn't be helped. Rising, she began to pace across the bedchamber. "I love being outdoors in nature, helping the birds and other wildlife. I'd like to travel as well, perhaps to Italy! Mama, you must see that I'm simply not cut out for marriage. There isn't a man alive who would allow me to do as I please, to freely tramp miles in the woods, on the cliffs, over the beaches, unsupervised. No, any re-spectable fellow would have a lot of notions about the proper way for a wife to behave. Overseeing a house-hold...how deadly dull that would be!" She shuddered. "And what about procreating? I cannot imagine being shut up inside for nine months, and then devoting the next two decades to raising not just that baby but others." Warming to this familiar topic, Camille continued, "No one places such restrictions on men, of course. They can do exactly as they please, even after marriage."

"And what if you met a man who was different, who would love you just the way you are?" Her mother raised both brows above her gold-rimmed spectacles.

Camille felt her face warming and looked away. "I've tried that experiment, and it was a failure."

"Are you referring to Lord Upton?" Isabella asked gently. She crossed to Camille's side and put a hand on her arm. "Papa and I were never certain, during his weeks in Cornwall, if you two developed feelings for one another. And then, after he returned to London, intending to wed Lady Barbara Framstead, we put it out of our minds. Darling, have you been suffering from a broken heart?"

Camille tried to banish the memory of Roger looming above her on the chaise at Lupine Cottage, grasping her hand, holding it to his bulging crotch as he rocked back and forth. "Certainly not!" she said briskly, even as bile rose in her throat. "Really, Mama, I think you have not been listening to a word I've said. Even if his lordship was not an aristocrat, and above my touch, I don't want a man in my life."

Just then Lillian reappeared with Camille's gown. "I just needed to press a few wrinkles from the hem," she explained.

The day dress was fashioned of pale honey-hued silk brocaded with tiny silk bluebells. The wide, lace collar was designed to show the tops of Camille's creamy shoulders, and she already wore a delicate gold locket engraved with a bird's feather that rested at the hollow of her throat. As Lillian fastened tiny buttons,

Camille glanced in the cheval mirror. She barely recognized the beauty who gazed back at her.

"I'll leave you to dress," Isabella said from the doorway. "I have a few finishing touches of my own to see to."

Camille raised a warning finger. "Don't forget, Mama. No feathers!"

* * *

IN PREPARATION for the party at Frenchman's Haven, Benedict arranged for Rafael to stay with Lazarus, who was improving and growing with each passing day. It seemed a bit ridiculous to appoint a minder for a kittiwake, but if anything should happen to the chick in Benedict's absence, Camille would be heartbroken.

He rode Max over to meet Camille and her family at Frenchman's Haven, located not far from the coastal village of Lansallos. The approach took him down a hill and into a leafy green tunnel, so characteristic of Cornwall. Max brought his head up in surprise when the narrow lane curved slightly, and a handsome stone manor house suddenly appeared in an open sweep of land.

As Benedict came up the drive, a liveried stableboy approached to take Max's reins. Perhaps two dozen finely garbed guests strolled on the sunlit grounds to the rear of the manor, while servants in midnight-blue livery circulated with trays of hors d'oeuvres and goblets of wine. Benedict dismounted and started toward the other guests.

"Ah, Mr. Hawke," called a deep, French-accented voice. "*Bonjour.*"

Turning, he saw Justin St. Briac striding toward him, strong and solid. In spite of a slight limp, his entire being was alight with a magnetic force. The

Frenchman's immaculate dark suit was set off by a crimson-trimmed white waistcoat, a black silk cravat, and a black eyepatch also edged in crimson. "You found the place without incident?"

"I did, thank you, sir."

"Justin," he insisted, pronouncing his own name in the French way.

Benedict nodded as a footman appeared with a tray. He accepted a goblet of red wine and took a generous sip. "It is kind of you to have me…Justin."

"My niece has been waiting for you," St. Briac said. Looking back toward the house, he raised a hand, and through the figures of other guests, Benedict caught a glimpse of Camille.

His breath caught for an instant as she waved back, face alight, and started toward them. What the devil was happening to him?

"She is ravishing, don't you agree?" Justin murmured. "Camille has been a great beauty since she was a baby, but now she is coming into full flower." He paused and sent Benedict a knowing glance. "Almost."

Benedict straightened and nodded. The man was clearly hoping to draw a reaction from him, but he refused to take the bait. Camille had mentioned that her uncle was once a pirate, which explained a great deal about his personality.

"Full flower indeed," he replied.

Camille reached them and took Justin's arm. "Hello, dear uncle. Are you behaving yourself?"

"Barely, *mon ange*." His smile widened as a beautiful dark-haired older woman appeared on his other side. "Ah, look, here is Mouette, come to remind me that today I am to play the amiable host."

"Look at the two of you!" exclaimed Camille. "How well you wear these two decades of marriage." She turned to Benedict. "I must present my Aunt Mouette to you, Mr. Hawke."

Mouette Raveneau St. Briac extended a graceful, gloved hand and said warmly, "I have been hearing a great deal about you, sir."

"I hope you will address me as Benedict." He bent and lightly kissed her hand. "Do I dare to ask what you've heard?"

"Only that there is a fascinating stranger living at Gull Cottage. Dark and handsome, rather brooding and mysterious!" Her lovely face lit up as she spoke. "And now you have come out among us. Rumor has it you have romantic intentions toward our darling Camille!"

"I thought I was the only one who had intercepted those signals," Justin remarked, arching a brow above his eyepatch.

His wife playfully cuffed his arm. "You were not paying attention when Izzie visited yesterday and told us Benedict would join us here. She clearly said that he has asked to court Camille."

"Ah," came his ironic reply. "In that case, I am grateful one of us was listening."

"It is one of the secrets to our marriage." She laughed and looked at Benedict and Camille. "And now, we will leave you two to socialize. There is food on the terrace, and a lovely buffet luncheon inside. We wait only for Justin's mother to arrive before we properly commence the celebrations."

"Grandmère is habitually late," Camille remarked.

"*Bien sûr*. Maman does that intentionally," Justin said in acid tones. "She likes all eyes to be on her when at last she sweeps into the room."

Mouette wrinkled her nose. "You are very harsh, especially considering she has not long been a widow. She is missing your papa."

He nodded, but his expression remained sardonic. "She misses Papa because he never spoke up to her."

"I am going to take you away now, darling," Mouette said calmly. To Benedict, she added, "It is Justin's way to be contrary. Do not imagine that he does not love his parents."

Benedict arched a brow at this. "In fact, I understand. Some parents are not very lovable."

Justin flashed a grin, as if in solidarity, then he waved at his brother, and they went to welcome Gabriel and Isabella. At last, Benedict found himself alone with Camille.

"I don't think I have had an opportunity to greet you," she said with a radiant smile. "Hello."

He took her gloved hand and tucked it into the crook of his arm, surprised by how neatly it fit there. "You're looking exceptionally beautiful today."

"Thank you. And you, too, are very well turned out, sir."

They gazed at one another, and Benedict knew they were both thinking of all the times they had been together when she was in trousers, dirt-smudged, her hair in a braid, and he had been writing, often unshaven, not even bothering to tie a proper neckcloth.

"Hopefully, if anyone is here who might have seen us in other circumstances," he began, lifting both brows for emphasis, "they won't realize we are the same people."

"Yes!" She lowered her voice and came near enough for him to breathe in her fragrance. "For example, anyone who might have been at the Old Ferry Inn in Bodinnick during your meetings with Jem."

"My thoughts exactly."

They had been strolling together behind the manor house, and now Benedict paused beside a colorful wildflower border. An assortment of butterflies danced back and forth over the delicate blossoms, vying with honeybees for the pollen. Looking toward the flagstone terrace, he recognized the couple he'd met in Bodinnick...Lord Sebastian and Julia Trevarre. The rare bird she had been carrying in a willow cage had never left his memory.

"Ah, my Uncle Sebastian and Aunt Julia are here," Camille said.

"Lord Sebastian is your mother's brother, as I recall?"

When she nodded, Benedict told her about his meeting with them near the ferry in Bodinnick. "I expressed a strong interest in your Aunt Julia's roseate tern, explaining that I am an ornithologist, but I don't think she approved of my occupation," he added.

"Because you shoot and stuff our beloved birds?" came Camille's tart response. "She and I are of one mind."

"In my own defense, I can assure you that I have not engaged in taxidermy since I came to Cornwall." This fact surprised even Benedict, and for a moment he stared into space, wondering what it meant.

"Is that so?" Camille looked up at him, her eyes softening. "Perhaps I have exerted a positive influence!"

"More likely, you have disrupted my routine so that I haven't had time for scientific study," Benedict parried dryly, yet inside a secret part of him felt warm yet uneasy.

* * *

AS THE OTHER guests began to move through the French doors that opened into the manor, Camille saw her mother gesture for them to join them. Although reluctant to end her time alone with Benedict, she took his arm, and they walked across the lawn to follow her assorted family members inside.

"Grandmère must have arrived," she said softly. "I love her very much, but she is a strong character. Don't be surprised if she does something outrageous."

"Your family is very colorful," he observed. "What is your absent sister like?"

"Louise is not colorful in the least," Camille assured him. "She is older than I am and a serious scientist. A paleontologist, actually. She works with the great Mary Anning in Lyme Regis."

"Indeed?" As they entered the large, flawlessly decorated drawing room, Benedict's eyes widened. "What a splendid room."

"It is." Looking around, she saw the treasures from Justin's travels to all corners of the world. Each piece told a story, Camille knew. The walls were lined with fine paintings, including landscapes of Cornwall painted by her own mother. The Sheraton furnishings were fashionable yet inviting, artfully arranged against the backdrop of French rugs. Even the fresh garden bouquets were impeccably arranged in opaline vases discovered by Mouette and Justin in Paris.

Camille led Benedict over to stand in a crowd with her parents and other relatives. The feeling of Benedict's hard body pressed against hers, even in this setting, made her feel a bit lightheaded. Finally, when the guests were all assembled, Justin rose to his feet and looked toward the doorway to the dining room.

"Before we can get on with the anniversary celebrations, let us take a moment to welcome my inimitable Maman. She lost Papa this year, so it is a testament to her strength that she insisted on coming today."

With that, a figure appeared in the doorway. It was Grandmère, reclining in an old-fashioned three-wheeled invalid chair, pushed by Adele, her latest long-suffering maid. She was clad in her favorite deep burgundy silk gown, dating back three decades, and an array of jewels. As she rolled farther into the drawing room, Camille saw that her grandmother was wearing a large, striking hat. To her relief, there were no tall egret or ostrich feathers fluttering above it, but then Benedict gripped her arm and Camille focused more closely on the headdress. Her heart pounded in horrified disbelief.

Like a queen among her court, Cerise St. Briac spoke to various guests in French as she slowly glided past. Turning first right and then left, she allowed everyone a clear view of her headdress...adorned on each side by an entire black-tipped, white kittiwake wing.

CHAPTER 17

Staring at the severed wings that decorated her grandmother's hat, Camille wondered if it all might be a nightmare. Could this truly be real? Her heart was pounding, and as she began to tremble, Benedict put an arm around her and held her still.

"Come with me," he whispered in her ear. It was not a request, but an order.

Camille knew a primal urge to stride over to Grandmère, rip the hat from her head, and deliver a furious, impassioned speech. However, Benedict had taken hold of both her arms and was surreptitiously guiding her away from the others. Fortunately, the party guests were occupied, greeting Cerise St. Briac and accepting goblets of champagne for an upcoming toast.

When Benedict silently opened a nearby door and virtually pushed her inside, Camille turned to face him. They were standing in her uncle's study, a bastion of masculinity.

"Did you see that?" Her voice broke on a sob.

His chiseled features were serious. "I did, and I can imagine how you must be feeling—but nothing can be gained by making a scene in front of that large group of guests. One of them might help lead us to our quarry."

"But what is *wrong* with people?" she cried.

Benedict closed the door completely and pulled her against him. "Quiet, minx. Unless you mean to ruin our chances for uncovering the bird killers responsible for your grandmother's hat, as well as countless others, you must control yourself."

Camille felt as if hot lava was boiling up inside of her. "You may be asking the impossible!"

"Take a few deep breaths. Think about what you are saying."

He held her firmly against him, his chest broad and hard beneath her cheek. She could feel the warmth of his body and hear his heart beating, slow and steady, and she clung to him.

"Better now?" he murmured. A stirring, husky note had crept into his voice.

"A bit...but I can't erase that image from my mind! Of course, I should not be surprised. Grandmère has favored such shocking hats as long as I can remember. Once, a decade ago, I visited her, and she was wearing a bonnet decorated with iridescent hummingbird skins!"

"No doubt, even at that young age, you tried to set her straight."

"I certainly did, but she never listens." Her throat thick with tears, Camille mourned, "I cannot get the image of those wings out of my mind. They could have belonged to poor Lazarus's father!"

"I suppose it is possible," he allowed. "But Lazarus would be better served if you channel your anger toward our greater mission."

Camille tipped her head back and looked up at him, eyes narrowed. "You are trying to distract me."

"I am," he agreed with mock solemnity. "And if that attempt did not succeed, I would be forced to kiss you."

"That would be a very reckless thing to do, here in my uncle's study."

A tentative smile touched Benedict's hard mouth, and she sensed he wanted to say more. Something in his face and the way he held her sent a fresh current of desire through Camille's body. As if he could feel it, too, he loosened his hold on her.

Camille swallowed. "I will consider your advice."

"Very wise. Your grandmother's millinery surprise may well be our first real clue, especially once you discover who created the kittiwake hat for her."

Closing her eyes, she drew in a deep breath and let it out again. "I am trying to be rational, but really I only want to shake her."

As if imagining that scene, Benedict flashed a grin. "I trust you can restrain yourself, but I'll stay close by, just in case."

Realizing that he was about to send her on her mission, Camille fretted, "I can't imagine how I can get her to reveal the milliner's identity! She knows I deplore those sorts of hats, and she is extremely perceptive."

"Ah, minx, I am confident that you will think of something. You are very resourceful!"

With that, Benedict opened the door only an inch or two. The lilting strains of violin music reached them, and Camille guessed that her gifted, older cousin, Cassandra Trevarre, must be playing for the guests. After looking through the crack in the door for a few moments, Benedict reached back and took her hand.

"Quickly," he whispered, and led her back out into the drawing room.

Servants were pouring more champagne, and during a lull in the music, Justin and Mouette moved to stand before the fireplace. Camille tried to block out the sight of Grandmère, whose invalid chair was positioned nearby.

"We want to thank each one of you for coming here today to join in our celebration," her uncle said in a rich, warm voice. "It is only fitting that we are here together at Frenchman's Haven, the very place where my beautiful wife first cast her spell on me. Little did I imagine, when I hired her to pretend to be my bride, we would create a home and family more real than I could have ever dreamed."

Mouette smiled up at him in a way that tugged at the corner of Camille's heart she'd long sought to keep under lock and key. Her eyes stung with emotion.

Benedict inclined his head. "Is something wrong?"

She managed a shaky nod. "I am…happy for them."

Justin then continued, "Some of you know that I am cynical by nature. I did not think I was capable of *love*." He infused the word with a hint of his typical mockery and shook his head. "I was a fool, as my beautiful wife gradually brought me to understand."

"Not a fool," protested Mouette. "Darling Justin, you were like the lion with a thorn in its paw. At last, we found a way to remove it." She leaned against him, adding, "Together."

Watching them, Camille reminded herself that such love stories were very rare. True, her parents had also enjoyed a happy marriage, but her mother was suited to wifely devotion in a way Camille could never be.

"I ask you to raise your glasses with me. *To love!*" Justin toasted lustily, drank along with everyone else, and flashed an irresistible smile. "Thank you all for coming from not only nearby but also as far away as London to celebrate with us."

Camille wondered briefly who the London visitor might be. All the family members who lived there were unable to be here today, as far as she knew, including Justin and Mouette's own children, Anthony and Emeline.

Mouette spoke up then. "Margaret, our faithful cook, and Baptiste, our treasured steward, have recreated the cake from our wedding day two decades ago." She gestured to the proud pair who stood in the doorway. "We hope you will all partake of luncheon and sample the cake as well."

As the chattering guests moved toward the buffet laid out in the dining room, Camille glanced over toward her grandmother. The exceedingly old woman was watching her under the brim of her kittiwake bonnet.

"*Ma fille*, do you take no notice of your *pauvre grandmère*?" She feigned a sobbing sound, the corners of her rouged lips turning down. "There was a time when you made special visits simply to cheer me."

Camille felt a slight nudge at the small of her back and knew it was Benedict, urging her to approach Grandmère. Of course, he was right. The kittiwake hat was the best clue they had. She must try to see it as a gift, not a curse. Summoning her resolve, Camille went forward and perched on a low stool beside the three-wheeled invalid chair.

"It is so nice to see you, Grandmère," she murmured. "I have been longing to visit you for a nice, long chat, but so much has been happening."

"*Vraiment*? Pardon me for asking if that is true, but in this very dull part of the world, one must wonder what could be so pressing to keep you from the side of your beloved *grandmère*."

"That is an excellent point." Camille pasted on her sweetest smile. With an effort of will, she managed to avoid looking directly at the black-and-white kittiwake wing that was just inches away. "You know me...I am ever in nature, and the hours fly by."

"Hmm! And who is that fellow who has been lurking near you?"

"Oh, that is Mr. Hawke." Camille was relieved to see that he had wandered off to chat with her handsome cousin, Lucas Trevarre. The two men looked to be about the same age, and soon they were engaged in an animated conversation. "He is visiting Cornwall for a short while."

"And how do you know him?"

Fearing that she might say the wrong thing, which her grandmother might then repeat to the wrong person, Camille shook her head. "Let us not waste this precious time talking about a man I barely know!" She gave a careless laugh. "I want to hear about you, Grand-mère. You are looking splendid, as usual."

Cerise St. Briac turned her face up to the light and preened. "Do you think so? I have acquired some very special Parisian cosmetics. My maid insists that I now appear decades younger."

The powder was caked in the deep lines around her eyes and mouth, and Adele had applied too much rouge, but Camille nodded and leaned forward to kiss a withered cheek. Her grandmother had claimed to be a death's door many times over the years, yet here she was, still vital in all the ways that mattered.

"You look lovely," Camille said sincerely. Then, summoning her nerve, she added in an offhand tone, "And I must say, that is quite a striking hat. Wherever did you get it?"

"Oh, *this*," Cerise lifted a thin hand to stroke one of the severed wings. "Of course, this creation is very unique to Cornwall. Do you know the birds they call kittiwakes? My milliner crafted this masterpiece for me, as a sort of *tribute* to my adopted home."

Camille could have burst with indignation and grief, but she bit her lip and nodded. "How inspired. Please remind me...who is your milliner?"

"I'll own I am surprised that you admire it so,"

Grandmère said, watching her with a faint glint of suspicion in her dark eyes. "Are you not the same child who has scolded me in the past about my love for feathers?"

Yes, she wanted to cry. *Yes, I am, and I am outraged by this monstrous hat you are wearing!* But then, from the corner of her eye, she glimpsed Benedict. His head was cocked slightly as he sent her a warning glance. Camille drew a deep breath, slowing her heartbeat.

"I suppose I have grown up," she told her grandmother. "I don't feel so…emotional. I can now admire your headdress as an object of beauty."

"*D'accord*! I am pleased to hear this." Cerise peered back toward her maid, who waited obediently behind the invalid chair. "Now I am hungry. My son tells me there will be a perfect summer *bouillabaisse*. Take me to the dining room, Adele."

Camille felt a rush of panic as she watched her grandmother begin to roll away, but after just a few feet, the old woman seemed to remember their aborted conversation. She stretched a gloved hand back, and when the maid halted, Camille hastened to Grandmère's side.

"It was lovely to talk to you today, *chérie*, and to find that you are at last becoming a true woman." The old woman clasped her fingers momentarily, then released them. "I shall tell Lady Daphne that you admired her creation when next we meet."

With that, Adele began to push the chair again, and Grandmère glided away into the dining room. Standing in her wake, Camille pressed a fist to her mouth, pondering what she had heard.

She sensed Benedict's nearness before he came into view beside her. "Well?" His voice was husky.

"How very curious. I believe Grandmère said the

milliner's name is 'Lady Daphne.' Is it possible that she could be a noblewoman?"

* * *

BENEDICT CONSIDERED THIS INFORMATION. "Perhaps Lady Daphne is a name the milliner has assumed to sound grand. London is rife with English dressmakers and even tailors who have taken fancy French names to impress their would-be clients." Dryly, he added, "They even affect false accents."

"I suppose our next challenge will be to discover who exactly this Lady Daphne person might be." She caught her lower lip with her teeth and gazed off into space. "Oddly, I seem to have a memory of her, or at least of her name. I shall consult with Mama later."

Fragrant aromas drifted out from the dining room, where many of the guests were filling their plates with food. Some had gone out to the terrace to enjoy their meal at the long table, while others were taking seats in the drawing room. Suddenly Benedict's stomach sent an audible signal that it wanted to be fed.

"Oh, you must be hungry," Camille teased, showing him her dimples.

"If you heard my stomach grumble, I'm quite certain you should not mention it," he pretended to reprimand her.

They were just taking up plates when Benedict noticed a young man staring at Camille from the other side of the table. His memory stirred. The fellow was tall and slim, with waves of thinning fair hair, and a long nose in his otherwise handsome face. He looked as if he had just come from the shop of Weston himself, his clothing fashionable and yet so tasteful that Benedict assumed he must be an aristocrat.

When Camille glanced up and met the newcomer's eyes, she went very pale and then pink. Benedict watched her blink several times, then turn back to the food, taking a spoonful of marinated pilchards. Her hand shook slightly.

Something flared white-hot inside Benedict. Who the devil was that man, and why was Camille clearly disturbed by his presence? Or perhaps she felt an attraction to him!

They moved along, around the table, which was lined with a selection of dishes that were unique to Brittany and Cornwall. Camille explained about the Cornish specialties he didn't recognize, like saffron cake and crab with devil sauce. Glancing up, Benedict was relieved to see that the unexpected guest had disappeared.

Unfortunately, as they emerged from the dining room, plates in hand, the young man was there, chatting with Justin St. Briac. When he broke off in midsentence at the sight of Camille, their host took his cue.

"Ah, yes, Lord Upton, as I recall you and my niece became acquainted during your visit to Frenchman's Haven, last year." He looked at Camille. "*Mon ange*, I surely do not need to reacquaint you with our friend from London, the Viscount Upton?"

"Yes, of course I remember." Camille had gone white again, but she smiled as if nothing was amiss. "So, you have returned to Cornwall, my lord."

"The memories of my last sojourn here compelled me to return," Upton intoned smoothly. He wore a wide, charming smile that never quite reached his pale blue eyes.

Sweeping a hand toward Benedict, Justin said, "May I also present M'sieur Benedict Hawke, who is visiting Cornwall for a time?"

Before Justin could divulge any further information to Upton, Benedict extended his hand. "Good afternoon, my lord."

"Good afternoon, Mr. Hawke."

"Is it possible that we have met before?" Benedict ventured.

"I doubt it," came Upton's cool reply.

The viscount glanced away as if speaking to a servant, and Benedict's memory bristled. However, before he could respond, Upton returned his attention to Camille.

"Miss St. Briac, I understand you have become quite the crusader since last we met," he said, bending down slightly to look into her eyes.

"I believe I have always been a crusader, my lord." She straightened her back. "Perhaps you simply did not take notice."

Upton angled his body slightly, blocking Benedict in a way meant to exclude him from the conversation. In that moment, the past came into sharp focus. Benedict saw Upton as a young man during their years at Oxford, his head thick with blond curls, his manner superior. In one of many similar incidents, Upton emerged suddenly from Oriel College and purposely brushed up against Benedict as he passed on Grove Street. The nobleman had glanced over with feigned surprise and continued on his way, as if he could not be bothered to speak to a commoner.

Now, giving Benedict his back, Upton was fully focused on Camille. "I should like very much to hear more about your crusades…as well as all your other news from the past year."

"Oh, I don't know." Camille shook her head. "There really isn't much to tell, my lord." She gave him her gloved hand. "I hope you enjoy your visit to Cornwall."

What a spitfire! Benedict thought admiringly as he turned to follow her onto the terrace. Glancing back for only a moment, he flicked up both brows to bid Upton an ironic farewell.

CHAPTER 18

When at last the guests began to depart, Benedict felt a long-suppressed surge of relief. Engaging in polite conversation with so many strangers was more exhausting than a trek through the Amazon in search of rare birds.

Meanwhile, his peace was further disturbed by the situation with Camille and the deuced Viscount Upton. He should get to the bottom of that, he knew, but at the moment he craved freedom. He had to breathe the sea air and feel the wind on his face, far away from *people*.

However, he waited for Upton to bid his hosts goodbye before making his own move to go. Nothing could compel Benedict to leave Camille in the company of Viscount Upton, especially since the two appeared to have some sort of history. Benedict told himself it might not amount to more than a few shared pleasantries when Upton was last in Cornwall, but it was harder to dispel the memory of Camille's flushed cheeks.

Tomorrow he would find out the truth, but today he had bloody done enough.

Outside on the terrace, he found Camille watching Damien and Zeus run on the lawn. "Do you see the fruit trees bordering the property?" she asked as her brother threw a stick for the black dog. "Papa began planting them soon after Uncle Justin and Aunt Mouette were married, when they were still transforming Frenchman's Haven from a very plain, empty house into the warm and beautiful home it is today."

Benedict tried without success to imagine this scenario of domestic bliss. "Very nice." He forced a smile. "I must go now." Clearly, that wasn't enough. She was looking at him in consternation. "I may have forgotten to mention that I have an appointment."

"Yes, you did forget." She took a slight step backward, and a part of him wanted to reach for her. "I will let you know if I find out more about the true identity of Lady Daphne." Glancing away, she added, "I could ask Rafael to take word to you."

He wanted to tell her he would be outside her door tomorrow morning, or that she could bring a message to Gull Cottage herself, but then he remembered how her hand shook at the sight of Lord Upton. *Curse him.*

"Yes. I will be in touch." Benedict took his gloves from a pocket and drew them on. "It was a worthwhile afternoon, in spite of the hat."

She looked up at him and widened her blue eyes, as if she'd forgotten all about the kittiwake wings. "Oh, yes—the hat!" She nodded, once. "I agree."

* * *

RIDING across the wildly beautiful Cornish cliffs, Benedict pressed his knees against Max's flanks, urging him to gallop faster. As the wind blew his hair back, he leaned into it and looked out to the blue sweep of the English Channel. In the distance, a magnificent, three-masted sailing vessel glided westward toward the Atlantic Ocean. Perhaps it was bound for

Australia? The thought of escaping from Cornwall and the newly evolving structure of his life was tempting.

But impossible.

As Benedict rode on, it came to him that perhaps the cause of his gnawing sense of disquiet was Pa. Of course, there was nothing new about that. No matter how far he might stay away from Prudence's house, or even from Polruan itself, the real issue remained unchanged, lodged deep in his soul.

Just a visit, he told himself as he turned Max onto the narrow lane leading from the cliffs toward the hillside village of Polruan. His sister was about to deliver another child. Her husband was away from dawn to dusk, operating the small ferry that crossed to Fowey, and Benedict knew she needed help. Was he not her brother? It wasn't as if he would be forced to endure a difficult scene with Pa. The old man couldn't even speak or move, for God's sake, and Benedict was free to walk away.

Outside Prue's narrow house overlooking the waterfront, he tied Max to a hitching post and went up to knock at the door. Soon, the portal swung open to reveal Fletcher, leaning heavily on his blackthorn walking stick.

"I suppose I shouldn't be surprised to find you here, old fellow," Benedict said wryly.

"Not a bit, sir. You instructed me to look after your father, did you not?"

A part of him hadn't wanted to think about the reality of this situation. He'd been able to tell himself that his own obligation was being fulfilled, but exactly what happened when Fletcher went off to Polruan each day remained a mystery as long as he didn't probe.

"Is my sister at home?"

"Mistress Johns approaches her time, sir. She is resting." Fletcher was interrupted then by the fretful crying of a baby. "Ah, that will be baby Jenny. I'll see to her."

Good God, it seemed that Fletcher was virtually managing the entire household! Watching as his manservant limped off into the cramped cottage, Benedict had no choice but to close the door and follow him.

"What brings you here today, sir?" Fletcher inquired as he scooped little Jenny up from her cradle.

"Why shouldn't I be here?" He couldn't seem to keep the defensive note from his voice. "It's my family, is it not?"

"Indeed, it is," the manservant murmured. Taking a chair, he held Jenny against his chest and began to rock gently. After a few moments, she emitted a satisfied belch and Fletcher smiled. "Perhaps you've come to visit your father."

"Right." Benedict nodded but didn't move.

"I was nearly finished feeding Mr. Hawke when you knocked."

"I'll go and see him, then."

Wending his way through toward the back of the cottage, Benedict thought of the enchanted scene he had just left at Frenchman's Haven. The spacious, light-filled rooms, the scents of saffron bread and summer flowers, the laughter and love among the members of the St. Briac family. It seemed that a gulf yawned between his family and Camille's, but then, what did it matter? It wasn't as if they were really courting.

As Benedict approached the small room attached to Prue's house, he heard a muffled moan. Again, he questioned himself for coming there at all. He thought of summoning Fletcher to assist, but then Benedict remembered the baby. Doubtless by now Fletcher was changing her nappy.

He pushed aside the thin curtain separating Pa's

space from the rest of the house. The last time he was here, his father had resembled a wraith, left arm bent and pressed in against his side, one knee poking out at an angle, cheeks sunken and mouth slack. Benedict steeled himself to meet that same distorted version of Pa once again, but instead the old man was up in a chair, leaning against a pillow. He clutched a fork in his right hand and endeavored to spear a bite of potato. Each time he stabbed at it, the buttery wedge slipped away.

Seeing Benedict, he scowled. "Blast." The word was somewhat garbled, but still understandable. He awkwardly waved the fork in the air.

Shocked, Benedict remembered then that Fletcher had recently told him Pa was improving, but he hadn't inquired further. Of course not. He would rather pretend none of it existed, leaving the thorny matter to Fletcher. *I can be a bastard*, Benedict thought. Like father, like son.

"Hello, Pa. Do you want me to help you?"

As soon as the words were out, he knew he'd made a mistake. Pa's face went red, and he tried again to poke the fork into the potato. This time, the tines engaged. "Huh!" Pa held the prize aloft with a look of triumph before aiming it into his mouth. While chewing, he pointed to the bed with its tangle of blankets. "Sit!"

Benedict didn't want to touch the place where Pa spent his days and nights, but he obeyed, lowering himself to sit far away from the pillow. When he glanced down, he saw the rim of a chamber pot pushed under the bed, piss still visible inside.

Silence stretched for a long, painful minute. "I thought I should come by to see how you're getting on," he said at last.

Pa gave a grunt as he hunted down another bite of

potato. Surveying Benedict's fine clothing, he pointed the fork again and challenged, "Ye! Care not."

It came to Benedict that his father had always been able to say the dark things Benedict couldn't or wouldn't admit to. And now he was right, again. Benedict didn't care how he was getting on.

Did he?

"High…mighty."

Benedict was perhaps the only person in the world who could easily play this word game with his father. Every twisted thought Pa had was readily apparent to him. Although the scattering of words Pa managed to employ since his stroke were helpful clues, often all that was needed was a curl of his lip or a piercing look that was meant to belittle Benedict's ambitions and station in life.

This 'high and mighty' comment was all too familiar. From the moment Lady Far intervened and suggested that Benedict was gifted and should go away to a proper school, Pa had accused him of being proud, arrogant, and putting himself above the rest of his family. He strove to turn every one of his son's accomplishments into a cause for derision. Eventually, Benedict stopped coming home, which led Pa to write him angry, disjointed letters.

"I never thought I was better," Benedict said in a low, hard voice. "I simply chose a different path." He wanted to openly confess that all he had ever longed for was a word of approval, a sign that his father was proud of him, but he now knew better than to invite Pa's mockery. Instead, he challenged quietly, "In spite of all the harsh words between us, I am still your son."

Pa twisted his drooping mouth into a scowl and threw down the fork, signaling an end to that subject.

"I've been staying at Gull Cottage," Benedict said, "and taking care of your cat."

He watched the old man for a reaction, but Pa looked out the window.

"I found him in a hiding place under the cottage floor..." At this, Pa's gaze swiveled back to Benedict, sharp and focused. "At first, I thought it might be an old smuggling tunnel, but perhaps it has another use of late?"

Pa shook his head, but Benedict could see the flash of alarm in his black eyes. His heart thumped. He felt both triumphant and sick. Before he could probe deeper, the old man tried to point at the curtained doorway.

"Out!"

Benedict rose and left the tiny room, relieved to get away. Pa's body and tongue might be weakened, but his deadly power to wound remained intact.

* * *

"AH, SIR, THERE YOU ARE." Fletcher met him on the other side of the curtain. "I was just about to retrieve Mr. Hawke's dishes. Your visit is ended?"

For an instant, Benedict's throat closed. He nodded. "Yes. Thank God."

"Mistress Johns has come downstairs," the manservant said, briefly touching Benedict's arm. "You'll find her in the parlor."

Entering the narrow room, Benedict saw little Gareth rolling a ball on the floor for his sister. Jenny sat on a blanket, pudgy legs outstretched. She laughed as the ball came toward her but could not work out how to send it back.

Prue's voice came to him from a shadowed corner. "This is a surprise."

He crossed to her, affection welling up inside, and

bent to kiss her. "Look at you! How did you manage the stairs?"

"I know." She gave a weak laugh. "If a wheelbarrow would fit through our door, I'd ask Fletcher to push me to and fro in it." For a moment, she clung to his arm. "Thank you for lending him to us. You were right, Fletcher has been more help than you ever could be, especially with Pa."

This should have pleased him, but his heart squeezed. "Right. If I'd been caring for Pa, one of us would doubtless be dead by now. He clearly despises me."

"Oh, I'm certain that's not really true." Prue's eyes were soft. "Sit for a moment. How have you been? You're looking quite the toff in those fine clothes."

"I'm not certain if that was a compliment or an insult," he parried, arching a brow. "I have a lot of fine clothes, but rarely put them on, to Fletcher's dismay. Today I attended a party at an estate called Frenchman's Haven, near Lansallos. Do you know it?"

"My!" She pretended to be awestruck. "Of course, I know it. Justin St. Briac is rather legendary in these parts. Why on earth would he invite you to a party?"

That was a question he was not prepared to answer. "Is it so shocking to think I've made a friend or two since coming here?" Benedict punctuated this question with an arched brow.

"I simply thought you were all alone, locked away at Gull Cottage, examining your specimens and writing," Prue replied, smiling. "I don't suppose you want to tell me more about your new friendships?"

"Not yet."

"Uncle Ben'dick." It was little Gareth, tugging at Benedict's coat sleeve. "Do come for my birthday!"

"Ah, that's right." Benedict put an arm around the little boy, whose fair hair smelled freshly washed. He wondered if Fletcher bathed the child when both parents were consumed with other demands. Feeling an unfamiliar pang, he looked up at Prudence. "When will this birthday take place?"

"Friday next. Gareth turns four on the same day as the new queen's coronation!"

"I mean to have a party," the boy announced. "Like the queen!"

"Darling," Prue said gently, "it's not possible to have a party right now. The new baby is coming any day now, remember? That can be your special present."

For a moment, it seemed Gareth might burst into tears. "Oh." He sniffed. "Arright, Mama."

Benedict felt an odd tug inside as a long-buried memory returned. He had been a little boy, not much older than Gareth, and they were still living at Windsor Great Park, where Pa was an undergardener. After overhearing tales of London from the royal children, Benedict had begged his parents to take him to see the exotic animals and birds in the Royal Menagerie for his birthday. Pa had been brutal in his refusal, quashing Benedict's dream. "Ye want to travel to bloody London and lark about at the Menagerie? I s'pose ye expect *me* to pay the entrance fee!" Pa had let out a bark of laughter. "Nay, be thankful for a wooden top and an apple for your birthday." Although that rebuff had been crushing, Benedict had no way of knowing then that a cruel pattern had begun.

Through the years, the message remained: *You are worthless, so don't bother trying to rise above your station.*

And now, from the back of Prue's house, Benedict heard Pa's voice rise, his words broken, unintelligible. The walls seemed to close in. His heart pounded in his chest, and his throat constricted.

"I have to go now," he said hoarsely and pushed to his feet.

"I know," Prue murmured, as if something in his bearing revealed his battered heart.

"Sorry I'm not more use to you these days." He reached down to smooth Gareth's hair.

His sister suddenly tried to sit up straight. "Oh, Benedict, I nearly forgot…a letter came for you in the post. Addressed to Benedict Hawke, in Polruan, so the postman took a chance and brought it to us. I intended to send it to you with Fletcher." She struggled to her feet and went to a tiny desk against one wall. "I think it has come from London!"

Moving to accept the letter, Benedict looked down at the unfamiliar, spidery script.

What the devil could it be about?

In the next moment, an inner voice whispered, *Deliverance?*

CHAPTER 19

*L*ong after the other guests had departed, Camille's extended family lingered in the garden at Frenchman's Haven, enjoying the warm afternoon weather. Baptiste, who had served her uncle in nearly every capacity for more than three decades, directed the footmen to transfer the rest of the food from the dining room to the long table in the courtyard.

When Camille saw Grandmère dozing in her invalid chair under the spreading branches of a plum tree, she decided to seize the opportunity. Adele was off filling a plate of her own, while the other family members who remained were seated around the table, engaged in animated conversation.

Camille perched on a bench near her grandmother's three-wheeled reclining chair and reached out to touch her bony fingers. "Grandmère?" she whispered. "It's Camille."

"Ah." Her eyes fluttered open. "And where is Louise?"

"Do you recall...my sister has been in Lyme Regis for some years. She is doing important work, uncovering fossils with Mary Anning."

"*Oui*, I do recall." The old woman nodded slowly, as if returning from a distant place. "Poor girl, perhaps it is the best she can do, for we both know Louise was not blessed with your great beauty. Her options are sadly limited, and now that she has left society and spends all her days *digging*, who will want her?"

A familiar spark caught inside Camille. "I believe my sister is very happy all the same."

"Such a pity." She shook her head so that the kittiwake wings on her headdress moved from side to side. "But what of you, *ma belle*? You grow older, yet the men flock to you, even when you do not invite them. You could still return to London in time for the coronation, *n'est-ce pas*? Properly gowned and coiffed, you would set the *haut ton* on its ear." Leaning forward a bit, Grandmère went on in conspiratorial tones, "I took note of the Viscount Upton gazing at you, *petite*. I vow, you could have him, yet he is but a small fish in the sea." She flicked her fingertips in a way meant to minimize Roger's worth. "Why not set your sights on a *marquis*, or even a *duc*? Having achieved such a union, you might arrange for your dear Grandmère to live in the dower house!"

It was a torturously familiar conversation, but Camille forced a smile. "I do not want a marquess or even a duke. Have I not explained to you that such a life holds no appeal for me?"

"But that is ridiculous." Her voice rose. "Are you mad?"

Camille realized she must find a way to change the subject as quickly as possible. "I promise to think about all you have said." Smiling, she made herself add, "Clearly, you have my best interests in mind."

"Ah. *Bon!* Perhaps there is hope for you after all."

"Thank you for your faith in me." Fearing that the old woman was about to close her eyes again, Camille took her hand. "Wasn't it a lively party? So many interesting guests." Almost as an afterthought, she continued, "And I have found myself wondering about something you mentioned. You said your milliner's name is Lady Dahlia…or was it Lady Deidre?"

"No, that's not right. Lady *Daphne!*" the old woman exclaimed, relishing the chance to utter a correction. Then, accentuating each word as if Camille might not understand, she added, "Her name is *Lady Daphne Leyton*…But perhaps not Leyton any longer, for she married an elderly squire. Callywith or some sort."

Camille gave a friendly nod. "I know someone who is looking for a talented milliner. Perhaps I will refer her to Lady Daphne."

"No, she has retired from the millinery trade! Lady Daphne worked with your Uncle Justin for some years. Don't you remember? He purchased a building in Polperro, and she oversaw the workroom where they made lovely hats. I believe my son's intention was to help the townspeople earn a living after storms destroyed the fishing boats." She wagged a finger in the air. "But, after marrying more than a decade ago, Lady Daphne naturally turned to domestic pursuits. It was her dream to have babies, but alas, that has transpired."

Camille didn't bother to remind her grandmother that she had been a child when all of this occurred, too young to notice or remember the name of a milliner.

"I see. So, this kittiwake bonnet of yours was created some years ago?" She paused. "It is very distinctive, but I don't recall seeing it before."

"Lady Daphne has been known to undertake special projects for me." Grandmère gave a cryptic shrug and glanced away. "*Eh bien,* I do not understand your interest in a milliner. Have you changed your opinion of feathers on hats?"

Just then, Adele appeared, holding out a plate of

small tarts. Grandmère's eyes lit up. "I was longing for a sweet! And, perhaps, a small glass of Calvados brandy?"

It was the perfect opportunity for Camille to excuse herself. She crossed the terrace to sit down at the table beside her Uncle Justin and Aunt Mouette.

After a few minutes of friendly conversation, Camille said warmly, "I can't remember a more wonderful party!"

"Oh, I'm so glad you think so," Mouette replied. "I'll own I was a bit concerned that your grandmother's terrible hat might ruin the day for you. I know how you feel about feathers, and that headdress is particularly grotesque."

She wanted to throw her arms around her beautiful aunt. Instead, she leaned closer, lowering her voice. "Please do not tell Grandmère I said this, but you are right. It is truly horrifying. I find I am curious about the sort of person who could make that shocking hat." It took every ounce of restraint she possessed not to tell Mouette and Justin the whole story, but Camille knew Benedict would warn against that. "I understand her name is Lady Daphne Leyton? And, Uncle Justin, you were once her business partner?"

Mouette and Justin exchanged a glance that was heavy with meaning. Camille's pulse raced. What could it signify? Justin leaned across, in front of Mouette, and stared at Camille. Even though one of his eyes was covered by a silk eyepatch, his gaze seemed to pin her to the spot.

"You may recall that I own the net loft, the large stone and timber structure on Peak Rock in Polperro harbor?" He waited for her hesitant nod before continuing, "Lady Daphne was a noblewoman who fell on hard times and took up the millinery trade. She employed Polperro women in a workroom on the upper story, making hats. Eventually we parted ways…"

Mouette gave a disdainful sniff. "She is ruthless. Even immoral if truth be told."

"*Chérie*," rumbled Justin. "You might curb your tongue."

"I hardly think you can counsel others on the art of self-control, my dear husband," she murmured.

Camille intervened, whispering fiercely, "I am not surprised to hear that a person who would decorate a foolish *hat* with the wings of innocent, beautiful kittiwakes is possessed of many terrible qualities! But is it true that she no longer is engaged in that wicked trade?"

"Daphne married a squire a decade ago," Mouette confirmed. "However, that didn't stop her from engaging in other sorts of misdeeds."

Justin leaned close to his wife's ear. "Did you not vow to put that in the past?"

Her face softened. "Oh yes, I did. I apologize." Turning back to Camille, she said, "Suffice it to say, Daphne has committed her share of mischief in the past, but as far as I know, she has reformed. After persuading the squire to dispose of his family estate near Fowey and purchase a grander manor house up Lerryn Creek, she appears to be living a quiet life. We have not seen her, even in town, for many months."

"I am glad to hear that this person has changed her ways and is no longer a threat to our kittiwakes or any other birds," Camille said firmly.

Was that true, however? She could scarcely wait to share everything she had learned with Benedict! He had been rather abrupt in his leave-taking, and now Camille regretted her own rather crisp response. A part of her wanted to set out for Gull Cottage at that very moment and simply knock on the door, yet it came to her that their relationship had changed, shifted, in an utterly foreign way. The thought of doing something so bold gave her butterflies, and her stomach felt odd.

Camille closed her eyes. *What is happening to me?*

* * *

AT DAWN, the view from Benedict's window overlooking the English Channel was breathtaking. The world was quiet except for the sounds of birds and small animals foraging for their breakfast, and the golden-rose light lent a magical quality to the water.

The countless, individually tagged bird corpses that had lined his desk were temporarily packed away. In their place was the small drawer containing a fuzzy kittiwake hatchling who had just been fed drops of water and two grubs. Benedict reminded himself that Fletcher had put Ember the cat in the smugglers tunnel that morning, allowing Lazarus to leave the bedchamber. The kittiwake now lifted his head and gave a small peep.

Reassured, Benedict turned his attention to the letter Prue had delivered the day before. He had already read it at least ten times and had awakened in the night to ponder its contents, but now he unfolded the page again.

Fletcher loomed up behind him, offering a cup of strong black tea.

"Sir?"

"I suppose you are wondering about this letter." Benedict took the tea and sipped, appreciating that only Fletcher knew to add but a splash of milk, just the way he liked it.

"A bit, sir." The manservant kept his expression neutral. "Only because I've seen you open it and study the contents at least three times since last night."

"It is from William Swainson, perhaps the only

British ornithologist whose reputation rivals that of John Gould."

"I see."

Sharing the contents of the letter made his stomach clench, and yet it was a relief as well.

"You might as well sit down." He pointed to the chair he'd once pulled over for Camille.

"I am listening, sir, and of course you may depend upon my discretion."

This caused Benedict to push to his feet and pace in front of Fletcher's chair. "Swainson writes that he intends to sail to Australia and New Zealand in the coming months. He was informed by a Zoological Society colleague that I had to bow out of Gould's expedition due to a family illness. However, he writes…if I still want to go, he can offer me a position with him." Even as he spoke, Benedict heard his heart begin to pound in his ears.

"I see," Fletcher said again. "That would solve everything, would it not? I know how crushing it was for you to miss that golden opportunity with Mr. Gould."

Ignoring this question, Benedict went on, "Swainson declares that he would welcome me as a member of his expedition. In addition, if I chose to join Gould after arriving in Australia, I would be free to do so."

"Better and better."

Benedict pressed a fist to his chest. "Right."

"How soon must you reply?"

He raked a hand through his already disheveled hair. "Once I write to express my interest, Swainson promises to keep me apprised of the plans as they develop. I believe the voyage is yet a few months away."

"Ah! Perhaps such an arrangement would make it easier for you to endure your stay in Cornwall." Fletcher paused, watching him. "May I be frank, sir?"

Benedict winced. "Have at it."

"I know that the situation with Mr. Hawke is very taxing. Also, you are accustomed to coming and going as you please, so there's that as well. It's almost as if you have been forced into a kind of exile here! If you accept Mr. Swainson's invitation, you can enjoy the sense that your freedom is at hand during the weeks that remain."

"But can I simply leave? I mean…there's Pa."

Fletcher straightened his spine. "Leave all of that to me, sir. You may sail to Australia, and I shall be honored to remain behind to look after your family."

"Right." Benedict stared out the window at the blue expanse of the Channel. Thoughts of Camille raced unbidden through his mind, as every muscle in his body tightened. "I will think about it."

* * *

As CAMILLE ATE the last bite of her rather enormous breakfast, she felt a rush of excitement. Soon she would be out in the sunshine, walking on the cliff path toward Gull Cottage. She could scarcely wait to see Benedict, not only to tell him all she had learned about Lady Daphne Leyton, but also to be close to him. The memory arose of his arms drawing her against his hard body, his mouth covering hers, and heat blossomed at her core.

She had just leaned back in her chair, sighing, when her mother appeared in the doorway.

"My, don't you look lovely!" Isabella smiled and tilted her head to one side.

"Do I?" Camille glanced down, cheeks warming. That morning, she'd reached into her armoire for her favorite breeches, but something had caused her to choose a printed lavender cotton dress instead. After all, she was perfectly capable of walking outdoors in a skirt!

"That color sets off your beautiful eyes," her mother continued. She crossed over to perch on the edge of the chair next to Camille. "I wonder if your decision to wear a dress has anything to do with the two very handsome men who were vying for your attention yesterday."

"Mama, really—"

"But wasn't it a surprise to see Lord Upton at the party? Your Uncle Justin has informed me that his lordship did not wed after all. I know that you deny that you ever had feelings for him, but the way he gazed at you yesterday seemed to tell another tale."

"Mama, I beg you to stop this." Camille shook her head. "I am going out now. I must see how Lazarus fares."

"The rescued chick who is being cared for by Mr. Hawke?" Her mother gave her a searching look.

Before Camille could reply, Claire appeared in the doorway, eyes wide. "Mistress, there be a caller, askin' for ye."

When Isabella nodded in reply, the housekeeper shook her head. "Nay, it be the young mistress he bade me fetch."

Camille's heart sped up. *Benedict!* She rose quickly, but her elation vanished as a tall, fair-haired young man strode into the dining room.

"Lovely ladies, I bid you good morning." Lord Upton came forward, one pale hand outstretched. To Isabella he said, "Please accept my apology for this unplanned visit, my lady, but I find that I cannot rest until I speak with your daughter." Roger directed a fervent look at Camille and added, "*Privately*, if Miss St. Briac will do me the honor."

CHAPTER 20

For a moment, Camille considered refusing to have a conversation with Roger. A familiar cloud of shame closed in around her, but she tried to push it away. As tempting as it was to avoid any further contact with the man, perhaps the best path was to face him.

On her terms.

"I do have other plans, my lord, but I can spare a few minutes," Camille said politely. "Shall we walk in the garden?"

Upton agreed, and they walked out, past the conservatory. Camille was relieved to see her father through the glass panes, repotting a dwarf citrus tree. She waved to him, and he lifted his chin, nodding.

"My dear, how good it is to see you," Roger said as they strolled along the same narrow path where Benedict had kissed her just days ago. "Will you sit with me and allow me to speak to you from my heart?" He gestured toward a bench tucked away in a corner, under a trimmed boxwood arch.

Instinctive panic set her heart racing, but Camille reassured herself, *I am not in danger.* Nodding, she spread her skirts as she perched on the bench, hoping to create a barrier between them.

"I have waited so long for this moment," Roger said. His pale blue eyes were so earnest, she almost believed him. "I know that it might have been rather confusing for you when I had to leave Cornwall last year…"

Confusing? Bile rose in her throat. "You told me that your family was depending on you to marry Lady Barbara Framstead, that you had no choice."

"That was true!" Color crept into his pale face. "I mean, of course, I had a duty." He coughed. "As a man of honor."

She had only allowed fragments of her past with Roger to trouble her memory, but now all of it returned in a sickening rush…Roger's frequent visits to Elysium during his fortnight in Cornwall, his kind attentions to her. His gentlemanly treatment even when they were walking in the woods and she showed him many of her favorite spots, pointing out birds he had never heard of. He had professed first to admire and understand her, and then to care for her. In her innocence, Camille believed she was falling in love. Then came the day they walked a bit farther than planned, and Lupine Cottage came into sight on the cliffs. Roger said he had twisted his ankle and wondered if they might go inside so he could rest. Once they were seated on the chaise, it wasn't long before he was kissing her, gently, then more forcefully, kneading her breasts, telling her he *needed* her, he was in the grip of a pain unique to men. He was desperate for release, he begged, and only she could help him. Between kisses and caresses that were at once arousing yet confusing, Roger murmured that of course she needn't fear he meant to take her virginity. No such thing! There were other ways she could ease his torment, without even lifting her skirts. Finally, he had seemed to bare his soul to her: *You are so beautiful, so special, my darling. Show me, please, that you care for me as well!* Perhaps this was what it meant to be in love, she had thought, allowing Roger to draw her down onto the chaise. He rose above her on one arm and grasped her hand, pressing it to his erection, begging her to squeeze, harder, thrusting himself against her palm...

For the past year, Camille had tried to bury the shameful memory, but today she let every degrading moment of it play out in her mind.

"Roger, I am glad to be able to say this." It was very hard to look directly at him, or to find her voice, but she knew she must. "I regret what happened between us in the cottage."

He looked genuinely shocked. "Really, my dear, you need not speak of that—interlude. I implore you to lock the memory away, as I have. I assure you, I think of you today as the same innocent girl you have always been."

"If I am no longer innocent, it was your doing," she said, her voice shaking only slightly. "You forced your-self on me—"

"I did no such thing!" came his offended reply. "Per-haps you have forgotten that we were fully clothed."

"I remember every detail clearly. I also recall how amorous your attentions became toward me...when we were alone. If I had been more astute, I would have re-alized that you never declared yourself to my parents. Privately, however, you led me to believe you were falling in love with me!"

Shaking his head, Upton broke in again. "I beg your pardon, but you were mistaken. I never spoke the word *love.*"

Perhaps the scene in the cottage wouldn't now feel sordid if it had all ended differently. If Roger had meant any of the romantic words he had spoken. Instead, after achieving his own release, he became distant as they left

Lupine Cottage and walked back to Elysium. Camille's throat ached now as she remembered how Roger had told her parents that, regrettably, he would return to London on the morrow. *My betrothal to Lady Barbara Framstead will be announced...it's been on Father's calendar since we were babes...*He bade Camille goodbye in the presence of her parents, kindly thanking her for their nature walks, wishing her all the best in the future, leaving her feeling confused, betrayed, ashamed, heartbroken.

"I must admit, I blame myself," Roger was saying now. "I was carried away by your great beauty, you see, and your charm. Never have I known a girl like you, Camille."

She blinked. "How can you talk this way?"

Roger seemed not to hear her. "You see, I couldn't do it, couldn't marry Lady Barbara." He inched closer to her. "It crushed my parents, but since the moment I left here, I have been haunted by thoughts of you. My dear, tell me that you feel the same."

* * *

"SHE'S GONE for a stroll with Lord Upton." Pointing through the conservatory window, Gabriel St. Briac added, "They became friends when he visited Cornwall last year. I think Camille taught him a bit about birds and nature."

Benedict pressed, "Friends, only, then?"

"I couldn't say precisely. Camille has a very independent spirit. She was of age, and Upton seemed a good sort." He shrugged slightly. "Before departing, he said he was about to be betrothed, so my wife and I assumed his intentions toward Camille had been strictly platonic."

"I see." Benedict felt a muscle move in his jaw but

managed to smile. "Well, your daughter and I agreed to meet today and discuss what we learned at the party. If you don't mind, I'll go and join them."

"I'm happy for you to do so." Gabriel reached for his trowel, adding, "Upton asked to speak to Camille alone about something, and of course she is her own mistress." His brows flicked upward.

"I take your meaning, sir."

Heading off on the narrow path, Benedict listened for voices. He passed the various glass cold frames, open to the summer morning, and an occasional gardener working in one of the vegetable plots. Just as he was about to circle back, he heard Upton's cultured voice.

"Tell me that you feel the same."

A strange feeling coursed through Benedict's body, something akin to blind aggression. *Bloody hell.* He came up behind a half-dozen fig trees and, through the pattern of their leaves, he saw Camille sitting on a bench with Upton. What the devil was going on?

"Roger," he heard her say, "I must tell you that I do not share those feelings."

His brain focused on her use Upton's Christian name: *Roger.* It felt like a blow. There had been something between them, curse it, in spite of Upton's planned betrothal to Lady Barbara, and now he was trying to rekindle Camille's affections. Benedict wanted to challenge the cur to a duel. Dimly, he was aware that he had no right to claim her, but in that moment, it didn't matter.

He came out into the open and started toward the bench that was intimately tucked under an arch of clipped boxwood. "Ah, there you are, my dear," he said. Camille looked up, surprise and relief mingling in her eyes. Reaching the bench, Benedict drew her to her feet. "I confess, I could not wait another moment to see you."

A radiant smile lit her face. "You are very bold, sir."

"You have that effect on me," he replied in a husky voice.

Looking on in disbelief, Upton cleared his throat and stood. "I beg your pardon." He frowned, pretending to forget Benedict's name. "Is it—Hawke?"

"That is correct." He rested a proprietary hand at the small of Camille's back. "It was good of you to help Camille pass the time, but now I have arrived, and you are free to go." Pausing for a beat, he added coolly, "your *lordship*."

To his delight, Camille interceded, leaning closer to him. She gave Upton a polite nod and said, "Yes, Benedict is right. You mustn't give up another moment of your day, lingering here with us."

"I see." Upton frowned. "Am I to understand that you two are...*courting*?"

"That's one word for it," Benedict replied with a faint smile.

Camille looked up at him, as if they were sharing a secret, before turning back to Upton. "Goodbye, my lord."

The man had no choice but to take his leave. When they were alone, Benedict drew Camille back down next to him on the bench.

"What the devil was that all about?"

"If I didn't know better, I might think you were jealous."

He was not prepared to admit, even to himself, the truth of that. "I knew Upton at Oxford. I don't like him."

"What did he do to you?" Her gaze was fixed on him.

Benedict gave his head a negligent shake. "Just a lot

of small things, designed to put me in my place." Turning, he let his eyes burn into hers. "What I want to know, is what he did to *you*."

Camille stared, a flash of panic in her wide eyes, and then heat stained her cheeks. His gut hurt.

"He pretended to court me, and I was momentarily taken in, but that was long ago. In this moment, I don't give a fig for Lord Upton!" The shadow had passed, and now her tone was bright. "Let us speak of other things. I have so much to tell you!"

She leaned closer and he breathed in a fragrance of summer flowers. Suddenly all Benedict wanted to do was kiss her mouth, her neck, unfasten the bodice of her gown, caress her bare skin, taste every inch of her. *Possess* her.

"Tell me, then," he managed at last. His voice was hoarse.

"I had a very enlightening conversation with Grandmère after you left yesterday!"

This was not what he was expecting. "You want to talk about your grandmother?"

"Have you forgotten about her terrible headdress with the kittiwake wings?"

"No, but—what about Upton?"

"I have put that man from my mind, and I beg you to do the same!" Camille took his hands, her enthusiasm palpable. "Grandmère told me about Lady Daphne Leyton, the erstwhile milliner who created that monstrosity." In a rush, she told him all she had learned from not only her grandmother, but also her uncle and aunt. "It seems she lives in a manor house near the village of Lerryn. I thought I might enlist Rafael to come with me to visit her! I shall take an assumed name and dress the part, so she won't be able to track me down later." She was glowing, her hands warm in his. "I shall tell Lady Daphne that I saw Madame St. Briac's magnificent kittiwake headdress at a party, then I will beg her to create one for me, and I will offer her an extravagant sum of money."

"I see." He arched a brow. "Where will you get the funds?"

"Oh, I won't really *pay* her." She shook her head, laughing, and one long curl came loose from its pin. "I just want to lure her into my trap!"

Benedict imagined that this was how Camille must have been while planning to abduct him and hold him captive at Lupine Cottage. Ravishing, irresistible, passionate. A feeling surged over him, deeper than desire, verging on pain.

"Forget about Rafael," he ground out. "I will go with you, or you won't go at all."

Camille threw her arms around his neck, then drew back to gaze boldly into his eyes. "Do you imagine you can dominate me?"

He was lost. Their mouths met, joining in a feverish kiss that took his breath away. Her tongue was eager, meeting his stroke for stroke, and Benedict heard her whimper in a way that made him want to take her right there in the sunlit garden. Her hands pushed into his thick hair, he kissed his way over to her ear, and she gasped with surprise and pleasure.

In the next moment, he lightly caressed her breast and she pressed closer, giving a little moan. Even through the cotton fabric of her gown and chemise, he felt the firm, warm fullness of her, and wanted more. Wanted all of her, and yet he couldn't ignore the undercurrent in her passion.

"You are killing me," he muttered, trying to draw back.

She glanced down at the evidence of his need and caught her lip between her teeth. "I'm sorry."

"Don't be." Leaning forward, he kissed her once, and

their lips clung. "But this is dangerous, for more reasons than one. We're in your family's garden, for God's sake."

"Oh, yes." Her eyes were heavy with longing, all the more enticing because it was clearly new to her. "That is true."

Benedict shifted away from her, and in that moment, he glimpsed the distraction in Camille's eyes. Again, he wondered what had really happened between her and Upton. Why did she adamantly refuse to talk about it? It came to him that her passion had a slightly desperate edge to it, as if she hoped to extinguish other feelings, memories…

"Hello, did you hear me?" Camille put a hand on his coat sleeve, and he realized she had been speaking. "When shall we go on our adventure to meet Lady Daphne?"

"The sooner the better. I can't keep Jem and his crew waiting much longer." Resisting the urge to touch her again, Benedict added, "Shall we travel to Callywith Manor in my gig?"

"I was planning to row up the River Fowey," Camille replied. "Uncle Sebastian keeps a small boat that I often borrow. It will be a wonderful outing!"

"All right. Two days hence?"

"Excellent!" She clapped her hands. "I will meet you at the swan's nest, near the footbridge crossing Pont Pill. Nearby is the small shed where Sebastian and Julia keep their boat."

Aware that he was venturing into risky territory, Benedict nodded. "Nine o'clock."

CHAPTER 21

The path leading down to Pont Pill was enclosed on all sides by a lush blend of trees and greenery sprinkled with bluebells, pink foxgloves, and golden saxifrage. Delicate spider webs glimmered in the sunbeams, and on this warm morning, Camille breathed in the damp scent of growing plants. Best of all, birds fluttered all around, gathering seeds and pecking for insects. When she spied a plump English robin peeping out at her from a blackthorn bush, Camille paused.

"Oh, look at you, sir," she said warmly. "How handsome you are."

The tiny bird seemed to puff out his russet-hued breast in reply. A moment later, he disappeared back among the white blossoms, and she continued on her way.

Nearing the banks of the tidal creek, she paused before a humble farmhouse and its adjacent lime kiln. Just around the corner, Camille would see her Uncle Sebastian's little boat tied up among a tangle of low-hanging branches.

Was Benedict already there, waiting for her? Her

breath hitched at the thought of him, the kisses they had recklessly shared in the garden at Elysium…and the questions he asked about Roger.

If only Roger hadn't come back to Cornwall! Why couldn't he stay away and leave her alone? As shame and anger mingled anew inside her, Camille blinked against the sting of tears and renewed her vow to never speak of that terrible day again. Somehow, she would find a way to bury it forever.

With that, Camille straightened her shoulders and started off again, turning south at the little footbridge. She had only gone a short distance when she glimpsed a tall, dark-haired male figure on the bank of the creek. *Benedict.* As she watched, he removed his coat and slung it over a tree branch, then lightly crouched at the edge of the water to watch a swan glide by, two petite cygnets paddling in her wake. His shoulders were wide, his tapering back well-muscled under the fine linen of his shirt, and the sun shone on his tousled black curls.

The moment Benedict sensed her presence and glanced up, shading his eyes against the sun, desire washed over Camille in a warm, effervescent wave. Roger had nearly killed that part of her, but Benedict had brought about a reawakening. She drew a breath, uncertain whether to be grateful or terrified, to open herself to it or hide away.

"Ah, there you are," he said, and rose effortlessly to his full height.

"Am I late?" Camille hesitated, remembering how she had thrown herself at him on the garden bench in a desperate effort to blot Roger from her mind.

"Not a bit. In fact, I may be early. I have come from a visit to Trevarre Hall." Benedict pointed up the path on the other side of Pont Pill, to the estate of her uncle and aunt. Picking up the handsome midnight-blue coat, he approached her. "When I spoke with your Aunt Julia at the party, she kindly offered to oversee the remainder of Lazarus's recovery. I took him there earlier this morning."

The mention of Julia caused her to relax. "Oh, lovely! Isn't she wonderful?"

"She is an impressive naturalist in her own right," he agreed, smiling. "I'm looking forward to talking more with her about the habits of the many birds she has watched and rescued in these woods."

"Since she was a small child, Aunt Julia has kept notebooks with all her observations and sketches of birds, animals, plants, rocks, insects, even shells and fish."

"Ah, has she?" A moment of silence passed, then he revealed, "I too began keeping notebooks when I was young."

"I'm so glad you have become better acquainted with Julia." Impulsively, she put a hand on his arm. "She will take excellent care of Lazarus."

Benedict nodded and glanced back toward the small boathouse. "I suppose, if we are truly going to Callywith Manor, we should make a start," he said. "Your Uncle Sebastian invited me to use their rowboat, and Julia sent a hamper of food for us." A glint of mischief in his eyes, he added, "She insisted you would be glad for it."

"Perhaps you have noticed, I have a rather prodigious appetite," Camille said cheerfully. "Let us go now and see the rowboat."

Flowering vines known as "traveler's joy" clung to the trees and Benedict pushed them aside as they made their way along the water's edge. Just ahead was the picturesque rubble-slate boathouse that featured in many of Camille's favorite childhood memories. She felt a frisson of anticipation for the adventure that lay ahead of them. Would this be the day when they would discover a clue that would lead them to the feather thieves' leader?

The doors to the boathouse creaked in protest when Benedict pried them open. Inside waited the rowboat, brightened with a fresh coat of periwinkle-blue paint. When he had dragged it partway into the water and set the hamper inside, he held out a tanned, strong hand to her and arched a brow.

"Are you ready to sail away with me, my lady?"

Was she imagining the note of seduction in his voice? Camille, who was not the sort of female who swooned, could have done so at that moment.

"Yes, please." She couldn't suppress a wide smile.

They both surveyed the space between Camille and the stern of the boat. If only she could have worn breeches today! It would have been so much easier to clamber over the twisted tree roots and into the boat. She had just lifted her skirts when Benedict stepped forward.

"Allow me." With one smooth movement, he caught her up in his strong arms and carried her to the rowboat.

When she was seated on the forward bench, she beamed at him. "Thank you, sir."

Benedict handed her his coat, then climbed into the stern and used one oar to push off from the bank. Sitting opposite her, he began to row them out into the wide, calm tidal creek. Camille watched the play of muscles under his snowy shirt as he pulled on the oars, a few black locks of hair falling over his brow. Never had she experienced these feelings about another man, not even Roger during the time when she thought she might be falling in love with him. Now it was clear that she had been deluded, for those fitful responses were nothing like this.

Just then, Benedict looked up and met her dreamy gaze. He seemed to look directly into her thoughts.

"I think you may like me after all," he said, eyes agleam.

"I do like you…at times," she allowed. Longing to take the attention off herself, Camille added, "I find you rather a puzzle, however. Just as I think I've found a piece that fits, it disappears."

"Have you ever considered the notion that some puzzles are better left unsolved?"

"I have not," she replied firmly. "Never."

He looked out at the water that sparkled in the sun. There were small boats at anchor near the place where Pont Pill met the River Fowey, and now they had a clear view of the ancient town of Fowey on the opposite bank of the river.

"I never realized how beautiful, even enchanted, this place is," he said, almost to himself. "I was oblivious."

"You're doing it again," she accused.

"What do you mean?" He was watching a kingfisher dive into the water, its wings a blur of turquoise.

"You're withholding the pieces from me."

Their eyes met, and for a long minute, the only sound was the splash and whoosh of the oars moving in and out of the water. Camille saw a muscle flex in his jaw before he finally spoke again. "I've been thinking about my nephew, Gareth, who will soon be four years old."

She nodded. "Oh, yes, I saw him with his mother outside Gull Cottage." How long ago that day now seemed!

"I stopped at Prue's on my way back from Frenchman's Haven. Gareth was begging my sister for a birthday party. She told him it isn't possible because her confinement is at hand, and soon he will have a new brother or sister." He closed his eyes for a moment. "In truth, no one has time for Gareth these days. He even lost his miserable little room when Prue brought our father there to live, after his stroke."

The very mention of Josiah Hawke caused Benedict's face to harden. She thought of how he had come to Polruan to assist with his father, yet it seemed Benedict rarely left Gull Cottage. True, he was writing a book, but it seemed another piece of the puzzle was missing.

"Perhaps you might organize something?" she said hesitantly.

Benedict stared. "Impossible."

"It sounds as if your sister's house could use a bit of joy…"

It was as if a black cloud had suddenly descended from the clear, azure sky to hover over Benedict. Frowning, he pulled harder on the oars. "You have no idea. My father…"

He stopped speaking, yet Camille sensed an opening. "Papa has told me that Mr. Hawke was a gardener, first at Windsor Great Park, and then at Tremethyck. Is that true?"

Benedict nodded. "It should have been an idyllic life for a boy like me…and I suppose it was, for a time. Pa let me follow him around all day when I was small. He taught me all about nature, plants, animals, birds, and I soaked it up like a sponge."

Camille nodded. "I had a rather similar experience at Elysium with my own father."

"The two men couldn't be more different," he said shortly. For one long minute, there was only the swoosh of the rowboat sweeping through the water, and then Benedict spoke again. "As I grew older, I began to read. I wanted to understand the science of what I was learning. We moved from Windsor to Tremethyck Park, where Lady Far loaned me books by François Daudin, Carl Linnaeus, Alexander von Humboldt—"

"Oh, yes!" Camille broke in. "Papa keeps those books in our library, and so many more!"

He nodded. "I now have my own volumes. They go with me everywhere, in a special trunk."

The notion that they loved many of the same books made her glow inside. Yet, although his life sounded quite wonderful, the shadow continued to hover over Benedict. Gently, she inquired, "Your father didn't approve of the books?"

"When I tried to talk to Pa about all I was learning, he grew enraged." His shoulders broadened as he pulled at the oars, bringing their boat closer to the Fowey Estuary. "He accused me of putting on airs and graces, getting a lot of fancy ideas above my station. It all came to a head when Lady Far made it possible for me to go away to good schools, and then to Oxford. In Pa's mind, it was worse than if I'd committed murder. He delighted in—" As if realizing that the floodgates were opening, Benedict suddenly broke off.

Camille ached to know what he was going to say. "Please, do go on."

"No, never mind. You have a loving, supportive family. A golden life, really." His handsome face had shuttered. "You couldn't possibly understand my situation."

Outrage surged through her body. "What a thing to say!" She wanted to come out of her seat, but that might cause the boat to capsize. "I certainly *do* understand what happens when one has the courage to rebel against expectations. People don't like it! Since I was a child, I haven't fit in, and as a female I encountered resistance from nearly everyone I met. My own grandmother strongly disapproved of all my interests. Grandmère was always prosing on about the great *gift* of my beauty and how I must embrace it and allow it to carry me to great heights. She still reminds me that I can marry very well and have a life other females would only dream of."

"Lord Upton, I presume," he said in a hard voice.

"Oh, no, he isn't good enough for Grandmère! She cannot understand why I don't go to London and endeavor to capture a marquess or even a duke!"

At last, Benedict slowed the cadence of his rowing. He studied her, as if seeing her in a new light. One he understood. "What stopped you from doing that?"

"You of all people know the answer to that. I have a passion for nature, and especially for birds. It is my calling." Camille couldn't help the throb of emotion in her voice. "My gift. And fortunately, my own parents have accepted it, though I know they worry. I suppose it's much easier when a child conforms."

"That's true." He leaned forward, holding her gaze. "That was the situation for my mother. When I insisted on a path different from the one Pa had set for me, her existence became more difficult as well."

"And yet you persevered," she said, tears threatening. Once again, she wanted to go into his arms, but for new reasons.

"We only have one life, don't we? Every moment matters."

"Exactly."

Even as Camille felt a throb of connection to Benedict, she remembered his plan to join John Gould on an expedition to Australia, in search of new and rare birds. He'd been forced to abandon it to come to his sister's aid, but surely he had not given up.

"Look, here is our turning," she said, pointing to the place where Lerryn Creek flowed into the estuary.

Ancient oak woodlands lined the banks of the creek, and as they continued on, Camille and Benedict took turns pointing out egrets, wagtails, cormorants, and even an otter. They rowed past the fine boathouse and quay at Ethy rock and approached the village of Lerryn. The creek narrowed until Camille held up her hand.

"I think that is the place." She pointed toward a small beach boasting a new quay, the name Callywith carved into the stone. A worn path led into the trees, and in the distance the shape of a manor house was visible.

After they disembarked on the shore and Benedict tied up the boat, he shrugged into his coat and looked at her.

"Is my cravat straight?" He leaned over to open the hamper that was stowed in the bow of the rowboat and withdrew a fine beaver hat. "You may be surprised to know I own a proper hat. It's an Aylesbury. Height of fashion."

He donned the hat, and Camille thought that it made him look even more handsome. "Now your rather distinctive black hair is hidden, all the better to conceal your true identity." Smiling, she reached up to smooth the edges of his cravat. "What about me? Am I terribly disheveled?"

"Do you want the truth?"

Camille felt herself grow pale. She swept a look over her fashionable morning gown of cream muslin with a trailing floral print in raspberry and green. It did not appear to be torn or stained. Her caramel tresses were drawn back under a fetching bonnet with a large brim that tilted up to frame her face in a way she had hoped was flattering.

"Of course you must be honest," she said, biting her lip. "This entire outing depends on us fooling Lady

Daphne into thinking we are a prosperous married couple."

He bit back a smile. "The truth is…you look ravishing, minx."

"Oh…thank you!" Was it her imagination, or had his gaze lingered on her bodice? Her nipples tingled.

"Shall we go, Mrs. Andrews?" Using the name that had chosen for their masquerade, Benedict offered his arm.

Pulse quickening, she tucked her hand into the crook of his elbow, and wondered for an instant what it would be like to be the wife of this splendid, complicated man. Together, they started up the stone steps leading toward the distant manor house. Just as they were about to enter the canopy of trees, Benedict glanced up at the sky. Fast moving soot-gray clouds scudded across the sun, and the breeze sharpened.

"I hope it isn't going to rain," he murmured.

Camille scarcely heard him, for just then she glimpsed a tall, lanky man striding toward them down the path. He looked rather ill-at-ease in his fancy bottle-green livery.

"Do ye be lost?" the man shouted, looking them over.

Benedict smiled jauntily and started toward him. "Good morning! I am Sir Reginald Andrews, and this is my wife, Dame Helen. She begged me to bring her here to speak to Squire Callywith's wife, Lady Daphne, on a matter of some personal urgency. Will you please tell her ladyship that we are here?"

Clearly unimpressed, the servant shook his big head and said, "No visitors be expected."

Camille began to feel uneasy. Had they come all this way for nothing? "Sir, I beg you to convey our regards to her ladyship. You might tell her that Madame Cerise St. Briac has recommended her to us."

He scowled. "Wait here."

When they were alone again, Benedict turned to her, the corners of his mouth quirking upward. "You are very bold. What do you suppose Lady Daphne will think you meant by 'recommended'?"

"I hope she will be curious enough to come out and speak to us!"

In the distance, Camille surveyed the rather grand manor house and recalled her Aunt Mouette saying that Lady Daphne had compelled her husband to move here from a modest ancestral estate near Fowey. Where had they gotten the means for such a purchase?

Just then, the front door opened, and the liveried servant reemerged. "I'll ask you to follow me," he said in more respectful tones, leading them around the side of the house. "Kindly wait here in the garden, if you please."

They found themselves standing beside a fountain that overlooked elegant flowerbeds and paths of crushed golden limestone, still being created in that moment by a dozen gardeners. Jewel-toned peacocks skittered about on the lawns, occasionally flaunting their tail feathers.

When the servant had gone away again, Camille glanced up at Benedict. "It's not what I was expecting at all...so very grand for Cornwall."

He was staring at the workmen, pensive, but before he could speak, a door opened at the back of the house and a rather fragile-looking, middle-aged woman with faded gold hair appeared. Camille's gaze was immediately drawn to her simple but striking headdress that featured the feathers of a magnificent white egret.

"Hello." Walking toward them, the woman's full profile came into view as she extended a pale, gloved hand. "I am Lady Daphne Leyton. I do not recall inviting anyone to visit today. Can it be true that my dear Cerise St. Briac has sent you to me?"

Camille tried not to stare, but it was difficult to contain her surprise. Grandmère had said that Lady Daphne had been unable to conceive for many years, yet this woman was great with child—seemingly mere weeks away from giving birth!

CHAPTER 22

Lady Daphne wore a gown of pale-yellow silk with fashionable gigot sleeves, but where the waistline should have tapered in, the gown billowed out over her large belly. She seemed to emphasize its size by resting a hand on the highest curve.

After introductions were completed, their hostess inclined her head. "Are you surprised to see that I am *enceinte*, Sir Reginald and Dame Helen?" As Lady Daphne spoke, Camille noticed the many fine wrinkles that radiated out from the corners of her eyes. The woman appeared to be at least five-and-forty. "Indeed, it is so. Of course, I have avoided mingling in society for many months, but today there is no choice because you have arrived here uninvited." She smiled suddenly. "Not that I mind very much. In truth, my life has grown terribly dull."

The door opened again, and a liveried footman wheeled out a small cart laden with covered dishes and a tea service. In his wake an invalid chair appeared, one wheel squeaking as it rolled along, pushed by the same tall, unfriendly servant who had greeted them earlier. The chair's occupant was a rotund, balding gentleman of perhaps eight decades.

"I am Callywith!" the old man proclaimed loudly, waving a fist.

Lady Daphne looked momentarily embarrassed, but quickly recovered and hurried to his side. "Indeed you are, my darling." After introductions were performed, she poured tea for her husband. "Why not allow Herridge to take you round the grounds, to inspect the work of the gardeners?" She paused. "You have such an excellent eye for spotting their mistakes."

Squire Callywith thrust out his lower lip. "I do, don't I?"

Watching the servant called Herridge push the squire away in the invalid chair, Camille glanced back at Lady Daphne. Of course, she had no personal experience with the marriage bed, but she wondered all the same how Squire Callywith had managed to get his wife with child at this late date.

Once tea was served, Lady Daphne made no move to take a seat on one of the nearby benches. Instead, she continued to stand, leaning against a low garden wall. This was apparently a signal that their interview with her must be very brief.

"I know you must be eager to be on your way," their hostess said, "and as you may imagine, my ability to socialize is limited by my delicate condition. Tell me now, what brings you here?"

Benedict wasted no time getting to the point. "We recently attended a small party near Polperro, and Madame Cerise St. Briac was also a guest," he said. "She was wearing a very striking headdress that featured the wings of a kittiwake."

Lady Daphne inclined her head. "A *what?*" She drew the second word out in apparent confusion.

"A kittiwake," he said patiently. "It is a kind of gull that breeds along the Cornwall cliffs. My wife is quite taken with their wings. They are pure white, but the tips look as if they've been dipped in black ink." Pausing, he drew a breath. "Quite striking."

Camille spoke up in a tremulous voice. "I vow, when I saw Madame St. Briac's headdress, I told my husband that I must have one for myself!"

He patted her hand. "Fear not, my love. I mean to make your dream come true." Turning back to Lady Daphne, he said, "We understand that you have retired from the millinery trade. No doubt you have no need for it any longer, but I must implore you to create one more unique hat for my beloved bride." Benedict leaned forward slightly and added in an undertone, "Price is no object, my lady."

Lady Daphne blinked her green eyes, and Camille could see that she was clearly tempted. However, she murmured, "It is impossible. As you can see, I am otherwise engaged."

"Would it be so great a burden to create just one more hat?" He rubbed his brow, as if searching for another path forward. "Ah. But perhaps you do not have access to kittiwake wings. If you direct me, perhaps I could be of assistance?"

Camille spoke up then. "I have heard that there are even feather sellers, called...*plumassiers*, in London!" Feigning uncertainty, she stumbled over the French word. "I wonder where they get their exotic feathers?"

"Bah! Are you not aware that birds shed their feathers all the time?" Lady Daphne gestured toward the peacocks. "They simply drop off, just as hairs are lost from our heads."

Benedict leaned forward, eyes wide, as if he had just learned something fascinating. "I had not considered that. So, people gather stray feathers from the ground and supply them to milliners and *plumassiers*!"

Their hostess nodded briskly. "That's right. At least, that is what I have always understood." Lady Daphne set down her teacup. "I fear I must bid you goodbye, for I am fatigued and must go inside for a rest." She touched her belly to underscore her point. "I am sorry I could not help you in your quest."

"If you should change your mind—" Benedict began.

Lady Daphne cut him off with one raised hand. "I can assure you, I will not do so! I may have been celebrated for my creative gifts, but my life has changed drastically since the days when I made hats." She gave a little shake of her head. "In fact, I have chosen another path entirely."

* * *

"THAT WOMAN!" Camille burst out as soon as he handed her back into their little boat. "I couldn't believe my ears when she began claiming that feathers for hats are simply gathered where birds drop them on the ground!" She gave her head an angry shake. "Of course, she is not the first milliner to utter that lie."

Benedict pushed the boat off from the quay and stepped in at the last moment. "You concealed your outrage well, minx." Taking up his oars, he sat down on the bench.

"Indeed! It took all my powers of self-control not to ask Lady Daphne if she also found her kittiwake wings scattered about on the ground!"

He bit back a laugh. "I confess that until today, I wasn't aware that you possessed powers of self-control."

"I'm in too much of a temper to bear your teasing," she retorted.

Benedict watched as her inner glow intensified. *So beautiful.* "I'll bear that in mind, Dame Helen."

Camille was leaning forward, rummaging inside the hamper of food. "All that drama has made me ravenous!" She brought out fresh-baked loaf of brown bread and a thick slice of cheese. "I love to eat, you know."

"So you have mentioned," he replied dryly, leaning forward to accept the bites of bread with cheese tucked inside it that she proffered.

"Oh, look! Blackberries!" Camille beamed as she put two of the juicy berries in her mouth, then fed two more to him. "Delicious!"

Lerryn Creek widened as Benedict rowed back toward the River Fowey. Glancing up again at the sky, Benedict realized the clouds had darkened further and the air felt heavy. Could they possibly make it back to Pont Pill before the rain began?

"As strange as our meeting with Lady Daphne was, I have to admit I enjoyed pretending to be someone else," Camille said. "I thought you also did rather well, Sir Reginald!"

He sent her an appreciative grin. "I suppose it was worth it to go and see her, though it seems we can rule her out as the leader of the feather thieves."

"She doesn't seem to be in any condition to even leave her garden," Camille agreed.

"Meanwhile, take a look at the sky. We must decide on a course of action if the rain comes."

"Are you afraid of a few raindrops?" she challenged. "I have tramped through these woods in all sorts of weather."

"Were you wearing a fancy gown and bonnet?" Benedict arched a brow at her. "In any event, it is different to be caught in a storm on the water, especially in so small a boat. Once we are out on the open river, it could be treacherous." Even as he spoke, the wind picked up, and their rowboat began to bob.

Camille stopped chewing and looked around. "I hadn't thought of that."

"I think we should look for shelter. Do you know anyone else who lives along this stretch of the creek?"

"Only Viscount Senwyck. But we have already passed the turning for his estate, Lanwyllow. It is a distance up the tributary, beyond Ethy Rock." As she spoke, she replaced the food in the hamper.

Just then, raindrops began to spit from the leaden sky. "There isn't time to go back, and the tide would be against us." Benedict raised his voice above the roughening wind. "But look, there is a small beach just ahead. I will tie up there and we can at least take shelter in the woods until the storm has passed."

Moments before they reached the shore, the burgeoning clouds burst open, and the rain fell thicker and faster by the second. Benedict rowed them onto the tiny spit of sand, jumped out, and reached in to grasp Camille around her small waist. Of course, she leaned away, resisting this sort of male assistance, but Benedict easily lifted her onto the ground. Her bonnet was dripping, her face was wet, and her ruined gown clung to her body in ways that stirred every male fiber of his being.

Silently, Benedict warned his cock, *Stay where you are*, but as always it rebelled. Turning away from Camille, he tied the rowboat to a stubby tree and hoped it would still be there when the storm passed. Almost as an afterthought, he brought the hamper out as well.

"Come on." Carrying the hamper, he led the way until they found an opening in the trees.

"I feel as if I know this place," she said as they came upon a narrow path. "Long ago, I once spent an entire day exploring these woods. There may be shelter for us..."

Benedict let her go ahead. The rain was pouring down, and he pinned the hamper under one arm so he could use his other hand to push wet hair back from his face. The wind and rain made the summer day feel chilly, causing him to shiver under his sodden clothing.

"Oh, excellent! My memory did not fail me," cried Camille. She turned back suddenly, her face alight, and pointed. "In that little glade just ahead, there is an old summerhouse. We can wait inside until the storm has passed!"

He peered through the rain-lashed trees and saw a small, rustic dwelling with double doors. It seemed that it must be a mirage, but Camille was hurrying toward it, gesturing for him to follow.

* * *

THROWING open one of the doors to the little summerhouse, Camille ran for cover, chased inside by the rain. As her gown dripped water onto the wide floorboards, she turned back and reached out to take the hamper from Benedict. A moment later, he was standing beside her.

Camille set the hamper down as Benedict reached for her hand. Wild sounds of raindrops and wind battering the roof filled the space around them. For one long minute, they simply stood close together and watched the storm outside.

"It's rather stirring, isn't it?" she murmured.

Benedict made no reply but turned to look at her. Camille drank in the sight of him. Shadows played over his lean, broad-shouldered physique, accentuated by wet clothing, his damp, disheveled curls, and the chiseled contours of his face. As their eyes met, a familiar thrill raced through her.

"Where the devil are we?" he wondered aloud.

They both turned to survey their surroundings. One side of the room contained a few mismatched chairs and a small table covered by a floral-patterned cloth. The far wall was dominated by a low, simple bed with a feather tick, a bright, worn quilt tossed to one side.

"I came upon this summerhouse during the long walk I told you about," Camille said. "It's part of our friend Tristan's vast estate, Lanwyllow. I suspect that he and his wife, Sarah, have used this as a..." She felt herself blushing. "A trysting place, especially when their children were young. When I mentioned to them that I had come upon this place, they exchanged what I could only describe as a secret smile."

"Ah. Good for them," Benedict said, watching her. "I suppose it would be a fine place for a tryst on a different sort of day."

"I love it! Truly, I think it may be enchanted." Even as she spoke, Camille felt herself begin to shiver in her sodden clothing. She untied her bonnet and set it, dripping, on the floor. Silently, they removed their shoes.

"You should get out of those wet things before you grow chilled," he said, his neutral tone belied by the words he spoke. "Perhaps you could wrap yourself in that quilt?"

"And what about you?" she asked. Although her own voice was even, inside her heart had begun to pound again. They were stranded, completely alone, and now Benedict was suggesting that she take off her clothes! Forbidden thoughts began to race through her mind.

"Perhaps I might wear the tablecloth." His smile flashed white in the shadows. "Do you suppose there is enough of it to fashion a toga?"

Her face grew warm. "I don't know, but we might try." She licked her dry lips and dared to ask, "Will you help me undress? It's difficult enough to get out of these dratted gowns, even with the help of a maid, but a wet garment is nearly impossible."

"Impossible?" His husky voice fanned the flame of desire inside her. "Not for me."

Moving to stand close behind her, he began to unfasten the tiny buttons that marched down the back of her gown. Each touch of his fingers along her spine sent a throb of desire to her intimate places. When the buttons were all undone, Benedict quietly lifted the garment over her head.

Camille stood there, heart racing, in her chemise and corset. Oh God, had she lost her mind, inviting him to strip her naked? It was outrageous! Yet an inner voice whispered, *You want this*. Yes, she did, quite desperately.

His fingertips brushed her naked back and heat blossomed between her legs.

"Camille..." he whispered, and she heard the hitch in his voice. "Do you—"

"Yes. Yes, I do." She wanted to beg, *Please don't stop*.

She turned around to face him. His eyes darkened as they met hers, thrillingly. It came to Camille that everything about this moment was different from the haunting episode with Roger. Since she intended never to marry, this might be her only chance to make a new and wonderful memory; one that could last a lifetime.

Even the corset was damp, her breasts swelling above it. The garment laced up the back, but there were three little ties in front that held it in place. Camille reached for Benedict's tanned, masculine hands and pressed them to her breasts. Her nipples were hard peaks, chilly and aroused all at once. Benedict molded his hands to her, squeezing just enough to drive her mad with a need she didn't fully comprehend.

"You are..." he began hoarsely.

"Say anything you like, but do not tell me I am beautiful," she warned in a low voice. "I have heard that from all the wrong men."

Suddenly, his control seemed to snap, and he took her in his arms. "I am not like them."

Her eyes stung. "I know that."

Benedict seemed to recognize what she needed, how she felt, and he drew back just enough to find the ties at the front of her corset. He undid them and soon he had tossed the thing to one side. His gaze seemed to burn through the thin batiste of her chemise, and her nipples grew taut, aching.

"Camille, I am human. If you don't stop me, I'm going to finish undressing you and take you to bed," he warned. The outline of his impressive erection was clearly visible through the wet fabric of his trousers, and she found it shocking, tantalizing, arousing.

"I will not stop you," she assured him, lifting her chin. "On the contrary. Neither one of us wants the constraints of marriage. Yet, as a man, you are free to lie with anyone you please. I cannot enjoy such liberty." She glanced around just as a golden sunbeam broke through the rain and illuminated the secluded summerhouse. "I have thought about this. Don't you see, this is my chance. Perhaps my only chance, ever. And it's you I want."

"You've *thought* about it...but—" He arched a dubious brow, so sinfully handsome her heart skipped a beat.

"You needn't worry that I've fallen in love with you and, when this is over, you'll have broken my heart. I-I'm not that sort of female." Even as she spoke, Camille knew it was a lie. Her feelings for Benedict were powerful, even uncontrollable. Could it truly be love?

She stepped closer to him and reached for the lapels of his midnight-blue coat. "Please."

* * *

BENEDICT STARED down at Camille and wondered again if he might be dreaming. All the signs were certainly there…The summerhouse, appearing like an apparition in a wild rainstorm. This woman, unspeakably beautiful and yet so, so much more. Fiercely independent, brave, intelligent, and she was practically demanding that he make love to her.

Through her gossamer-thin chemise, he saw the curves of her body, inviting his touch. When Camille tugged again at his wet coat, he began to strip off his clothing. First the frock coat, then his intricately tied cravat, then the waistcoat and the linen shirt that clung to his torso. One by one, he tossed them over chairbacks along with the rest of their discarded garments. Standing there in only his damp trousers, Benedict was glad for the summer afternoon. It might be storming, but inside the air felt sultry, almost warm, and their bodies grew drier by the minute.

"You are a very splendid looking man," murmured Camille. Her gaze turned dreamy in a way that only heightened his arousal.

"I thought comments like that were not allowed." He lightly touched her shoulders and slid his hands down her bare arms. "Or are your rules one-sided?"

She gave a low laugh. "You know me too well."

"Yes." He brought her against him, his hard cock pressing against her belly. "I do."

"I want to be brazen," Camille confessed, molding herself to him.

"My God," he groaned.

Benedict bent to cover her waiting mouth with his, and they kissed with mutual urgency.

At length, he scooped her up into his arms. They

were still kissing as he carried her to the bed and lay her down on the clean feather tick.

Looking down at Camille, her hair spilling across the pillow, Benedict knew a surge of lust mingled with tenderness. A voice in the back of his mind urged caution, but when she stretched up her arms to him, he was lost.

CHAPTER 23

Camille's chemise was all that separated her body from a man so magnificent he scarcely seemed real. As he braced himself inches above her, he reached for the hem, and she held her breath to keep from gasping aloud.

But then, to her surprise, his rough cheek brushed hers and he murmured, "Do you remember that night when you abducted me and tied me to a chair?"

Her heartbeat kicked up. "Yes." How could she possibly forget?

"I couldn't touch you then. I could only kiss you and taste your mouth when you deigned to offer it to me." Leaning closer, he traced the shell of her ear with the edge of his tongue, and every intimate nerve in her body awoke. "But now, I am the one in control."

Aching, Camille arched her hips closer to him. "Yes."

"You have never been with a man." Was it meant to be a question?

She shook her head, forcing back the dark memories of Roger. "No. Never...like this."

Benedict drew back for an instant and studied her blushing face, something unreadable flickering in his green eyes. Could he see her secret?

"Please," she said again. "I won't change my mind."

"It's madness," he breathed, eyes hooded with desire.

His mouth was tender and deft as he kissed his way down her throat, all the while lifting the hem of her barely-damp chemise with one hand. He trailed fingertips all the way up her inner thigh in a way that made her feel mad with longing. She heard herself pant.

"Go on," he encouraged her.

Something broke free inside of Camille. She lifted her arms to help him slip off the garment, and then she was naked beneath him. Oh, it felt glorious to feel his strong, warm male chest against the swell of her breasts! Yet he still wore trousers, and she reached down to push at his waistband. Benedict leaned to one side, agile as a panther, and shucked off the last barrier between their bodies. Now, crouching above her, he feasted his eyes on her in a way that made her feel hungry as well.

He cupped her chin in one dark hand and kissed her again, his tongue questing in a sensual promise of what was to come. Meanwhile he slowly caressed one of her breasts, his fingertips like feathers. How did he know exactly what she liked, needed? Her breathing quickened, and she felt the moisture between her legs.

But then Benedict moved to lightly lick the sensitive peak of her nipple before closing his mouth over it, alternately suckling and bathing it with his tongue. Camille heard herself whimper. She sank her fingers into his damp, black curls and pressed him nearer.

For an instant, he raised his eyes to her face, and she mouthed one word, *More*.

Long minutes passed as Benedict continued to worship her breasts. She arched closer to him, soaking up each erotic sensation, until it was not enough. Her hands traced the back of his neck and the hard-muscled breadth of his shoulders. His body was warm, alive, pulsing with male energy, and Camille understood at last what she had been missing.

This is my chance, she had told him. *Perhaps my only chance, ever.*

Uttering a low, appreciative sound, he kissed the tender undersides of her breasts, the border of her ribcage, the curve of one hip.

He had braced himself on one elbow, and Camille looked down, drinking in the sight of his wide chest with its dusting of dark hair, the lean ridges of his belly, and finally...his stunning erection. Aroused yet wary, she caught her breath. How in the world could *that* fit inside her? Just then, she saw him watching her and knew he had read her thoughts again.

"Touch me," he invited, angling his body for better access.

When Camille reached out and brushed her fingertips over the side of it, she heard Benedict draw a harsh breath. Emboldened, she wrapped her hand around his straining length and felt him swell and harden more with each caress. Just as she began to relax into the power she seemed to have over him, Benedict nudged her thighs apart.

The look he gave her then stopped her heart. He reached to trace a fingertip from her hipbone down into the nest of soft curls, and Camille knew a wild mixture of longing and trepidation. His hand strayed farther, and she realized how wet and swollen she was. When he touched her, a lightning bolt of sensation went to her very core, and his fingertip made lazy circles, dipping down to venture inside her in a way that made her hips come off the bed.

"Is this what you like," he murmured, glancing up. "You can tell me."

He must know that she sometimes touched herself, hoping to find ways to satisfy herself so she might never need a man. Even her best efforts paled in comparison to *this*. Meeting his gaze, Camille managed a mute nod, but her eyes widened a moment later as Benedict bent his dark head and kissed along the same path his fingers had blazed.

His mouth moved lower, exploring her inner thighs, each brush of his lips heightening her arousal. Then, what must have been the tip of his tongue flicked over the very core of her, and she wanted to sob. What was he doing? Again, his tongue touched, then probed, the swollen petals that concealed the bud of her desire. Oh, how she ached for more! A tidal wave of exquisite sensation, building for so long, began to surge. But Benedict waited, maddeningly, licking, even nipping, until she opened her legs even farther and tried to show him what she needed.

"Ah, love," he muttered. She could almost feel his smile.

At last, his mouth fastened over the tender, aching nub, and Camille whimpered. She grabbed fistfuls of his hair and pressed him nearer, even as he worked magic on her with his expert tongue. Swirling, circling, suckling…somehow knowing exactly how to take her higher, then higher still. His long fingers entered her, then withdrew, and penetrated again, discovering a hidden spot deep inside her. When Camille climaxed at last, she saw stars, and it felt as if a firestorm of sparks had been unleashed throughout her body. Her legs trembled as waves of pleasure carried her to a place beyond her wildest imaginings.

And yet, when she lay in a euphoric daze, she knew there was more to come. Benedict rose up to kiss her, and she tasted herself on his lips.

"Am I allowed to say that you are a goddess?" came his hoarse whisper.

She nodded, filled with a joy she had never known

before. "And now…?" Caressing the length of him, she said, "I want to feel you inside me."

Their eyes met even as the air seemed to change. Benedict glanced away. "We shouldn't—"

"What?" She blinked in confusion. "I don't understand."

The hours of enchantment they had shared could not end this way! For reasons she didn't fully comprehend, Camille ached for something beyond the bliss she had just experienced in Benedict's arms. She needed him inside of her, filling her, their bodies joined, finding complete fulfillment together.

He shifted in her embrace. "There is nothing I'd like more than to finish what we have started…but I now realize it would be a mistake. Even if I withdraw at the crucial moment, there is no guarantee I won't get you with child."

Finish what we have started? The impersonal words were a blow, yet something in Benedict's shuttered face told a different story. In her heart, Camille felt certain that he burned to possess her completely, even to leave part of himself inside her. She wrapped her arms around his wide back. "But it is what I want. I'm not afraid of the consequences."

He shook his head slightly. "You know, darling minx, you're a bit mad." Abruptly, he reached up to loosen her embrace. "We cannot do it. If you were to get with child, I would never forgive myself."

In the grip of an emotion she couldn't name, Camille began to shiver. She was cold as ice.

Benedict reached for the quilt and wrapped her in it, pausing for a moment to touch her cheek. "For once in my life, I am trying to do the right thing," he said tersely.

She watched in disbelief as he swung lean-muscled legs over the side of the bed. *It shouldn't be like this!* At that very moment, they could be making love, and when it was over, they would doze together, sated and warm, limbs entwined. The hamper still waited for them...Camille's eyes stung as she imagined them spreading the remaining feast out over the quilt, laughing and feeding each other.

Instead, Benedict had begun to dress, turned away from her. "The clothes are beginning to dry," he said, glancing back over one shoulder. "And the rain is letting up. We will be able to leave soon."

She watched him pull on his trousers and then the linen shirt, now barely damp. It came to her that she couldn't stay huddled in the bed, naked, like a child whose feelings were hurt. No matter how bitter her disappointment and confusion, she must not let him see. Lifting her chin and straightening her back, she plucked her chemise from a nearby chair, donned it, and rose to fetch her gown.

Benedict walked over to the hamper and looked inside. "There is still a lot of food here, Camille," he said. "You must be as hungry as I am."

"Oh, yes. I am famished," she lied. Her heart stung, yet she managed to smile. "If you'll help me with these fastenings, we shall see what else my Aunt Julia has sent for us to eat."

Outside, Camille saw that the rain had stopped. The sun broke through the clouds, shimmering rays of light illuminating the clearing.

Their idyll was truly at an end.

* * *

"FLETCHER!" yelled Benedict, barely looking up from the papers on his desk.

The manservant came in from the kitchen, holding a large spoon in one hand and his walking stick in the other. His bushy white brows were raised in surprise. "Is something amiss, sir?"

"No." He realized that he must seem very disagreeable but didn't care. "I merely wanted to inform you that, from now on, I will be spending a great deal of time writing. All my time, in fact."

"Indeed, sir?" Slowly, Fletcher advanced toward the desk.

Benedict nearly put up a hand to ward him off. "There's really nothing else to say about it."

The older man dared to take a chair, the same one where Camille liked to sit. "Not long ago, I had a notion that you might be in higher spirits than before, perhaps due to the invitation from Mr. Swainson to join his Australian expedition? You even smiled at me when you went off to take the little bird to Trevarre Hall."

"Oh right, Australia," Benedict said, and drew a harsh breath. He stared back into Fletcher's calm gray eyes, wanting to confess, *Yes, my life was improving, but now I've bungled it.* But he could hardly explain what had happened with Camille. The memory of their interlude in the summerhouse made his stomach clench.

At night, Benedict tossed restlessly, alone in his bed. His loins ached as he remembered how right it had felt to hold her, kiss her, awaken her beautiful, passionate soul to the joys of physical love. By God, how he had wanted to take her fully, to show her what lovemaking could be, but his conscience had flared up, white-hot, at the last moment. Camille's bewildered, hurt reaction continued to haunt him.

Now, Fletcher cleared his throat, watching him patiently, still waiting for a real response.

Benedict dipped his pen in the inkpot. "I may have smiled then, but not any longer." He pointed from the notes spread before him across to the dozens of bird specimens lining the desk to his right. "I have a lot of work to do, especially if I am to go to Australia."

"I see." The manservant pushed up on the chair arms and steadied himself with his blackthorn stick. "I too have a great deal to do. As you may recall, it is Master Gareth's birthday tomorrow."

Suddenly, Benedict remembered his conversation with Camille during their journey by boat to see Lady Daphne Leyton. When he had spoken of poor little Gareth's life, especially with another babe coming, Camille had said, *Perhaps you might organize something?* Her kind suggestion had been a shock, prompting Benedict to slowly reveal to her a host of personal memories and feelings about his cursed father, his past, his own pain. He blinked in disbelief at the memory. What the devil had come over him?

Yet he heard himself say, "Perhaps I might organize something for Gareth's birthday."

Fletcher, by now halfway across the room, turned and stared as if Benedict had proposed marriage. "Sir?" He visibly swallowed, quickly regaining his composure. "I think that is a splendid idea! It needn't be anything grand. Perhaps just a few people? I will prepare a small cake, just the sort Master Gareth loves best. If we could only contrive to find a gift—"

Stunned by this outburst, Benedict put up a silencing hand. "Yes, fine. Tomorrow afternoon then. There's space in that house for only a few of us. I suspect Gareth will be happy simply to receive some attention."

"I agree, sir." He paused, lips pursed, then seemed to gather his courage. "Might we invite Mistress St. Briac? She would bring a bit of sunshine to the gathering."

"Have you gone mad?" Benedict felt as if the manservant had just set off a bomb on the floor in front of him. "I don't want Camille mixed up with my twisted family, and in any event, she doesn't bloody know Gareth."

"Ah. I see." Fletcher took a cautious step backward. "Very well, sir."

* * *

CLAD AGAIN in her favorite breeches and a boy's shirt, Camille tramped along the Hall Walk high above the River Fowey. She had just spent a lovely afternoon visiting Lazarus, along with her Uncle Sebastian and Aunt Julia. The kittiwake was doing splendidly, and it seemed that he soon might be able to fly. The thought of releasing him on the cliffs, to join the others, filled her with both elation and uncertainty. The danger that Lazarus might be killed in a future raid by the feather thieves was real, for the younger kittiwakes' wings were prized most.

The visit to Trevarre Hall had been a welcome distraction from the intense emotions that had plagued Camille since the episode in the summerhouse. She found it hard to sleep, and her normally robust appetite had deserted her, causing her parents to wonder if she might be ill.

Yes, Camille wanted to tell them, *I am suffering from heartache.* Yet in truth, she didn't understand what Benedict's rejection really meant, especially since it came at the moment when she so longed for more.

There was nothing for it but to stay busy, Camille decided as she followed the footbridge across Pont Pill and up the wooded hill toward Polruan. She had promised to bring Damien's mended boots home from the cobbler, or she might not pass this way. Not that she was afraid of seeing Benedict! When they had parted after the summerhouse interlude, Camille had refused to let him see her confusion and pain. In fact, back at Pont Pill, she had given him a kiss on the cheek, her manner almost jaunty.

The path narrowed now as it wound down through a low tunnel of greenery, into the village. After a moment's indecision, Camille turned onto Chapel Lane, avoiding the town quay and the home of Prudence Johns and her family. Yet, rounding the corner of Fore Street, mere steps away from the cobbler's tiny shop, she heard someone call her name.

"Mistress St. Briac?"

Instantly, Camille recognized the familiar voice of Fletcher, Benedict's longtime manservant. A part of her wanted to pretend she hadn't heard, but after a moment, she turned.

"Oh, hello, Mr. Fletcher. This is…unexpected!"

His expression was warm and friendly. "I was just on my way to the home of Mr. Hawke's sister," the older man said, leaning on his walking stick as he drew near. "How fortuitous to encounter you here, today."

"Is it?" She put on a bright smile, suddenly tired of smiling when she had no heart for it. "I am on a simple errand to the cobbler."

"I won't keep you," he assured her. "However…" Behind his spectacles, she could almost see the wheels turning in his mind. "I hope you might consent to attend a very small party for Mr. Hawke's nephew, Gareth. Tomorrow is the lad's fourth birthday."

"Oh, yes, I know!" Camille exclaimed, her own concerns forgotten. "I'm so glad to hear that there will be party. Has Benedict organized it?"

"Indeed, he has, miss! I believe that your presence will bring a special cheer to the gathering, especially since Gareth's own mother may be, uh, indisposed. Will you consent to join us?"

Although Camille wanted to agree, she felt torn. One hand on the latch to the cobbler's shop, she bit her lip. "It is kind of you to invite me, Mr. Fletcher, but to-morrow I may be otherwise occupied."

He swayed a bit, looking crestfallen. "I see."

Wavering, she added, "However, if you will kindly share the particulars of this gathering, I shall consult my calendar when I return home."

"Ah, of course, miss." Fletcher bowed, but she glimpsed his smile. "I shall be pleased to do so."

The sound of Zeus barking drew Camille through the low door in the walled garden. Standing on the other side, she waited. Moments later, the curly-coated black retriever came bounding along the path from the Sundial Garden, her father's latest creation.

"Show me, Zeus," she greeted him, smiling, and the dog did her bidding.

Camille had to lift her skirts to negotiate the sloping pathway. Through a gap between the willow trees, she caught sight of her brother, squirming at the edge of the shallow reflection pool.

"Mama, how much longer must I sit here like this? It's *torture*."

Her mother, who perched on a stool in front of her easel, soothed, "Just a few minutes more, love."

"You have said that for at least an hour," complained Damien.

"It only feels like that," came Mama's amused reply.

Camille stood back for a few moments, surveying the scene. The long, rectangular pool was bordered by a low wall and boasted floating water hyacinths, lilies, and plants Papa called Neptune's Crown. A spherical sundial rose up from the center of the pool, its hidden fountain spewing delicate streams of water.

"I think this garden may be my favorite," Camille said as she joined her mother. For a moment, she looked at the portrait of her brother and marveled at Isabella's gift for capturing the inner spirit of her subjects. In the painting, Damien was perched on the edge of the foot-high wall that surrounded the pool, feet staggered, one hand on his knee as if he were about to push off and run away. Her mother had added Zeus to the painting. He leaned attentively against his young master, as if waiting for their shared signal to bolt.

Mama looked over with a smile. "Each time your father finishes a garden, you say it is your favorite."

"Did someone say *finished*?" Damien interjected hopefully, and Zeus added a loud bark of agreement.

"Go on then," their mother said, pretending to sigh. Before she could add, "But we will have to do this again tomorrow!" Damien and Zeus had disappeared into the woods.

"That portrait is simply perfect," Camille pronounced.

"Thank you." With a rueful smile, she set down her palette and brush. "The hardest part is getting him to sit still. Your sister Louise is the only one of my children who would deign to pose properly."

Camille nodded. "I miss her."

"There was a time when I thought only Louise could persuade you to put on a proper gown and behave like a lady, if only for a few hours, but look at you!" Isabella swept an arm through the air. "First the party at Frenchman's Haven, then your outing to meet Lady Daphne, and now today! Are you off to rendezvous with your suitor, Mr. Hawke?"

Glancing down at her simple but pretty gown of

gold and gray patterned cambric, Camille felt herself blush slightly. "Benedict is not my suitor, Mama!"

"Oh yes, that's right." Isabella nodded, but her eyes danced behind her spectacles. "I meant to say *pretend* suitor. Still, my intuition tells me there is more to it."

Deciding to ignore this, Camille pressed on. "Actually, I am going into Polruan, and I hope you can spare Rafael to drive me in the gig. I have been invited to a little party to celebrate the fourth birthday of Benedict's nephew."

"How sweet!" Isabella sat up straighter.

She put up a hand. "It is not what you imagine. In fact..."

In the silence that followed, her mother rose and looked into her eyes. "You can talk to me, you know. Your father and I had quite a tempestuous courtship." Telltale color washed her cheeks. "Truly, you cannot shock me."

That might be, but Camille simply could not imagine confiding all that had happened in the summerhouse. "Your instincts are correct, Mama. There has been...a romantic interlude between us, but—" She drew a breath and continued, "Benedict rejected me, at a very awkward moment."

"Oh, I see." Isabella wrapped her in a comforting embrace, and Camille clung to her, tears threatening. "My darling girl, if you have true feelings for him, I can only advise you not to give up. Sometimes men push love away when they want it the most."

Their eyes met again, and Camille managed a wry laugh. "How very vexing."

"Indeed!" Isabella patted her cheek. "But perhaps there is hope for him. Has he not invited you to this little party?"

"No." She shook her head. "In fact, it was Fletcher, the manservant, who bade me come when we met by chance in Polruan. I don't even know if Benedict would want me there."

"But you are going all the same?"

Camille nodded. "My heart goes out to little Gareth. His father is the ferry master and spends all day, from dawn to dark, on the River Fowey. His mother is about to give birth to her third child in four years, so I fear he has to settle for crumbs of attention. A little party would be a way to let him know he is special."

"You have a tender heart, darling. Do not be afraid to let it lead you."

Camille let herself lean, briefly, against her mother's soft cheek. "Sometimes I would rather stay in my little shell, walking in the woods and on the cliffs, looking after the birds—alone."

"I know." Isabella tightened her embrace, then opened her arms to set her free. "But now you have been awakened as a woman. Do you think it's even possible to go back to the way it used to be?"

* * *

BENEDICT STOOD outside his sister's house holding a small wooden box with a carved lid. Was he making a mistake, getting involved in the goings-on at Prue's house? As if on cue, a dark cloud blocked the sun and began to pelt him with tiny raindrops. Drawing a deep breath, he knocked.

A moment later, the door swung open to reveal the harried face of Caleb Johns. His brother-in-law's thinning ginger hair stood out as if he'd been struck by lightning, and he looked as if he hadn't slept for days.

"I'm surprised to see you," Benedict said. "Who is piloting the ferry?"

Ignoring this, Caleb grabbed his arm and pulled him into the cramped entry. "Ye do come just in time! Sally, the midwife, and my Ma be here. Prue's laboring begins!"

With that, Caleb whirled around and vaulted back up the narrow steps to the bedroom. As Benedict stood there, his head nearly touching the ceiling, he wondered where the devil Fletcher might be. The manservant bloody well knew how hard it was for Benedict to be here, especially with Pa under the same roof. He ought to be rushing out to ease the way.

Just then a small voice piped, "Uncle Ben'dick?"

Benedict's stomach clenched as he slowly went forward into the tiny parlor and looked around. In the midst of a lot of clutter, he spied his young nephew sitting at one end of the frayed sofa, all alone except for baby Jenny, who slept in her nearby cradle.

Even as he cursed inwardly, Benedict went forward, moving aside a book, a blanket, and a cup as he made room for himself next to Gareth. Just then, he heard his sister wailing in her room above them.

The boy glanced upward, wincing. "Do ye come t' wait for the babe?"

"In truth, I have come to see you, my boy," Benedict told him warmly, smiling. "I happen to know that today is your birthday."

Gareth's eyes grew very wide. "Aye!"

"I am here for your party." He felt a wave of compassion for this child who was so accustomed to being shunted aside. "Didn't you know about it?"

"N-no!" Even as Gareth shook his head, his voice shook. "Ma does say there can be no party."

"Well, your ma has a lot on her mind right now, so we shall forgive her for getting this wrong. There is definitely a party. Do you see? I have brought a present." He held up the small wooden box.

"But—is it to be only you and me?"

When the boy's lip began to quiver, Benedict resisted an urge to lift him onto his lap and hold him very close. "Oh, no. My horse, Max, wanted to come but he wouldn't fit through the door." This drew a small, uncertain laugh from Gareth. "And of course, there's little Jenny here."

As if she had heard her name, the baby awoke and began to whimper, louder by the moment.

"Devil take it," Benedict burst out, "where is Fletcher?"

The little boy stood up and pointed toward Pa's makeshift room at the back of the house. "Wit' Gran'-pa," he said, and reached into the cradle as if he might pick up the crying Jenny.

Benedict wanted to shout to summon Fletcher, but Gareth was already struggling to lift the baby. "Wait. Don't do that!"

With one motion, he leaned close enough to wrap both hands around Jenny's pudgy middle and brought her easily up into his strong arms. The baby took one look at his unfamiliar face and her cries swelled to shrieks. When he tried inexpertly to pat her back, she spit up mucus and what looked like cheese curds all over his tailored coat of gray superfine.

At that moment, a knock sounded at the front door. Nerves stretched taut, Benedict had no patience for an unexpected caller. Couldn't he simply ignore the knocking until they went away?

Footsteps pounded above them, and Caleb yelled down from the landing, "Benedict! See who it is, will you?"

* * *

HER HEART IN HER THROAT, Camille stood outside the narrow stone house overlooking Polruan's small boatyard. She closed her eyes and imagined the door swinging open. Fletcher would greet her, shepherding her inside, and he would then smooth the way with Benedict.

Lifting her hand, she knocked. Her palms were damp, and her mouth was dry. What would Benedict say when he first saw her? Before her imagination could run completely wild, the door swung open with a loud creak.

Camille had an immediate impression of a tall, dark-haired man carrying a wailing baby of perhaps eighteen months, his face obscured by the toddler's mass of coppery curls. This must be Prudence's husband, the ferryman! Camille had just summoned a friendly smile when the man barked a greeting.

"Yes? What do you want?"

Her heart sank at the sound of his voice. Oh, dash it! It was Benedict, and he sounded ominously out of temper. She wanted to run away before he could focus on her face, but at that moment, he leaned sideways around the squirming baby and their eyes met.

"What the deuce are *you* doing here?" His voice felt like a slap.

Straightening, she lifted her chin. "What sort of greeting is that?"

"As you can see," he ground out, "I am rather busy at the moment."

"I am here at Mr. Fletcher's invitation. He was quite insistent, so I assumed you knew!" Camille turned around and took a step toward East Street, where Rafael waited with the gig. "I apologize for disturbing you, sir."

Benedict secured the crying baby with one large hand and reached out to grasp the back of her gown with the other, stopping her progress. "No. Don't bloody go. Prue is preparing to give birth upstairs, and Caleb is with her. I am the only guest at Gareth's party."

Forced to stop, Camille turned back only halfway. It was tempting to leave him to muddle through on his own, but just then she caught sight of little Gareth, peeking out at her from the shadows.

"Are you suggesting that you need my help?" she asked crisply.

His jaw tightened, but he nodded. "I do."

* * *

BENEDICT FELT as if he were balanced on a treacherous cliff with no clear way forward. Camille under the same roof with his monstrous father was the last thing he wanted. And now, watching her make her way into the cramped, dim little house made his gut clench in a way he didn't fully understand.

"Hello," Gareth was saying. "Who're you?"

Camille bent her knees and, even in her dress, easily lowered herself to his level. "Hello, Gareth. My name is Camille. Word reached me of this very special day, and I came to join the party. I hope you don't mind."

"Oh, no!" He was staring at her in wonder. "Did you know? They do give the queen her crown on my birthday."

Benedict approached them, still carrying Jenny, who was now squirming mightily to get down. Wondering what seat he might offer Camille, he tried to make more space on the aged sofa.

"Would you like to sit down?" he asked her.

Gareth marched over and planted himself on the place Benedict had indicated for Camille. "I sit here." Moments later, he was flanked by his uncle on one side and the surprise visitor on the other. To Benedict's further consternation, Camille picked up Jenny and held her on her lap.

"Someone has left you a present," she remarked,

wrinkling her pretty nose at the curdled spit-up on Benedict's lapel. "It has a perfume all its own."

Her eyes, too beautiful for words, were dancing.

Before he could reply, Fletcher appeared in the doorway to the kitchen, holding a plate with a cake on it. His white brows went up at the sight of Camille.

"Ah, Miss St. Briac," he said. "It is a pleasure to see you."

"My cake!" crowed Gareth, clapping.

Fletcher was advancing toward them without his walking stick. A moment later, Benedict had crossed the room and taken the blue plate. "Let me help you. Where is your stick?"

"Really, sir, this isn't necessary. The room is small and there are many objects for me to reach out for."

"Not when you're carrying a cake." Benedict set the plate on a stool in front of the guests, then turned back to bring Fletcher to join them. "Sit down. We need every guest for this small gathering."

"I made a little crown of sorts and left it out in the kitchen, sir," Fletcher whispered. His smile was rare, tender. "For little Gareth, you see."

Glad for an excuse to shed the stained, pungent-smelling coat, Benedict went into the kitchen and left it on a hook beside Caleb's rain gear. He had just picked up the gold-painted paper crown and started back when a faint groan reached him through the thin wall. He flinched. *Pa.*

The last thing Benedict wanted to do was go into Pa's room. Reminding himself that the old man often uttered unintelligible sounds, he returned to the little party.

"Oh, look," Camille exclaimed to Gareth. "Uncle Benedict has brought your special birthday crown."

The child's eyes were wide. As Benedict set the

painted crown on his head, Gareth sniffed and blinked back tears.

"It's your day," Benedict told him.

"Yes," Camille chimed in. "Yours and Queen Victoria's!"

Benedict, Camille, and Fletcher applauded and gave a little cheer, then Fletcher began to cut the cake. The top was decorated with custard and a pattern of berries, and Gareth licked his lips as he sampled the first bite.

He swallowed, then looked around at his three smiling guests and gave a little sigh. "I do be so very happy."

"You are now four years old," Benedict declared. "Old enough for some proper toys." He reached for the wooden box and held it out.

Gareth jiggled the lid until it came off and then peered inside. "Oh!" he gasped. One by one, he took out some small, rather crudely carved animals and birds: an owl, hedgehog, duck, badger, wren, sheep, and even a gull. They were just the right size for a little boy to play with. Gareth immediately picked up the hedgehog and owl, one in each hand, and turned them toward each other as if they were meeting.

"How wonderful." Camille gazed at Benedict with unexpected warmth. "Did you carve them yourself?"

He shook his head as his throat swelled. "No. Pa made them for me when he was the gardener at Windsor Great Park. I was no bigger than Gareth."

When he met Camille's eyes, he could see what she wanted to say: *You have carried them with you for all these years?* He wanted to protest that he had simply kept the small wooden box—also made by Pa—tucked away deep in the same trunk with his favorite books. He wanted to say that he'd forgotten all about the toys Pa had carved just for him, they meant nothing to him, but it would be a lie and Camille would know it.

"Am I truly to keep them, Uncle?" breathed the child.

"Yes, of course." His voice was husky. "They are meant to be enjoyed by a little boy just like you."

"But not Jenny," Gareth pronounced. "Or a new babe."

Fletcher had taken Jenny onto his lap and was feeding her little bites of sponge cake. "I'll help to guard them," he assured Gareth.

From upstairs came more urgent cries from Prue, followed by the muted voice of the midwife. Gareth looked worried until Camille patted his knee.

"As it happens, I too have brought a gift," she said. Under her skirts, a pocket was tied around her small waist, and now she reached through a slit to access it. A moment later, she withdrew a small, loosely bound book and handed it to Gareth. "This is something you can keep for your very own."

As the child turned the pages, Benedict saw that the little book featured watercolor illustrations of birds, each page embellished with a few words printed in ink. Camille had clearly made it herself, even cutting tiny holes along one edge and using ribbon to bind the pages together. Why was he surprised to see that each painting was an exquisite work of art?

"Do you like birds, Gareth?" she asked.

He was nodding, gazing at the little book as if he couldn't believe it belonged to him.

Camille put an arm around him, and he leaned against her breast until his crown was askew. "Perhaps one day, if you'd like, we'll take a little walk and discover some of the birds in your book."

Benedict found that he wanted to be included in this plan, but of course she had distanced herself from him ever since he ended their interlude in the summerhouse. Was it simply that her pride was hurt, or was it something more?

"I do like birds," said Gareth. "And I like you." With that, he climbed down to the floor and began to play with his new carved toys.

It seemed a signal that the party was ending. Camille began to make her farewells. After rising to her feet, she smiled and spoke to Benedict as if he were a polite acquaintance. "I must thank you for allowing me to attend this family party."

"Right. Yes." Benedict stood up as well. "Fletcher was right to invite you. I—" He wanted to tell her why it was so damned hard for him to let her into this house, into his family, but how the devil could he explain something he didn't even properly understand himself? "That is, I am glad you came."

Perhaps she saw something in his face, for she took a step closer. "Benedict, is there any possibility you might introduce me to your father?" She paused. "Since I am here, I mean?"

"God, no!" He was surprised to hear how loud his voice was. He must sound like a madman. "I mean, I would rather not..."

Before he could say another word, a loud crashing sound came from the room at the back of the house, followed by muted cries of pain.

Fletcher immediately pushed to his feet and grabbed for his walking stick. "Don't move, sir!" he said to Benedict. "I will see to Mr. Hawke."

CHAPTER 25

*W*atching Fletcher limp away toward Pa's room, Benedict felt paralyzed. But then, Camille's gaze burned into his back, and he turned to meet her shocked stare.

"It is your *father*," she whispered hotly.

Indeed. That was exactly the reason he wished to leave it all up to Fletcher, yet suddenly Benedict didn't want to be that sort of person. In seconds, he was pushing aside the curtain that served as Pa's door. Inside the crude, lean-to room, he saw his father sprawled across the floor in front of his cot. Fletcher bent beside the old man, pulling at him, urging him to hold on, to get to his knees.

In that moment, Benedict's revulsion was forgotten. He went forward and gripped Fletcher's thin shoulder.

"We both know you can't do this."

"But, sir—"

Camille's voice interrupted as she came up behind them and extended a hand to the manservant. "Please, Mr. Fletcher, you must let him help."

For one burning moment, Benedict couldn't breathe. *Camille*. He felt raw, naked, exposed, as his two worlds collided. Perhaps his heart had stopped, and if so, it might be for the best. Anything but this.

But then Pa was clutching at his shirt sleeve, grunting. Benedict dropped to one knee, put an arm around him and hooked another under his knees, and rose, lifting him up like a baby. Gently, he laid him back on the cot, heard Pa's grunt of protest. It was a shock to feel his bones through the nightshirt he wore, to realize how utterly frail he had become.

Fletcher spoke, his voice thick. "Oh, well done, sir."

As Benedict adjusted his father so that he was reclining against the pillows, Camille came close to arrange his scrawny legs. Benedict didn't want to meet her penetrating gaze or even imagine what she might be thinking. He had an even stronger aversion to looking at Pa, who was so close he could smell the old man's fetid breath and feel the erratic beating of his heart through his bedclothes.

"Son," rasped Pa, scowling.

"Never mind," he managed to reply. "You're all right now."

In a different sort of story, Benedict would have seen tears of remorse in his father's bloodshot eyes, and the decades of bitterness and distrust would have melted away. But he could not even think of that. Instead, he pried Pa's clawlike fingers from his pristine white sleeve and rose to his full height. He turned his gaze on Fletcher.

"You cannot manage here on your own," he said flatly. "I have been a fool to think otherwise."

The manservant blinked several times. "But, sir, what do you mean to do?"

"I don't bloody know yet." Benedict made his escape then, grasping Camille's arm and bringing her with him. "I will have to think."

* * *

WHEN THEY WERE outside the house, Camille watched as Benedict stopped, closed his eyes, and took a deep breath.

"Really," she ventured, "was it right for us to take our leave so abruptly?"

"If you are referring to Pa, he was settled and already dozing before we were out of the room. Caleb and Mrs. Johns are both there if Fletcher needs them." Pinching the bridge of his nose between thumb and forefinger, he added, "There's nothing you or I can do for Prue at this moment, and Gareth is content with his new toys. By God, if anyone is in distress, it's me."

She caught her breath and searched his hard face. "What is it? Are you ill?"

"You might say that." Benedict shot her a dark look. "But never fear, I'm not physically ill. It's just that the walls were closing in on me. I had to get out, and I would not leave you behind—with him."

Camille's emotions were in a tangle. She remembered every memory Benedict had shared with her about his youth and his father as he rowed them up the River Fowey. Clearly, he had a great deal of pain stored inside, like the carved toys he had held onto since childhood. Yet now he was a man, and his father was incapacitated. It felt wrong for Benedict to continue to direct his anger toward that helpless, broken man.

"I hardly know what to say," she murmured, biting her lower lip.

"There's nothing you can say. No doubt you feel sorry for him, trapped in that ruined body." He walked a short distance along the waterfront and Camille kept pace with him. "When I see him, I pity him, too, but then I look into his eyes. The father who bullied, mocked, and beat me is still alive and well inside of Pa. He hasn't changed." Benedict glanced down at her, eyes flashing. "I think he hates me more than ever because I am free, and he is a prisoner."

"I see." She felt sick. "And…do you mean to live like this forever?"

"I don't want to, but I may not have a choice." He turned, his tall, broad-shouldered form silhouetted against the gray sky. For an instant, she saw the raw hunger in his eyes and thought he might take her in his arms. Instead, he took a step back. "Go home, Camille."

"But…what about the feather thieves?"

"I'll send word when I know more about the next raid." Glancing away, Benedict shook his head. "Our little courtship masquerade hasn't led to any real discoveries, so we might as well put an end to it."

She wondered if he had forgotten completely about Lazarus, whom she had visited each day since the kittiwake chick had gone to Trevarre Hall to be nursed by Julia. Had Benedict's tenderness toward the orphaned hatchling been false?

Before Camille could speak, he reached back. His fingertips grazed her cheek, sending potent currents of longing to her very core. "I am grateful to you for coming today, for helping to make Gareth's day special."

Camille nodded and stood there as he walked back to fetch Max, his horse, from the post in front of Prudence's house. He swung lightly up into the saddle, and she watched until they were out of sight, fighting back an urge to weep.

"My lady?"

It was Rafael, coming toward her from the gig. She was glad when he took her arm and helped her into the small equipage. When he had settled onto the seat beside her, reins in hand, he glanced over, brow furrowed.

"Something is wrong, I suspect."

"No." Camille shook her head and sat up straighter. "It's just been a day filled with emotion. Little Gareth's birthday, you know…and his mother's confinement has begun. Very soon there will be a new baby."

The gig, pulled by Pegasus, had begun its slow ascent up Fore Street. "You're very pale, my lady." When she made no reply to this, he added, "Perhaps you should rest."

Camille was about to close her eyes when she spied a familiar figure walking down the hill as they passed by. The man wore a silk hat, its broad brim pulled rather low to conceal part of his face. Could it possibly be Lord Upton? She leaned out for a better look, but now only his fashionably garbed back was visible as he continued down the steep street toward the waterfront. Why would Roger still be in the area, and what business could he possibly have in the tiny village of Polruan?

* * *

As DAWN BROKE the next morning, Benedict began to pack away the dozens of specimens collected during expeditions throughout England and Scotland as well as to America, Spain, and Brazil. Reaching for a prized, rare white skylark, he remembered the thrill of first sighting, then shooting it near Falmouth.

Of course, the only way to gather specimens for use in ornithological study was to kill them. Yet, as he cradled the feathered corpse in his big hand, Benedict felt an unsettling pang of guilt. He could almost hear Camille admonishing him to allow this beautiful bird to live in nature, as God intended.

Just then, the door opened, and Fletcher entered the cottage as if he'd been there all along. Surveying the open trunk and the half-empty desktop, he said, "Ah, sir, what have we here?"

"I'm packing these away for the moment." Benedict hoped the manservant wouldn't question him further, for he had no good answer. How the devil was he to write a book about the birds of the Cornwall coast without his collection of specimens at hand? The truth was, he found it hard to look at them now.

Fletcher merely nodded. "I've just returned from your sister's house."

"Oh, God—Prue!" He crossed the room in a few strides. "What news do you bring?"

"You have another wee niece, born at midnight. I believe they mean to call her Amelia, after her maternal grandmother, Mrs. Hawke."

Benedict felt the sting of tears as he thought of his mother and all she had endured, living with Pa and then dying just as her life should have gotten easier, enjoying the pleasures of grandchildren. "Excellent," he murmured. "Did you get any rest at all, old boy?"

"I did. After you left, your father slept almost continuously until this morning. I made a bed on the sofa." Fletcher set down the little bag that he took back and forth to Prue's house. "I'll just have a wash-up and have something to eat before I go back."

"Is Caleb there, looking after Gareth?"

Fletcher nodded as he started toward the kitchen. "He is. And Mrs. Johns, his mother, has stayed to help with the new babe."

Left unspoken was any reference to Pa. No one outside their three-person circle wanted to sit with him, and Benedict certainly couldn't blame them.

"I've been thinking about...all of this, Fletch." He paused, swept by a wave of nausea. "It isn't right that you are shouldering the burden of my father alone. I'll go down later today." Quickly, he added, "I can't promise to be his minder, but I would be there if needed."

Fletcher blinked. "Thank you, sir. I know it cannot be easy for you."

Just then, Ember the cat scampered into the kitchen, and the manservant followed, murmuring to him in the same tone one might use with a baby. After a moment, he reappeared in the doorway, holding the cat's dish.

"Sir, I thought I should mention something that happened after you left your sister's house yesterday." As Fletcher spoke, Ember rubbed insistently against his legs. "A man came to the door, asking to speak to Mr. Hawke."

"To me, do you mean?"

"I assumed so, but when I inquired, he said no…he was looking for Mr. Josiah Hawke. The man said he understood Mr. Hawke no longer lived at Gull Cottage, but now resided in the home of his daughter, Prudence Johns."

Benedict arched a sardonic brow. "Doubtless Pa is in deep to the fellow. He always has lived beyond his means."

"Hmm. Perhaps." Fletcher seemed to consider this, while Ember began to make low yowling sounds of complaint. "I did mention that Mr. Hawke had suffered a serious attack of apoplexy and was no longer receiving guests, but he wanted to see him all the same. I had the feeling it was about something other than the repayment of a debt."

"He didn't give his name?"

"No. When I offered to relay a message to Mr. Hawke, the man frowned and went off in a dudgeon."

"Odd." Benedict rubbed his jaw. "What did he look like?"

"Unremarkable. Rather young, tall, slender. Fair, I would guess, though he wore a hat that shadowed his face." Ember began to prick his claws through Fletcher's trousers, finally driving the manservant back to the kitchen. He paused just long enough to add, "Oh, there was one thing. The man wore a signet ring on his left hand, and I saw it was inscribed with a crest. Mayhap he is an aristocrat?"

Benedict felt an abrupt shock at Fletcher's words. Good God, could it be Upton? And if so, what could his lordship possibly want with Pa?

CHAPTER 26

*T*hree long days passed without word from Benedict.

Camille carried on as always. She looked after all the nesting birds who came to the kitchen gardens. She joined Damien and Zeus to race paper boats in the lake and spent hours sketching woodland birds. Each day, she walked to Trevarre Hall to visit little Lazarus, who continued to grow stronger. Julia always enticed her to stay longer. The two of them shared tea on the stone terrace, had a look at other wild creatures that were being rehabilitated in the barn, or set out to explore the magically beautiful estate. Later, returning home over the footbridge at Pont Pill, Camille couldn't help glancing down to the shore at the rubble-slate boathouse. Vivid images returned of the morning Benedict had carried her into the little boat and then rowed them all the way to Lerryn Creek.

Camille felt utterly changed by their stolen hours in the summerhouse, when rain had rattled the window-panes and she had lain with Benedict, naked, vulnerable, reveling in each sensual moment of her awakening. In the end, he had broken the spell, yet as the days passed, she made a choice not to close off her heart. Slowly, she began to reflect in a different way about their time there together. She thought, briefly, of Roger, who had cared only for his own satisfaction...and then it came to Camille that Benedict had unselfishly given her pleasure beyond imagining yet denied his own release.

Who could say what might still lie ahead?

Eventually, Camille donned her breeches again and returned to the cliffs, carrying her sketchbook and crayons in an old leather satchel that once belonged to her father. She followed the coastal path, up and down through the fog, past Palace Cove and Lantic Beach. Occasionally, spying a plover or curlew below on the sand, she scrambled down to make a sketch.

It wasn't until Camille was nearing Polruan that Roger appeared like an apparition, striding toward her out of the mist. He wore proper riding clothes, but there was no horse in sight. A long gun case was slung over one of his shoulders.

"Ah, Camille, this is a pleasant surprise," he called genially. "And look at you in your boy's garb. You were ever an original."

She seemed to have no choice but to stop. "Hello, my lord."

He was beside her now, gazing into her eyes. "Did I not give you leave, long ago, to call me by my Christian name?"

He was a bit too close, his tone too intimate. Camille glanced away. "I don't understand why you have lingered in Cornwall."

"I think you know exactly why I linger," came his low reply.

"If you are referring to your attempt to resume our...friendship, I have told you plainly that is not possible."

When he moved as if to take her arm, Camille knew

a pang of alarm. Why was he carrying a gun? Perhaps she should have brought Rafael with her, as Papa suggested. They stood on a particularly precarious stretch of pathway, and if one of them should misstep, it would be very easy to tumble down to the rocks below. The wind had picked up, and in the distance, Camille saw a pair of kittiwakes wheeling and calling near their cliffside nests.

"Do you reject me because you are enamored of that fellow Hawke?" He pressed his lips together. "You are too fine for him. What has he to offer you? That plain little cottage on the cliff that is not even his own?" Roger was so close she could hear his ragged breathing. "Camille, I am a wealthy man, even more wealthy than I was a year ago."

"What do you know about Benedict's circumstances?" she demanded.

"Oh, I know all about him. We were at Oxford together, didn't you know? He had no good right to be there, yet he behaved as if he were the same as the rest of us." Roger's eyes flashed. "It seems he has always had ideas above his station."

"This conversation is pointless, sir." As waves crashed against the sheer cliffs far below, Camille tried to move around him. "The path is narrow. Do, please, step aside."

He glared at her for a long moment, but then allowed her to pass. "You'll regret the choices you are making, my dear," he called after her.

Camille did not look back. Was he following her? How could she have ever found him attractive or interesting? The thought of her brief, misguided infatuation with Roger now filled her with revulsion. As she hurried onward into the wind, it came to Camille that she had wanted Benedict to share the painful aspects of his past, yet there was something in her own history that she could never reveal.

Never.

The kittiwake parents she had spied just minutes earlier had now settled on their nests, where the growing chicks were devouring their breakfasts of small fish and worms. Before long, they would fledge, and all the birds would leave the rock ledges to return to ocean life. Perhaps the feather thieves would be too late?

"Camille?"

She glimpsed a tall figure ahead, beyond a rocky outcropping. *Benedict.* Her heart swelled at the sight of him, so handsome in top boots and a white shirt tucked loosely into snug, fawn trousers. When he stretched out a hand and started forward, she wondered if he could see Roger behind her. She scrambled toward him and threw herself into his arms.

"What is it?" Benedict said, holding her fast against his strong body. "Are you hurt?"

"No. No! It's him..." She canted her head to gesture back toward Roger. "Lord Upton."

"There is no one there, love. And you're safe."

For a moment, Camille simply absorbed that single word: *love.* Could it mean something? Then she turned her head to look at the path behind her. There was no sign of Roger.

"He was just here. Following me!" She was about to tell Benedict more, but what good would come of repeating the terrible things Roger had said about him? "And he was carrying a long gun case over his shoulder."

"Perhaps a rook rifle? No doubt he was hunting," Benedict said in a distracted tone, looking out to sea. "It would seem that you disturbed his peace."

"If I stopped him from shooting any living creature, I am grateful."

"This fierce wind is driving me back up to the cottage for a cup of tea. Come with me, just in case that buffoon is still lurking about."

"Yes, all right." Camille nodded. Inwardly she was elated, alone with Benedict for the first time since the day at the summerhouse. "I heard the news that you have a new baby niece. What is her name? Is everyone well?"

"She is called Amelia," he replied. "Mother, babe, and all the family are doing well." After a brief pause, he added, "I have tried to go by daily to help Fletcher."

"I'm so pleased to hear it."

"I thought you might be." His voice held a tender note.

As they started together up the path toward Gull Cottage, Benedict touched the small of her back. The pressure of his fingertips sent a thrill of recognition to every intimate corner of her body. How she had missed him!

After a moment, she saw a sketchbook and a small folder of pencils ahead on one of the rocks. They were so similar to her own that she had to feel the satchel she carried to be certain she had them. Before she could point the items out, Benedict reached for the items and continued walking.

"Are those yours?" Camille asked in surprise. "You have been sketching this morning?"

He nodded. "Ornithologists do more than just kill and preserve birds, you know," he said with a trace of irony. "We are trained as artists as well."

"I do know that," she protested. "When I was young, I was a great admirer of John James Audubon, until I realized that he *shot* the magnificent birds he then painted. How disillusioned I felt!"

"Yet there is more to it, isn't there? Audubon began a new tradition, showing the birds moving, engaged in their natural behaviors instead of the flat, profile paintings of the past." He paused before adding, "Two years ago, I worked alongside Audubon in the bayous of Louisiana. He explained to me that the only way he could make his subjects more lifelike was to watch them in the wild and make preliminary sketches."

"Hmph," Camille sniffed. "How noble he was to linger for a bit, appreciating the splendor of the birds—before he murdered them and orphaned their chicks."

She felt him glance over at her as they walked and rued her own short temper.

"I think you are quite harsh," Benedict said at last, "but I admit, I have come to agree with many of your views. I suppose I've been conflicted. It felt heretical to question the cornerstones of my profession, such as gathering and preserving specimens for study. Yet you not only question those practices, you condemn them, and now it seems I can't look away any longer." One corner of his mouth crooked upward as he added, "Yes, my persistent minx, you have spoiled it for me."

Camille wanted to beam at this admission from the man she loved, but instead she gave him an earnest look. "I'll own I am proud to have done so."

* * *

IT WAS madness to invite Camille back to Gull Cottage. Even if he didn't touch her or kiss her, just walking next to her reawakened all his deeper longings. There was a bond of companionship between them that he had never known with another woman, especially one he desired so much. It came to him that their friendship was a thornier issue than the physical ache to lie with her. It had crept up on him, and now he wasn't certain how to get free.

"Will you show me your sketches while we have tea?" she was asking.

"Perhaps, if you promise not to laugh," he said wryly. "I haven't your gift."

"I can't really take credit for any ability I have. My mother is a great artist, you know, so I suppose I was simply born with artistic talent."

How charming she was, chin tilted up, guilelessly accepting his praise rather than feigning false modesty as so many females were taught to do. When she sent him a radiant smile, Benedict felt something stir deep inside, a longing he didn't want to examine.

"If you can manage to capture the finer details of the birds without...uh, rendering them immobile, you could change the entire practice of ornithology," he mused.

"That would be a worthy goal for my life's work," came Camille's firm reply.

They were approaching the two tall, narrow rocks that marked the entrance to the smugglers tunnel. Since the night of the raid, when he and Camille had discovered the passage, Benedict had meant to return and investigate further, but there had been too many other distractions.

"Let's go inside, shall we? Just to have a look around by daylight."

"Oh, yes, excellent! Perhaps we shall find some clues."

When she fearlessly went ahead, Benedict reached out to grasp the back of her boy's waistcoat. "Let me go first, minx."

Even now, the tunnel was dark and shadowed, only faintly illuminated by the sliver of light passing through the narrow entrance. Benedict looked around as they went farther inside but saw only the rocky walls. Inhaling the scents of damp earth and rotting organic matter, he decided it was pointless to stay longer.

"I hate this place," he said to Camille. "Let us go back."

They were just turning around when she drew a quick breath. "Look over there."

He squinted in the direction of her extended finger. In the shadows, behind the stone that served as a step up to the cottage floor, Benedict glimpsed a dark object with square corners.

"What can it be?" He went forward, sat back on his heels, and touched the object. It was a flat, shallow wooden box, and someone had carved a niche in the rock to store it. When Benedict ran his fingers over the top, he felt the carvings…just the sort Pa had liked to make, when he was still able. Bile rose in Benedict's throat. Were his worst fears coming true? Pa could be the one who had overseen the gang of feather thieves, and now that he was incapacitated, they weren't certain how to proceed.

Camille watched, waiting. "Are you unwell?"

"No. I'm fine. Let's take this up into the cottage for a better look, shall we?"

Holding the box along with his sketchbook and pencils, Benedict went ahead, pushing up the loose floorboard and setting his things and Camille's satchel on the floor above them. Then he extended a hand to her, and she climbed up with him into the cottage.

Ember jumped from the sofa and rushed over to greet them. The cat seemed to recognize the box, rubbing against the corners and purring.

"Look," said Camille, "the carvings on the lid are rather like the little wooden case you gave Gareth. Do you think your father made this, too?"

"I don't know," he said, unable to meet her questing gaze. He pointed to the brass lock on the front of the box. "Until I find a key, the contents will remain a mystery."

Benedict decided then not to bring her into this, at least not until he knew more. Maybe never. He continued to feel revolted by the prospect of Camille and Pa mingling in any way. Every time he remembered her appearance in Pa's awful room, wanting to help in the wake of his fall, Benedict's stomach clenched like a fist.

"I promised you a cup of tea," he said. "Would you care to sit down while I go and brew it?"

"Oh." Camille smiled politely, but he saw the confusion in her beautiful eyes. "Yes, I will wait here for you."

With that, he took the cursed box and went into the kitchen, relieved to get the thing away, out of her sight.

*　*　*

CAMILLE PERCHED on the edge of the sagging sofa, and Ember leaped lightly up to lie nearby. Her thoughts whirled. How elusive Benedict was, tugging her heart and her hopes this way and that. One moment, they had been sharing views about topics important to both of them, and he had let his hand ride at the small of her back. It had felt so right! Now, a short time later, he had closed himself off again, not only avoiding her gaze but leaving the room entirely.

As Camille surveyed the cottage, she realized that the dozens of ornithological specimens no longer marched in rows across the long table under the window. She felt a wave of new hope. Rising, she approached the table that served as Benedict's desk and looked all around. There was no sign of the dead, stuffed birds that had dominated the space, not even a box nearby. She remembered what he'd said today about coming to question that aspect of his scientific craft. It must be true! He couldn't look at them any longer.

Camille put a hand to her breast and felt the beating of her own heart. Tears welled in her eyes. *I love him,* she thought. *God help me, I do.*

Just as she was about to turn back to the sofa, she saw something next to Benedict's spectacles and the notes for his book. Sunlight spilled across the desk to illuminate a long piece of heavy paper, unfolded to reveal what appeared to be a letter, written in an ornate hand. The signature at the bottom was bold: *William Swainson.* Her breath caught. What business could that respected London ornithologist have with Benedict now that he was in Cornwall? This was his private correspondence, yet she felt an irresistible urge to learn more.

My dear Mister Hawke. After only a few lines, Camille's curiosity darkened to foreboding. She was unable to stop reading, to turn away from reality. The great William Swainson was inviting Benedict to sail with him to Australia, offering him passage as well as a choice. Once they arrived, if Benedict wished to travel to join John Gould's party, he would be free to do so.

Camille's heart was in turmoil as she put down the letter and moved to look out the window. In the distance, the English Channel glimmered in the sunlight as sailing vessels passed by on their way to the open sea.

She could only imagine Benedict's elation, relief, and joy upon receiving Swainson's letter. Of course he had not shared this news with her, but this explained why he held himself at arm's length, and why he had broken off their interlude in the summerhouse. It would have been cruel to encourage her to fall in love with him when he doubtless already knew he was going away. Perhaps that was even a sign that he cared for her, at least a little.

Of course, it was too late to save Camille's heart. She was already hopelessly in love with Benedict...and that was why she must let him go. This was his chance to fulfill the great dream he had thought was broken when he was compelled to come to Cornwall instead of sailing with Gould on the *Parsee*. Yes, it was for the best. He could never be happy here, and she had learned from her own parents that real love was much bigger than one's own selfish needs.

"I apologize for making you wait." Benedict was setting a tray on the small table. "I have our tea."

Camille turned from the window, conscious of his watchful green eyes. She picked up her satchel, smiled as brightly as she could, and hurried across the room. "How kind. But I have just remembered that Rafael is going to meet me near here with the gig, and I am already late."

"Are you certain?" He cocked his dark head, one of his gestures she loved most. "The tea is hot, and I was about to offer you a scone with Prue's own blackberry jam."

"That sounds delicious. I wish I could stay, truly, but...not today."

"Ah." His smile was self-deprecating. "Does this mean you don't want to see my sketches after all?"

"Oh, I do." Hearing the catch in her own voice, she knew she must go before he perceived her pain. "Another time. Goodbye!"

Closing the cottage door behind her, Camille began to run, stopping only when she reached the windswept pine tree. As she leaned against its bent trunk, the tears came at last. She allowed herself a long, blessed minute of release before swiping at her eyes.

You will be all right, she told herself. *Besides...didn't you always know, deep inside, it couldn't be real?*

CHAPTER 27

*A*lone at last, Benedict stared at the box with the carved top as if it were a poisonous snake. His first impulse was to break the bloody lock to get inside, but then he remembered his father's keys. Taking the ring of rusted keys that hung inside the back door, he began to try them one by one. His heart thumped louder with each new key. If none of them worked, perhaps it would mean that Pa was innocent. That simple thought ignited a flicker of hope inside him.

Benedict came to the last key. Steeling himself, he put it into the lock and tried it. It turned. *Damn.* When he slowly lifted the lid, he saw a broken pencil sharpened to a rough point, an assortment of coins, mainly sovereigns and crowns, a stack of £5 notes, and many stained scraps of paper, folded in half.

It was quite possible that Pa had been involved in smuggling at some point. Yet, in his gut, Benedict knew better. He picked up one of the papers and saw a kittiwake feather lying under it. Cursing, he opened the paper.

The writing inside was little more than a lot of faded pencil scratches, but he thought he made out the number 52 and then the word *wings*. His stomach roiled in horror and disbelief. There were more faint scratches which seemed to record a massive payment from someone. Benedict carried the paper to a bright window and stared at the initials: *R U.*

Bloody hell.

* * *

HE WANTED to take the entire box to Prue's house. He wanted to demand that they leave him alone with Pa, and then he would shove the thing under his nose and thunder that he wanted *answers*! Perhaps there was even a way to have Pa arrested, he mused irrationally. Hanged! His body tossed into the sea for the birds to pick clean.

In the end, Benedict merely took one of the dirty, nearly illegible receipts from the box, shoved it in his pocket, and walked down the path to Polruan. Outside Prue's door, he paused and drew a few deep, harsh breaths. There was a babe inside, as well as Jenny and sweet Gareth, who was always so happy to see him. It wouldn't do for him to burst in and threaten to murder pitiful, helpless Pa in front of all of them.

And so, he went inside as he usually did these days, smiling and ruffling Gareth's hair, lifting Jenny high until she giggled, and inquiring after the wellbeing of his sister and her newborn infant. Caleb's mother, Mrs. Johns, was looking after the little ones, while it seemed Fletcher was with Pa.

After allowing Gareth to "read" him the book of bird paintings created by Camille, Benedict rose to his feet. "I suppose I ought to look in on Pa," he said to Mrs. Johns.

She made a sad face. "He be quite fretful today."

"Ah, well. Perhaps I can distract him a bit."

With that, Benedict walked to the back of the

house, pushed aside the thin curtain, and bent to enter the cramped room. Fletcher seemed to be feeding him a last spoonful of soup from a now-empty bowl.

"I want to speak to my father," Benedict said. "Alone."

Fletcher's eyes grew big behind his spectacles as he looked between them. "Sir, I am not certain this is—"

He cut him off. "None of your speeches. Leave us."

Pa made a strangled sound, but the manservant rose from his stool. "I should take away these dishes." Clearly, he wanted to say more, but when he met Benedict's hard gaze, he seemed to think better of it.

When Fletcher had taken a few steps, Benedict picked up the blackthorn walking stick and handed it to him. "If you fall, old boy, I would be forced to play nursemaid to both of you." He lifted both brows for emphasis.

"Point taken, sir." Fletcher nodded as he left the room.

Although the air was warm in the small, enclosed space, Pa was covered by a blanket. Benedict perched on the stool beside the bed and stared hard at the feeble old man.

"I have been in your tunnel, under the cottage," he said in a low, deadly tone. It was satisfying to watch Pa try to shrink back into his pillows. "I want to know what the devil you've been up to, in league with the feather thieves."

Pa curled his lip and shook his head. "Unhh."

"I know you can speak if you want to," Benedict ground out, frustrated.

But then he remembered a recent conversation with Fletcher. The manservant explained that apoplexy had caused Pa's powers of speech to ebb and flow, often depending on how tired he was. If Pa had been trying to talk to Fletcher before Benedict came in, that ability might now be depleted.

"Never mind, I'll do the talking for now." He leaned closer. "It's no use shaking your head. I found your cursed box, the one where you kept your payments from the thieves and crude little receipts like this one." Taking the paper from his pocket, he flicked it open and brought it close to his father's face. "Were you the one who killed the kittiwakes and cut their wings off? Or perhaps you were the leader who paid the feather thieves, and then you sold the wings to someone else?"

Blinking, Pa turned the corners of his mouth down. "Nuh!"

"Who was in charge, then?" Benedict pointed to the faint initials R.U. on the scrap of paper and demanded, "Was it Upton?"

Their eyes met for a long, blazing moment. When, abruptly, tears welled in his father's eyes, something seemed to crack open inside of Benedict.

"Pa!" He heard his own voice break. "For God's sake, I am your *son*. Yet from the moment I dared to think for myself, you have tried to crush my spirit. I once dreamed of making you proud..." To his horror, he felt his throat swell with emotion. "If you want it to be this way between us until you die, so be it. But heed me! This may be your only chance at redemption."

Had he gone mad, speaking of such things to this wicked man?

After a charged silence, he prodded, "Tell me! This leader—who is he?"

A tear rolled down Pa's withered cheek, but Benedict refused to trust it.

"Not he," Pa croaked at last. "*She.*"

* * *

LATER THAT AFTERNOON, Benedict was still wondering what the devil his father had meant by "*She*", when he stopped at the Lugger Inn to check for messages from Jem. There had been no communication between them since Benedict had warned about the customs officers, but today when he inquired at the bar, a note marked *Pascoe* was put into his hand. The crudely written missive from Jem demanded a meeting in the Lanteglos churchyard at dusk. Although the location was much closer than the Old Ferry Inn in Bodinnick, the change was vaguely unsettling.

In fact, Benedict had felt deeply unsettled all day. He couldn't stop thinking about the exchange with Pa. Those moments lingered like a chill mist, deep in his bones, his heart. A part of him wished he'd never allowed himself to strip away a piece of his protective shell. A voice whispered, *He was acting! It was all lies.* Benedict's very soul had felt raw, flayed, and yet the next moments were like the burn of cleansing alcohol followed by a healing balm.

Deep, years-old wounds could not be cured in one day, but perhaps Pa's revelation was a first, tentative step toward truth telling...and even healing. Whether his father was acting or not, Benedict had begun to realize that opening himself to this risk was necessary if he hoped to become a better man.

As he rode toward the parish church of Lanteglos, Benedict tried to put his own personal feelings to one side and focus on the feather thieves. He thought of Lord Upton, appearing to Camille on the cliffs, armed with a rook rifle. Could the RU on Pa's receipts refer to Upton? Even though the initials were a match, it seemed a mad notion. Why would a deuced viscount get involved in the feather trade? And if Pa's garbled "she" was correct, what could it mean? He and Camille had stalled for time long enough. Their outing to learn more from Lady Daphne had become a blind alley, and his meeting with Pa spawned more questions than it answered.

Spying the square Norman tower of Lanteglos church, Benedict pulled his tricorne lower to shade more of his face. The time had come to act, even if that meant laying a dangerous trap.

Lanteglos was tucked into a verdant fold of hills. The grassy churchyard was liberally dotted with cowslips, violets, and foxgloves decorating the graves of those who had gone before. As Benedict dismounted and walked Max along the pathway, he saw a tall, time-worn stone shaft with a gothic, lantern-head cross at its peak. He remembered hearing of this at the party at Frenchman's Haven. It seemed the 13th century artifact had recently been uncovered in a ditch in the church-yard, probably hidden away since the Reformation.

"Psst! Over here, guv'nor."

Looking around, he saw Jem standing near the shaded path that led down to Pont Pill. Still leading Max by the reins, Benedict walked over to join him.

"I hadn't heard from you for so long, I thought mayhap you gave it up," he remarked in husky tones. "Become a shipwright or a limeburner."

Jem seemed to consider these suggestions. "One day I might do, but for now the feather trade be my choice."

"Have you a new plan?" Remembering the feather thief's terror of being arrested and hanged, Benedict added, "No doubt the customs men moved on to other areas."

"Aye, it be time, the master say," Jem agreed, thrusting out his heavy chin. "We raid again, two days hence, at dusk, when the birds be bringin' dinner to the chicks." He paused, then leaned closer, as if he suspected the trees had ears. "We need thee! What be your answer?"

Benedict nodded. "You may depend on me."

"We'll gather on the beach below the nests. The master says ye will be paid later, Pascoe, only if the raid be successful." Jem narrowed his eyes for an instant. "Yer name *do* be Pascoe, aye?"

"Oh, aye." Benedict managed to smile, even as a chill ran down his spine. "Pascoe."

CHAPTER 28

*T*wilight would be gathering soon, thought Camille as she hurried quickly along the flower-lined path toward Lupine Cottage. She slowed her pace just long enough to reach into the pocket in her skirts and find the message from Benedict. It was difficult to believe it was real.

Leaving his cottage just yesterday, Camille had imagined she might never be alone with Benedict again. She had made up her mind to let him go, to sail to Australia and discover birds no one had ever seen before on this side of the world. It would be the most exciting adventure imaginable, and Benedict had been born to experience it.

Knowing all of this, it was better to avoid him from now on. It seemed he must realize it too, but this note told a different story. Inside the cottage, she perched on a small bench, took out the folded paper, and spread it open on her lap.

My love, I must see you. Come to me at Lupine Cottage just before the sun sets. B.

It was so romantic and mysterious that Camille felt

a pang of doubt, yet the words *My love* overrode all else. *Come to me*, Benedict had implored. Just reading the words again sent a warm, sensual shiver through her body. Tonight, they would be together.

She had carried a basket of food over one arm, and now she began to take out its contents and set it on a small table near the window. Madame Kerjean had given her a fresh baguette, a tiny crock of soft cheese, a bunch of purple grapes from Papa's arbor, and an assortment of raw baby vegetables. Camille opened a bottle of Beaujolais wine, one her parents kept on hand for their own occasional trysts and took out two glasses.

The room felt warm, or perhaps it was her own body. She pushed on a window casement enough to let in the breeze from the English Channel. How quickly her heart was beating! Perhaps a few sips of wine would have a calming effect. Camille poured a small quantity of the dark liquid into her glass and drank, but soon realized the wine only heightened her arousal.

A knock sounded at the door. "Camille!"

She rushed to open the door and there was Benedict, so impossibly, sinfully handsome that for a moment, she stopped breathing.

"You've really come," she heard herself say.

He filled the small doorway, coatless, black curls windblown, wearing a midnight-blue-striped waistcoat over his loose linen shirt. "Did you doubt it? Of course I have come. Do you have need of me?"

His deep voice and heated gaze made Camille feel giddy. She caught his hand and drew him into the cottage. "Need of you?" She allowed a radiant smile to shine from her heart. "Indeed."

My love, he had written. *Come to me...*

Camille boldly stood on tiptoe and wrapped her arms around his wide shoulders, reaching up for his kiss. When his mouth slanted over hers, hot and assertive, the world fell away. Their mutual arousal was palpable, like a brushfire ignited by the heat of their bodies. He held her fast against him, cupped her buttocks through her thin muslin skirts and brought her hips against his. He was already so hard, Camille nearly gasped aloud to feel him pressing against the swelling bud of her own need.

Benedict broke their kiss to meet her eyes, and she replied by pressing her hips forward. It all felt completely natural and right. He caught her up in his arms and carried her across the room to the chaise, bending to lay her down across the green velvet. Only when Camille realized where they were did she panic.

"No!" came her hoarse cry. "Not here."

Benedict drew back to search her face, but he made no protest. Instead, he set Camille lightly on her feet, reached for a blanket and draped it across the woven rug. At last, he drew her down into his arms.

She clung to him with primal urgency. His hard, warm body, his musky sea-air scent, the taste of his mouth, the way he responded to her in such a personal yet powerful way...for Camille, he was a potent aphrodisiac. Perhaps she had been storing up this need since Benedict had turned away from her at the summerhouse, and now she felt like a fizzy bottle of champagne about to be opened.

Lying on their sides, they faced each other, kissing for long minutes, oh such delicious, intoxicating kisses! Camille's fingers groped to open the buttons on his waistcoat, and then his shirt. She could scarcely wait to press her face to his chest and inhale his masculine essence.

"You—" he managed to accuse.

She licked the flat disk of his nipple, and Benedict muttered a curse. Encouraged, she sucked at it, imitating what he had done in the summerhouse, and eventually his hands framed her hips and he pushed her back into the blanket.

With deft fingers, he unfastened the bodice of her simple day dress. There was no easy way to free her of the garment, and so he simply opened her bodice and blinked. "Where are your terrible female undergarments?" he murmured.

"I thought I might not need them today..." Camille knew her lids were heavy with passion, and for once she embraced the role of temptress. "Are you shocked?"

"Only in the best sense of the word," Benedict murmured, covering each breast with a hand so that her nipples stood up against his palms.

Bending, he trailed kisses over one breast, then fastened his mouth over the nipple and began to suckle. Camille didn't know if she could bear the exquisite, aching pleasure that tingled between her legs. She was swollen with need, and when he reached down with one hand to lift her skirts, she heard herself beg, "Touch me. Oh, God, please."

Somehow, they managed to undress one another, all the while kissing, caressing, with unbridled urgency. Camille thrilled to the feeling of his tall, masculine body against her softer form. With his skilled fingers and then his mouth, he brought her to another blinding climax, the need between them like a fire. Camille sank her hands into his hair, gasping as the contractions shook her to her core.

"You..." was all she could say.

"I know," came his muffled, smiling response.

When her senses returned, she pushed Benedict onto his back and straddled him. "Now you are mine, sir."

Camille bent to kiss from his mouth down over the lean-muscled surface of his chest. She loved the sensation of his warm skin, the intoxicating scent of him. Soft golden light streamed in through the window, bathing his body in its glow. He was fully erect, pulsing with the need to possess her, and she turned her soft cheek against him. Although Benedict let her have her way with him for a while, kissing and tasting him, eventually she heard him groan and he drew her up his body.

"Sorceress," he accused. Suddenly he was on top again.

"Lover," she countered. Their flushed faces were inches apart, and it seemed that all the protective layers had been stripped away between them. Camille reached up to trace the rough edge of his jaw with her fingertips.

"God, yes. Lover." As he positioned himself between her thighs, he added, "My darling, you are the most beautiful woman alive."

She heard the faint edge of defiance in his voice. How many times had she warned him not to speak of her beauty? Yet today, those words melted her heart.

"I am yours." Camille vowed, reaching down to guide him to her entrance. She was wet and so ready. "Please...take me."

This time, Benedict uttered no protest. Instead, he came slowly into her, looking into her eyes. "I have wanted this, wanted *you* for so long."

She lifted her hips to receive him as he bent to kiss her, slowly, deeply. It was a delicious distraction from the momentary burn of pain when he pushed past her inner resistance. Then their bodies were joined, and the sensation of Benedict filling her was a kind of bliss Camille had never imagined. He partially withdrew and thrust again, and she met him, over and over, clinging to his broad back, feeling his heart pound against her damp breasts. It was a rhythm as old as time, and yet could it have ever been like this for anyone else? Sensual fulfillment warmed every corner of her body...and each urgent thrust felt like a renewed vow of love.

The moment came when Benedict tensed in her arms and uttered a sound deep in his throat. He was pulling back from her. Camille felt something warm and wet on her stomach and remembered what he had said in the summerhouse. *Even if I withdraw, there is no guarantee I won't get you with child.*

As she pressed her face into the crook of his neck, breathing in his scent, Camille knew a bittersweet ache. It came to her that if a babe should grow within her after Benedict sailed for Australia with William Swainson, she would welcome the child with all her heart. Hadn't she always gone her own way?

Still holding her, Benedict propped himself on one elbow and reached for a napkin that lay forgotten on a nearby stool. After gently cleaning her off, he kissed her again before saying, "Camille, I have something to tell you."

Abruptly, she thought of her own secret. Had the time come at last to tell him the truth about her past with Roger?

"I love you." His voice was rough. "I love you." He tipped up her chin and she saw the telltale gleam in his eyes. "I don't know why it took me so damned long to admit the truth, even to myself."

She couldn't help smiling, even as her own eyes stung with emotion. "Mama says that men can be cowards when it comes to matters of the heart."

"Your mother is a wise woman."

Should she mention Australia? How could she tell him that she had violated his privacy and read the letter lying on his desk? It came to her that, just because he said he loved her, it didn't mean he intended to give up his work as an ornithologist. And she would not want him to make such a choice!

Enjoy this moment, counseled her inner voice. *Worry later.*

And so, Camille wrapped her arms around his neck. "I love you, too. I knew it in the summerhouse. Perhaps from the first, when I thought you were a villain. My life hasn't been the same since that first day in Hyde Park when you interrupted my scolding of Lady Rockbridge."

They laughed together and, a few moments later, Benedict murmured, "There's nothing I'd rather do than lie here with you for hours, but perhaps we should put on some clothing, in case someone like your father wanders by." He got to his feet and reached for his trousers.

She took the hand he extended, loving it when his eyes caressed her naked body as she rose. Would they ever be together again like this? When Benedict sailed to Australia, everything might change. Allowing herself a tiny sigh, Camille slipped on her light gown and Benedict did the fastenings, leaning close to murmur in her ear.

"Has anyone told you how closely you resemble Botticelli's painting of Venus? You could have been the model, my love." He kissed a sensitive spot on her neck.

She wanted to say that only he had seen her like this, but then the nagging memory of Roger returned... the two of them in this very room. It was true that she hadn't been naked with him, but there had been intimacy all the same. Whether she wanted it or not, had she not allowed it to go too far?

"No doubt you are as ravenous as I am." Benedict moved to the table where Camille had laid out food and wine on a tea tray. He sent her a faintly wicked smile.

"Let us enjoy a small picnic, shall we? We can feed each other."

She watched as he carried the tray over to the chaise and sat down. Her stomach was in turmoil. Perched on the very edge of the seat, she accepted the plate Benedict made for her and tried to eat some of the food.

"Grapes from the arbor at Elysium?" As he spoke, he ate one and held another close to her mouth until she parted her lips to accept it.

"Yes." *Tell him, just tell him.* There was a chance Benedict would be so disturbed by her secret, it would change things between them, but Camille knew her moment had come. "Actually, there is a private matter I must speak to you about."

"Anything." He moved to sit so that their bodies were touching, and his smoldering gaze told her that he couldn't wait to make love to her again. "You are always brave enough to say what is in your heart. Thank God you sent word today, asking me to meet you here." He brought a small, folded piece of paper out of his pocket and held it up as if it were a diamond.

She stared at the note he held, all else forgotten. "But...*you* sent word to me!"

Benedict's brow furrowed. He shook his head once, then opened the note so she could see it. Camille's heart jumped in her chest as she read the words: *My love, I must see you. Come to me at Lupine Cottage just before the sun sets. C.*

* * *

"WHERE DID YOU GET THIS?" Camille had gone so pale Benedict felt alarmed.

"It was under my door when I returned from a ride this morning," he said. "I assumed you had sent Rafael to deliver it."

316

Camille immediately reached into the pocket hidden in her skirt and withdrew a folded piece of paper identical to his. "A young boy rode over to Elysium today and gave *this* to Claire, our housekeeper."

Dread clutched at him as he opened it and read: *My love, I must see you. Come to me at Lupine Cottage just before the sun sets. B.*

"Who the devil is behind this?" he demanded, searching his memory for a key to this puzzle. "Could it be someone in your family, playing matchmaker?"

Camille looked sick. "I don't think so. More likely, it was someone who has…special knowledge of Lupine Cottage." Her voice shook slightly. "Oh, Benedict, now you must heed me!"

He was pondering the odd feeling he'd had during the meeting with Jem. Was there a clue there? When Camille tugged at his bare arm, he forced himself back to the present moment. "Go on. I'm listening, but—"

In anguished tones, she broke in, "I have wanted to tell you, but I have been afraid. Afraid you might feel disgust each time you looked at me. You see…last year, when Roger spent time here in Cornwall, we came here once." As she spoke these last words, color flooded her pale cheeks. "Alone."

Raw, blazing fury gripped him as he realized she felt *shame* for what had happened with Upton. "He tried to have his way with you right here, didn't he? That's why you turned away from the chaise with me." Benedict stood and drew her to her feet.

"Yes. I…I let it go on too long, but at least we did not…" Camille turned her exquisite face up to him and his heart tore at the sight of her tears. In a whisper, she added, "We did not undress."

Burning, he silently swore, *I will tear him limb from limb.*

In the next moment, aching for Camille, he

wrapped her tightly in his arms. "Never mind, my darling. For God's sake, you needn't say more. And I will not allow you to blame yourself in any way! Now that you've told me, you are free."

"I love you." Her voice was thick with emotion, as if no other words mattered now.

"And I love you." He kissed her roughly, letting her feel the cleansing force of his love for her. "But now time demands that we deal with this other matter. You clearly think that Upton sent the notes to us."

"Who else could it possibly be? He knows about Lupine Cottage, knows I come here alone. And when I think of him on the cliffs with that awful rifle, it seems that he must have something to do with the feather thieves."

"He does. I have learned that much, but still haven't put all the pieces together." Releasing Camille, Benedict continued talking as he sat down to pull on boots, shirt, and waistcoat. "When I met with Jem last night, he told me the raid was planned for Wednesday. Tomorrow!" Grimly, he shook his head. "But I had a feeling that he might now be suspicious of me in my guise as Tom Pascoe." He drew a harsh breath and buttoned his waistcoat. Through the windows, he saw that the sun was lower in the sky. Dusk would soon be upon them. "Clearly, they misled me about the raid. It's doubtless happening at this very moment—and that's why they lured both of us away to this cottage."

"We must hurry!" cried Camille. As she spoke, she twisted her long, luxuriant hair up into a knot atop her head and quickly secured it with pins.

Benedict stopped her midway to the door, a hand on each shoulder. "You are not going. It's far too dangerous!"

She looked back at him, and he could see her thinking. "Perhaps you are right, especially since I am wearing skirts. I would only slow you down."

Relieved that she was not going to fight him on this, Benedict replied, "I have Max. I will take you to Elysium on my way."

"No, there isn't time! Look, we can see the rooftops of my home in the distance," Camille said, throwing open the door and stepping outside. "I can easily walk there on my own. Don't worry about me! If there is still a chance of stopping the raid, you must go!"

He watched as she rushed down the path, past Max, pausing only long enough to turn back and urge, "Hurry, Benedict! Make haste to save our kittiwakes."

When Camille lifted her skirts and half-ran up the drive to Elysium, she was surprised to find that no one was about. She opened the door and went inside, thinking only of finding her father to ask for help. The aroma of one of Madame Kerjean's delicious peasant soups wafted to her, but for a second time today, she could not think of food.

Just then, the solitary form of Zeus appeared, wagging his big tail, like a black-clad canine butler.

Camille asked, "Where is everyone?" and he turned to lead her to the library. As they came to the open double doors, male laughter reached her ears. Inside, seated around a hexagonal table near the fireplace, she saw a convivial group engaged in a game of Faro.

"Hello, darling," called her mother as she began to deal the cards, two at a time, to her right and left. "Can you believe it? I am the banker! Would you care to join the play?"

When the other players turned in their chairs to greet her, she saw not only her father, but Uncle Justin, Uncle Sebastian, Rafael, and even Damien. The three rakishly handsome men were drinking, and young

Rafael and her little brother looked completely excited to be among them.

"No, Mama, I cannot, but how wonderful that all of you are gathered here!" Camille lost no time in hurrying to her mother's chair, where she held up a hand. "Please, everyone, attend me! I need your help."

"Cam, what happened to you?" exclaimed Damien. "You look a mess!"

"I ran here from Lupine Cottage. But that doesn't matter." They were all staring at her, waiting. "I need you, Papa, and I hope that my uncles will join us. Benedict and I believe there is a raid commencing any moment on the kittiwake nests near Polruan. He has gone ahead to try to stop them, but it may be dangerous."

Uncle Justin narrowed his eyes. "The blackguards deserve to be caught and punished, but what penalty exists for killing *birds*? None that I know of."

Her father was rising to his feet, and Uncle Sebastian joined him. "There may be no law," her uncle said. "But perhaps I can bring to bear some power as the Lord of Trevarre Hall."

"Oh yes!" cried Camille. "You must threaten to expose them as the villains they are if they do not immediately give up their evil ways!"

Papa put an arm around her and glanced toward the others. "It seems there is no time to waste. We should leave immediately. Rafael, I will ask you to bring the horses round."

"Of course, sir!" The Brazilian youth jumped up. "But I must go as well, as your guide. I know exactly the place where they do this wicked deed."

"I will go, too!" cried Damien, leaping up from his chair. "I'll bring my wooden sword. I have been sharpening it!"

Gabriel pointed at the boy. "Not this time, son. I am trusting you to guard the women in our absence."

Camille was about to exclaim that she would not be left behind but feared an argument from her parents, and there was no time for that. Instead, she rushed up to her bedchamber and changed into her boy's clothing more quickly than ever before. Her fingers flew as she plaited her hair into a long braid and pulled a cap over her head. By the time the men emerged onto the drive and mounted their waiting horses, Camille was passing through the entrance hall.

"So, you are going, too," said Isabella's voice from the library entrance. "I knew you couldn't have turned all your power over to the men that easily."

Camille turned to see her mother standing there, smiling with a mixture of pride and concern. In the background, Damien had dozed off in one of the comfortable leather chairs, wooden sword by his side.

"Oh, Mama, I have to go." A moment later, she was embracing her tightly. Drawing back, she let her see the happy tears in her eyes. "I love him, and he loves me."

"I know." Isabella caressed her cheek. "We recognized it from the first. Go, my darling. I know you must."

Camille started away, then glanced back briefly. "It is not only for Benedict, you see, but for the defenseless birds. Someone has to stand up and fight for them."

"They couldn't wish for a better champion than you...our own firebrand."

Just then, Rafael appeared in the open doorway, framed by the glow of sunset. He gave her a jaunty bow. "My lady, I have your Pegasus here. Do you come? The others are just ahead."

"Yes!" As she ran to join him, Camille felt the deep thrill of their purpose that night. "Thank you for waiting, dear Rafael."

The boy gave her a slightly raffish bow as she

mounted her horse. "I am ever your servant, my lady. Let us be away!"

* * *

Twilight painted the summer sky in shades of gold and plum as Benedict galloped over the coastal path toward the cliffs. In those minutes, he realized that he couldn't just appear on the scene and stop an entire gang of men from carrying out their plot. Camille might feel that they were committing a hanging offense, but Jem had spoken the truth himself during the last raid: killing kittiwakes was hardly on a par with smuggling. In fact, it was not a crime at all, legally speaking. It was only the presence of the customs officers that had caused them to stop that night, for doubtless most of the feather thieves were wanted for other crimes.

Could Benedict use a simple warning that the king's men were coming? It seemed unlikely that the trick could work twice. Besides, he suspected his Tom Pascoe identity had been pierced, or Jem wouldn't have given him the wrong day for the raid.

Benedict could hear the kittiwakes crying and the waves crashing as he came to Gull Cottage. Quickly, he dismounted and led Max inside the small shed, out of sight. The birds might already be dying by now, he knew, and there was not a moment to spare.

Inside the cottage, he went into the bedroom and pulled on the worn brown coat and tricorne hat that he wore as Tom Pascoe. He opened the case containing his pistol and put it in the waistband of his trousers, concealed by the coat. The place was silent; not even Ember was about. Crossing to his desk, Benedict quickly pried up the loose floorboards and lowered himself down into the tunnel. Just in case anyone was checking, he had put the carved box back in its hiding place. The sight of it now reminded him of how many questions remained unanswered.

One thing Benedict did know: all the signs pointed to Lord Roger Upton as the mastermind behind the feather thieves' plot. The initials RU on the receipts in the box, Upton turning up at Prue's house and asking for Pa, Upton skulking about on the cliffs with his rook rifle, and finally, Camille's strong belief that Upton had sent the messages luring them both to Lupine Cottage.

Quickly, quietly, Benedict made his way through the tunnel, pausing between the two tall, narrow rocks at the entrance to scan the pathway outside. The ledges lining the cliffs where the kittiwakes nested were still a fair distance away, though their cries seemed to grow louder. No one was in sight. His heart began to pound as he silently left the tunnel and crouched behind a giant rock.

Soon, the sound of grumbling voices reached his ears. Mist was gathering in the gloaming, blurring the shapes of raggedly garbed men on a rocky outcropping just below him.

"Wait, I tell ye!" A Cornish-accented voice that sounded like Jem's rose above the others. "Look 'ee! There she be."

Had he heard Jem say *she*? Was he talking about Camille? Nothing made sense. As Benedict caught sight of the kittiwakes circling back toward their nests, bearing tiny fish for their hatchlings' dinners, he knew that there was no time to wait for answers.

All that mattered was stopping the slaughter. Remembering the day he'd watched them cut the wings off a live bird and toss it into the Channel, raw fury churned inside him. He moved behind a taller rock to get a better view of the cliffs below and was surprised to spy a small boat rowing onto the beach. A thin man wearing a coat and brimmed hat climbed out, pulled the boat fully onto land, then raised a hand to the men above. Jem and his band of feather thieves started down the precarious cliff path to meet the new arrival. Was it Upton?

A short distance eastward, Benedict could see the nests where growing chicks were straining to greet their kittiwake parents as they swooped toward them with food. The group of men, armed with clubs and canvas bags for the severed wings, began to point at the birds and move in that direction.

As he emerged into the open, Benedict reached under his coat to lightly rest a hand on his pistol.

"Ho there!" he called. When all of them had turned in surprise to look up the slope, he lifted his free hand and waved. "Jem, did you not intend that I should lead this raid?"

The stocky man in the striped cap scowled, then turned to confer with the slender newcomer. At last, Jem replied, "Nay, Pascoe, go on your way. Our true leader be among us tonight."

Who the devil was it? Benedict tried to get a better look at the man who now stood near his boat. This person, who must be the "true leader" Jem referred to, appeared barely bigger than young Rafael!

"Ah, I understand now," said Benedict. "You gave me the wrong date for the raid so I wouldn't meet your leader. Don't you trust me?" He started toward them, down the rugged path, one hand still resting on the pistol concealed at his waistband.

"Go back," shouted Jem, using his thick body to block the fellow who'd come by sea.

"I am afraid there is really no place for me to go. You see," Benedict paused to point back toward Gull Cottage. "That is my home."

"Nay. It be the home of Josiah Hawke!" argued Jem.

He almost revealed his true identity, but there was no time. Instead, he took a chance. "Hawke no longer lives here. It is my home now. It is my land, and I require that you all take your leave."

"Even if it be true, ye cannot order us from the cliffs!" scoffed Jem, peering up at him through the mist. "No man owns the beaches."

The motley band of feather thieves muttered their agreement and began to move again toward the nests, clubs in hand.

Benedict drew his pistol and pointed it at the group. "Are the wings of a few helpless birds worth your lives?" he shouted. "Go home and I will forget who I saw here tonight."

At that very moment, a hard object jammed between his shoulder blades and a sickeningly familiar voice warned, "Lay down your pistol, Hawke, and say your prayers."

His heart sank like a stone. "Ah, Upton. You have ever been a snake." Bending his knees, he set the pistol close by on the ground, and stood again.

"Brave words from a man about to die! Insult me if you will, but the beauteous Camille sang quite a different tune the day I sampled her wares in Lupine Cottage. Oh, but of course you wouldn't know that she is now little better than soiled goods. When she was there with you today, she was doubtless pining for me, remembering our tryst." He pushed the barrel of the gun harder against the center of Benedict's back. "That must be the reason your rendezvous ended so soon! I had been hoping you would stay much longer."

Ignoring Upton's taunts, Benedict pressed, "It's been you all along, hasn't it? Hiding behind your noble title while slaughtering the kittiwakes and selling their wings to the *plumassiers* in London and Paris. The people of Cornwall, including the St. Briac families, were generous enough to befriend you and you repaid their kindness with treachery."

"Say what you will." Upton managed a shaky laugh, and Benedict heard a note of hysteria in his voice. "You are about to have an unfortunate accident."

Would he really do it? A cold chill spread like a stain through Benedict as he imagined dying here, losing every precious thing he had struggled to attain if Upton simply discharged the pistol into his back. *Camille...*

Just then, the sound of distant hoofbeats reached his ears, and he sensed that Upton had stiffened his arm, perhaps even craned his neck to look. Moments later, among the clamor of horses being reined in, Benedict heard a shout from the clifftops above them.

"I am Lord Sebastian Trevarre!" thundered a commanding voice. "I am here in the company of many more men, all of us armed. More are close behind. I demand that all of you come up the path and surrender your weapons."

On the cliff behind Benedict, there came the sound of pebbles crunching under boots as Sebastian and his companions started down the steep path. He could sense Upton's increasingly nervous indecision and knew he must act. Spinning around, Benedict grasped the wrist holding the pistol. Upton put up a fight, forcing Benedict to twist the man's wrist. Then, at the very moment he wrested it from Upton's grasp, the gun discharged in a deafening blast that scattered the adult kittiwakes. Smoke burned Benedict's eyes, and the acrid scent of powder stung his nostrils.

"I've been hit!" cried Upton over the sound of the birds' cries of alarm.

Benedict would not risk the chance that Upton was trying to trick him. In one swift movement, he bent to snatch up his own pistol from the ground and aimed it at the other man's chest. Face to face, he saw that Upton had gone dead white.

"I don't see any wounds," Benedict muttered, sweeping him with a hard gaze. "Where were you hit?"

"At this moment, I couldn't tell you—but I am in terrible pain!"

Sebastian came into sight then, followed close behind by Gabriel St. Briac and his older brother, Justin. Rafael was bringing up the rear.

"Thank God you've come," cried Upton, pointing at Benedict and the pistol aimed at Upton's chest. "This blackguard is trying to *kill* me!"

"Ah, but we know differently, my lord," Justin St. Briac said with a dark smile. "I suppose I should have known when I encountered you so frequently at White's, losing badly at Hazard, that you were very desperate. Selling kittiwake wings to the *plumassiers* must have seemed far preferable to confessing your deep debts to your stern father, Earl Helford."

As St. Briac spoke, Benedict lowered his weapon and waited with the others for Upton's response.

"My father would cut me off without a farthing!" cried Upton. His expression turned pleading. "Don't you see, I was only trying to spare Father the humiliation of being laughed at by the *ton*. Instead, having discovered this—uh, alternative means of income, I have been able to keep up appearances quite brilliantly, and thereby maintain our good name."

Sebastian arched a brow and glanced at the other men, one by one, before proclaiming sardonically, "I perceive that his lordship believes himself to be a bloody hero!"

Benedict nodded. "Yet I must take issue with the countless birds he has slaughtered to pay his creditors and line his own pockets." He fixed Upton with a cold stare. "Have you been leading this entire gruesome enterprise?"

"No! How could I do so? I am merely the one who purchases the wings and sells them in London and Paris. Your own father, Josiah Hawke, was my broker!" Adopting a scornful tone, Upton exclaimed, "We committed no crime. Need I may remind you? It is hardly unlawful to kill wild birds!" He paused, nostrils flared. "Is it?"

"Perhaps not," Sebastian replied grimly, "but as Lord of Trevarre Hall, I am committed to protect the wild birds and animals of our Fowey Estuary. Needless to say, I have a great deal of power, and I have many friends among the king's officers. I suggest you be grateful to escape with your life, my lord. We never want to see you in Cornwall again."

"I see," Upton said stiffly, nodding, clearly attempting to salvage the shreds of his pride. "Fair enough, I suppose."

"And the rest of you!" Lord Sebastian shouted into the breeze, pointing to the group of men still gathered farther down the sloping cliff. "Unless you wish me to give your names to the authorities, suggesting they investigate *all* of your clandestine activities, I would advise you to leave this place and never return."

Amid scattered calls of "Aye, my lord!", the feather thieves began to disband. Then, as Benedict watched, one thin figure broke away from behind the taller men and scrambled down toward the little boat pushed up on the beach. In the fellow's haste, he jumped suddenly from a ledge of rock, then struggled back to his feet and limped forward.

It was, Benedict realized, the person Jem had pointed out as the mysterious leader.

"Stop him!" he shouted, gesturing, and gave chase. It was encouraging to hear others following him down the steep path, occasionally skidding over the loose rocks.

"I am right behind," called Justin.

They pushed through the feather thieves and then Benedict dropped from a ledge onto the beach, reaching out to grasp the villain's coat just as he climbed back into his boat and grappled with the oars. With a roar of frustration, he heaved the slight, struggling figure back onto the beach, turned him on his back. He pulled off first a wide-brimmed hat, and then a knit cap. Long, pale blonde tresses spilled out across the sand.

Breathing hard, Benedict blinked in disbelief. To his utter shock, he found himself staring at the angry yet beautiful face of Lady Daphne Callywith.

* * *

HER HEART IN HER THROAT, Camille crowded in behind her father and uncles on the stony ledge above the beach. She had arrived just in time to hear Roger admit his role in the cruel slaughter of numberless kittiwakes, and now as Benedict unmasked a second villain, she held her breath.

The instant the knit cap was removed and long, golden locks tumbled free, Uncle Justin spoke first: "*Sangdieu!* It is Daphne, up to more of her tricks!"

"Lady Daphne?" repeated Camille in disbelief. "It cannot be. We just saw her a few days ago at Callywith Manor. She was heavy with child!"

"Do you imagine that this woman is her twin?" Justin slanted a sardonic glance her way, clearly not surprised to find that his niece had ridden to join them. "No, it is all another of her hoaxes. It seems everything in her life is a deception."

With that, he jumped down to the beach along with

her father and Sebastian, and Camille followed. Papa shook his head, sighing, at the sight of her. "*Ma petite,* you are incorrigible," he murmured, wrapping an arm around her shoulders and kissing her brow.

"I had to come," she whispered. "I belong here!"

Near the rowboat, Benedict had allowed Lady Daphne to get to her feet but held her by one slender wrist.

"What the devil is this all about?" he demanded in scathing tones.

"You have no right to keep me here like this," she replied haughtily. "I insist that you release me and let me go my way."

Camille couldn't stay in the background another moment. She went to Benedict's side, expecting him to exhibit shock at the sight of her, but instead he only flashed a grin. His green eyes told her *I missed you!* After their brief, wordless exchange, she turned to Lady Daphne.

"All of you feather thieves protest that murdering defenseless birds like these kittiwakes, simply to harvest their wings for a lot of ridiculous hats, is not a criminal offense and thus you are blameless!" Camille said in clear, ringing tones. "Perhaps it is not a crime punishable by the law, but it is clearly an offense to God and Nature. Every evil deed you commit, every life you harm, darkens your very soul."

Daphne was defiant. "What else was I to do? Callywith's ancestral estate was falling down around us, and he was losing his reason! Was I meant to simply sit by the fire and endure it?" Her voice rose. "I had to *do* something! Once Roger and I conceived of providing kittiwake wings to milliners and *plumassiers,* my life was transformed!"

"That's how you could move to the larger, grander manor house near Lerryn," Benedict interjected.

"Oh, yes, and it was far more fitting. I was born a noblewoman, after all."

Camille stared at Daphne's slim figure, then pointed. "But what about—?"

The other woman smiled proudly. "You two were quite fooled by my disguise, weren't you?" She motioned with both hands to mimic her girth during their previous meeting. "Of course, I had good reason…first, so that no one would suspect that I could be leading these men, and also because it has long been my greatest dream to have a child." Her gaze strayed to Justin.

"Your plot, a decade ago, for *me* to father your child sent tremors through my marriage," he said, brows aloft. "I should not be surprised that you have now taken matters into your own hands, fooling your husband and the world by pretending to be with child. What have you planned next? A journey to London to purchase a baby?"

"Certainly not!" Daphne sniffed, offended. "*Paris.*" Her voice rose as if she were speaking from a stage. "Callywith must have an heir, and so I am going to provide one. I mean to use some of the funds from this little enterprise to travel to France. Then, in a few weeks, I shall return with Callywith's new son!" No sooner were the words out than she put a hand to her mouth, as if realizing the mistake she had made by revealing too much.

Camille spoke bluntly. "My lady, I think you are mad."

"Ha! I believe you must mean bold, daring, and unconquerable," came Daphne's imperious reply. Turning to Benedict, she ordered, "Release your hold, sir, so that I may be on my way to Paris."

Utterly mad! thought Camille as she exchanged a speaking glance with Benedict.

Sebastian stepped forward. "Lady Daphne, if you are wise, you will not return to Cornwall. Remain in France, where one imagines you may well discover a new circle of friends to bewitch."

"Indeed," agreed Justin, fixing her with a hard look. "Now that you have so proudly divulged your plan to put an imposter heir in Squire Callywith's nest, we would tell the world if you ever dare to return to England."

When Benedict released her wrist, Daphne lifted her chin, climbed into her rowboat, and took up her oars. It was Justin who came forward to push the small craft off into the English Channel. As the moon rose in the gathering darkness and the kittiwakes once again settled contently on their nests, Lady Daphne and her tiny boat grew smaller and smaller on the water, eventually disappearing from sight.

CHAPTER 30

The moon was bright overhead, silvering the cliffs near Gull Cottage, when Camille's father, uncles, and Rafael all left to ride back to Elysium. Only Camille remained behind.

"I want to stay with Benedict for now," she had told her father. "Can you understand, Papa?"

"I should forbid it, you know, but I can see how it is," he murmured with a trace of irony, holding her fast for a long moment before he opened his arms. "Have a care, darling Cam."

When the last of their hoofbeats had died away, Camille stood with Benedict on the cliffs above the kittiwake nests, drinking in the quiet. The gulls were on their nests, safe, the threats against them banished.

"It is the best sound of all," she whispered and leaned against his strong shoulder.

He nodded. "The silence? Agreed."

"Soon the last of the chicks will fledge and they will all fly out to sea for another year." Camille's throat felt tight. "But what about next spring, and all the years to come? If they return here, will new feather hunters come for them?"

"They may, as long as there is a demand for birds'

feathers and wings to decorate hats," Benedict allowed. "But they don't know who they are up against, minx."

His confidence fueled a warm glow that spread inside her. Looking up at the shadowed planes of his face, Camille vowed, "I will never stop fighting those terrible men. Never!" She paused. "Perhaps I ought to go to London and petition Parliament to pass a bill, protecting birds like the kittiwakes! Does that sound absurd?"

"A bit, perhaps, in this harsh world," he allowed. "But if anyone can do it, you can."

Bending, he kissed her tenderly. As his mouth covered hers, the spark flared between them, and Camille's body came alive. She wrapped her arms around his neck, opened to his kiss, felt him harden against her. It was a beautiful sort of ecstasy.

Dimly, she wondered what lay ahead for them. She ached to surrender to this moment and the evening ahead, to further deepen the connection between them...even though it was surely destined to end in heartbreak when Benedict sailed to Australia with William Swainson.

He drew back just enough to meet her eyes. "Come inside with me and let's find some supper, shall we? We need to talk."

They walked back to Gull Cottage hand in hand. Inside, Benedict lit a fire to dispel the slight, misty chill of the summer night while Camille discovered fresh eggs and hard cheese in the larder.

"I shall prepare an omelet for our supper," she told him. "Papa taught me how when I was a little girl. I am half French, you know."

After pouring water into the kitchen basin, she washed her hands and face and looked up to find him holding out a towel. Laughing, Camille dried herself and said, "I must look a mess." She glanced down at her boy's clothing. "Are you put off?"

This drew a husky laugh from Benedict. "You know better than that." With one hand, he unfastened her braid and loosened the long waves of her hair. "You have never been more radiant."

While Camille expertly cooked the omelet, creating mouth-watering aromas, he poured small glasses of red wine and found scones for them to share with their meal. At last, they sat down at the little table. Benedict drew his chair close to hers, and a candle flickered between their plates.

"I was ravenous," he said. "My God, this is delicious! You have more talents than I ever could have dreamed."

"I love food, so I had to learn to cook at a young age, or I might not get enough to eat!"

Laughing softly, he fed her a bite of omelet. "You're a wonder."

She felt herself glowing. Was it possible to be any happier than this? Looking around, she thought that even the cottage looked better than she remembered. "Have you changed something here? It feels different."

One of his dark brows flicked up as he set down his fork. "I have added a few of Ma's things that Pa stored away after she died. A rug, some cushions, other small touches." He pointed to a small blue vase on the table, displaying a bouquet of bright pink thrift and white sea campion. "It seems a good idea to make the cottage more…inhabitable. Not just a place to exist, if you take my meaning."

Her heart swelled. "Aunt Mouette is in the midst of redecorating again. She asked Mama if we needed some new furniture, but we don't." Her cheeks grew warm. "A lovely green velvet sofa…and a simple bed in the Empire style. Perhaps you would like to have them?"

Leaning toward her, Benedict brushed his mouth over her temple, and murmured, "Will you help me with those changes?"

Enjoy this moment, her inner voice counseled again.

"Of course." Unbidden, tears stung her eyes. "And where is Ember?"

Benedict straightened and took a sip of wine. At last, he met her gaze. "This morning, I took Ember to Prue's, to be with Pa. I—" He paused, and she sensed the raw edge of his discomfort. "I thought it might be good for both of them."

"It couldn't have been easy to do something so kind for your father, considering the past," she whispered.

"No. I would rather turn my back forever." Benedict's jaw hardened, and he closed his eyes for a long moment. "Yet—I have been haunted by something you said."

She blinked in surprise. "Something *I* said?"

"When we left there, after Pa fell at Gareth's little party, you asked me if I intended to live like that forever. I had time over these past days to think about that. I finally realized it wasn't Pa who kept me imprisoned by bitterness. I was doing it to myself."

Each word seemed to be torn from a place deep inside him, and Camille felt a spear of grief for the boy who had suffered so much, whose every attempt to win his father's approval had been met by mocking rejection. She dared to reach for his hand, and he gripped her fingers.

"You don't have to forgive him, not yet at least," she said softly.

"Right. He doesn't bloody deserve it." His eyes gleamed with unshed tears. "But Pa has lately shown contrition, I believe." He told her then about the carved box he had found in the tunnel, filled with receipts. "I took it to Pa and told him this might be his only chance for redemption. I demanded to know if Upton was the leader. He couldn't speak except to say it was not he, but *she*."

Camille gasped. "He was trying to tell you about Lady Daphne!"

"It would seem so. I couldn't imagine then what he meant, given her misleading appearance at Callywith Manor, but I perceived something in his eyes. And that helped me come to the decision about Ember."

"Perhaps that's how your healing will unfold... slowly, with small moments."

Benedict drew a ragged breath and nodded. "You may be right." He reached out to grasp her waist with both hands, bringing her onto his lap. "I only know I don't want that cursed pain any longer." Holding her close, he buried his face in her hair. "I want this." His embrace tightened. "I want you."

Her heart raced with a mixture of joy and uncertainty. "I want that, too."

"Do you think you could live here, with me? I thought I hated this place because Pa lived here, but I've begun to imagine it transformed into a real home. Together we could add rooms to the cottage, make a proper garden, build a stable...and guard the nests on the cliffs."

Camille quavered, "But, I don't understand."

"I love you." His smile flashed in the candlelight. "What else is there to understand?"

"What about...Australia?"

"What about it?" He looked puzzled. "Do you mean the expedition with Gould that I had to refuse when Pa fell ill?"

She glanced away. "No. I mean...a more recent opportunity."

Drawing back, Benedict looked at her and cocked

his head. "Camille, have you been reading my private correspondence?"

"I didn't mean to!" Her face burned. "You were making tea, and I simply went over to the desk because I noticed all the specimens had disappeared from sight. And then—"

"Never mind, I can guess rest." He shook his head and gave a rueful laugh. "That's why you left in such haste that day."

"Yes." She bit her lip. "I know it is your life's dream to go to Australia with an ornithological expedition. And I understand! I love you and I would never stand in the way of that."

"Very noble! However, you don't have to stand in the way because I already decided not to go. I've done enough of that...and in any event, how could I be part of such a project when I no longer shoot and preserve specimens?"

Camille felt dizzy. "Truly? I thought perhaps that was simply a passing phase."

"Darling minx, can't you see, knowing you has changed me?" Now there were tears in his eyes as well, and she reached up to touch them. "I did my best to cling to my old ideas, but that only made me more miserable. I don't want to live that way any longer. I want to be happy...with you."

"Oh, Benedict," she sobbed. "I want that, too! And I also have changed."

For long minutes, they held each other, tears mingling, their hearts beating in unison as the candle flame guttered on the table. When Benedict finally rose, he brought her with him, one arm crooked under her knees, the other firmly supporting her back.

"I realize you have vowed repeatedly never to marry, but I promise you we will make an unconventional marriage that pleases us rather than society. My love, allow me to wear down your resistance." A wicked gleam lit his eyes as he added, "Like this."

His intoxicating kiss left Camille swimming in a sea of pleasure. "Oh, my," she managed to whisper.

He drew back, watching her. "Is it working?"

"Almost..." She gave him a rather giddy smile. "But I fear there may be only one sure way to successfully breach my defenses."

Benedict gave a soft laugh as he carried her off to the bedroom. "I thought you would never ask."

EPILOGUE

JULY 1838

On Benedict's wedding day, he woke at dawn and walked alone on the cliffs. The last of the kittiwake hatchlings would fledge any day now, and the compelling birds would leave their nests and return to sea for another year.

Benedict thought back to the long-ago day in London when he had read Prue's letter. He'd thought her gut-wrenching news marked the end of the life he'd been creating, but in truth it was the beginning of a miraculous new chapter that continued to unfold. He wouldn't have believed, then, that he could find happiness in Cornwall, but it was true. He wouldn't have believed then that the wounds in his relationship with Pa could begin to heal, just a bit, but it was true.

A fortnight had passed since Prudence went to Pa's room and discovered him dead, one slack arm curved around Ember's soft, protective form. The news had felt like a sword through Benedict's midsection, but that raw pain was soon followed by a kind of peace. Pa would never have recovered, and he was miserable, trapped in a body he could not control. Fletcher had put a hand on Benedict's shoulder and said, "I think, if he had found the words, this would have been his wish. Perhaps he willed it."

But first, Benedict realized, Pa had shown a sliver of remorse. He had tried to tell Benedict about Lady Daphne and, looking back, it seemed he'd stretched out a hand and offered that single word "*She*" as a gift to the son he'd mistreated so bitterly.

It wasn't enough, but it was something, and Benedict had pried open his heart to accept it…for his own sake as much as Pa's.

"Sir!" called Fletcher's familiar voice from the cottage door. "Do you not have an important appointment today?"

"Ah, yes!" Benedict couldn't help grinning as he started back. It was time to bathe, shave, and dress for his wedding. The very word made him shake his head with bemused joy. "I do, indeed."

He had never expected to find a woman like Camille…and the chance to fashion marriage into something of their very own. But like everything else in his life these days, the unthinkable was now quite real.

* * *

CAMILLE STOOD JUST inside the medieval chapel near Trevarre Hall, her heart beating like a drum. She wore the simplest of gowns, fashioned of sunshine-yellow silk, and her tawny-gold locks were caught up in an Apollo knot, tendrils escaping to frame her face. Her bouquet was a cluster of flowers from the gardens at Elysium: buttercups, poppies, violet lupine, and frothy Queen Anne's lace. Camille held her father's strong arm, and he looked over at her and smiled with so much love she felt teary. Just behind her stood her sister, Louise, who had traveled from Lyme Regis to join in her wedding.

Surveying the guests who swiveled to look at her, Camille recognized her own family who resided in Cornwall, and many more beloved faces. Grandmère was present, watching from her invalid chair, and today she had deigned to wear a hat decorated with flowers rather than feathers. Beside her was Cousin Emeline along with her older brother Anthony, his wife Frederica, and their newborn son, Oliver. Camille also recognized a striking, older couple: Mouette's parents, André and Devon Raveneau.

In the back row she saw the Trevarre family, including her cousins Cassandra and Lucas, with their spouses and children. And in the front row sat Prudence and Caleb with their little ones. There was only one person Camille did not recognize...a distinguished, bejeweled old lady who sat close to Prudence.

Just as Cassandra rose and took up her violin to play the lilting "Fairy Dance," Benedict appeared at the front of the chapel, Fletcher proudly standing by his side.

He wore a finely tailored suit of soot-gray broadcloth, a sapphire-blue waistcoat, and an expertly knotted white neckcloth. A beam of sunlight streamed through one of the stone windows, shining on his windblown black hair. Camille drank in the sight of him. If possible, Benedict was more handsome than ever, perhaps because he was finally allowing himself to be happy.

Louise leaned over to whisper in her ear. "Are you ready?"

"Oh, yes." Camille nodded, blinking back tears. "I never knew how ready I could be."

***

THE SUNLIGHT WAS BURNISHED by the time the newlywed couple made their farewells to family and friends on the garden terrace at Trevarre Hall. The last person Benedict stopped to embrace was the one guest Camille had not recognized.

"I can never thank you enough for coming today," he said, taking a seat beside the grand lady who wore a collar of emeralds round her aged neck. As Camille came to join them, he spoke to her. "My love, was this your doing?"

"Bringing Lady Far to our wedding? No!" She smiled. "Mama went to Tremethyck Park to see her ladyship, I believe, though she kept it a secret until today. You may recall that Mama's parents were killed in a carriage accident when she was still in the schoolroom. Mama has never forgotten Lady Far's kindness to her in the aftermath of that tragedy."

"It brought me great joy to be reunited with my dear Isabella last week." The old woman beamed. "Yet neither of us knew if I could travel here for the wedding. I have suffered this year with pain in my joints, but today was a good day." Looking between them, she added, "How marvelous, to see Benedict at such a happy point in his life." Her eyes held his. "My dear, I could help you achieve an education and rise to a higher level in society, but you had deeper wounds that only you could heal."

His throat tightened. "Yes, but it was Camille who helped me to recognize them and realize what I had to do."

Lady Far reached out with a wrinkled hand to caress first his cheek, and then Camille's. "Many people spend their entire lives in search of a love like yours. There is no greater treasure."

"I will not forget," he nodded, reaching for Camille's hand. "And now, I am going to take my bride away. We have another important task to accomplish before the sun sets."

* * *

GULL COTTAGE HAD BEEN LARGELY TRANSFORMED during the past two weeks since Benedict's marriage proposal. Some of Justin and Mouette's cast-off furniture now replaced Pa's tattered pieces. There were bookshelves, filled with volumes belonging to both of them. Pictures hung on the walls, not only landscapes painted by Isabella, but also newly framed watercolors and sketches of birds made by both Camille and Benedict.

Prudence had sewn white curtains for the windows, and they now fluttered in the summer breeze. As Benedict waited for Camille to finish changing her clothes, he stood in the parlor and looked around. Tears pricked his eyes. If it were possible for joy to be tangible, he felt it in this cottage.

Camille emerged from the bedroom, bright as a sunbeam, clad in her favorite pair of trousers and a soft linen shirt. Following at her heels was Ember.

"I think she is hungry!" Camille observed, and the cat began to purr so loudly Benedict heard it across the room.

"That cat can wait a few minutes." He crossed to take her hand. "Come outside with me."

She laughed a little as they went toward the door. "I'll own I didn't expect you to ask me to put on breeches and come outside with you. Instead, I felt quite certain you would demand that I undress and confine myself to your bed for the next twenty-four hours."

His brows flicked up as he sent her a sideways glance. "Oh, don't worry, that part of the plan is yet to come...right after we take care of one more bit of business."

Outside, he went to the shed. Moments later, he returned with a cage made of willow twigs that Sebastian Trevarre had brought over earlier that day.

Camille gasped aloud as Benedict drew closer.

"Lazarus!" Instantly, tears welled in her beautiful eyes, and she ran to his side. "Oh, Benedict!"

"It's time, love. The kittiwakes have begun to leave, back to sea with their fledglings, and Julia assures me that Lazarus is now fit to make the journey with his flock."

"Of course." She nodded, her chin trembling a little. "It's the way it must be."

They walked in silence to the edge of the cliff overlooking the vast English Channel. Below, many of the ledges that had once held scores of kittiwake nests were now bare. The sky was layered with soft pinks and azure, the water glimmered in the setting sun, and in the distance, a three-masted brigantine was bound for the ocean.

Camille opened the door to the cage, and they stood back to wait. Lazarus seemed to be in no hurry to reemerge into the wild.

"I've been thinking," Benedict said, standing behind Camille and wrapping his arms around her. When she leaned back against him and he inhaled the fragrance of her hair, a wave of contentment broke over him. "About our future."

"Since you can't be a proper ornithologist any longer, I too have wondered how we shall live." Her voice held no note of concern. "I could plant and tend a vegetable garden. We could have laying chickens, but I'm afraid I cannot condone hunting."

"It is true, unless we can find another way to study the birds, my ornithology days are over," he said. "But perhaps there is another path forward, something more than harvesting vegetables and gathering eggs."

Her soft body shook a little with laughter. "I was hoping you might say that."

"I don't think you and I alone can stop the feather hunters, but we can show people the way birds live in the wild. We could make Gull Cottage into a place where others can learn about the kittiwakes, and even spend time observing them."

He could feel the heat and energy in her body as she turned in his arms and looked up.

"Yes!" cried Camille. "I will make little books about the kittiwakes and everyone who comes will take one away. If they begin to appreciate the birds, they will want to save them." She paused before adding excitedly, "Perhaps we could also take groups to see my outdoor aviary at Elysium! And you know, I have always thought that Papa's many nature gardens should be enjoyed by others outside our family."

"All of this could be a start," Benedict agreed, longing now to go back inside and take her to bed. "Who knows where it might lead?"

As he bent to kiss her, a movement near the cliff's edge caught his eye. *Lazarus!* Good God, he'd almost forgotten. Turning Camille around, he touched a silencing finger to her mouth, then pointed.

They watched together as Lazarus slowly emerged from his cage and stepped uncertainly to the grassy edge of the cliff. As he did so, one of the other kittiwakes flew high, then swept back toward them. When it circled away again, as if leading the way, Lazarus suddenly spread his wings and flew out into the open. It seemed impossible, but the bedraggled chick who recently seemed doomed now soared away over the water, healthy and whole, bound for a future with his flock.

Benedict wanted to cheer, to call out good wishes to the valiant kittiwake. Instead, he tightened his embrace and felt Camille's tears soak through his shirt sleeve.

"There he goes," he whispered. "We did it."

"It feels like a miracle," came Camille's fervent response. "But I believe, for us, it is just the beginning."

~THANK YOU ~

I am honored that you've read my book and I sincerely hope you enjoyed it!

Would you like to be the first to know when I have a new release, a contest, sale, or a giveaway? You can sign up here for my occasional newsletter: www.cynthiawrightauthor.com.

You're invited to join my private "Cynthia Wright's Rakes & Readers Group" on Facebook. You'll be the first to see my coziest posts and "Behind the Book" tidbits. You'll also be included in special previews and giveaways and have a chance to interact with me—and with new friends who enjoy reading historical romances. I hope you'll come by now to join us—just click HERE.

You can also follow me on Twitter @CynthiaWright1 and on Instagram @CynthiaWrightAuthor.

In response to reader requests for a family tree, you can now access one on my website, under "Extras"! It shows all the connections between the characters in my books, most of whom are related in one way or another. I'd love to know what you think.

If you enjoyed reading this book, please consider posting a brief review. It's the very best way to say thank you to an author, and your review will help other readers make a choice

Members of the irresistible St. Briac and Raveneau families reappear throughout the Rakes & Rebels series:

The St. Briac Family:

1 – HIS MAKE-BELIEVE BRIDE(Justin & Mouette)

2 – HER IMPOSSIBLE HUSBAND (Justin & Mouette)

3 – HER SECRET ROGUE (Anthony & Frederica)

4 – HIS FIERY ANGEL (Benedict & Camille)

The Raveneau Family:

1 – SILVER STORM(André & Devon)

2 – HER HUSBAND, THE RAKE a sequel novella (André & Devon)

3 – SMUGGLER'S MOON (Sebastian & Julia

4 – THE SECRET OF LOVE (Gabriel & Isabella)

5 – SURRENDER THE STARS (Ryan & Lindsay)

6 – HIS RECKLESS BARGAIN (Nathan & Adrienne)

7 – TEMPEST(Adam & Cathy)

The Beauvisage Family:

1 – STOLEN BY A PIRATE: a novella prequel to CAROLINE (Jean-Philippe & Antonia)

2 – RESCUED BY A ROGUE BY A ROGUE (Alec & Caro)

3 – TOUCH THE SUN (Lion & Meagan)

4 – SPRING FIRES (Nicholai & Lisette)

5 – HER DANGEROUS VISCOUNT (Grey & Natalya)

Do you love audiobooks as much as I do? Most of my titles are now available in audio format, with special prices on Chirpbooks.com. You can listen to samples of my audiobooks here.

A special excerpt of the next book in this series is just ahead! And if you haven't yet read SILVER STORM, the bestselling romance of André and Devon Raveneau that started it all, you can download your copy now!

Once again, my heartfelt thanks for your support, interest, and encouragement for my books. I welcome your comments and suggestions, and I hope that you'll write to me at Cynthia@CynthiaWrightAuthor.com. I promise to reply!

Warmest wishes,
~ Cynthia

~ AUTHOR'S NOTE ~

I hope you've enjoyed Camille and Benedict's romance in His Fiery Angel!

If you've been following this series, you know that natural history plays a major role in the stories. The 1820's and 1830's were a fascinating time when amazing scientific discoveries were being made, and many brilliant naturalists and ornithologists were emerging, including John Gould and William Swainson. Their voyages to Australia in search of new species of birds occurred as described in His Fiery Angel.

During the creation of His Fiery Angel, I was able to return to one of my favorite places in the world: Cornwall's Fowey River Valley. It was my sixth trip to Cornwall and as always, I was caught up in the timeless magic of the special area where I've now set five historical romance novels. (Smuggler's Moon, The Secret of Love, His Make-Believe Bride, Her Impossible Husband, and His Fiery Angel.) On this particular research trip, my husband and I were joined by my daughter and her family. It was a dream come true to show my best-loved places, like the Hall Walk, Pont Pill, and the Lost Gardens of Heligan, to my young grandsons.

Our heroine, Camille St. Briac, has appeared in several books, beginning at age four in His Make-Believe Bride. She has always had a fascination for birds – and abhorred the use of feathers in women's hats. This scandal didn't reach epic proportions until later in the 19th century, but of course Camille was ahead of her time! When I searched for a Cornwall bird that was hunted for its feathers, I discovered the humble kittiwake. I am not certain that kittiwakes bred on the cliffs near Polruan, but I do know that they lived elsewhere on the Cornwall cliffs, and who can say where they might have nested in 1838?

If you'd like to see more of the images "behind the book" for His Fiery Angel, I hope you'll visit its <u>Pinterest</u> page.

If you page ahead, you'll find an excerpt of HER BRIDEGROOM LIST, set in 1842 London and Suffolk and featuring the irrepressible Emeline St. Briac and a libertine hero she can't resist. You'll also reunite with many familiar characters, including Justin and Mouette St. Briac.

Thank you, as always, for your friendship and support!

Warmest regards,
Cynthia

HER BRIDEGROOM LIST

RAKES & REBELS: ST.
BRIAC FAMILY, BOOK 5

PROLOGUE

*L*ord Jasper Hartcliffe, widely known as Hart the Heartless, reclined against a pillar in the magnificent ballroom of Riven Court. Under hooded lids, he surveyed the throng of glittering guests and closed his fingers around a small, folded note.

The hostess of this predictably dull Spring Ball, Susanna, Countess of Riven, had pressed the paper into his hand just minutes before.

Hart's blood pulsed as he thought of her brazen invitation to rendezvous with her at two o'clock in the morning. *I yearn for you. I will be waiting in the bedchamber at the top of the stairs.* Although the ball would be winding down by then, Susanna's overbearing husband would still be occupied in the library, deep in his usual game of whist. Lord Riven cared far more for cards than the ample charms of his countess.

Still, Hart mused, it would be mad to cuckold the man under his own roof.

Wouldn't it? The edges of his hard mouth flickered as he considered this.

"Scanning the crowd for your next conquest, I surmise," a voice murmured just behind Hart's left shoulder.

No need to look back, for the speaker was his brother, Austell, 9th Duke of Caversham.

"Envious, Your Grace?" Hart taunted lightly.

"Envious?" Austell repeated, pausing for effect. "Far from it."

"Ah." This finally drew a brief glance from Hart. "That's right, you are still besotted with your duchess. Or is it simply that we agree that all of these young beauties are as monotonous as an array of porcelain dolls with painted smiles?"

This was one reason Hart rarely attended formal gatherings among the haut ton. He could not be bothered to play their tedious social games, especially because they usually involved yet another insipid female in her first Season, angling for a titled husband. In truth, he'd really come tonight to see how his brother was getting on.

"Even if I were not devoted to Margaret," replied Austell, "I would have the good sense to realize that, at one-and-thirty, you and I are too old for this sort of marriage mart."

Too old? Hart narrowed his eyes. "Speak for yourself." The jest was rapier-sharp, for they were fraternal twins, sharing a birthday and yet opposites in both looks and personality.

"I may be older by a few minutes, but hard living has left its mark on you," Austell persisted, gesturing toward the silver hairs glinting liberally throughout Hart's dark locks. "And it's not only your age..." He seemed to consider whether to go on, but put up his chin and finished, "You are an infamous libertine. No respectable mama who loves her daughter would dream of handing her over to the likes of you."

"That's just as well." Hart lifted a dark brow. "I have no interest in respectable females."

If Austell hadn't been born just minutes ahead of

him, Hart would have been the one to assume the dukedom when their father died two years ago. Ever since Papa had brought the fraternal twin brothers, on their fifth birthday, into the drawing room and announced that Austell was first born and thus would one day be the duke, Hart had felt a bittersweet mixture of rejection and relief.

Thank God he'd come to realize that, in truth, *he* was the fortunate one. Each morning, he awoke to a surge of freedom that his tradition-bound brother would never know. He could do as he damned well pleased, with no concern for society's censure.

He turned now and met Austell's soft brown gaze, the opposite of his own crisp midnight-blue eyes. In a nearby mirrored wall, Hart glimpsed their reflections. He was tall, lean, some said imposing, with chiseled features and cropped black hair heavily salted with silver. Austell was slighter, paler, his chestnut curls thinning. No wonder people were doubtful upon hearing that they were twins.

"Clearly, you do not envy me my debauched libertine's existence." Hart endeavored to keep the cynical edge from his voice as he added, "And why would you? You have achieved your life's dreams. You're a duke, after all, and you are smitten with your duchess."

His brother looked oddly nervous, even as he nodded. "You're quite right, of course. I am terribly fortunate."

What lingered in the air, unspoken, was the reality that Austell and Margaret had yet to produce an heir after five years of marriage. And Hart suspected something more lurked behind his brother's tense expression. Did he really want to learn what it was? God, no.

Hart glanced away before reluctantly asking, "Have you found that investment you were seeking?"

"I believe so! In the shipping sector!" Austell's eyes

were a bit too bright. "You have no doubt heard there are brilliant new *steamships* being built, driven by propellers rather than paddle wheels." Austell's voice rose with excitement. "Iron and steel replacing wood."

Hart knew a pang of relief that he had no ties to the family fortune. Austell wanted the title and all that went with it, and he was damned welcome to it.

Yet it was disorienting to realize that Austell had actually replaced their shrewd father overseeing the vast holdings of Caversham Castle. The old duke had been conservative with the estate funds, avoiding risk. However, two years into Austell's dukedom, Hart suspected that his brother might be running up debts, and not the sort that came about from improvements to the estates. When Hart had last visited Hartcliffe House in London, the duke, after a few brandies, had very casually inquired if Hart knew of any splendid investments.

"You are acquainted with a lot of those cits, aren't you?" Austell had pressed. "The vulgar fellows who are building railroads and factories?"

"I have an aversion to vulgar fellows," Hart had replied drily, sidestepping the question. In the next moment, his sister-in-law, Margaret, had appeared in the doorway, ending the awkward conversation.

Now, Hart suppressed a sigh. "I hope the new steamships make you very rich."

"Yes, I believe they are bound to do so," Austell replied. "*Very* rich."

Sensing the gray cloud that continued to hover over his brother, Hart wished he could walk away and leave him to it. This was what Austell had dreamed of his entire life: the dukedom, the estates, the title, an exalted position in Society. Hart hoped His Grace could simply occupy himself taking care of it all, as their father had done, and Hart could continue to go off and seek his own forms of pleasure.

Across the ballroom, illuminated by an array of new gas-lit, crystal chandeliers, elegantly clad guests were taking their places for the next dance. Hart turned his head as the musicians began to play Chopin's latest waltz, an appealingly lively piece. His gaze followed the pairs of dancers as they dipped and turned, stopping abruptly on one arresting female.

"Who is that beauty with old Lord Fulham? I've never seen her before."

Austell craned his neck and blinked. "Never seen her? Why, that's Emeline St. Briac. They call her the Exquisite." He paused, then added, "Her father's a pirate, you know. One of those notorious corsairs from St. Malo. Retired now, but rich as Croesus." He paused for a long moment, staring at the girl. "She's enchanting, but they say she goes against the current."

"Does she indeed?" Intrigued, Hart leaned negligently against the pillar but continued to follow the movements of the spirited brunette. Radiant in a simple, elegant gown of amethyst silk, her ebony locks smoothed into a chignon at the base of her neck and decorated with a single white English rose, the girl was enchanting. She was nothing like the others, with their schooled, polite expressions. On the contrary, her countenance displayed her thoughts and feelings for all to see, whether she realized it or not.

The chit didn't want to be here anymore than he did.

"She is on the husband hunt?" Hart wondered in an offhand tone.

"More like the other way round! By Jupiter, man, you have been absent from polite society longer than I realized."

"It would seem that I am sadly ignorant."

"Emeline St. Briac came out nearly two years ago," Austell reported. "Margaret says she's had many excellent offers and turned them all down for one reason or another. It's rumored that she means to run out the clock so her papa will surrender and allow her to go off and live independently."

"How very...unexpected," Hart murmured. "What do you think she means to do?"

His brother snorted. "Search for *fossils*, or so they say."

Fossils! Hart decided he could not have heard Austell correctly. However, before he could question him further, Margaret, Duchess of Caversham, motioned from across the room with a subtle movement of her silk fan.

"I must go. My bride beckons." Austell straightened his cuffs.

Hart looked at him. "I'm leaving for Italy next week."

"Are you indeed! You only appeared tonight to say goodbye?"

Discovering his glass on a nearby side table, Hart drank down the champagne and nodded. "I wanted to see you before I go. I mean, in case you should need me for any reason."

"And what if I did?"

He had a point. "We are brothers, after all…"

Austell gave him a half-smile as he turned to go. "So we are."

A moment later, the clock struck two. The note in Hart's pocket seemed to catch fire, urging him on to the forbidden assignation with his hostess, Lady Riven.

It was mad. Licentious. Reckless!

Just the sort of thing Hart badly needed to feel alive.

* * *

Lord Fulham was looming so close to Emeline, she caught a whiff of his breath, a mixture of cigar and port. She would have been annoyed if not for his air of menace.

"Sir, it is good of you to ask me, but I cannot possibly stand up with you for another waltz," Emeline said firmly. "My slippers have begun to pinch."

"Can't hear a word over the din in this room," came his shouted reply. He caught her arm and began to lead her toward the doorway. "Do come this way for just a moment."

Should she try to wrest her arm from his? Emeline looked around and saw that no one was paying the least bit of attention to them. Fulham, with his thick graying side-whiskers, was a powerful, respected figure in Parliament, after all, and heir to a fortune. No one would challenge him. Newly widowed at forty, he was sought after on the marriage mart in spite of his age.

When they came into the wide, dimly lit corridor, Emeline saw that they were completely alone. Her heart kicked up, even as she scolded herself for being frightened of this man. Of any man!

He was smiling down at her. No, *leering*. Emeline tried to free her arm, but he held her fast and attempted to force her against the wall.

"I must ask that you release me, sir," she said.

"Ask away." Fulham leaned closer, staring at her mouth.

Emeline's palms began to sweat. "Let me go."

"You cannot have any notion how desirable you are, my sweet." He came closer, and she glimpsed the bulge in his trousers.

"You must be mad. Do you imagine I am some doxie that you can accost at will?" She attempted to twist free, and Lord Fulham scowled.

"You've been teasing every gentleman in London for the past two Seasons, my girl. It seems that you are begging to be taught a good *lesson*!"

Even as he spoke, Emeline reached with her free hand to lift her gown and petticoats. Fulham glanced down in confusion just as she brought one knee up and struck, hard, at his groin. Eyes protruding, he emitted a howl of pain, grabbed himself with both hands, and staggered back.

Without a second glance, Emeline turned and sped away. Down the corridor, up the broad staircase, past a startled young footman on the landing. From the top step, she spied a closed door. There was no time to think about the risks of her actions. Grasping the brass knob, Emeline twisted and pushed it open. To her immense relief, she found herself in a silent, darkened room.

Alone.

Heart pounding in her ears, she closed herself inside. Surely Fulham must be following her. She felt for a key in the lock, to no avail. Hide! She felt her way across the room, moving through a sea of inky darkness, until she encountered a waist-high obstacle.

A bed! Just as Emeline was wondering if she might conceal herself under it, a low, male voice spoke.

"I'd begun to think you were not coming."

She froze and stopped breathing. Was this real? The voice was husky, seductive, tinged with amusement. To Emeline's surprise, her primal self took notice. Good sense told her to go the other way, that this stranger was probably worse than Fulham, yet she felt paralyzed. From the shadows, powerful arms reached out to enfold her, lifting her up onto the high bed.

"We are very bad," he murmured. His hands, strong and warm, lightly caressed her bare arms, grazed the curves of her breasts that swelled above her silk bodice, and she knew a shock of pleasure.

Emeline felt drugged as the stranger drew her down on the bed. Dimly, she made out a sculpted face, saw the glimmer of his eyes as he bent over her.

"It's been too long." His mouth scorched a trail

along the tender line of her throat, her neck. "Sweet. God, so sweet."

Emeline felt herself tremble helplessly. This was utter madness! Madness on a grand scale. Just as she was about to speak, to protest, the stranger began to kiss her. She'd been kissed before, but this was something completely different... He used the tip of his tongue to coax her lips to part for him. He tasted her slowly as if she were the most delicious morsel in the world, and she felt compelled to brush his questing tongue with her own. A tantalizing heat spread over her entire body, a kind of *wanting*, and her nipples ached. Her hands fluttered, not daring to touch his broad, bare chest, to feel his heartbeat.

A moan rose in her throat.

At that, the stranger drew back in the shadows. He was staring at her as moonlight stole between the bed draperies. His face remained in dark silhouette above her, but Emeline realized that he doubtless could see now that she was the wrong woman.

"What the devil...?"

Emeline's face flamed. "Unhand me, sir," she managed to croak in tones of mortified outrage. Scrambling off the bed, she made for the door.

Just as she turned the knob, a low laugh reached her ears. "Methinks the lady doth protest too much," taunted the stranger.

This is the last straw, she vowed. *If I never come near another man, it will be too soon!*

* * *

Download HER BRIDEGROOM LIST now!

~ MEET CYNTHIA WRIGHT ~

Cynthia Wright is the *New York Times* and *USA Today* bestselling author of the two *Rakes & Rebels* series, 14 intertwining historical romances starring the irresistible Raveneau and Beauvisage families. She has also written beloved series set during the Renaissance in France, England, and Scotland, and in the 19th century American West. Cynthia has won numerous awards over the years, and Romantic Times Magazine hails her novels as "Romance the way it was meant to be."

Cynthia lives in northern California. She enjoys riding a tandem bike and taking road trips in an airstream trailer with her Colombian-born husband, Alvaro and their corgi, Watson. She is also devoted to her two adorable grandsons who live nearby.

You are invited to visit Cynthia's website (where you can sign up for her newsletter and peruse the Books Page):
http://cynthiawrightauthor.com/

You can join Cynthia's Facebook Reader's Group here:
https://www.facebook.com/cynthiawrightauthor/

View her "Behind the Books" boards on Pinterest:
http://pinterest.com/cynthiawright77/

CROWNS & KILTS

The St. Briac Family

YOU AND NO OTHER

OF ONE HEART

ABDUCTED AT THE ALTAR

RETURN OF THE LOST BRIDE

QUEST OF THE HIGHLANDER

* * *

ROGUES GO WEST

BRIGHTER THAN GOLD

IN A RENEGADE'S EMBRACE

THE DUKE AND THE COWGIRL

* * *

BOXED SETS

RAKES & REBELS: THE RAVENEAU FAMILY 1

(Silver Storm, Her Husband, the Rake)

RAKES & REBELS: THE RAVENEAU FAMILY 2

(Smuggler's Moon, The Secret of Love, Surrender the Stars)

RAKES & REBELS: THE RAVENEAU FAMILY 3

(His Make-Believe Bride, His Reckless Bargain, Tempest)

THE RAVENEAU FAMILY IN CORNWALL

(Smuggler's Moon, The Secret of Love, His Make-Believe
Bride)

RAKES & REBELS: THE BEAUVISAGE FAMILY 1

(Stolen by a Pirate, Rescued by a Rogue)

RAKES & REBELS: THE BEAUVISAGE FAMILY 2
(Touch the Sun, Spring Fires, Her Dangerous Viscount)

CROWNS & KILTS: COLLECTION 1 – CROWNS
(You and No Other, Of One Heart)

CROWNS & KILTS: COLLECTION 2 – KILTS
(Abducted at the Altar, Return of the Lost Bride, Quest of the
Highlander)

ROGUES GO WEST
(Brighter than Gold, In a Renegade's Embrace, The Duke and
the Cowgirl)

A small press bound by the belief that every voice matters.

Sign up for our newsletter to learn about new releases and more.
https://oliver-heberbooks.com/subscribe/

Follow us on social media:

facebook.com/oliverheberbooks
instagram.com/oliverheberbooks
amazon.com/oliverheberbooks
youtube.com/@OliverHeberBooksPublisher

www.ingramcontent.com/pod-product-compliance
Lightning Source LLC
Chambersburg PA
CBHW010523100726
47903CB00011B/2875